PLEX PRESENTS

LOVE & THUGGIN'

By Bo Brown

CAN'T STOP WON'T STOP

LOVE & THUGGIN'
Copyright © 2011 by: Bo Brown & PLEX
Written by Bo Brown
Cover Design Created by: Cedric "Ckillz" Killings & Bo Brown
Cover Graphics by: Cedric "Ckillz" Killings
Book Design by: Pam Quigley
Co-Authored by: PLEX
Edited and Perfected by: PLEX and Pam Quigley

This novel is an absolute work of Fiction. Any resemblance to real, living or dead, establishments, actual events, organizations, or locales is intended to give the Fiction a heightened sense of reality and authenticity. Names, characters, places, events, and incidents are products of the authors' vast imagination and is used fictitiously, as are those fictionalized events and incidents that may seem to involve real people and did not occur are set in the future.

A PLEX PRESENTS BOOK
Published With Permission By BADLAND PUBLISHING
PO Box 11623
Riviera Beach, FL 33149-1623
ISBN: 978-0-9825018-6-3

First Edition

www.badlandpub.com

Dedication

I dedicate this book to Susan Gibson (I love you Ma), Leslie "Bee" Taylor (I'm blessed to have 2 moms), Shanika Brown (don't know where I'd be without you as my backbone), Adrian "Lottie" Hall (you're my Connie), L.C. Brown (Be patient) and Shod Brown (I can't wait to show you I walk it how I talk it).

Acknowledgements

To all the people that matter, I salute yall: Bobby Bellamy (When Pac said "Never had a friend like me," he meant you my nigga). Clifford and Devonda Sands (What's understood need not be explained, I love yall). Lilly, Franmeka and Shawntavia Wright (We got a lot to sort out but I owe yall the world, thanks). Johnnie Mae Green (nothing but love). Diane and Princess Hughes (Family forever). Traquia "Duke" Viel (thank you, and stop tripping). Adrian Hadley (Are you stable yet? Yeah, right). Patricia "Ms. Pat" Dismuke (Can't wait to go to that casino with you). Angela Williams (I ain't mad at cha). Hasina Baillou and Aleatrina Issacs (Keep up the good work with my girls). Avonda "Black Girl" Dowling (Towner 4 life is in my blood no matter what ☺). Kanren "Candy" Ridley (You certified gangsta). Kelvonia "K-Cutta" Clarke (Match Box till the end). Peaches and Tangarey (Can't forget yall). Red Girl (Good looking even though you only get a check next to your name). Tina Meadows (You came through when you aint have to, thanks). Reginald Abel (I'ma show you how it suppose to really be done). Nukey, Visha and Freddie (I should be getting more pictures of those kids ☹). Bertron Hobes (Still waiting on pictures of the baby). Ketha, Lisa and Khailia (We all family so get used to it). Trenece and Tameka Lee (Thought I'd forget yall?) Tammie (Bout time I got my pictures back). Angel (Stop being fiesty). Butta (Step ya game up). Snook (It's not hard, trust me). Levante Brown (Grow up to be better than us). Kayla (Please don't have your mother's ways). Nini (Don't make me show off on you). Qua (Same applied to Nini applies to you). Chey (Stay smart shorty). Wil'Shon Graham (Stop being so bad all the time). Leonard "Lil Bo" Brown Jr. (At the end of the day, it's my blood that's running through you). There's a bunch more cousins, nieces, nephews and great nieces and nephews. I love all yall. I want to thank Kim over at Badland and Chico and Plex for supporting a nigga. Last, thanks Rossy. You sent me that Screenwriters Bible and that set all this into play. Can't forget Rat, E-4, Dee (Resurrection), Fats, Earl (Ice Man), Ernest Knight, Victor Williams (Lil Boomer), Bunky Brown, Junkie Jit (Scott's representer), T-Funk (St. Pete) and Rick Brownlee (The Mayor).

R.I.P.

T.J., Phillip, Dominique, Albert, Pork Chop, Alex, Pee-Wee, Louise Hall (Mother), Aunt Lean, Grandma Bee, Fish Grease, Marvin (cold rida), Shortman, Terry, Cheryl and Cenetra, Charlene Brown (miss you), Bear, Zette, Skinny, Tina, Greg and last but not least Lenard Brown a.k.a. Dutch. Miss yall. We all have lost someone close in life but as my brother would say "Life goes on, don't cry for me, ride with me!" As much as I wouldn't loved to ride, I couldn't. Sorry…All I can do is make everything back how we had it minus a couple of fake people, provide for our family and stay sucka free. You already know I'm gonna honor my end or die trying so don't trip. Wherever yall at just hold me a spot. Tell Marv and Terry I can't wait to see yall at heavens gate in ya all white and if its hell then have my glock with the 30 round clip waiting on my arrival cause wherever we end up gonna be about survival. I Love and Miss You My Nigga.

Stay Strong: I can't begin to name everybody but we'd start here and finish as the books come along. Sparks, Coop, Amir, Al, Junt, Spoon, Pop, Mark Bell, Lil E, E, Big E, 1-2, Boo Hound, Vee and D (St. L), Tut, Mo Brown, Wize, Vee (NY), Juvy, Rock (DC), Tammy Son (Towner), Snap, Head, Disco, K-1, Nard (Scotts), Big G-Moe, Dez, Joe Black, Bump, Shorty Black, Cheese (What's up son), Miller, Groove (Palm Beach stand up), Dirty Redz, Diesel, Block, G-Baby, K, Poppa Stoppa, Bootie (Monticelo), L (Alabama), Flaco, Red, Tarzan, Nardo and Big Ray (DC) Streeter, Jed (St. Pete's finest), Kenny and Popcorn (P-Cola),

Tom Cat – Styles P – Shorty dope (My Folks), E.R. (DC), Boomer Check, Los (What it do Zoe?), Spida, Champ, Rod, Jimbo, Pooky, Ro, Bino, JB, Al Dog (A-Town Hustler), G-Male (Broward), Blabber, D-Boi, Lill Bobbie, East Wood, Dion and Goo (DC), Chuck (Ohio) and if I missed yall don't trip. I had to save room for the next one.

JUST FOR YOU

This is to one person and one person only. If you ever read this book then you know I'm talking directly to you and at you. Where did we go wrong? I know I can reach out and it'll be all love but why should I? I remember it was us all day everyday. Now a nigga can't get a fuck you card. What part of the game is that? Yeah, you make the effort to make sure all my people always have your numbers in case I want to holla but that's sucka shit. You know what it's hitting for. A picture or two of you and the kids will do. I heard you had another one too. That's been a minute so you might've had more. I don't know where we went wrong and I'd bet it all that it'll all be love once a nigga touch back down, but then it will all be in vain. Why? Who will I need once I'm home? It's been years now but I take part of the blame. But I'm the one who's info hardly ever changes so what's your excuse? Ain't that much caught up or busy. This me. I know how shit works. We bosses so we set our own standards. We make our own schedules. Anything we want to do we do it. I bet you make extra time for them bitches? I'm good though. I figured we all need reality checks. This was yours. I was just looking at some pictures of you and Nard. Yall were out somewhere clowning. I know niggas grow apart from bitches and vice versa, but us? You won't believe it if I told you some of the niggas who get at me. That actually take time out to write or make one of their bitches write to check for a nigga. I know once this book is published you gonna read it, so maybe after you read this you'll sit and think and reanalyze all that 'my dog shit' or how much love you suppose to have had for a nigga. I meant to call you but didn't. I put it in the book cause this just don't apply to you and me. There's thousands of niggas in my shoes and thousands in yours. So this applies to all the You's out there who forgot about all the Me's in here. All I can say is grin when you see it again 'cause it's never over until the fat lady start hitting high notes and the bitch ain't even hit the stage yet. Figure the rest out!!

THUGGIN' STILL
BO

vi

OFF DA' RULER'S DESK

Working on this project with Bo Brown was special to me because Bo's a very special person in my life. He and I have been to hell and back, and we did it like G's. So for that [his love, respect, and continued support] and bringing this project to the table, I want to thank him once for every copy that we're going to sell [that's a million thanks, homie]. One Love and thank you for coming to PLEX PRESENTS, because I know personally that hella' people wanted this book...Especially with Mrs. Shanika Brown on the cover...One love!!!

Yo, Disco [my lil' brother Troy Jones]! Tell me how you love it...It's your year [2011]. I'm almost finished with editing your book, YOUNG & THUGGIN'. So get ready to hustle real hard! Our destination, the moon!

Skip and LaLa Coleman, I owe yall big and I'ma pay yall in full. Ya' heard me?! Everything happens for a reason and everybody has their season. It's just our time, so let's get it!!!...and I cannot forget Monica Harvey, my Gangsta Boo. Shorty, you just don't know.

A lot has happened over the years [both great and terrible] and people who were riding then are not riding now. So for those that believed, understood, and stood beside me in the paint, I would like to take this time to extend my love: Dorothy A Killings, Cedric L. Killings, Michael G. Harper, my lovely big sister Kimberly Adams, Arthur C. Pless III [Lil' Plex], Artoria J. Pless [the sweetest little female me], Troy Cannon [my dog for life], Marquiesha A. Pless [my babygirl], Ms. Summer Rose [Wifey!], Arlexus C. Pless [Daddy's little girl], Jai N. Pless [my heart!], Monisha B. Wimberly [I love you with all my heart!], Bernard 'Big Gemo' Moore [I got the house on you, Junior...don't let the ole-boy down], my sons [Marquis, Artraveous, Travis, Isaiah, Diamond] I love yall like I love myself. And as I expect the best from myself I also expect the very best from you all [Like father like son!]

What I do I do it for yall, yet without yall I'd be lost and most likely unpublished; so with much love and sincerity I thank my book-family: Chuck [out of Ohio], Black [out of Detroit], my homie K-1 [I love you lil' homie], Spoon [from Overtown], Sharon Pless [thanks for the love and support], Buffy Uter [thank you for everything! I love and owe you big!], Tracey Carter [Lovingly yours, ma], Steven Polk [the best of the best!], Dwayne Gladden [my brother from another mother], Ms. Tonetta Chester [Lady, you better stop playing with me!?], Bling [Let's get it, lil' bruh!], Jimbo & Pookey [we got 'em hatin' bruh bruh!], Willie Dutch [You're my mutha f#@kin' dog! Stay down, homie…Until we come up!], Seth Ferranti & LaMont 'Big Fridge' Needeum [Yall hear that? They screaming let's get it from another planet], so let's get!!!

Love and PLEX are the two greatest things that God ever created, and Pam Quigley, you deserve them both [smile]. I needed you and you didn't hesitate to step up for me. I'll owe you forever. And baby, all I see is BOOK GANG!

Yall know I ain't sh@# without my homeboys?! Big Bino, Big Joe Hollywood, Marlo Moore, Banks [out of Chi-town], Bundy [out of Orlando], Bo Rizzim [my Co-D], Fats [Big Wayne], E-4 [my Ace in the hole], Chris [Young Hit 'em Up out of Palm Beach], Muhjah [Arab Money. I love you bruh bruh!], Palmer Bradshaw [I owe it all to you! Thanks a million, bruh bruh. And when we touch down, we gon' spend a million!], Nathan 'Big Nation' Welch [You see what patience gets us? Bruh bruh, we writing our own checks now!], Jonathan Carter [thanks for the plug], Debra Harrel [thanks for the love], Theresa [my uncle Ronnie's girlfriend] thank you for reading all of my books and taking the time out to promote and pass them around…Bronco [from down South], Capo Cat Freeman, Jim Beam, Lenny 'Mac' Harrison [out of Jersey]…Nephew [Mall], Chrizac [I need you bruh-bruh! We're all we got!]…

D-Boi, Mike Brown, and Bug Sleezze. Yeah, yall serious, yall some fools with it…To all my ni@gas @ dumbnigga.com [where keeping it real has gone wrong], I wanna say, yall some dumb niggas! Starting with the president and CEO, Mr. Dumb Nigga himself, what it do Showtime Shawdy aka ATL Shawty aka Put Ya' Hands Up Shawdy aka Playboy Wayne; Blue [Worm], aka Keep Des Trap Jumpin'; Montrae aka Wallstreet Shawdy aka Curtain Up Shawdy aka The Stock Down Shawdy aka Dollar Tree

Shawdy aka Bad Investment Shawdy; Money Roy aka EZ-Money aka Get 'im Some Help Shawdy aka My Grill Comin' Shawdy aka Make Da Bomb Jump Ay'; Chicago Black aka Sentimental Shawdy aka Jericho Shawdy aka Black Down aka Thump The Bible Shawdy...ay' oookayyy'!

Let me stop bullshitin'. They say the first will be last and the last will be first, so these last list of people may be closest to heart: Lisa 'Baby' Banks and Altonise 'Treasure' Hills, the two hottest chicks on the planet! Thank you both sooo' much. I've had a lot of bright and not-so-bright ideas over the years, and you both have always been receptive and willing to help me go to the next level. You two are the best!...Adielsie de la Rosa and Khernan [Thank yall for gracing the new BOO BABY cover].

Robert Thomas [I can always depend on you! Thank you so much. And I love you forever!], Mark Bell, Malik Yarborough-EL, JP Graham, Carlos Dubois [my lil' bruh bruh out the BANG 'EM], T-Mac [outta Chi-Town], Long Hair Don't Care [DaDa outta Chat-Town], Christopher Ross [Thanks for the love!], Oscar Fowler, that lil' goon-ass-ni#@a Frank Hill, Johnny 'Crusher' Jackson [One Love, bruh bruh!] George Ross, David Trotter, Devon Tyler [Thanks for the love!] David Harris [One Love, bruh bruh!] Michael Prophete [I couldn't do it without real dudes like you!], Edward Harper [Your support is greatly appreciated!] URBAN CELEBRITY MAGAZINE [Thanks for the look!], and Abman Glaster [Yall go online and cop FOREIGN EXCHANGE. It's pure Heat!]...What's up? DC BOOK DIVA, Kwame Teague: Yall killing 'em with Dynasty! I got it yesterday and finished it yesterday. Your pen-game is the best. ONE LOVE!!!...Damie 'Day-Day' Anwour [Devil's Assistant], Kevin R. Davis [my go-to-man!] Seven Supreme, Snap & Head, James 'Pop' Long, The Snowman [Out of DC], BOOK GANG MEDIA, the whole PLEX PRESENTS staff, and finally, PLEX [Head up, Eyes Open, Gun Locked and Loaded...now let's get it!]...

BOOK 1NE

✳ ✳ ✳ ✳ ✳

LOVE

By
Bo Brown

YEARNING FOR LOVE [Poem by John T. Bussey]

Dear Reader
Please Be Obliged
And Let My Words take You On A Horse and Carriage Ride
There Are Times When we All Are Alone
And Hurting So Very Much
In Need Of That Special Someone
To Touch Our Heart With That Special Touch
That Special Blessing From Above
Entwined Feelings And Emotions
Together Like A Hand In Glove
Knowing That If Love Is To Be A Color
It Is To Be Gold
So Perfect And Precious Enough For Only Love To Hold
Optimistic Of Love
Because Love Is The Bearer
The Refuge Of Pain
Life's Umbrella
Sheltering Your Heart From The Rain
Love Adds Joy To The Stirring Of The Soul
Causing It To Sing
Blossoming Chords As Beautiful As A Crows In The Spring
Still Love Has Caused Many To Cry Themselves To Sleep
Confused At The Understanding
Of Why Love Makes Them Weak
Unique Is Love
Joyful Because I Believe I've Found Love
She's Beautiful
For Love Has Landed
I Only Pray She's Here To Stay
For I'd Be Devastated
If She [My Love] Was To Fly Away

Chapter 1

BO

I sat in the corner of the huge 50 man tank desperately craving a smoke. It was as if my lungs and brain were about to shut down. Lucky for me Big Will's fat ass was a C-O at the county. Diablo had him on the payroll, so he would bring me a hand grenade if I told him to. I had a CD player, cell phone, cash money, and plenty of weed and Newports. The only problem was finding a quiet private spot to go up because niggas in the county jail weren't just crabs, they were rats. So I didn't wanna put Big Will on front-street, and cause the chump to lose his job, because I would never hear the end of that shit from Diablo.

Anyway, I finally found me a duck-off and was filling my lungs with tar and nicotine when crazy ass, trouble starting ass, Dewey the iron-lung walked up.

"Damn boy, what's up?" he said smiling and reaching for my Newport.

I couldn't deny the nigga, he was outta the 40's and used to run with my brother.

"Ain't shit, Dewey."

"I heard that, fool." He said, steady smoking up my square. "Bo, boy, I can't believe I ran into you again like this…shiid', the last time I saw you you was a lil' ass nigga holdin' a big ass gun. We was over at the gambling house on 22nd. You was with that nigga, um', what his name?"

"G."

"Yeah, the nigga G. I remember that nigga. Yall niggas was droppin' stacks with no pressure." Dewey went on.

I hated I knew the nigga. Not on no crab shit, because I had it. But the nigga sat there and smoked my whole square and didn't know whether I had another one or not. Dewey had always been that way – aggressive. He was a little skinny ass red nigga, 'bout 5'11" in height, with a reddish blonde bush and big beard. Everything he did was done 100 mph.

As he ran his mouth I twisted a joint of 'dro. The nigga's eyes lit up when he saw my P.S., but he didn't stop rapping. He was running down how the crackas' was trying to railroad him on an armed robbery and attempted murder beef. The victim had pointed him out and all.

"Bo, I can't believe these crackas' talkin' 'bout 65 years," he lamented, taking the joint from me.

"You do it?"

"Huh?"

He did it. I could tell by the way he responded. Talking 'bout "huh." If a nigga can *huh* he can *hear*. Dewey was buying time though. He hadn't expected me to ask him that, because for real, you don't ask niggas about their case.

"I ain't trippin', Dewey." I took my joint back before it disappeared into his lungs. "You gon' make 'em run it?"

He dilly-dallied for a second. "Maann', I don't know. This hoe-ass nigga Trent --"

"Trent?" I cut him off. "Yo' cousin, Trent?"

"Yeah, fool talkin' 'bout I ran up in his house and tied up his lil' daughter, and some more hoe-ass shit."

100 mph, right? Yeah, Dewey did that shit. His cousin Trent was outta Carol City, soft as cotton candy, but he was *getting it-getting it!*

"You a wild nigga, Dewey."

He reached for the joint but I double pumped on him, changed hands and hit it again. He ain't like that shit, but it was my weed.

"Oh, I'm wild 'cause a nigga tryna' get it? Bo, my nigga, ain't nobody doin' shit for me. Niggas pushin' all types of G-wagons and Q-45's and shit. Buyin' bars and rainin' on hoes. My nigga, a nigga ain't got shit!"

Point seen. I passed the nigga the weed. He was on that 40's, Overtown ass shit. They mentality was real fucked up. Always thinking 'cause a nigga got something he owe something.

But a nigga don't owe nann' nigga nothing. I got arrested in a G-wagon and my bitch had a Q-45.

"You trippin', Dewey."

"Nah, fool, you trippin'. I ain't from Carol City."

"Nigga, me either!" I snapped. "And if I was, what that got to do with anything, my nigga?"

He killed the roach. "I'm just sayin', C-C niggas got all the work and yall ain't lookin' out."

I laughed. "Dewey, I ain't from Carol City, and I don't owe you or no other nigga shit."

"Nigga, you is from C-C."

"Nah, yo…" I twisted another joint and broke it down for him…

Chapter 2

BO

I came up in Overtown, plain and simple. In 1987 we lived in the
Pink buildings – three stories, 33 apartments, eleven on each floor.
The area that we lived in was one of the roughest and poorest areas
in Miami, Florida.

One day after school I was playing downstairs like I always
did. It was me and some fast-ass little girl that should've been in
the house doing her homework instead of outside letting me play in
her coochie. We were off in the cut doing us when I heard two
men exchanging words. It was Tommy Lee – a crackhead who'd
made it big overnight by pulling off a big robbery and turning into
a drug dealer instead of a drug user – and Frank, who's mom lived
in apartment #11 by the stairs. Frank was telling Tommy Lee that
he couldn't serve drugs in front of his mom's apartment.

"Nigga, make this here yo' last day…or else!"

That's what Frank told him. But Tommy Lee was a big
nigga, muscles everywhere, so he didn't see that shit Frank was
talking. I guess the money was so good that it blinded his ability
to reason. After all, that was the man's mommas crib he was
disrespecting.

The next day I was out there by myself waiting for the little
fast-ass girl to come out of her apartment when Tommy Lee pulled
up in his powder-blue Cadillac Eldorado. It was the baddest car in

Overtown is like a road to destruction for anyone that
travels through there. I'm a living witness to that. I've seen a lot
of things in my younger years, things that children my age
shouldn't have been exposed to – drug dealing, women being
pimped and beaten, and people getting killed. In fact, I was only in
the third grade when I witnessed my very first murder.

6

1232 building's parking lot. He had the blue double crush-velvet seats, rag-top, and 30's with mustard and blue-cheese. I was in love with that car.

Tommy Lee got out with no shirt on, four big rope-chains, and about three diamond rings on each hand. He was really cuttin' it!

"What's up, lil' man?"

Was all he said to me before he went and opened up shop in front of Frank's mother's house – like he always did. I didn't think anything of it, I was too busy waiting on my girl to come out. All of a sudden I saw Frank walking out of the alley [we call it the hallway] with a big chrome revolver.

Boom! Boom! Boom! Boom! Boom! Boom!

Frank emptied the .357. All six shots landed in the back of Tommy Lee's head – he never saw it coming. No mask, no co-defendants. Just Frank and his chrome .357 – in broad day light.

I couldn't even move. My momma had to step over Tommy Lee's dead body to pull me up the stairs. Blood had ran all the way down the stairs and into the courtyard. It was dark and thick! For the rest of our stay in the 1232 building I saw that blood. It was embedded in the concrete, as well as my mind.

But that's just how it was when I was growing up. The environment was fast and unforgiving. Tommy Lee died that day, but I lived to see many more men [and women] lose their miserable lives to senseless violence. Of course, at the time I didn't know what *miserable* or *senseless* meant. I only knew that this was life and that's how they played. Shit was 100% normal to me.

In our household was me, the ole-girl, my twin brother, and my other four siblings – three boys and three girls. My Pops was a rolling stone. Not to mention a certified hood legend. So we had other sisters and brothers scattered out everywhere. Again, that shit was normal in the hood. But as I got older I realized that it was fucked up, and I decided that I wanted more for my family. And that when I had children, we were going to live under the same roof as one family. I love my ole-boy to death, but I did not want to be like him.

My brother and me are fourteen minutes apart – I'm the oldest. I was so big that they never even knew he was in there. I got the nick-name Bo because I was so bowlegged as a shorty that they had to break my legs and reset them. My brother's nick-name was Dutch. Yeah, Dutch, and you'll see why in a minute…

Chapter 3

BO

Fast forward this shit to 1993. We're no longer living in the Pink 1232 building, and my brother and me are on the verge of quitting school altogether. A couple of months shy of our sixteenth birthday and school is not at the top of our agenda. We were on some money shit. Nothing major, but nothing in life ever is in its infancy.

Shop was set up at our old building. They were now blue and wide open. Everybody came through there looking to double their money, so my brother and me had the juggler bombs out there booming! You could cop a $5 juggler from us, chop it down and resell that shit for $10 to $15. So not just crack-heads were coming through, but up and coming hustlers were coming through copping too.

We had weed, cocaine, and jugglers. The workers would be out there screaming "base, butter, and sense!" all day long. There were three shift – 7 a.m. to 3 p.m., 3 p.m. to 11 p.m., and 11 p.m. to 7 a.m. Each shift had a bomb man, a gun man, a watch-out man, and a Lieutenant. The titles are self explanatory so I'm not going to get into that, but everybody played their role and everybody got paid. We had two apartments in the building – one for storing drugs and the other one was strictly for lamping.

$ $ $

One day, I'll never forget it because it was the day that shit really changed for us, I was chilling in the spot smoking a blunt. At the building we were hustling out of there was a parking lot on the side. That's where I was, sitting on the hood of my 1976 Chevy Impala listening to the Ghetto Boy's SIX FEET DEEP album, when Dutch pulled up. He had a badass 1971 Impala Vert.

"Bo, when you finished down here I need to holla atcha'."

I said "bet" and kept chilling. My little man Boomer was out there with me, and we were messing with some little sack-chasers that hung around the building. Dutch was more of a business man than me, so he really didn't have time to bullshit with me, because I stayed on bullshit.

Anyway, me and Boomer playing tennis with the hoes – going back and forth – when one of the workers, Jit came telling us that Dutch wanted us.

As I was walking into the apartment I could hear Dutch rapping with someone on the phone. He was saying, "We'll be out there later, yo." So I figured that it had to be our cousin Diablo, because Dutch never explained his self to nobody, and he never told muthafuckas when he was coming or going.

Yet shit was different with Diablo. Dutch looked up to cuz. For real, everybody did. He was originally from Overtown, like us, but had moved to Carol City a while back. Diablo was making some big moves and had the Match Box projects on lock.

"What's good, yo?" I asked my brother as he hung up the phone. "You wanted me?"

"Yeah, we gotta slide through the Match Box a lil' later, yo…cuz got something for us, so be ready. Right now, I'm going home to count up."

At that time we wasn't buying nothing but a half of a brick. But whatever we bought, Diablo would *throw us* the same thang'. So if we bought a half, he'd front a half. Which was big for two young niggas our age.

Dutch was sort of living with this older bitch, so I mostly had the apartment 'olo. It was dropped too: 50" screen TV, big boy leather living room set, plush carpet throughout, and a top-shelf bedroom set. Me and my brother are big movie critics, so we had everything that was out – bootleg and all. Plus all the games and game-systems we had, the crib was laced.

So I just fell back in the a/c and smoked me a blunt, waiting for Dutch to come back so we could clear it, when I heard

10

somebody knock on the door. Getting up from the plush leather sofa, I adjusted the 9mm Glock in my pants and went to peep out the peep-hole. It was this animal bitch name Angie. She was older than me by four or five years. The bitch went to school with my older sister and had a cool ass little boy.

I was like, "What's up?"

Angie didn't say shit in return, she just walked past me into the apartment and sat down. I just closed the door and went back to my spot on the sofa.

Angie was aiight, I guess. I used to always look-out for her when hot shit came through the trap, because like I said, her son was my little man. I made sure that she always had groceries in her spot, because I used to lamp at her crib in spots.

Bullshit aside, Angie could've been some big-money nigga's wifey. She was a real good looking chick, and always smelt good enough to eat. This particular day she was playing a little tennis skirt outfit and some fresh white K-Swiss.

I passed her the blunt, she smoking and talking about going to the movies between puffs, but my mind was on the last time we'd fucked. I guess she was trying to hook me, because she sucked the skin off of my dick. But before I could get the blunt back and crack for some throat, somebody knocked on the damn door.

"Yeah, who is it?" I asked, peeping through the peep-hole.

It was my crazy ass sister Lottie. She was smiling as I opened the door. Probably because she was feeling good about the money she was about to beat me out of. But when she walked in and saw Angie, her whole   attitude changed.

Angie was like, "What's up, Lottie?"

Lottie frowned like, "I see you still robbin' the cradle."

Angie wasn't bothered by my sister's remark, because she was used to it. The two of them always had those types of greetings.

"Lottie, what's up, yo?" I asked, trying to diffuse the bullshit.

"I need some money," she said all nasty. "I gotta buy my baby something to wear."

11

I knew it was game. Every fiend, booster, and robber in 'Town knew to bring all of the baby clothes to us, because we'd buy that shit and give it to somebody if my sisters, cousins, or Angie couldn't used any of it.

But nonetheless, I was like, "Aiight, I got you when I get back." And knowing that my sister smoked like a freight train, I broke her off a quarter ounce of my P.S. "Here, now go somewhere."

"Yeah, aiight…" Lottie said, taking the weed. "I'ma let you get back to whatever ole' Angie came over her to give you." And she left.

With the bullshit out the window, I sat back down next to Angie and started playing with her. I had two fingers in her box and the blunt between my lips --- love was in the air. As soon as I slid my fingers in her she started leaking.

"Oooh, Bo…" she was singing as she leaned over and unzipped my shorts like a bad girl's supposed to.

You see, Angie was that baby, baby. She really knew how to please a nigga. And being as I was programmed to get boss-migraine before I Bobby Valentino [Beat! Beat! Beat!] a chick, she straight *put-on*.

I was fingering the box from the back, smoking my blunt, and trying to take her clothes off all at once. Before I knew it though, I busted-off in her mouth. But Angie ain't play with it, she went harder! Milking my shit like a boss-bitch do a boss-nigga…you feel me?

Once I rocked back up and she knew it was all good, she stood up and pulled her panties off. Pussy was hairy as a Muslim's chin. Straight up! I kept rubbers because safe sex was boss-sex to me. Angie was that baby, but she wasn't my lady and I was not about to contract no disease from her or nobody else. Plus I wasn't tryna' have no children. Because like I said, I wanted my children to be all from one woman – the woman that I absolutely loved. And at that point and time, Angie was not her.

Anyway, as she was getting the condoms off the entertainment center I came up outta my shit. She came back and rolled the rubber on. Then laid flat out on the couch, on her back with her head on the arm rest. With no words spoken I entered her.

12

My aggressive nature, compiled with my desire to feel the warmth of her insides, made me a little to anxious. Angie tensed up and placed her soft hands on my stomach.

"Do it slow, ba-be..." she whispered in my ear.

As I moved in and out of her I started sucking on her neck...her left nipple. Then the right one. After about five minutes her breathing got heavy and her body started shaking.

"Oooh God, Bo, I'm cummin'."

Her hands were on my ass, and with each stroke she tried to drive me deeper insider of her.

"Yes...yes...yes..." she chanted and the pussy got wet...wetter...wettest I've ever had! "I'm cummin' a-a-again, ba-be."

And then it happened – the bitch tried to kiss me! Angie had a fucking habit of trying to kiss me whenever we fucked – as if we were making love. I pulled out and turned her ass over. I ain't gon' lie, Angie had the prettiest body! I just had to look at her – admire the way her ass sat up and her pussy hung down – before I entered her again.

"What's wrong, baby?" she asked, looking back at it.

"If only you knew, ma." I replied as I dug in and rode out.

"So damn, ma, we gon' do that or what?" I asked Angie after our fuck session was over.

"What?" she answered, playing stupid.

But the bitch knew exactly what I was talking about. I had brought the subject up the last time we did our thang'.

"The shit with you and Brenda...and me." I was smiling and smoking another blunt.

I already knew what it was. She just ain't know that I knew. My sister had told me that Angie and her best-friend Brenda were sucking the life outta each other. This old nigga that was eating good Overtown had turned them out for a few stacks. Now I wanted my issue. Only I wasn't about to give them no two stacks! That was out...

Remember I said that Angie was that baby, baby? Well, Brenda was that baby, baby, baby! On a scale of one to ten I'd have to say that Brenda was a twelve.

"Bo, I…I don't know…I'm feelin' you for real…and, and you…I just, for real…I don't know…" Angie whined between puffs of the 'dro.

My dick got hard as fuck thinking about the ménage trios with her and Brenda. Because I knew what "I don't know" meant. "I'll do it if I have to." True bill! Because if she wasn't with it she would've just said, "hell nawl."

So we started playing tennis – going back and forth with *what if's* and *just don'ts* – but my serve was too much pressure for her. I cleared up all of her concerns and eased her every worry.

"So we straight?"

"Yeah, we straight…" she hesitated. "Brenda like you anyway."

"Oh yeah?" I was surprised to hear that.

"Yeah," she hit the blunt. "She see the way that you be lookin' out for me and my son, when you really don't have to…plus, she say you a cool lil' nigga."

"Lil nigga?" I questioned. "I'm bein' referred to as a lil' nigga?"

She laughed. Angie had a real pretty persona, and I loved to hear her laugh.

"Look, just put it together and hit me with the time." I told her and handed her $250.

$ $ $

When I walked Angie out of the building I found Dutch across the street at the dice-game. They were shooting three-dice. I wasn't really with that dice shit, because the dice-game was where nigga got their little jabs in. All the "L" and "slight" that niggas feel for a nigga comes out when them craps roll.

It was about seven or eight dudes out there – nothing major. The bet was $20 or better and Dutch had the bank. Dudes were dropping 'ifties and bees, praying for a dick-roll, but Dutch was issuing nothing but Haitians (fours), police (fives), and headcracks (sixes). I was sweeping the money and them niggas was hating it.

14

Of course, they knew what it was, because every time I swept I had to re-adjust the Glock. After about thirty minutes niggas was broke and the game was over. Dutch had raped them for about $1,800.

We jumped in my Chevy and hit I-95. It took us about 25 to 30 minutes to get to the Match Box. When we got there Diablo – our older cousin by about nine or ten years – was in one of his fucking lecture moods "again!" It's like every time we came to cop he turned into a college professor or some shit. That day he was tripping because we – me and Dutch – was still buying a half a bird.

"Yall niggas content with a half? Yall think I'ma keep throwin' yall shit and yall ain't steppin' up?"

I ain't say shit.

"I'm sayin' though, cuz. We just --" Dutch tried to speak.

"Yall just spendin' too much money and spendin' too much time fuckin' with these two-dollar-hoes."

When he said the shit about the "two-dollar-hoes" he was looking dead at me. But I really didn't give a fuck what Diablo was talking about. He didn't know how much money me and Dutch had saved, or what we was coming to cop. He just saw us and jumped into preacher mode…Even though we did want a half and didn't have shit saved. We was only sixteen though.

$$$

The streets were snatching squares for $19—19,500. We were getting them from Diablo for $15—16,500, easy. Ounces were going for $550-600 already cooked, and we were sort of like the only niggas in 'Town with the resources to get it. So for real, cuz was right, we should've had plenty money.

"Aiight then, you right," Dutch said. "Give us a whole one then."

Diablo beamed with pride. "Yall got brick fare?"

15

Dutch shook his head yes. I pulled out a 'gar and started rolling me a blunt. I didn't see what the big deal was. He was acting like a father seeing his child take its very first steps.

"Look," Diablo said, passing us two kilos. "I'm proud of yall boys...just bring back $15,000 for the one yall buying, and give me $16,000 for the one I'm frontin' you...Yall niggas save up and buy more the price'll get sweeter."

$$$

A lot of shit changed for us that day – financially. We had more room to play, so we started putting out bigger work. Not to mention our powder was cleaner now – pure. We was already stopping traffic, but with the extra work on hand we was killing the game! Especially with the whip that Diablo showed us. I could easily turn an ounce and a half into two and a quarter.

Diablo and all of his homeboys were big on rental cars with dark-boys on them, so me and Dutch parked the Chevy's and started splurging in rentals too. We was changing them bitches out every week or two. I guess we wanted to be just like our big cousin, and my momma hated that shit. She was a "G" and all, did time for killing a nigga before me and Dutch was born, and she really had love for Diablo, she just wasn't feeling the direction that our lives were taking. Nonetheless, she gave us advice and even let us keep work at her crib. "Don't keep all your eggs in one basket," she used to always say.

$$$

That night after we left Carol City, we shot straight to the ole-girl crib. She wasn't there so me and Dutch rocked-up half and busted it down. The other half we bagged up clean. It was close to the first so that shit wasn't going to last no more than three or four days.

16

As soon as we finished Dutch left to go take care of something and I called Angie.

"Hello?"

"What's up, yo?"

"Boy, where you at?" Angie screamed into the phone. "I been callin' yo' ass for the longest!"

"Aiight, well here I go, ma. What's the national emergency?"

"Brenda right here, and it's all good."

"Oh, yeah?"

"Yeah, unless you scared." Angie said, laughing.

"Meet me at the crib in 45 minutes." I said and hung up.

I hit the shower and jumped fresh. But before I could get with the babies I had to make sure the workers were straight and dropped the other work off to the stash apartment. It took me about 30 minutes to handle that and pop in New Jack City, that was one of my favorite movies at the time. I had a blunt burning while G-Money's animal ass hoe performed to "I Wanna Sex You Up," when I heard a knock at the door.

It was Brenda and Angie. They looked like they'd already been drinking and smoking. Brenda had on a little dress with the thin shoulder straps, it came just to her thick pretty thighs. She had a big-girl shoe-game with the six inch heels popping off. Baby looked good enough to eat – I mean really eat!

Angie had on a gray Nike outfit made out of that stretch material, with the matching Air Max. She sat down next to Brenda and picked up the blunt that was burning in the ash-tray.

As I sat down G-Money's hoe was still dancing, so I cracked at Angie. "Can you work it like that, ma?"

It was a bottle of Remy Martin X.O. on the coffee table – priced at $275. Angie poured herself a shot, downed it, and started doing her thang'. I poured a shot for me and Brenda while we watched the show.

Shorty on the movie ain't have shit on Angie. She snaked her body so slick and smooth that my dick almost jumped out of my shorts. By the time Angie was completely naked, so was me and Brenda. She had my swollen dick in her hand, admiring it.

17

Then she looked at Angie and said, "you wasn't lyin'," before she started sucking me up.

I turned Angie around and went to playing with her hairy pussy. She was so wet! And I couldn't take it. It hadn't been three minutes of Brenda's skull-game and I was nutting-up. Brenda looked up at me, smiling.

"Can you do Angie like that?" I asked the bitch.

"Hmmp," was all that she said before she stood and started sucking Angie's breast. As she sucked one, then the other, she eased Angie onto the couch. Brenda kissed her way down Angie's body, stopping at her pussy. She pushed her legs up and fucked Angie with her tongue. She had her making noises and faces that I'd never made her do. At first I thought the shit was all an act, but then Angie just started trembling and spraying rich white paste all over Brenda's nose and upper lip.

"Oh yyeess, baaabee, yyeessss!" Angie whined.

Brenda kissed her way back up Angie's body and locked lips with her. They moved and touched each other so soft and delicately. It was like they'd been practicing and could anticipate the others' forthcoming desires. I'd never ever seen two people express so much passion.

Brenda was laid back with her legs busted wide-open and Angie was eating her up. By now I was harder than I'd ever been. I slid on a rubber and started fucking Angie from the back. The X.O. had me numb, so I wasn't about to nut again for a long time.

Angie's pussy was wet, but it was gripping me good. Every time I dug into her I pulled out with even more cum' covering the rubber.

"I'm cummin', ba-be!" Brenda sang.

I pushed Angie out of the way and starting beating Brenda. Her pussy was so good and tight! Angie laid down and played with her clit while I rode out on Brenda. Everytime she came — which was about three times — she'd close her eyes and bust her legs open wider.

We went at it for about three hours, and by 3:00 a.m. we were out of it! I couldn't get on hard and their pussies were dry. So we just sat up smoking weed, talking, and watching movies.

$$$

The next morning I got up, broke the two animals off $250 a piece, and went out in front of the building to get some fresh air and smoke one. As I was posted-up, doing me, this nigga out of Swamp City projects pulled up. Niggas out of Swamp City were known for robbing, but Trav – the nigga – did a little hustling and bought ounces from us in spots.

"What's good, Bo?" he said, jumping out his car.

"Ain't shit," I responded and passed him the blunt.

"This lace?"

"Hell nawl."

"I'm good," he passed it back. "You straight?"

I took the blunt back and looked at Trav. "Yeah, I'm straight. Whatchew' need, a 28?"

"Um', nah. You gotta nine piece?" Trav asked, looking all around and shit. "And I need it hard."

I hit the blunt and thought about the profit. Shiid', that was a nice little lick. $600 an ounce, times nine, which was really only six – because I turned one and a half into two and a quarter, was like $900 an onion.

"Gimme a hour, Trav, I got that."

It ain't take me no time to *whip-it* and *weigh-it-up*. I put the shit in a zip-lock and then put the zip-lock in a brown paper bag. Trav had a baby-momma that lived in the projects and that's where he wanted to meet.

When I pulled up it was beaucoup niggas out there. But I ain't trip because they knew me, and they knew that I kept that 21 shot Glock on me at all times. Soon as I stepped out of the car Trav walked over.

"That was fast."

"Where my money?" I asked, passing him the bag.

"Let me run in and grab it."

He jogged off to the apartment and I leaned on my car. Niggas looking all side ways at me, but it ain't no real pressure. Five minutes went by and Trav still ain't came back. *Fuck this nigga doin'?* I asked myself, walking over to the apartment. I knocked and this other nigga opened the door.

"What?" he asked, his unit all balled up.

"Where Trav at, yo?"

"Lil' nigga, Trav said 'write that off'."

"What?"

"Write that off, nigga. That's took!"

He was an older nigger. Matter-of-fact, all them niggas was older niggas.

I jumped in the car and cleared it. Tears were in my eyes I was so mad. I called Dutch and told him how the niggas tried me.

$ $ $

Ten minutes later Dutch busted through the door with Terry. Terry had a Tec-22 with a 50 round clip on that bitch, and Dutch had a Mac-II that shot 32 times. We jumped in my car, no ski-masks, and shot right back around there.

It's a little alley that connects the street that they were on to the next street over. That's where we parked and came through on them. It was about 20 niggas out there when we went to letting loose.

Tat! Tat! Tat! Tat! Tat! Tat! Tat! Tat! Tat! Tat! everybody was bussing and them niggas was running like hoes. About seven of them got lit up. We jumped back in my car and shot straight to the Match Box.

We explained everything to Diablo and waited as he made a few calls. As fate would have it, the person that he was trying to holla at was busy trying to get in touch with him. The nigga's name was James – an O.G. cat who controlled the Swamps and all of the niggas in them. He was also one of the seven niggas that we shot the fuck up. Lucky nigga too, he only got hit in the arm.

Anyway, they talked for about five minutes, and thirty minutes after they'd hung up two car loads of niggas pulled up – James and his crew. I knew all of them because we were all from 'Town.

James got out with his little Unit on and shit, but niggas knew Diablo and they knew what time it was with us – especially after we had done put that fi' on they ass.

Anyway, him and Diablo hugged and dapped each other before they walked off talking. When they returned from their walk James pulled me and Dutch up and told us that he respected what we'd done because he would've done the same thing, *blah blah blah blah*. He was rapping his ass off about the shooting and the respect shit, but wasn't nobody saying shit about us getting our nine ounces back.

So I was like, "Yo, I'm sorry shit had to happen like this, but it's gon' be worse if we don't get our shit back."

He smiled and said, "Why can't the young niggas 'round me be like yall."

It was agreed that we would get our nine ounces – and we did. Niggas like James were platinum, they never went back on their word.

We stayed out of the way for about two weeks, then shit went back to normal. Well, for us it did, not for Trav. Somebody – two dudes with AK-47's – gunned him down in front of his baby-mommas house a month later. After those series of events nothing major happened until about a year later.

Chapter 4

BO

Shit was gravy. We was getting big-boy money and saving like crazy. Not only was the spot still jumping off the hinges, but our clientele with dudes buying weight was growing as well. So we started hanging out – Rolex, Coco's, Lukes on the beach, Miami Nights. Diablo had introduced us to his man Forty, so we didn't have to go to the Match Box to see him anymore.

Dealing with Forty was cool. He always had work and he loved to hang out. Which seemed a little crazy at first, because he was Spanish. But he lived in a black neighborhood and had three black baby-mommas. It was through him that I really started hanging out and got beat for my head.

$$$

One day I was lamping in front of the spot. Me and about three of the fellas were out there smoking weed and shit when Shana walked up. She was a bad little round the way chick that fucked with this basketball star. They both were like three or four years older than me.

"What's up, Bo?"

"Shiid', me…sometimes you." I kicked it to her.

"You fallin' to the game?"

The bitch knew I was going to the game, everybody was. The game was a real big game and her nigga was playing.

"Yeah, all us goin', what's up?"

"I'm tryna go with yall…if it's alright. I'll fill yo' tank up and break you off."

I laughed in that hoe face. Break me off? I was breaking off, and that slick Overtown bitch knew it. I had plenty money and didn't need hers. But being as she was the homegirl and we were already going – about ten cars deep – I took her money and let her ride with me. Good thing I took her bread, because as soon as we got to the game she ditched. It was another two months before I ran into her again. I was in Miami Nights with Forty and my brother.

"What's up, Bo?" she tapped me on the shoulder, smiling. "Buy yo' girl a drink."

"Bitch, what I'ma buy yo' loose conniving ass, they don't sell in here…now get the fuck outta my face!"

I don't know what possessed that bitch to try me like that. Maybe it was because I was young – she thought I was dumb. But I assured her that I wasn't by cussing her ass out. I called Shana every name under the sun. Yet she would not leave until I had heard her out.

"Look Bo, please. I'm sorry for ghostin' you like that. But the timin' was bad," she explained.

"Man, whatever."

"No Bo, it's not whatever. I said I fucked up," she whined and grabbed my hand. "Please Bo," she was rubbing the inside of my palm as she spoke. "Take me to the Fair with you and I'll make it up…I promise, it'll be all good."

The Fair that she was speaking of was the Dade County Youth Fair. It was the Fair of all Fairs – roller coasters, faris wheels, bumper cars, ski left, haunted house, all kinds of food and games. It's a real live event.

Anyway, I gave in and agreed to let her fall through with us. Me and my brother took the whole hood! We probably dropped about eight grand that night. It was worth it though. To see the little project children and their ole-girls laughing and having fun. They could ride whatever ride or eat whatever they wanted with no pressure. It was their world that night, even if it was only for that one night.

I didn't spend that much time with Shana that night. But every time I glanced in her direction I'd catch her eyeing me. The looks that she gave me said that she was really impressed with my financial status. So when the night ended we exchanged numbers and made plans to rendezvous that following week. We started doing it every weekend. And before I knew it, Shana and I were living together.

$$$

I ain't gon' lie, home cooking, live in pussy, waking up to brains for breakfast; all that shit was new to me. And truth be told, as I reflect back on the situation, Shana was a cool chick. I was just young, having money, and couldn't help but to do me. Clubbing and fucking bitches was my forte. Especially fucking with Forty! Dude was an all out party-animal, and I was his party-partner. For that reason alone it wasn't long before Shana had had enough. But I didn't give a fuck! I was having shit my way.

Me and my brother were sending work out of town here and there. $9,000 back off of nine ounces was religion! So we got religious and started sending eighteen up there. The money always came back faithfully. We kept three or four rentals and our jewelry-game was top-shelf. So naturally suckas' started hating, whispering all under their breath like bitches – *who them young niggas thank they is? Oh, they couldn't put down in the Swamps like that...They only stuntin' 'cause of they cousin, but he pie too...* That's just some of the shit that I used to hear – never directly from the source. Shit always came to a nigga from round the block. While at the same time – we didn't know this then – our cousin Diablo was beefing with this older nigga from 'Town. Of course, Diablo didn't play no game when it came to beef, so he quickly sent dude on his way. And that older nigga getting killed sparked some more shit that's still brewing, on the low.

Anyway, Trav's homeboys saw this as their opportunity to retaliate for Trav getting murked. Shit ws crazy, and Overtown was divided like a muthafucka. Nobody wasn't trusting nobody.

24

Muthafuckas that were eating together yesterday and expressing love for each other were now aiming for one another's head.

Now the building where we were trapping from was also the building where my grandmother lived. My momma, aunties, sisters and cousins hung out over there everyday. While me and Dutch had closed down shop and stopped hanging Overtown altogether. Not because we were scared or nothing like that, but because we were on some other shit – some get money shit! That's all we thought about, money.

The ole-girl was living in Liberty City at the sametime, so we mostly chilled over there. Clubbing, fucking hoes, and moving big weight. There were still some loyal people from 'Town that fucked with us – some we brought with us. One was my dog Pressure World. He was a little older than me and Dutch, but he was my muthafuckin' dog! Most of the weed being pumped Overtown was pumping out of his spot – one block over from our old spot. I kept telling him to hold fast and stop going over there about that little money. I had something in the works for him, but he was impatient.

Me and Dutch had financed these two dyke hoes trip to Texas for some fire weed at $150 a pound. That was going to be his thang. All he had to do was *wait*. The first trip netted twenty pounds – ten for them and ten for us. Only Pressure wasn't there to get the weed and profit from it because he was in the hospital, *shot-the-fuck-up*.

You see, Pressure was lying to me and Dutch, and sneeking back Overtown to his weed trap. The nigga who he had running the trap was a real fuck-nigga, and thought that by setting Pressure World up for the kill he'd be able to keep everything that my dog had worked and sweated blood for.

Me and Shana were no longer exclusive at this point, but I still fell through form time-to-time, fucked, broke her off, and went on about mine. So when she called me this particular night I started not to answer because I didn't feel like fucking her. But something inside of me pushed me to push *send*.

"Yeah?" I answered, high as fuck off some of the weed that the dyke hoes had delivered.

"Bo, somebody done shot Pressure," she said.

"Where at?!"

"Overtown."

I just hung up. My sister had a Nissan Altima that I had thrown some dark tints on. That's what I was driving at the time. I hit I-95 and did everything on the dash board getting to my dog. By the time I pulled up the ambulance had already driven him to Jackson. I was fucked up! High blown and mad as fuck! Not understanding at the time how Pressure got shot and why he was even over there, I sent somebody to tell his sister to meet me by Gibson Park on 12th Street and 3rd Avenue – right across the street from Douglas Elementary School. As I sat in the car smoking a blunt, I spotted Pumpkin looking around. I flashed the high beams. She quickly jogged over and jumped in.

It was a very short ride over to the Trama Unit at Jackson Hospital. Nothing was said during the trip. Head-bussin' was on my mind, and poor Pumpkin was lost to the fact that her brother might not make it.

Once we got there she jumped out and rushed in.

30 minutes later she got back in with a tight smile on her face.

"He gon' be okay. They shot him five times, but nothing was fucked up on the inside."

"Good," I breathed a little easier. "You straight?"

"Yeah, I'm straight," she said real low. "You just be careful, Bo."

"Don't trip off me, I'm good...but, who did it?"

Pumpkin paused for a long minute. I could see that she really didn't want to tell me. Not because she didn't want to see the dudes that shot her brother get their due, but because she didn't want me to be the one to give it to them. Pumpkin just wanted the whole shit to be over and done with. So she told me.

"My daddy was on the porch...and, and he said that it was Ty, Man, and Cash."

"Thanks."

"Aiight. You can leave me though, my momma is on her way."

"Aiight, Pumpkin, I'ma see you later."

An hour later, me, Dutch and Terry were in the Swamp posted up. I was driving the splack, Terry was riding shot-gun, while Dutch took knife handle. We had Cle posted up two blocks over in a rental for the clean getaway.

The objective was to strike hard and fast! Nobody would expect us – two jits – to hit back the very same night. Especially within the hour, so the element of surprise was on our side. We were going to knock them off balance and keep them off balance.

I had the Mazda parked on 5th Street and 5th Avenue, which gave us a clear view straight up to 8th Street and 5th Avenue. 30 minutes had passed and there was no sign of Ty, Cash, or the hoe-ass-nigga Man.

"Man, I ain't tryna be out here all night, dog." Terry said.

Me and my brother just ignored the nigga. If killing them hoe-ass-niggas meant sitting out there until sunrise, then that's what the fuck we were going to do. So that's what we did. And bingo! Look who pulled up – the bitch-ass-nigga Cash. Ain't no picks, so we masked up and rolled down on the nigga, lights out.

Cash was sitting drinking with four or five other niggas. Probably celebrating shooting my dog. Before they knew it we were out and on their ass – Cash never stood a chance.

Tat! Tat! Tat! Tat! Tat! Tat! Tat! Tat! Tat! Tat! Dutch and Terry busted off, clearing the way to our intended target.

Right there where Cash stood is exactly where I dropped him. *Yak! Yak! Yak! Yak!* the AK exploded, sending four .762's through the center of his face.

We jumped back into the splack and sped off. Cle was right there waiting by Booker T. Washington Middle School. We jumped out quick and Cle cleared it.

The ride to Carol City was quiet. Everybody was caught up in their own thoughts. I was thinking about killing Ty and Man when my phone rung.

"Yeah?"

"Where you at?" My ole-girl asked without even saying hello.

"In Carol City."

"Where yo' brutha'?"

"He right here, why?"

"I'm just checkin' on yall, because I heard Pressure got shot earlier and now somebody done killed Cash...Bo, I hope –"

"Ma, chill." I cut her off. "We out here with some chicks and we ain't gettin' in no trouble."

"Well, I hope yall wearin' rubbers with them lil' fast ass hoes," my ole-girl preached. "And tell Dutch to call me." With that said she hung up.

"Who that?" Dutch asked me.

"The ole-girl."

"What she want?"

"Nothing really. Just givin' me the *tee* on what happened to Cash. He outta there."

"Good!" Terry said with excitement. "We should get Ty and Man at the wake."

"I hope so," Dutch replied. "Sorta' like killin' two birds with one stone."

By now we were pulling up into the Match Box.

Dutch and Terry jumped out and me and Cle pulled off.

We had hide-outs everywhere – an apartment in Miami Lakes, the duplex in Liberty City, another duplex in Carol City, and the townhouses in Pembroke and Miramar. So our security was pretty much straight – as far as laying our heads down.

I shot over to the Pork-N-Bean Projects to see my little animal. I call her Red Girl, and she's like that. Ass, titties, and a fire head! The bitch couldn't think pass go though. But that didn't matter to me. Red Girl was just a cool little chick that I fucked from time-to-time.

I picked Red Girl up and shot straight to the hotel. We wasn't even in the room good and she was chewing me up – all tongue and throat! I couldn't believe how violently tender her lips were. She might've had the best head-game in the world.

We got up early the next morning. I always rose with the sun. My ole-girl used to always say, "you scared you gon' miss something." But that was just me. Red Girl went in the bathroom to get herself together while I rolled and blew me an early morning blunt on the balcony. The air was cool. Sitting out there under the heavens in so much peace and harmony was strange for me. No noise, nobody with their hand out, and nobody threatening to harm what was mine. I thought at that instance that maybe my life could be as peaceful. But my phone rung. I already knew who it was and knew that life wasn't going to be as that brief moment had promised.

"Yeah?" I answered.

"Meet me at Frank's house," Dutch said.

"Aiight," I said and hung up.

Frank was a bitch that lived around the corner from the ole-girl's house. So I dropped Red Girl off and shot straight 'round there. Dutch was already there reading the newspaper and drinking an orange juice.

"What's up?"

"Ain't nothing," Dutch replied and kept reading.

"Why you called me over here?"

"So we can go check on Pressure," Dutch said and folded up the paper. "Let's go."

We jumped in my rental and cleared it. I was bumping that THUG LIFE. Dutch turned it down and started explaining how we needed to focus more on our money after we fucked-over those other two niggas. I just listened. We already had a little over $150,000 cash, a few bricks up the road, and every bitch in Dade County on our 16 year old dicks. How much more focused could we be? But I didn't say shit. He was more of the thinker.

"Bruh, my nigga, I was with Diablo all last night, dog." Dutch continued. "We ran through a little over two tickets."

"Two million?" I asked him.

"Yeah, my nigga. That's why we gotta step our shit up." Dutch let his window down a little to let some of the week smoke out, because he didn't smoke. He did drink though. "He wanna holla at us later on."

"For what?" I said, "another lecture."

We both busted out laughing.

"Nah, but on the real, Bo. We gotta get this bread and get us a plan, bruh. We got advantages that other niggas ain't got, but they don't do us no good if we don't use 'em to the fullest."

"I feel you," I said, blowing smoke out of my nose.

$$\$ \$ \$$$

Pressure had been out of surgery, but he was still heavily sedated. So he was *out-of-it* when we got there. Still, we sat with dog for three hours. That was our new routine until he got released from the hospital. We'd sit with him and kick it, then flush it over to the bar. That's where Forty and them hung out at. The shit sat right on the corner of 89th Street and 22nd Avenue. Chico owned the spot so our whole circle lamped there. Plus the little gambling house was right 'cross the street. If you've ever read that book STREET LEGENDS VOL. 2 by Seth Ferranti, these are the same niggas that he was talking about: Bush, Vinny, Chuck, Chico, Fats, Diddy (Nitty), Fish Grease, Piere, Red Boy, and a few other kats that Diablo was cool with. Everybody was always either shooting pool, shooting dice, or shooting the shit.

Dutch and me really didn't hang up to the bar, but we'd come through though. It was some funny muthafuckas up there, as well as a wealth of game. Like Bush and Vinny, they was always arguing with niggas, Chuck and Fats were always out to beat a nigga outta something – mainly your money or dope, and Red Boy wanted to rob and kill everybody. 'Til this day I still don't know what the fuck Fish Grease was on, but Dutch and me got a little bit from everybody. Mainly Diddy and Chico though. They were on their business shit. Diddy was a dreamer. The niggas was always rapping bout having the hottest label in the south – on some southern Bad Boy shit, that's why we called the nigga Diddy. Now Chico, the nigga was next level. He didn't have the bread that Diablo had, but he was legally getting it good. Dutch had told me that Chico owned a dry cleaners in Palm Beach, but come to find out, the nigga owned the whole plaza.

Anyway, after kicking it with them for about an hour Diablo pulled up. Everybody hollered, because it was love at the bar. Wasn't no boss-man and it didn't matter how much money you had, everybody was equal.

Diablo pulled me and my brother to the side. He was concerned about the shit with Cash. I guess Dutch had said something to him last night, because I sure hadn't said shit to nobody. He never directly asked us "did we do it?" or even "what it was about?" Nor did we volunteer those answers, because we all lived by rules and the main one was, "if yo' ass wasn't there it ain't none of yo' business!"

Still, Diablo carried on for twenty minutes about, "how it should be done" and "what should be done next." My mind was back at the hotel on that balcony, smoking a blunt under the heavens. It was peace up there, and this shit was getting to fucking complicated for me. I mean, all I really wanted was a family and a comfortable place to live where I could give my children more than I was given. I guess Diablo peeped that I wasn't there – mentally.

"Well look, I'm not tryna tell yall what to do or run yall lives. I'm just tryna make sure yall straight," he continued. "So at least holla at somebody up here to assist yall in whatever…aiight?"

We agreed and he went on talking. The subject was now big money in small towns. Up until that moment I didn't know just how serious Diablo was. He had work in VA, North Click, and B-more. On some STREET RAISED shit, he had work all over the East Coast like Chino and Saph. Only this wasn't no fucking book, shit was *all-the-way* real.

Because of the shit with Cash our trap in Overtown was closed. So Diablo offered to sell us ten bricks for $135,000, and send them up the road for us.

"I'm gonna guarantee the work gets there and that the money gets back safe."

"What we gettin' off each bird?" Dutch asked.

"I'ma double yall shit." Diablo shot back. "Plus I'm not chargin' yall for my cars or drivers."

We already knew that it was $1,000 for each bird and that nothing was guaranteed, normally, so Dutch jumped on the offer without me having to say anything. Then, somehow, the conversation turned to Cash's wake. Diablo was against riding through it.

"It's gonna be a lot of family and children there, lil' cuz. People that don't have nothing to do with this shit…nah, that ain't a good look." He thought for a minute. "Yall gotta throw some money around. Give them niggas and bitches a few stacks for the info' yall need. Find out these niggas habbits…yall already at an advantage over these niggas 'cause they broke! So they gotta be out on somebody's corner to get paid, we don't…start using yo' resources. All them hoes that wanna be down, they gotta choose up. It's us or them! Then start hittin' the niggas that count. Ain't no sense in hittin' the followers. You kill the head and the body's dead!"

Me and Dutch just stood there. Shit was really heating up.

"What? Yall niggas scared or something?" Diablo asked.

"Fuck nawl!" I screamed and I meant that shit.

"Well you better not be. Fuck 'cause a nigga be strapped. Eight-five percent of the niggas that get they shit blowed off be strapped. Yall just can't be fakin'…be aggressive, and once you commit, you can't stop until you got your man. You understand?"

I shook my head yes, because I definitely understood…

Chapter 5

DEWEY

I sat there listening to my lil' fool buck the dizzles, wondering when he was gonna put something else in the air. I needed me another square as bad as I needed to get my ass outta jail...no bullshit! I had a few niggas that I really needed to see about a few very important things. One was the bitch-ass-nigga Crab, Ty's cousin. Yeah, the same Ty that Bo and Dutch were going through it with.

See, I'ma G straight up and down – all black everythang! So I respect G's and always stick to the G-code. That's why I like Bo so much. His ole-girl, Ms. Sue was a G, his ole-boy, Top Cat was a G, and even though I didn't know that Diablo was his cousin, that nigga's a certified G too. I'm saying, I knew that lil' one was a G by blood, but I ain't know it was like that?!?! Straight up!

I had met the dude Crab on the 10th floor, on some juvenile shit. It wasn't but three niggas out them 40's, so we was paintin' every day, three-four times a day. And the nigga Crab wasn't ducking nothing! He faded every nigga that wanted one, like a G. So naturally we got *down-as-fuck* and carried that shit back to the streets. Only I wasn't out that long, because I robbed this soft-body ass nigga Ted–Stanka from 'Town put me on the lick – and came off sweet. I ain't gon' do numbers with you, but know it was enough to split three ways and fall back.

Anyway, about a week after I dropped that do-do brown Cadillac Brougham – ninety fronts and backs, Mirrors and blue-cheese, with pillow-crush and boom – Stanka called me yelling and shit.

"Man, some Carol City niggas done approached Sam 'bout that shit you touched Ted for."

"And?"

"You gotta give yo' share back."

I laughed in that nigga's face. "You, Sam, and them niggas got me fucked up! You better be the Red Cross talkin' 'bout gettin' mine...nye' play with it."

I hung the muthafuckin' phone up. Fuck Stanka! I called Crab and he assured me that he would holla at Sam about the bullshit. Because I wasn't giving no nigga nothing back! No Swamp nigga, no Buck Town nigga, and 'specially not no Carol City ass nigga.

About thirty minutes later my Mobile One went off. Only it wasn't Crab, it was his cousing Ty, talking about he'd just hung up with Sam and Sam gave 'us' the green light to smash the Carol City nigga and his two cousins.

I was like, "Green Light? Fuck you mean, 'Green Light?'" Because I didn't call Crab about no fucking 'Green Light!'

"Sam's with you, Dewey, my nigga. That's took, nye' it's time to ride." Ty explained.

Me being me – a true G at heart – I changed cars and got up with Ty, Crab, and Man. Ty knew a bitch who fucked with this nigga in Carol City that cut hair. The nigga was always bragging to the bitch about this nigga who's hair he cut. Long story short, it was the same nigga that stepped to Stanka's scary ass about the shit that I took.

The niggas was in a blue Audi parked in front of dude's barber shop when we whipped up, *Yak! Yak! Yak! Yak! Yak! Yak! Yak! Yak!* Me, Ty, and Man jumped out. Crab was the hoe-nigga on this caper, and he got us away clean. Only thang' though, dude wasn't in his car. One of his homeboys had the muthafucka. Shit really got crazy from there, 'cause two niggas emptied two AK-47's on Sam a week later and Stanka hauled ass. I was still in the blind as to who I was really fucking with.

So like a month after Sam's close-casket funeral, me and about five niggas from 'Town – Joe, Dorry, Conrad, Zack, Dell, and my dog Ty – got together to plot out the Carol City nigga's demise. Crab wasn't nowhere to be found, and of the six niggas present only Ty and Joe could really be trusted to *bang-it-out.* The others hadn't done anything impressive, and even Joe's only body was that of an innocent by-stander. Yet we needed each other to get rid of the Carol City nigga. Because even at this point I still didn't know who the nigga was.

"Look, we need to stop playin' and catch them lil' bitches at they mommas house." Joe said.

"But them lil' niggas ain't no real threat." Conrad stepped up. "They cousin outta C-C is the one we need to get."

"We just startin' with them." Ty said. "We gon' finish with ole-boy."

I didn't say shit, I just listened. Reason being, I just wanted to kill them niggas and get back in my Brougham…I got jammed up though. The crackas ran down on me coming out of FireBall on 60th and 14th and I had a .40 on me. Good thang' though, 'cause that same night some gangstas rolled up on 39th Street and 11th Avenue – two blocks from my crib – and fucked my dogs over. It had been three murders in less than a week, so the heat was on. Homicide was everywhere asking questions, leaving cards and building up a serious task force…

Chapter 6

BO

The next morning I was awakened to the sound of fat ass Willie calling my name. Without brushing my teeth or washing my face, I slipped on my sliders and walked across the dirty open-dorm to the sally port. Willie slipped me a package.

"That's the new Raw-Nitty, some Plies, and my new mix-tape...plus it's some L's, Newports and some fire ass 'dro I got from Pressure World. He say the crackas snatched a few of the guys and they lookin' for Dutch."

I didn't have to ask why or for what? Shit had been so crazy. I was surprised they wasn't already locked up.

The Box was on, so everybody was crowded around the TV watching some Luke shit. I looked over the tapes that Will had brought me – wondering what in the hell made him think that I'd wanna hear his mix-tape when I only funk that classic shit – and put Raw-Nitty in. He was only local, but he had that rider music. So I fired up a Newport and tried to think out my next move. But guess who crept up?

"What's good famalam?" Dewey said, smiling and reaching for my square.

I hit it again and passed it to him, knowing damn well I wasn't getting it back.

"Ain't shit, Dewey."

We sat listening to Raw as Dewey filled his lungs. I took the time to roll a L. Just as I put the flame to it Dewey deaded his short and hit me with the 21 questions.

"So what happened with fool 'em?"

"Who?" I asked, chest full of 'dro smoke.

"The nigga Ty."

36

"Shiid', we got 'im."

I passed Dewey the blunt and he went to the moon with it. This nigga really had a set of lungs.

"How?"

I took the L back and spilled the story.

$$$

Diablo must of really been feeling *some-type-of-way* about that whole Overtown shit that night, because he shocked the hell out of me when he jumped up.

"Do yall know where these niggas live or be at?"

Dutch looked at me and then answered, "Yeah."

Diablo turned and hollered for Vinny.

"What's up?" Vinny asked when he got to where we were standing.

Diablo gave him the run-down.

Vinny just stood there smiling.

"Yall gotta splack?" Diablo asked.

"Yeah." I answered

"Is it wiped down?" Vinny asked.

"Yeah."

"Go suit up and bring back three k-cutters." Diablo said. "And call me when yall get on the back street."

$$$

It took us about twenty minutes to get there and back. When we met Diablo and Vinny they were in a Galant rental, parked on the back street. Diablo jumped out and got into the back seat of our splack.

Few words were said as we headed towards Overtown. We passed by Ty's ole-girl crib en route – on 39th Street and 11th Avenue – and guess who was sitting out on the porch smoking a blunt? Ty and the nigga Man! It was around 9:22 p.m. So it was good and dark outside. They never saw us coming.

"Just watch my back and make sure nobody don't come outta the house and steal me." Diablo said as he eased out of the splack. "I got these two."

Yak! Yak! Yak! Yak! Yak! Yak! Yak! Yak! Diablo's AK sounded.

Dutch hopped out right behind him, *Yyyyyyyyaaaaaaaaaaaaakkkkkkkkkk'!*

They were charging the porch. I looked in time to see Ty up and fire a little 9mm. *Pop! Pop! Pop! Pop! Pop!*

The nigga had heart, I'll give him that. But it was useless. A shot hit Ty high in the chest and flipped him. Dutch stood over him and dogged him, *yyyaaaaaakkkkk!* I never saw what happened to Man, but 60 seconds after the first shot was fired we were in the change up car with Vinny.

"Yall straight?" Vinny asked, bringing the Galant across 12th.

"Nah! Damn, man, I'm hit." Diablo said.

He snatched off his bullet-proof vest and lifted his shirt. He had been hit once in the stomach, but the vest stopped the bullet – saving Diablo's life. That was another lesson learned – always vest-up when you ride because a nigga could easily get a lucky shot off. I could definitely see why my big cousin was so well respected, *he didn't fuckin' play!*

When Vinny pulled up to our car, me and Dutch got out.

"Yo!" Diablo called out.

We turned around.

"Now yall just focus on gettin' money. After you put yo' gangsta down niggas gonna respect it or be the next victims…It's survival! Either you ride or get rode on."

Vinny was smiling – showing all sixteen of his gold-teeth – as they drove off.

$$$

38

For the following few weeks we kind of laid low even though we kept our schedule with visiting Pressure everyday. With the new deal that Diablo had given us up the road we were getting more money, so our stocks sky-rocketed with the bitches and the niggas.

I was still me though, doing me. I kept my Glock .40 with the 30 round extended clip, and I continued to shop, party, and fuck bitches. Because that's what I enjoyed doing. I could never stop hitting the malls and the strip clubs with Forty.

One day Forty and me were out at Westland Mall in Hialeah shopping for his four little princesses. He was a male-whore when it came to running the streets, but dog always took care of home. I believe that's one of the things that I really admired about him. He went home everyday – even if it was four o'clock in the a.m. – and his daughters and wifey were straight.

Anyway, I wasn't really feeling the shopping shit that day. I don't know why, it's like something bigger than 'me' was on my mind. I'm saying, I had everything that a young nigga could need or want, but something was still missing in my life. While he spent grands I decided to call my down-south chick, Denise.

"Yeah, what you on?" I asked as soon as she said hello.

"Nothing…what's up with you?"

"At the mall."

"Oh…well, look Bo, I need to tell you something."

"Tell me then."

"I'm, I'm pregnant, Bo."

That was a relief to me. I thought she was about to say that she had AIDS. Because I strap-up and all, but Denise was one of the 'few' that had talked me out of the rubber.

"Ain't no pressure, Denise." I said calmly. "Who the daddy is?"

She hung up on me. Or maybe my cell phone was tripping. I was in the mall. So I called right back.

"Hello!" somebody screamed in the phone.

"Who this?"

"Tasha."

"Put Denise on the phone."

I could hear Tasha telling Denise to get the phone.

"What!" Denise yelled.

39

"Yo, I'll be down there."

"Whatever."

It was silence on the line. I didn't know what to think or say.

"Yo, look Denise, you caught me at a fucked up time. It's a lot goin' on and I gotta lot of shit on my mind."

Still silence. What did she expect me to say? She was 22 and I was like 16.

"Well, I'll holla at you later."

"Okay," she whispered and I hung up.

$$\$\,\$\,\$$

I couldn't wait for Forty to finish shopping. I really needed to holla at Denise – face to face. I needed to look shorty in the eyes when she said that the baby was mine. She was a cool chick and all, we'd been fucking on the regular for about a year, but having a baby was a big step! Because like I said, I wasn't going to be a "baby daddy" like my daddy was; I was going to be a "father" and loving husband to whoever had my child.

"Yo, drop me off in the hood." I told Forty as we cleared it from the mall. "I gotta handle something."

Big Mike's SOMETHING SERIOUS was playing as we rode. Forty was vibing to it, but my mind was down south. It seemed like we couldn't get to Carol City fast enough.

"I'ma holla at you later, yo." I said to Forty and jumped into my car.

My other little brother – Shod – lived in Carol City also, a couple of blocks from the Match Box. He was still in school at the time, so me and Dutch bought him everything that he could want – to keep him out of the streets. His mother died of cancer when we were all young, so Shod lived with his grandma. I called him to take the trip down south with me.

"Hello?" he answered.

"What you on?"

"Oh, I'm chillin'…I thought you and Dutch was supposed to come get me last night. I beeped both of yall."

"Just bring yo' ass outside, yo."

I was already out front. He got in and I pulled off.

"How's school goin'?" was the first thing that I asked him.

"Everythang' everythang'."

"You been skippin' class and shit?"

"Man, I done told yall niggas, yall ain't my daddy."

I guess he was supposed to have been straightening me. I just shook my head, because me and Shod both knew that I would buss' his ass. Still, I understood though. Shod was a rebel by blood. He couldn't help going hard and trying to be his own man even if he wanted to…now ask me how I know.

"Yo, I found a Chevy. They want ten stacks for it, it's runnin' too."

"I bet it is." I said.

"What's that supposed to mean, yo?"

I laughed at his young ass trying to be older than me.

"Just what I said, yo."

He sucked his teeth before whining, "man, I thought yall said yall was gonna get me a car."

"I thought I also said you wasn't gettin' no car that niggas gonna be tryin' to rob and kill you for."

He sucked his teeth again. "Niggas ain't crazy! They know what comes behind that."

"And what comes behind that? Mr. 'Fucking Know It All'."

He didn't say nothing. He just sat there looking stupid.

"I told you to stop listenin' to all that idle street gossip!" I blew on him. "Find you a clean lil' manly car and I'll cop it."

"Aiight pop," Shod laughed.

I laughed too. But I had to explain shit to him. Everybody had a lane in life, and he needed to stay in his. The last thing I needed was for something to happen to him because of the shit I was doing or because of the money that came from it.

"Just focus on school and rappin', yo. That's yo lane, run it."

We rode in silence. My mind was in a million different places that all led to one place in particular – Denise's house. Shorty had my mind fucked up! Pregnant? I was about to become a father, and Shod and Dutch were about to become uncles. And my old-girl? She was going to kill me! Because she always preached, "yall better be wearing rubbers with them fast ass girls!" And I'd always be like, "aiight ma, I heard you." Yet here I was expecting a child from a bitch that I'd only known for a year, and I wasn't even exclusive with her. Yeah, bitches will fuck if you don't have them locked down and put up.

You see, the bitch Tasha, Denise's best friend, I was fucking her. Of course, Denise did not know that me and Tasha was fucking. Reason being, Tasha could keep her own secrets, she just couldn't keep Denise's secrets. Every time I fucked her she had some new *tee* to give me on her best friend. So I already knew that she was pregnant. Just like I also knew that she was fucking the nigga Bert. So I didn't trust her or no other hoe as far as I could see them, because all of them were open season.

$$\$\$\$$$

When we pulled up to her crib, her and her little boosting crew was outside. They were all money-go-getters, and I truly respected that about them. Especially Denise, she was Ms. Independent. Whenever we got together money wasn't an issue. All Denise wanted a young nigga to do was *keep-it-hard* for her.

"What's up, Chanell?" I called out after lowering the dark-boys.

Chanell was Denise's loose ass sister. "Nothing, just chillin'," she replied with her sexy ass. She was a year younger than me, but she could get it too.

Denise started walking over to the car, so Shod passed me the blunt and jumped out to mess with Chanell while Denise and I talked. I could tell that she was nervous.

"What's up, ma?" I asked as soon as she closed the car door.

"Nothing," she mumbled.

I inhaled deeply and thought as I exhaled, *life as I knew it was about to change.*

"Look shorty, I'ma be real with you. I never planned on having no kids this early, 'cause I always said that if I did have kids that I was gonna be 'with' my baby-momma…and well, you know how a nigga livin' out here. I could be dead or locked up doin' forever tomorrow."

She looked at me real sad. "So, what's that supposed to mean, Bo? First you acted like the baby wasn't —"

I cut her off. "Denise, look, I don't question you. I let you run freely and do you. But what you're doin', with this baby and all, the stakes are about to rise…so you need to really consider my next question before you answer it." I paused to let the seriousness of the situation sink in, "was you fuckin' anybody else besides me?"

She dropped her head and started playing with her fingers. When she looked back up there were tears running down her face. "Yes."

I dropped my head, but I didn't cry. It did feel like the wind had been knocked out of me, and even though the truth hurt, I was glad that she didn't lie to me.

"Who?" I asked, head still down.

"Bert," she cried " A dude from around here."

"How many times?" I looked her in the eyes.

"Like once…or twice."

"Is he the only nigga you done fucked since we been kickin' it?"

"Yeah, Bo. I swear to God."

She was boo-who crying! I grabbed her and pulled her close to me.

"Don't worry, ma. We gon' make it right." I hugged her and rubbed the back of her neck as I spoke. She was still crying bad though. "Don't cry, ma. It's gon' be aiight…You with me now. But this is what it's gon' be from here on…" I lifted her head so that she could look me in my eyes. "Denise, if you cross me…I mean, if you do anything to betray my love, I will fuckin'

43

kill you. That's on stacks! If you 'ever' sleep 'round on me from this point on, I will fuckin' kill you...do you understand?"

She shook her head yes.

I then went on to explain my position. When I was finished Denise was still crying, but she now knew what I wanted and expected of her. I was going to do everything that a man was supposed to do for his woman. And when I said 'woman', I wasn't talking about no little girl running around stealing them crackas' shit. To be 'my woman' Denise was going to have to get a job or take her ass back to school. Because 'my woman' was going to have to be my back bone – like Sugar in STREET RAISED. Denise said that she clearly understood.

"Look shorty," I said, wiping tears from her face. "For real, it don't even matter if the baby's mine or not. You with me now, so it's whatever."

"But, but, Bo...it, it, it is yo's."

I kissed her lips. "It ain't no pressure, ma. You got a couple months to do all the hangin' out you gon' do. Slowly but surely, we gon' move you to the crib...now what are you bringin' to the table?"

She knew that I wasn't talking about her head and good pussy either. I was talking about money and baby knew it.

"I'll let you know later, if it's aiight with you." Denise said.

I took a few more minutes of my valuable time to reiterate my position. I didn't want her to feel forced into anything. She could turn everything down and we'd have to make other arrangements concerning the baby. There would be no more hanging out and fucking around.

"So maybe you need to think it over...'cause ma, this like a deal with the devil. One false move could cost you yo' life..."

"I got you, Bo," she simply said.

"Ain't no gettin' mad leavin' for days. Ain't no callin' the police. I'm yo' momma, daddy, friend, lover, or whatever...I'm yo' everythang, yo."

"I don't need to think it over. I know what I want and what I been wantin'."

"And what's that?"

"You."

44

"Then you got that."

I kissed her, she got out, and me and Shod cleared it.

"So," Shod asked, laughing as we traveled up US-1. "What's the verdict?"

"She straight."

"Shiid', didn't look like it. Shorty was boo-who cryin', yo."

"She'll be aiight."

I picked up my cell phone and hit Dutch.

"Yo, what the lick read?"

"Nothin', my nigga." Dutch said. "I'm chillin' in the Match Box. You comin' through?"

"Yeah, gimme 'bout a hour." I said and hung up.

Chapter 7

BO

I enjoyed spending time with Shod. Even more so, I got a real kick out of giving him shit. After all, I had it to give and I didn't want him out in the streets trying to get it. Money, clothes, and hoes – I gave Shod everything.

"You wanna hit this lil' animal I got?" I asked him as we rode.

"Hell yeah!"

"Dial this number," I called it out. "6-9-3-6-9-1-8, and ask for Peaches."

The little nigga called the number and asked for her, but when the bitch actually got on the phone he nutted-up and passed me the phone.

"Yeah?" I took the phone.

"Who this?" Peaches spoke with the true mannerism or a hoodrat.

"Bitch, who the fuck you thank it is?" I responded like a real hoodrat tamer.

Her whole demeanor changed. "Oh, what's up Bo?"

"Nothin', just ridin' and lookin'."

"I was just thinkin' 'bout you," she lied like a real bitch was supposed to.

"Yeah, I bet you was." I shot back and we both busted out laughing.

Peaches was a real cool chick if a dude had the swag and game to counter her bullshit. Because Peaches had plenty of shit with her.

"What you on over there?"

"Shiid', nothin'.   A bitch just got outta the shower."
Peaches slurred all sexy and shit.   "Gotta stay fresh, 'cause you
never know who gonna pop up tryna spend somethin'."

"Damn, you a mind reader, huh?"

"Why you say that?"

"'Cause I was just tellin' my lil' brutha' 'bout you, and he
dyin' to meet you."

"How old he is?"

"14 years old."

"14?" Peaches screamed.

"Ma, don't trip, I gotchu'."

Peaches was real hesitant about freaking off with a 14 year
old, yet she knew how I got down.   I always looked out for
Peaches and for that reason she was always willing to show me –
or anybody else that I brought with me – her appreciation.

"Since he yo' lil' brutha', I'll do the lil' nigga on the
strength." Peaches finally said. "Where yall at?"

"Jumpin' off I-95."

"Okay, by the time yall get here I'll be home by myself."

I hung up.

Peaches lived in the Scott Projects – off 74th Street and like
25th Avenue – where Cowboy had the SCUDDA hole.   They shit
was jumping-jumping and shit was always jumping-off 'round
there, so I didn't really like going through there too tough.

The closer we got the more nervous Shod looked. He had
reason to be nervous though, because Peaches was the real one.

"Don't trip, lil' nigga." I handed him three rubbers. "She
ain't gon' kill you."

"Fuck you," he said and snatched the rubbers.

I called Peaches' crib again once I crossed the tracks. She
walked outside just as we were pulling up.

"Damn! That bitch fine as fuck!" Shod yelled.

"I know…just don't take the rubber off and please…Shod,
please don't kiss her."

"Man, fuck you!" Shod replied.

By now Peaches was standing at the passenger-side
window. So I let it down for her. "Damn, yall niggas triplets or

somethin'?" she asked, looking from me to Shod. "Where yall been hidin' him?"

"Away from animals like you."

"Boy, I ain't no animal!" Peaches defended herself. "Have this boy thankin' I'm out there."

I looked at Peaches like, *bitch you is out there!* But all I said was, "Peaches, don't play no games with my brutha'."

She saw that I was dead ass serious. "Nigga, chill..." she opened the door for Shod to get out. "You too serious, Bo."

"Whatever, yo...Shod, call me when you ready, nigga."

$$\$\$\$$$

I bent a few corners and checked a few pussy-traps to pass time while Shod got served. It had been a few minutes (like two weeks) since I had cruised thorugh the city. Before I knew it a whole hour and a half had passed and Shod hadn't called me. That worried me a little, but I knew Peaches wasn't crazy enough to play with my brother's safety, because then I would have to kill everybody that the bitch ever knew in life – just on principle alone. Just as the thought cleared my mind the phone rang.

"Yeah?"

"I'm ready, yo." Shod said flatly.

I could hear Peaches in the background giggling like a little girl.

"What the fuck so funny?"

Shod started giggling just like the bitch. "I'on know, ask her."

"Put that bitch on the phone." I said.

"Hello?" Peaches got on the phone, still giggling.

"What the fuck so funny?" I blew on her. "Let me in on the joke."

"You trippin', boy...yo' brutha' just surprised me."

"Yeah, now you know why we real bruthas'." I laughed. "That young nigga's back strong as an ox, huh?"

48

"You ain't never lied." Peaches said and then went quiet. There was a long pause before she stuttered. "Um', Bo, I was wondering. Um', wou-would it be cool if…if I gave yo' brutha' my number?"

"Shod is his own man, ask him." I told the scary bitch. "But Peaches, know this now, Shod ain't no goon. He still in school and he ain't no street type nigga. So don't have him in no bullshit, 'cause that's not for him…'cause it's gon' be yo' ass on the line."

"I ain't dumb, nigga." Peaches shot back. "I know what you sayin'."

"Good," I told the dumb bitch. "Tell Shod I'm outside."

A minute or so later he emerged with the biggest smile a nigga ever seen. I didn't even have to ask if he was good.

"Spark one up, bruh," he said, sliding into the car.

I passed him a blunt as Peaches did her hoe-stroll around to my window. I let it down and slipped her ten $20 bills.

"Thanks, Bo…" she smiled. "You always lookin' out for me."

"Ain't nothin', ma."

"Yo, I'ma call you later, yo." Shod called over to Peaches.

Before she could respond I reminded her of my warning. "Peaches, don't forget what the fuck I told you."

And before she could fix her mouth to say anything slick I pulled off.

As we pulled up to the light I pulled Shod's coat to the hoe Peaches' game – because the bitch had plenty, and I didn't want my little brother falling for that shit. I explained that she was a super-cool bitch, great for sucking and fucking and a few limited conversations, but that was about it. I didn't want Shod to get too relaxed around the bitch, because once a bitch got a nigga to relax, she had him.

"She seems like she likes you and all, and that's cool, but don't make us have to fuck that bitch up." I warned him as well as I'd warned her. "I can't tell you who to fall for, but that bitch ain't the one. She's old and she's out there. She can't do nothin' but suck you, fuck you and break you off. Anything else is gon' bring you down…and that's on stacks."

He sat over there smoking weed and nodding his head like he heard me, but I could tell that the little muthafucka was going to try his hand. It was just in his nature to do the exact opposite of what a muthafucka told him. The ole-girl used to always tell me and Dutch, "a hard head makes a soft ass!" Well, Shod was going to be like Charmin when Peaches got finished with him.

$$\$\$\$$$

When we pulled in the Match Box I seen a crowd of people standing in front of the basketball court – we call that the middle. I parked and Dutch and Diablo walked over to the car. We all greeted each other, and Dutch just jumped on the subject of money. He was starting to act more and more like Diablo, *like when is enough?* I thought to myself. I didn't want to talk about no money or no killing people. I just wanted to chill, so I interrupted his spiel and ran my own.

"Denise pregnant, yo."

"That's crazy, my nigga." Dutch shook his head sadly. "From the pussy-nigga, Bert?"

"Hell nah, yo!" I checked my brother. "From me, dog."

"Oh," was all he said.

I could tell that he was thinking crazy. I hate that I had told him about Bert fucking Denise. But then again, how was I supposed to know that I was going to get the hoe pregnant? Either way, Dutch wasn't going to understand. As it was my situation and I didn't fully understand it.

"I'ma move her in the crib we got in Miramar."

"I don't care," was what he said. "Do you."

I knew he didn't care. Not about the crib, anyway. We'd had the spot for a little minute, but we hadn't even spent a week in it yet.

"Look, it ain't no rush, yo…I'ma move her in slowly. She already been told the rules before she signed on to be with 'us'…so it's her call."

Yeah, I said 'us' because me and Dutch were one. Diablo was our big cousin and big homie, Shod was our little brother, Ma was our ole-girl, and Denise had just made herself wifey, but none of that shit came before me and Dutch's relationship. I really wanted a family and to do right by Denise and the baby, but if Dutch wasn't with it, the bitch and the baby were out! No questions asked.

I knew that he didn't particularly dig the whole thing, with Denise having fucked Bert while we were together, but he respected my call and moved on.

"So you straight?" he asked.

"Yeah, I'm good."

"Aiight, so look. This is the plan."

He was right back on money. Dutch wanted to send ten bricks up the road with Diablo. I didn't give a flying fuck. He also wanted to cop ten to move in the City. I still didn't care. I was wondering what Denise was doing. *Was she gonna have a Lil' Bo or a cute Lil' Denise?*

"Bo!" Dutch yelled.

"Yeah, what's up?"

"You listenin', ny nigga?"

"Yeah," I lied.

"My nigga, you better shake that shit off." Dutch warned and continued his Diablo impersonation. "We got enough clientele to move about ten in a week or two. That will cover our monthly expenses. So the money from up the road will be all gravy. You feel me? That's $300,000 a month, minus our $150,000, for twelve months, we'll be at two tickets in no time! Not includin' the bread off the ten for down here."

He really had it all figured out. Diablo had even convinced him that 'we' were going to all pack up and leave the state in two years. Because by then, 'we' would all be filthy fucking rich.

"Well, it sounds good. But as of now, we ain't got but a hundred and some change. That's only enough for a ten piece. So we short." I stated.

"Don't worry 'bout that." Dutch smiled. "All them groupie ass niggas that we been meetin' in the club…wanna be down ass niggas, we gon' touch all of 'em."

"Man, I don't care how we get to the top. Let's just get there and get outta this shit."

Of course, I had no idea how we were going to just 'touch all of them' and not start WWIII. A lot of dudes were straight up groupies and didn't really belong in the game – especially at this level. But somehow or another they were. Which meant that they were plugged with somebody, who most likely wasn't as fragile. Nonetheless, when I ran those concerns by Dutch he had an answer for them.

"Niggas be fakin', Bo. Real talk!" Dutch continued. "These niggas, outside our circle, don't fuck with us. They just need an outlet to move they work and get in good with they connects. Plus by fuckin' with us, the wolves back off because they think the niggas are really with us. They using us, dog! But it's all good, because they 'bout to pay the tax that comes with fuckin' with us. You feel me?"

"Yeah," I answered, but that shit he'd said didn't answer my questions.

Maybe he sensed that in my facial expression or something, because he went on explaining.

"Look, we gon' finesse most of 'em. No guns or nothin'. The rest of 'em, we gon' strong arm 'em. Fuck 'em! We can let niggas run with our money, get 'em relaxed and comfortable, then set 'em up for the big one. 'Cause ain't none of 'em stupid enough to run off." "Not unless they death struck. 'Cause I'll ride all day everyday until I bust they ass 'bout mine." I said, mad at the mere thought.

Dutch just shook his head agreeingly, because he knew that I was as serious about killing a nigga's ass as he was about getting rich.

After that the subject switched to Shod. He'd already ran the shit down to Dutch about the Chevy he wanted. I could feel the little nigga, because what nigga at his age didn't want a fresh Chevy already dropped? The dude selling the car owed Chico for a nine piece, so we would be getting the Chevy for little or nothing.

Dutch didn't give a fuck. "It's yo' call," he said and that was that.

Dutch and all of the niggas from the bar had plans of hitting the Rollexx that night, but I passed. Which was a big-ass shock to everybody, because I was *Mr. Rollexx*. But for whatever reason I just wasn't feeling it. I had to take Shod home – and hopefully talk his crazy ass out of wanting that damn Chevy – and get Denise off of my mind. And the only way to get her off my mind was to get her into my arms. Yeah, I wanted to spend some time with my new wifey.

After dropping Shod off I just smoked weed and rode. I had beaucoup shit on my young mind. It was so much that had to be done. If Denise was going to be living at the crib, then we'd have to keep our money somewhere else. And since the crib was the only spot with a big floor safe, then we'd have to have one installed at the spot in Pembroke Pines.

Then, with all of the wild shit that Dutch was talking about – robbing niggas and basically running the City – we damn sure needed to cop the ole-girl a new house and a new car. Of course I already knew that she wasn't going to move too far away from her friends. That would be too much like right. Ma, our ole-girl, was as stubborn as we were.

Until everything formulated though, we were just going to lay low. Coming out and serving a few niggas and sliding back in.

Still riding 'olo, I picked up the cell phone and called Denise's house. Her sexy ass sister answered on the fifth ring.

"Hello, may I please speak to Denise?" I popped politely.

"Why you always soundin' proper and shit when you call people's house?" the little dumb bitch asked. "You know you thugged-ass-out. So act like it."

I wanted to tell her little smart-mouth ass to suck my dick. Not just because she had a slick mouth and sexy ass lips, but because I really wanted her to suck my dick. But I chilled and just asked Ms. Smart-Dumb-Ass, "How am I supposed to ask for her?"

She thought for a minute, which I know was really hard for her.

53

"Well, at least say, 'where yo sister' or 'put Denise on the phone'."

"Yes maam," I said laughing. "Put yo' sister on the phone."

She sucked her teeth, "here she go right here."

"Who this?" Denise took the phone.

"How many niggas you got callin'," I asked.

"Bo, don't play. I'm so used to you callin' my cell phone, you threw me off."

"Aiight, you gonna be ready by 9:30?"

"Yeah, just come on and call when you outside." Denise said sweetly.

"You thought about what we talked about earlier?"

"Yeah, I did."

"Good," I said and hung up.

Before going to Denise's crib I shot to my house. I backed the car into the two car garage and entered the five digit code to the security system.

Soon Denise would be here waiting for me to come home, I thought to myself as I jumped in the shower. The hard spray of the hot water felt good against my tired body. Everything about my life, as I had been living it, was about to change. I only prayed that the change was for the better.

$$\$\$\$$$

An hour later I was fresh and racing towards my baby's house. I called her on the way and told her to pack a bag for a week. My plan was to just kick back and enjoy Denise's company.

When I pulled up Denise was sitting on the porch waiting. I just sat and watched her as she walked to the car. Her body was one to be admired. Best of all, my baby was growing inside of it. The reality of being a father was really fucking my head up.

Denise got in and gave me a kiss.

"What's up, ma?"

"Nothin'."

"So what you gon' do?"

"I want us to be together," she paused then said. "And, well, I gotta stipulation too, Bo."

"And what's that?"

"Just respect me...don't bring no diseases home and don't bring home no babies, or I will fuckin' kill you."

I just looked at her like "yeah right, I'm scared." She was real cute trying to put her thing down and I had to respect it. Especially after she handed me the brown paper bag.

"What's this?" I asked.

"That's what I'm bringin' to the table, $29,000. I just gotta figure a way to keep up my car and house notes, plus look out for my ole-girl and sister."

"That ain't no pressure, you with me now." I said as I drove off. "A lot of shit gonna be different."

During the time that we rode to the $178,000 house that she would soon be living in, I ran shit down to Denise. To be fair I was going to match her $29,000 and be sure that all of her ends met. As far as I could see, Denise was stepping into a prime situation. Dutch and I had closed on the house a little over a year ago. We got it below market value – only $137,000 – and had over $95,000 worth of equity.

I knew that she would love the house – totally remodeled, a pool, two car garage, four and a half bath, and four bedrooms. The master bedroom was already dropped – brand new White Stone king sized bed, 64" screen TV, and surround sound. The bedroom set alone ran us ten stacks.

No other female had ever been to the crib, not even my ole-girl or sisters.

"You're free to decorate it however you want." I told her. "In fact, we can go tomorrow and pick out the living room set. We'll move your stuff in piece by piece."

I really opened up to Denise and I really think that she understood me for the most part. When you took away the money, cars, jewelry, women, and street prestige, I was a 16 year old child trying to figure out what happiness really was. So it was going to be an extreme task trying to convey true happiness to Denise.

"Say Denise, I ain't never really had no girl to call my own, or you know, to come home to every night. But I'm willin' to give it a real shot if you will just help me along the way. I'm sayin', I won't ask for mu—"

Denise cut me off. "Whatever it takes, Bo..." she smiled and rubbed my face as we drove along. "You're with me now."

"That's what's up." I said.

And before we reached the house or I finished talking, me and wifey had really come to terms...or at least I thought we had. As a couple with a baby on the way and love on the horizon, we agreed to save and spend wisely because money wasn't going to always come so freely. Denise decided to get rid of her Acura RL 3.5 – the big body coupe – to minimize our monthly expenses, in view of the fact that I wasn't going to be in the streets forever...Shorty had put her trust in me and I wasn't going to let her down.

"Can I at least work for a few more months? I mean, to help out." Denise asked softly.

She was asking me could she continue stealing them white folks shit with her roguish ass friends. That was one of the habits that she was definitely going to have to break...in due time.

"Yeah, go ahead, yo. But you pregnant, so you gonna have to give that shit up sooner than later."

"I know," she said. "I just want to help you out as much as I can."

I found that to be so sweet on her behalf. So far our new life together was so good. We rode along to the sounds of Mary J's REAL LOVE, both unsure, but so willing to meet the unexpected *together*.

Grand Pupa and Mary J. Blige were ping-ponging the 411 when the unexpected hit.

"Bo, which one of my friends you done slept with?" Denise asked out of nowhere.

"One?" I replied, laughing.

"That ain't funny." Denise punched me in the arm. "It's more than one?"

"What's this, a trick question?"

"No, I just wanna know. I promise I won't use it against you or throw it up in your face."

I thought for a minute then replied, "just look at it like I slept with all of 'em."

"That's not a good enough answer, Bo!"

"Okay," I smiled. "You know I don't lie. So go ahead and name names and I'll just say yes or no. Deal?"

"Deal."

"Are you sure you can handle this shit, because I don't wanna hear nothin' 'bout this later on."

"Boy, I'ma big girl," she sassed.

"It's on you then, shoot."

"Princess?"

"Yep."

"Trice?"

"Yep."

"Brina?"

"Did – I!?!"

Denise slapped me on the head.

"C.C.?"

"Yep."

"Tasha?"

"Yep."

"Bo! You slept with Tasha?"

"'Bout four-five times."

She slapped me again.

"Shantrell?"

"Yep."

"Val?"

"Sho' did."

"Venessa?"

"Yep."

"April?"

"Which one?"

"My friend April, Bo."

"Well, yeah, her and Keta Black sister, April."

"You make me sick!"

"You asked!"

"Toya?"

"No."

"Kim?"

"Almost."

"Sandra?"

"Do head count?"

She slapped me again.

"Shawn?"

"Yep."

"Londa?"

"Three times." I looked over at her and she was crying. "You had enough yet?"

She didn't answer me.

"Look, they was all before yo' time, anyway." I lied.

"Then why the fuck you ain't tell me?"

"Tell you what? I don't volunteer no information and you know that."

Especially no information against myself. Shiid', why she didn't volunteer the '*tee*' on her fucking Bert? Exactly! Because people with common fucking sense don't tell on their selves.

Denise was heated though, and I could tell. Reason being, she wasn't the kind of chick to curse, especially not at me.

"Look Denise, I knew you couldn't handle this shit from the jump. So let's just drop it, okay."

"No! 'Cause I want to know!" she yelled, still crying.

"Well I ain't tellin' you shit else." I blew on the nosey, naïve ass bitch. She was really about to piss me off. "Do I inquire about your past niggas?"

"No."

"Right, because I don't fuckin' care. You mine now! That's all that matters."

"Then give me your word you won't mess with any of my friends anymore."

"Are you fuckin' crazy, yo?"

"Why I gotta be crazy, Bo?"

"Because I don't even know who your friends are. Just like I didn't know that you knew most of them bitches until way after we was fuckin' 'round. Besides, my word don't come that easy."

58

"So I ain't worth yo' word? Is that it? My feelings ain't shit to you?"

"You trippin'." I said and kept my eyes on the road.

I was praying that she didn't slap me, because even though she was mad and I partly understood, I was also growing tired of the bullshit. Denise was acting like she was the muthafuckin' 16 year old and not me. So if she slapped me, I was going to beat her stupid ass.

"Denise, look, I told you not to even start this conversation."

"Whatever, Bo." She said dismissing me with a wave of her hand. "If you can't give me yo' word then all bets is off...you just keep doin' you and I'ma do me."

"Oh, you mean keep fuckin' Bert?"

"Whatever."

"Bitch, you ain't said shit. We can do it just like that."

I damn near tore them crackas' rental car up turning that bitch around. She was sitting over there looking stupid – tryna hold on and look cute, mad, and sad all at one time. I couldn't get that simple-minded shop-lifting ass hooker out of my car and out of my life fast enough. I was doing the dash board trying to get her back home with her slut sister and begging ass mammy. The faster I drove the more I wanted to stop and kick her ass. Because that's all she really needed. So 45 minutes later when we pulled up in front of her crib I'd already made up my mind to do just that.

"Look bit—" I started, but she snatched the car door open and walked off towards the house.

I jumped out behind her! Denise really had me fucked up! She wanted to leave? Cool. She was going to take an ass whuppin' with her.

She was almost at the foot of the steps that led to the porch when I caught up to her. Without saying one word I grabbed her...around her waist...she struggled...I held her tighter...I hugged her and whispered in her ear, "I give you my word."

Denise stopped struggling and allowed me to hold her. She felt so good in my arms. After about five minutes of complete silence had passed she turned around smiling.

"I love you, Bo." Denise kissed me. "I know you not gonna say it back, but those five words that you did say meant even more."

"You crazy," was all I said and turned to walk back to the car.

When I got in the car Denise was getting in as well, smiling ear-to-ear. In her mind she had proved two points to herself. One, she had made me break down and give her my word. Two, I had showed her a sign of jealousy on my part when I brought the nigga Bert's name up. They were two good points, too. Because when you added them up it kind of [sort of like] showed that I loved her…

Chapter 8

BO

Denise loved the house! I knew she would though. The spot was bigger and nicer than most urban resident's dream home. Especially since most inner-city folk dared to dream. However, I had plans of upgrading sooner than later.

After showing her the house we got our celebration drink on. I was never much of a drinker, so after a few drinks I was drunk, and we decided to hang out. We hit the movies and enjoyed some flick about a junkie-pimp name Boo Baby. The shit was off-the-chain! But as we were leaving there was a group of niggas standing by the exit – about five of them. One blurted out, "what's her name, dog?"

I looked around like *I know this nigga ain't talkin' to me!* That's the problem with niggas and music, movies, and books. They take them shits *literally*. Which is not always a good thing to do, because Boo Baby was about to get dog fucked-over!

When we made eye contact the nigga said, "yeah you!"

I looked again to be certain, then stopped.

"Come on, Bo, they trippin'." Denise tried to pull me on.

"Nah," I pulled away. Dude felt like he wanted something so I was going to give it to him. I stopped right in front of their little group and was like, "you said somethin', dog?"

He said, "Yeah, what's her name?"

"Here she go right there, ask her." I told the chump.

Denise was steady trying to pull me away, but I wasn't going nowhere. I had already sized them up. They were some neighborhood niggas that thought I was something sweet. Being as we were so far down south – a few blocks from the Homestead

Air Force Base – they didn't know me and I was in their *neck-of-the-woods*.

"Tell the nigga yo' name." I said to Denise.

She was really looking crazy now!

The nigga with more heart than brains was a lot bigger than me, but I was right up in front of him. The element of surprise was largely on my side – being as I was so much smaller than him, and he just knew that I was *ripe-for-the-picking*. But before he could utter one word I grabbed his shirt while upping my Glock at the same time. The first blow landed across the bridge of his nose and the gun went off, *BLOCKA!* Everybody got low and started breaking out except Mr. Big Mouth, who's ass I was crushing! I was coming from Texas with every blow across this nigga's head and face.

"You –" *Whop!* "still –" *Whop!* "wanna –" *Whop!* "know –" *Whop!* "her –" *Whop!* "name?" *Whop, whop, whop!* "Bitch ass nigga!"

"Bo! Stop! Please!" Denise grabbed me. "Stop, Bo! You gon' kill him!"

Blood was everywhere! Good thing we had parked out back because we had to get the fuck out of there. When we got to the car Denise was shook up and crying.

"You shot that dude, Bo...I can't believe you killed him...you crazy." Denise cried.

I knew that the nigga wasn't dead, because I didn't shoot him. The gun just went off when I hit him. But I didn't explain any of this to her.

"So what you would've had me do, huh?" I asked her. "I don't do no turnin' the other cheek, ma."

She sat shaking her head. "Where we goin'?" she asked.

"I need a drink."

It was a little liquor store up the street, but before I could get to it I spotted a strip club and whipped up in it. Denise frowned. I laughed.

"We might as well hang all the way out."

"Whatever, Bo."

I tucked my gun before we got out, then tucked my shirt in, making sure that my boxers were showing. That way the bouncer

62

would think I was green and he'd see that I wasn't holding anything around my waist line – where most niggas tote guns.

"Why you can't leave that in the car?" Denise asked as we walked towards the club's entrance.

"Are you crazy?"

When I walked through the metal detector at the door it beeped twice.

"I got metal in me, bruh." I told the bouncer.

He patted me down and Denise and I went on inside.

"I'll meet you in the V.I.P." I told Denise and shot straight to the restroom.

Unbuttoning my pants, I reached into my jock-strap and pulled out my Glock. When I got back to the V.I.P. Denise was shaking her head again.

"Boy, you are cra-z'."

I winked at her and ordered a bottle of Remy XO.

The night was live. Denise and I really enjoyed ourselves. We both danced girls and drunk like fish. The club – I think it was WET WETZ – had a real nice variety of chicks. Denise took heed.

"I see you like thick girls…all the girls you done danced are big blocks."

"Yeah?" I laughed. "I do like thick girls. That's how I ended up with you."

We stayed in there for about another hour after that. I was twisted! Every bitch in the club came through the V.I.P. and I danced them all. It's like Denise wasn't even there, because I was finger-fucking them and all. When it was all said and done Denise had to help me back to the car.

From there went looking for something to eat. I smoked a blunt as we rode and it helped to bring me down some. It also had me hungry as hell. Which was cool because Denise whipped up in Tony Romas. I ordered a whole slab of ribs, a few corns on the cob, and some shrimp on the stick. I ate and Denise talked.

$$$

I don't remember how we got home, I just remember Denise waking me up. We were in the garage of my crib. Denise had a real nasty smile on her face, and that's all it took to get my mind right. We started right there in the garage – fucking like animals and ended up making a movie in the bedroom.

That night was the beginning of something real special, and I truly thought that I was experiencing forever. Because I genuinely felt that Denise was the woman for me.

The next morning I woke up to head in bed and a big boy breakfast. She watched the news as I ate, my gun sat next to my plate.

"Can't you do anything wit'out that gun," she whined.

"Thanks for breakfast," I replied, totally ignoring her stupid ass statement.

I sparked an early morning blunt while she cleared the table and started washing the dishes. All she had on was one of my T-shirts. Eyeing her big ass as she moved around the kitchen reminded me of the boss-sex we'd shared last night, and my dick instantly got rock hard. I stood up and pushed Denise against the long counter next to the fridge. She looked a little startled at first, but I eased her fears by pushing my tongue down her throat. Grabbing both of her thick thighs, I lifted her up onto the counter top and slipped my rod into her moist opening.

"Oooh, baby." Denise moaned.

Her pussy was so good.

"Feed our baby, Bo."

Those words alone sent me into overdrive. "Our baby" was inside this beautiful chick that I was inside... wishing...hoping...praying that we could stay just like we were...forever.

$$$

The house needed a woman's touch since a woman was going to be living there, so I dropped Denise a nice piece of cash and gave her the keys to my Camaro Z28. I never really drove it, so when I did people thought that it was a rental car. Which was exactly what I wanted them to think.

With her off shopping I decided to get out in traffic as well. As I came through the City behind tints, I saw a lot of shit for what it really was. The niggas Ced and Black were posted up on 63rd and 15th; Jack, the hoe-ass-nigga Wease and Vet were squatting on 60th and 14th; and the bitches Lil' M, Von, and Netta were still stopping at every trap rapping slick and tryna come up on a session. This was life for them. I mean, all of them were at least five years older than I was and had been out in the streets at least ten years longer than I had. Yet they were still doing the exact same shit that they were doing years ago when my daddy used to bring me and Dutch through here. And truth be told, they'll probably be doing it long after I'm gone – if somebody don't kill them or the crackas don't throw the book at them.

I didn't stop to holla at nobody. I just blazed my blunt, rode and looked. I thought about Pressure and realized that today was the first day that I hadn't gone over to Jackson to see him. He'd be alright though. Just as I turned off 22nd Avenue my cell phone rung.

"Yeah?" I answered.

"What's up, cuz?" Diablo said.

"Nothin' for real, just ridin', seein' what I can see."

"I heard that. Where Dutch?"

"I'on know. I ain't rap with 'im yet."

"Aiight, look, catch him and yall meet me at Lums 'bout 2 o'clock."

"Aiight, but yo, I'ma bring Denise."

Diablo got quiet when I said that. Today was normally our day, reserved just for me, him, and Dutch. We always got together and ate, rode jet-skis, or went to the gun range.

"Aiight cuz," Diablo finally said. "I'll see you later."

I hung up and before I could put the phone down it started ringing again.

"Yeah, what?"

"You rude." Denise said.

"What's up, ma?"

65

"You. Oh bay, I found some nice furniture," she said excitedly. "Come up to Modernage."

"Give me ten minutes."

I hung up and made my way to Denise. For some reason I missed her and really wanted to be there in the furniture store with her. When I pulled up and hopped out I saw Denise standing up front waiting for me. She immediately gave me a big hug and a wet kiss.

"Come on," she grabbed my hand and started pulling me into the store. "I found the perfect set."

She stopped in front of a big ass light-green and beige six piece sectional. The shit was plush. It was perfect for the beige shag carpet that we had in the spot.

From there she dragged me over to see 'her' dining room set, new patio furniture, and a gang of 'whatnots' to go with the painting and throw-rugs. Of course, the money that I had gave her was not enough to cover her spree, so I dropped another stack and a half and we left. The stuff would be delivered the next day.

$$$

"Are you hungry?" I asked Denise when we got home from Modernage.

"Yeah, I was about to cook some steaks and make a salad."

"Nah, put somethin' on, we goin' to meet my cousin and Dutch."

She stood there looking lost.

"Ain't nothin' major, girl. I'm just puttin' everybody on the same page." I said.

It took her damn near two hours to get ready. You would've thought we were going to Café Bellagio out in Vegas instead of Lums on 111th Street and 7th Avenue.

Dutch and Diablo were already seated in our usual rear booth. I didn't have to introduce them because they already knew each other. Denise was from down-south, but she knew a lot of people in the City because they bought stuff from her and her stealing ass friends.

After we had all ordered I broke the news to Diablo about Denise being pregnant. He didn't seem too shocked. Which led me to believe that him and Dutch had already been talking about me. It didn't matter though, because they both damn near choked when I hit them with the next bit of news.

"We gettin' married, dog."

"What?" Diablo yelled.

Denise looked nervous as Dutch stared through her. I hadn't even discussed it with her yet.

"I'm ready to settle down, man." I explained. "And besides the ole-girl, yall two are my only real concern, so I'm askin' for yall blessings."

They were all really stunned. Tears ran down Denise's face. My heart pounded in my skinny chest as I waited for someone to say something. Diablo was the first to speak.

"Is this really what you want, lil' cuz?"

I shook my head yeah.

"My nigga, you trippin'." Dutch said. "But if it's what you want, then that's on you."

He then turned an evil stare back towards Denise and said, "I guess you with 'us' now... it's all good, but if you cross my brutha', I'ma be the one to come holla atcha'."

She shook her head up and down – still crying – like she understood.

I popped the magic phrase, "Denise, will you marry me?"

She just hugged me and said "yes, yes, Bo" like a thousand times. It was official. I was about to be the man my daddy never was. And for real, I couldn't believe it myself...

$$$

News of my coming wedding spreaded like cancer! How, I have no fucking clue. The only people I told was Dutch and Diablo. Yet it seemed that everybody and their momma was calling my

67

phone about invitations. My plans were not consistent with a big wedding. I wanted to just go down to the court house and *do the muthafacka*. So I played the nut role with everybody until the ole-girl called.

"Hello?" I answered.

"Who is this bitch?" my momma screamed.

"Damn, ma. No hello?" I laughed.

"Bo, don't play with me! Who is this lil' bitch done whipped you?"

I could hear my sisters Lottie and Wholee in the background putting the cables on the ole-girl. They were talking cash shit!

"Ma, look, I –"

My mother cut me off. "Bo, I'm just playin' with you baby...I'm happy for you. I really am." My mother told me. "And I'm real proud of you. You're growin' up. Be good to her, Bo, and don't treat her like a object. You treat her like you'd want a man to treat me or your sistas."

I felt good when I hung the phone up. Better than I'd felt in a long time. I went to place the phone back on the seat and it started ringing again.

"Hello?" I answered.

"Who is the bitch, and when is I'ma meet her?" Bee yelled.

Bee was like my second mother. She used to smoke crack back when I was growing up, yet we were always cool. Especially after she got shot and was partially paralyzed. It was fucked up how it happened, but the situation caused Bee to straighten her life up and we grew closer as a result. Bee was truly my heart.

"Soon, Bee." I laughed. "Why you talkin' crazy?"

"'Cause I haven't heard nothin' from you or yo' brutha. That ain't like you and Dutch to not come by and see me." Bee complained. "Then, yo' ma had to tell me you talkin' 'bout gettin' married."

Damn the ole-girl was fast with giving up the 'tee', I thought as I rode. *I had just hung up!* Shaking my head I explained it to Bee.

"Bee, it just happened. You ain't even give a nigga time to holla at you."

"Well how much time you needed, nigga?"

I laughed. "You cooked?"

"Child, you know I cooked."

"I'll be through there later so we can talk."

"Aiight, but I ain't comin' back from the afternoon church service until after 3 o'clock. So call my cell phone in case I ain't home."

I hung up with Bee and I'll be damned if the phone didn't ring again.

"Yeah, who this?" I answered for the third time in less than eight minutes.

"What's up?" Angie replied. "What happened to you? I thought you was 'posed to hit me back last week."

I could hear that something was wrong. It was in her voice. The way she accented her words and toned her voice spelled argument. I sure as hell hoped – prayed – that she hadn't heard about the wedding. Angie and I were not together – never really were and most likely would never be – but I dug her for some reason.

When I didn't respond fast enough for her she talked on. "Shortman was sick and you ain't even come through like you was 'posed to."

"I ain't know he was sick. Why you ain't call me back?" I felt bad about that, but I wasn't about to let Angie stress me. "Yo' ass call me for everythang else."

"What-eva', Bo."

"Put Shortman on the phone." I told her dumb ass.

Angie began yelling for Shortman. It took him three minutes to get to the phone, but he finally came – out of breath.

"Hello?" he said, excitedly.

"What's up, boy?"

"Nothin', just playin' the game you bought me."

"Aiight, you feelin' better?"

"Yep."

"How's school?"

"I got all A's and B's."

Shortman was my little man. I loved shorty.

69

"Yo' momma told me you had a fight in school. Did you win?"

"Yeah," Shortman answered slowly. "Fool tried me, talkin' 'bout I ain't got no daddy."

"Well, you know you do, right?"

"Yep, you my daddy." Shortman said with a touch of sunshine in his little voice.

"Sho' nuff is! And anybody that says anything bad to you, just tell me…I got somethin' for they ass, aiight?"

"Okay."

"And I got some more stuff for you when I come back in town, aiight."

Before he could answer, Angie got back on the phone.

"Why you keep tellin' him you his daddy?"

"'Cause I look out for yall. I been fuckin' with that lil' nigga since before I started fuckin' with you. I'm the nigga you call whenever he needs somethin'! I'm the nigga that breaks his neck for shorty. I am his fuckin' daddy, that's why I keep tellin' him that! And if you wasn't so stupid and small-minded you would've been moved yo' ass from 'round there so I could spend more time with 'im. Bit—" I caught myself and hung up on her simple ass.

Within seconds my phone was ringing again. *Fuck Angie*, I said as I sparked a blunt and kept bending corners. I didn't have the time or energy to waste arguing with her, so I ignored her calls. Only problem was, the bitch wouldn't stop calling.

"What, Angie? What the fuck do you want?" I blasted her. "This better be a fuckin' emergency the way you blowin' my shit up!"

"Bo, why you yellin'?"

"'Cause I don't have time for no bullshit."

"Can you just please hear me out?"

"What?"

"I know you do a lot for us….I mean, that shit I said just came out wrong. I did not mean it like that."

"Well how did you mean it? Because people usually say what they mean, or how they feel."

70

"Bo," Angie blew out a soft sigh of frustration. "I just...I don't wanna confuse my baby, Bo. He's all –"

"Confuse him? How the fuck you gon' confuse him? Is it another nigga he need to know? 'Cause he calls my momma granny and my sistas auntie! What's confusin', ma?"

She sighed again. "Look, I ain't tryna really argue with you. I just called 'cause I just heard that somebody 'posed to be lookin' for you and yo' brutha."

"Who?"

"Them niggas out the projects."

"How you know?"

"Brenda mess with Conrad and he was askin' her all types of questions 'bout me and you."

Bitch ass nigga! I thought to myself. We were laying back on our styles and these niggas were plotting our demise.

"Now you see why I be tellin' you to keep Brenda outta our business?"

"Yeah, but anyway, I want to hook up." She said as if niggas trying to murder me and my brother was common place.

"I'll hit you back later and let you know what's up. But yo, you gotta get from over there if you gon' be fuckin' with me."

"I know what you said, Bo." Angie whined.

I had told her lazy ass 'months ago' to find a job or take her ass to school and I would sponsor the whole move. Why? Because I dug the chick. Yet it was bigger than the chick. Remember my ole-girl said, "You treat her like you'd want a man to treat me or your sisters." I know that she was talking about Denise – not Angie – when she said that. But what if a nigga – bitch ass Conrad for example – was to catch me and Dutch down bad and slaughter us? That would leave Denise and my seed out here alone to fend for themselves. Well, God forbid, if it went down like that, I'd want a real man to step up and hold my people down. So I was doing the same thing for Angie.

But she was dragging her lazy ass. She couldn't seem to understand that time was running out, because I wasn't going to always be in position to help.

"You can keep playin', but you gonna have to be able to be there for me one day. I know you're tired of the lectures, but life ain't sweet, yo."

She just changed the subject all-together. "Shortman's birthday is coming up."

"I already know."

"We gon' throw him a party or somethin'?" she asked.

It wasn't Shortman that was confused. It was this bitch!

"Look, just get with my ole-girl. She'll handle the party. I gotta go."

"Aiight, just call me...please, when you free, okay?"

I said yeah and hung up.

Chapter 9

BO

Angie was strong on my mind. She really did not know what she wanted out of life. Talking about not confusing Shortman while she was personally all discombobulated. The hoe had me, Shortman, and life fucked up.

But I wasn't about to be stressed over her and her situation. If she liked living in a war zone and have nothing in life, I loved it for her. Because I was loving my thuggin'. And I was about to upgrade in life.

Puffing on a blunt I finally made it to the hide out we had in Miami Lakes. I knew that I would find Dutch out there. He had started fucking this stripper bitch and the two of them stayed ducked off at this particular spot. It didn't really matter though. The duck off was a two bedroom – like all of our honeycombs – so he had his space and I still had mine.

When I came through the door Passion was in the kitchen cooking Dutch a steak.

"What's up, bruh?" Passion turned and greeted me.

"Bitch, what I told you 'bout callin' me bruh?"

"Oh, he trippin' again." Passion quickly turned her ass back around and finished cooking.

"Friendly ass bitch!" I continued berating the sympathetic stripper hoe. "Don't talk to me unless I talk to you."

With that I walked off towards Dutch's room. He was sitting in there watching TV and talking on the phone. I put my blunt out and sat on his bed. Who he was rapping with, I don't know, but he quickly ended his call.

"What's up, nigga?" he said, all excited and shit.

My brother was just 'like that'. Always full of energy and wanting to have fun. He was truly about 'our' money and seemed to always see the better part of a situation no matter how crazy it looked.

"Just chillin', yo."

"That was Rome right there." Dutch told me, referring to his phone call.

Rome was a nigga that we'd been setting up for the kill. He needed to impress his connect – get in good by bammin' the product – so we moved it for him, *all of it*. Shit started out slow, three here, four there, but before long we were calling Diablo and Chico to borrow two or three hundred stacks, just to sweeten the deal. Not to mention we had bread as well as customers that spent $60,000 to $130,000. We would always let Rome run with the money and come back with the work. *Trust*, we did, and he *believed*.

Anyway, Dutch went on to tell me how we were going to go with the money for 30 units, and since Rome knew that we were always on other shit, we'd stage a call in front of him while we're counting the money and step off. Then we'd simply come back and order an extra 20 bricks. It wasn't nothing we hadn't done before and paid the extra within an hour. *Trust*, remember?

Passion walked her fine gold-digging ass in as we discussed the outcome.

"Didn't I tell you whenever I'm 'round to stay the fuck outta the room 'till I leave, bitch?"

She looked at me, *scared-to-death*, then at Dutch. He laughed and told her to go take a shower.

"Why you always trippin' on Passion?" my brother asked me.

"'Cause it's somethin' 'bout that hoe I don't like."

Dutch shook his head. "Well, I got Blink lined up for tonight. His ass gon' get it just like Rome. You feel me?"

"Just line it, I don't give a fuck." I said. "We just gotta hit 'em fast, as many as we can, 'cause once other niggas find out they ain't gonna want to fuck with us."

"Don't worry 'bout other niggas findin' out. 'Cause when niggas get stuck for this much money they wanna keep it as quiet as possible. 'Cause they ain't gon' do shit, and they don't want other niggas to start takin' 'em bad too...but fuck 'em! We gon' be so far gone in a few more weeks that it ain't gon' even matter, my nigga."

I shook my head and stood up. "I'm out. Finna go by Bee house. She called me today talkin' cash shit."

"I know, she called me too."

I dapped my brother up and walked out of the room. On my way pass the bathroom I pulled the door open. Passion jumped and tried to cover up her naked body. She was one fine ass bitch.

"Bitch, what you covering up for? I done seen yo' triflin' ass naked a million times! You done forgot you a fuckin' stripper?"

Then Captain Save A Triflin' Slut walked up. "That's enough, bruh. Leave the bitch along," he said and walked me to the door.

$$$

As soon as I got in the car I sparked up a blunt and called Denise to tell her about Bee. Then I called Bee to let her know that I was on my way. She was still talking shit. I just hung up on Bee like, "I'll see you when I get there."

I hit the Match Box to see who was out there. I needed somebody to ride through the Beans with me, because ain't no telling who a nigga might run into in the Pork-N-Beans or who might run into me.

It was quite a few niggas out there. I saw my man E and his other half Dick.

"What yall boys on?" I asked.

"Nothin'," Dick returned.

"Good, come roll with me to the City."

They both jumped in. Dick rode shotgun with his little Nina, while E sat in the back with a fully automatic MAC-11 – the kind that shot .45 caliber bullets. We smoked blunt after blunt until we got to Bee's crib in the Beans. I jumped out the car.

75

"Yall boys come back and snatch me when I call."

When I reached the back door Bee's son, Gary, opened it and Dick pulled off.

Bee hugged and kissed me. She was so happy to see me.

"Na-ooo-mi!" Bee yelled.

Naomi was her daughter, which made her my sister. She was my age, but still in school, so I considered myself much more advanced than her.

"What?" Naomi screamed back from her bedroom.

"Bo out here!" Bee yelled again. "Come fix him a plate!"

Naomi entered the room smiling. She had on some little skimpy ass hoe-shorts. The girl was really growing up.

"Damn nigga, when was we gonna find out you finna get married?" Naomi said with attitude.

I laughed and shook my head. "Why yall treatin' me like the bad guy?"

"Whatever, bruh. Who's the bitch, anyway?" Naomi asked.

I looked at Bee. Bee just shrugged her shoulders like, "that's on yall" and started laughing.

Seeing that I wasn't going to get my plate until I answered her, I told Naomi everything about Denise – the baby, the coming wedding, how we met, and how long we'd been vibing. Bee already knew all of this, because she had been gossiping with my ole-girl and my ole-girl couldn't hold water.

"Now can I get my plate?"

"I guess."

I watched Naomi from where I sat piling all kind of food on my plate – pigeon peas and rice, potato salad, corn bread, collard greens, BBQ chicken – and she brought me a sweet ass glass of cherry, grape, and lemon [ghetto mix] Kool Aid.

Bee could really throw down, or as we say in the south, put her foot in some food. And I didn't want to waste nann' minute playing. I ran through that shit so fast Bee couldn't believed it.

"I sho' hope that bitch can cook, 'cause you sho' can eat!" Bee said, laughing. "Yall gon' go broke eatin' at fast food spots."

Bee and I sat out in the living room and rapped for about an hour. Bee had really been through a lot in life and was a really smart lady because of it. Every experience that Bee had suffered in life taught her something in life.

After sliding her a few hundred dollars and breaking Gary off some change, I walked back to Naomi's room to holla at her. It had been a minute since our last heart-to-heart.

"What's up, shorty?" I popped, entering her space.

"Nothin."

"So it's prom time, I heard."

"Yeah, it is." Naomi smiled. "You wanna take me?"

I laughed as I took a seat next to her on the bed. Naomi was a real heart breaker – *fine to death* and pretty as million dollar bundles of money – and both Bee and myself knew that she had a crush on me, but all three of us also knew that I wasn't for her. Not only was I thuggin' too hard, Bee was my second mom, so Naomi was off limits.

"Stop playin' so much, shorty." I told her. "Who takin' you?"

"This boy from school."

"You got yo' dress and shit?"

"No, not yet. I'm a little undecided."

"Well don't trip. I'ma pay for everythang. Have Bee rent you any kinda limo you want, a suite at whatever hotel you want, and I got it. 'Cause I know that nigga gonna want some."

"Well at least somebody want it," she sassed.

I laughed. *If she only knew what I did to a pussy.*

"I ain't for you, lil' sis'." I said and gave her a few hundred dollars. "I'll drop you a stack before prom time."

I called my ride and went back in the living room with Bee.

"I guess you done broke my baby's heart." Bee said.

"She'll be aiight. She's strong like her momma."

Bee smiled. She was still nice looking for her age. Especially considering all of the shit she'd been through.

While I waited for Dick and E to come get me, Bee and I rapped some more. I told her that I had Naomi on the prom shit so she didn't have to spend her money. She was real appreciative. Even though she kept popping slick about seeing more of me.

"Bee, you know what's up. So kill all that sentimental talk. Seein' me ain't nothin'. It's my love that counts."

Just then I heard my horn blowing. I hugged everybody and got back out in traffic.

Soon as E pulled off I called the nigga Rome to get the ball rolling. It didn't make no sense in playing. I'd made promises to a lot of good people, and I needed money to make good on them. Rome answered on the first ring. *Bling!*

"Yeah?"

"What they do, nigga?" I asked.

"Oh, nothing. What's up?"

"Money, nigga, what street you on?"

"I'm on 145th."

"Right now I'm on 30th Ave. I'll be through there in a minute."

"Cool."

I hung up and called Dutch so he could get the chips ready.

When we pulled up at the spot Dutch was already there, sitting in a dark-blue Chevy four door Blazer with the money. I jumped out, got the money bags from him, and jumped back in the car with E and Dick.

It took us thirty minutes to reach Rome's crib. He lived in the City with his girl, who was fucking and sucking everybody that looked like they had money. But it was all his fault, because not only was he over-pampering the bitch, he had the nosey slut sitting in on every fucking drug transaction that he did. That's how I fucked the hoe. How was a bitch supposed to resist all of those big pretty grand stacks?

Anyway, I sat down and handed him the two Nike bags so that he could count the money. This simple, sucker-ass nigga handed her one. That pissed me off! But I just sat there watching and smoking a blunt. Rome's hoe kept cutting her eyes at me every time I dumped my blunt ashes on their nice carpet.

"'Cuse me, but it's an ash tray over there," she spoke with attitude.

"Oh, aiight." I said and dumped some more ashes on the carpet.

Fuck her, the carpet and Rome's pussy ass. I thought as my cell phone started ringing. I already knew who it was.

"Yeah?" I answered, sure to let Rome hear me. "I'm runnin' through that paper right now…What?…Thirty more…Hold up…"

I got up and walked out of the room. Rome and his money-hungry bitch were both smiling and watching me close as I walked off talking. When I ended my pre-arranged conversation with Dutch I came and sat back down.

"Ay' Rome, my nigga, I'ma need 30 more, ya' heard me? So just bring the 60 and I can kill two birds with one stone, feel me?"

Rome looked up as if he had to think about it, and shook his head yeah. If only niggas would listen to their first-mind, because I'm sure that his told him, "don't do it!"

I just smiled and hit my blunt, saying to myself, "got his greedy ass!"

They finally finished counting the money. Rome gathered it all up and left. But can you believe he kissed the hoe before he left? I was thinking "incredible!" when she wrapped those same big pretty lips around my dick. Yeah! Rome wasn't even out of the driveway yet and she was sucking me up. By the time Rome came back with the 60 kilos I had done fucked his hoe in every hole that she had.

"I'll swing right back through with the rest of that lil' money." I capped like a big-boy.

"Aiight," he replied and walked me to the car.

$$$

"Here, boy!" I said excitedly.

"My nigga, bet!" E said, taking the kilo out of my hand.

"That's for you and Dick to split." I said as we rode.

"Good lookin' out," Dick said, smiling.

I knew it was. Especially when nann' one of them niggas ain't did shit to earn a half of a brick.

I hit Dutch and Diablo up. All I put in their pagers was 10-4-73. Diablo hit back first.

79

"Swing through, cuz." was all that I said.

I dropped Dick and E off and shot straight to the spot. Dutch was sitting on the butter-soft leather sofa smiling when I walked in. He didn't even have to ask, I threw all those blocks of pretty fish-scale down in front of him and he fell back laughing.

"We rich!" Dutch yelled. "We did it, my nigga!"

"You crazy, yo." was my reply.

I sat down, twisted me a blunt, and started telling him how I had fucked the air out of Rome's hoe and got the nigga for an extra 30 instead of the planned 20. Diablo walked in as we rapped.

"What?" Diablo looked puzzled. "Fuck yall done did?"

I laughed and ran everything down to him. The look on his face didn't say whether he was impressed or pissed off with our little lick. He shook his head, taking the four bricks of cocaine as he sat down. For two whole minutes the room was completely silent. I wasn't tripping at all. My blunt was still burning and life was about to get a whole lot better for me and mine. If Diablo was upset, that was his muthafuckin' problem.

"Yo," he started saying slowly. "Yall know yall gonna have to stay outta them clubs. And yall can't just fuck this bread up because it came easy. Yall gotta play it smart and invest wisely, because before it's all over with, this money gon' have blood on it."

"My nigga, a nigga ain't stupid, my nigga." Dutch said. "We can go ahead with yo' up the road plan now, my nigga. We got ten for the road, and plenty for the crib."

$$$

Later that night when I walked through the door of our crib, Denise was sitting on a stool eating fruit, wearing one of my T-shirts. It was a little after 12 o'clock. I smiled at her and we walked straight upstairs without a word being spoken. As soon as we got in the bedroom I grabbed her and pulled her to me.

"You missed me?" I asked before kissing her.

"Yep," she returned my kiss. "I always miss you."

80

I kissed Denise again as I lifted her T-shirt. She wasn't wearing anything underneath. Her breast were nice and firm. I couldn't help but to suck them, causing her to shiver. Each nipple grew hard under my suction. I laid Denise down and slid my hand between her legs, wetness all over.

Slowly I eased down between her legs and gave her my tongue.

"Ooooh, bay," she moaned, running her hands through my hair and pulling me deeper and deeper.

Licking and sucking her swollen clit, I fingered Denise slowly. Within minutes my fingers were covered with white cream and Denise was violently shaking, my face smothered with her vagina.

When she finally stopped shaking she released my head and pushed me back onto my back.

"Now it's my turn," she whined devilishly.

She started by just kissing and licking my penis up and down, never fully taking it into her mouth. No teeth or hands, just unadulterated lips and tongue – just how I like it. I was feeling all kinds of pleasure as Denise's warm mouth covered my entire dick. Then she came back up and wrapped her tongue around the head, slightly squeezing it. She continued to work me, deep throat, tongue, squeeze, until I was about to cum. Sensing my excitement Denise left my penis and began sucking my balls – teasing me. Unable to maintain my gangsta, I spun her around and ate her from the back – in a 69 – so that we could cum together.

"Oh bay, I'm cummin'. I'm cummin', baby." Denise sang.

I licked and sucked every drop of cum that she had to offer, and before long she was doing the same thing for me.

$$$

The next morning my eyes opened with the rising of the sun. We were cuddled up close – her back to my chest. My dick was still rock hard, so I entered her form the side. She was already wet, like she had been waiting for me. I stroked slowly for about five minutes, then I turned her over on her stomach. Without saying a word I pulled her ass up slightly and gave her the business. Denise started moaning and making sounds that I had never heard her make before.

"Oh, baby, yeess! Fuck, Bo! Fuck me!"

I rode out for twenty minutes before I came long and hard. Our breathing was heavy. Denise turned over slowly. She looked into my eyes and I saw real love, even before she said it.

"I'm so in love with you." Denise whispered.

I was never the mushy type. "How long have you felt this way?"

"Oh, so you blind? Nigga, you ain't dumb. Yo' butt saw every sign." Denise playfully rolled her eyes. "My every move was based around your calls. I jumped every time my phone rung, anticipatin' your calls."

"Why me?" I asked.

"You just had somethin' different about you...I don't know. It's like you ain't care how many outfits I could give you. And even though you had dealings with other hoes, you always treated me like I was the only one when we got together. You never showed off to me or on me. And when I found out how old you was it really turned me on! Because I've listened to my sista's phone conversations and I've seen niggas yo' age, but you don't act like them. You're way more mature than niggas twice your age."

I didn't say anything. It was what it was and we both knew it. Of course Denise didn't know just how much I really was loving her, because I never said it.

"Do you remember when you first took me to Universal Studios?" Denise asked.

"Yeah."

"Well, nobody ain't never took me nowhere or bought me nothin'. I was always the one buyin' niggas stuff." Denise said sadly. "You bought me gifts on Valentine's Day, Mother's Day, my birthday, and X-mas."

"It ain't nothin', ma. That's what a man's 'posed to do."

"I know that now, and I know that you done probably done the same for other hoes, but I don't care 'bout that. You done it for me and that's all that matters." Denise paused, then looked me in my eyes. "I saw your signs, Bo...You might not love me like I love you, but you like me a lot."

Chapter 10

DEWEY

I woke up feeling crazy as fuck! Like a all black lion locked in a cage with frail ass deer, being watched from all sides by white faces. Fucked up, right? Damn right it was! As a young nigga I always hated the zoo. It was like even then I identified with the wild being caged. Like, maybe I knew that the caged gorilla was my ass. Feel me?

Anyway, I needed a fucking square! But my dog Bo was over there on his rack knocked-ass-out. Sleeping like it was gravy up in this county. I guess it was for him, he was a Teflon Twin, Diablo's little cousin. Nigga probably had like three-four lawyers working to free him, while a real ass field-nigga like me was 'round here stressing. Tripping 'bout a little commissary and couldn't get Traci or Juliette to brang a nigga no non-filters or weed. *When I get out, I swear to God I'm gon'...nah, fuck that shit.* I had to get my ass out first.

Couldn't catch this bitch-ass-nigga Crab for nothing! Him or hoe-ass Stanka. Nigga had the Hound fucked up! No lawyer, no sack, no fuckin' love! I should've just took my ass over to Bo's rack and told the nigga everything. How Crab and Stanka had hoodwinked a nigga and had me bussin' at them boys. But then I'd have to tell him how a nigga put it all in his man's life. My lil' dog might not have liked that too tough, feel me? 'Cause the Hound really didn't need no niggas hitting all at the Brome. Nah, fuck that shit! I'd just have to handle Crab and them myself. You know, get free and play the middle against the ends.

"Middle against the ends?" I wondered. I wondered if my lil' dog Bo would get me a "L." I damn sho' needed one. Better yet, fuck a lawyer! I wondered would my lil' dog Bo get me some goons? Yeah, I needed some real live field-niggas to go holla at Trent's bitch ass. 'Cause if Trent fell short, then the case folded up. And boy, I could not do no muthafuckin' 65 years!

Fuck that shit! I took my ass over there and woke Bo up.

"Fam...Fam-a-lam'." I shook his shoulder. "What's up, boy? Get up and get yo' dog out the streets."

Bo looked like he wanted to kill my ass. I couldn't blame him, I would've been fucked up with me too if I'd done that shit to myself.

"Dewey, is you fuckin' crazy?"

I just smiled that million-dollar smile. "Nah, fam', let's rap. I really need to holla."

Bo was mad as fuck! But he got up and got his self together.

"This shit better be serious, Dewey, my nigga."

"Fam', you know me. I don't play no game, dog."

He mumbled something about killing somebody and something else about somebody finding them somebody to play with as he walked off. I sure was glad I wasn't nann' one of them that he was so fucked up at. Real talk!

When Bo came back from the bathroom we walked over to our little smoking area in the back of the cell-block. He twisted up two fat ass rollies and we sparked as I ran down my offer to Bo. I came all-the-way clean too. Not about me killing his mans and fucking over Pressure World, but about me running up in Trent's shit and coming off with those twelve and a half birds.

"I 'on know, Dewey." Bo shook his head. "That was some low-down ass shit."

"You right, fam'. But 65 muthafuckin' years? It ain't like I killed nobody. Just send somebody 'round there to tell the nigga I'm sorry, I'll give 'im eight birds back and I'll stay outta his way. Plus, my nigga, I'ma throw you two birds for ya' trouble."

Bo fell back and puffed his square. He didn't need the two kilos that I'd offered him, so I knew that wasn't what had him thinking. It was his conscious that made him consider and reconsider my deal. Part of him knew that I was a low-life muthafucka that probably deserved the electric chair for all of the fuck-shit that I had pulled. Yet that other part – the G part –

wouldn't allow him to leave another G down-bad if he could help it. It was that simple, right or wrong; I was a G, and even though I was wrong in my actions, Trent was breaking the G-code by telling the crackas on a nigga. So he was wronger than me! Being the G that he was, Bo had to help me.

"Hound, I'ma see what I can do." Bo eyed me. "But my nigga, you better give that man his shit back, and you damn sho' better have mine!"

"Fam', that ain't for us. My word, nigga, I gotchu."

"Nah, fuck all that. I'ma send somebody at the nigga on my word, that he gon' get his shit back and you ain't gon' fuck with 'im. If you violate dog, you gon' make my word look like shit...and my nigga, I can't have that. It's gon' be a real problem."

Boy, if I ain't needed that lil' nigga to duck this six-fizzle I was faced with, I would have told Bo, "nigga, fuck you!" Real talk! Nigga was talking to Dewey Hound like I was one of his bitches or some shit. "It's gon' be a real problem," I know the fuck it was! 'Cause my gun busted just like his. But I needed the nigga.

"Ain't gon' be no problems, Bo. I'ma give the nigga his shit back and I gotchu'. That's on Black Flag." I told him.

He just shook his head and kept smoking.

I asked the nigga to finish telling me the story. I loved to hear that get-money shit.

He rolled a fat ass blunt of 'dro and laced a nigga...

Chapter 11

BO

That next morning when I got up my pager was on overload. Of course, that was nothing new. It was mostly bitches wanting to know if I was going to come through and beat it up, and the other thirty-something pages were from Rome. I laughed and called up Dutch.

"What's up, boy?"

"Ain't shit, my nigga." Dutch said. "I started to swing through there, but I figured you was sleep. What's good?"

"The nigga Rome blowin' a nigga up."

"Fuck that nigga!" Dutch blew.

"Nah, I'ma hit him and break the bad news to him."

"My nigga, you ain't gotta tell that pussy-nigga shit."

"I know that. I'ma just tell him that's dead so he'll know what it is and stop callin' me."

"Whatever, my nigga. Just hit me when you come out."

"Cool."

I hung up and fired a blunt up. I could smell French toast, eggs, and bacon going down in the kitchen. Denise was on her job and I was feeling that. My money was stacking up proper and my house was in order. What more could a fool ask for?

Feeling the 'dro, I thought about Angie. Why? I don't know. It's like shorty was a real part of my life that I couldn't just up and walk away from. So I picked up the phone and called her.

"Hello?" Shortman answered.

"Where yo' momma?"

"Who is this?"

"Lil' nigga, this Bo."

"Oh, she sleep."

"Give her the phone."

I already knew how she hated to be woke up.

A sleepy voice came across the line, "hello?"

"Why you ain't call my ole-girl?" I questioned her.

"Bo, I know this ain't why you woke me up. 'Cause Shortman birthday ain't 'til next month."

Angie was lightweight heated with me, like I knew she would be. But I didn't care. Angie was my bitch and that's just what it was.

"So you gonna wait 'til the last minute?"

Angie sucked her teeth. "Why you always on my back?"

I puffed on my blunt. "'Cause I want better for you and my lil' nigga. But you act like you can't see that."

I could hear her sigh on the other end. Probably rolling her eyes and all.

"Look, am I gonna see you today?" she asked.

"Yeah, go to my ole-girl crib and call me. Make sure you bring Shortman too."

She didn't say anything.

"You heard me?" I asked.

"Yeah man, I'll call you when I get there. Bye."

"Bye."

I hung up the phone wishing that I'd never called. My patience was running way thin with Angie's ass. She was the real deal, I knew that, but a nigga could only take so much before he snapped.

$$\$\$\$$$

When I left the crib I shot over by the hide-out to holla at Dutch. It really seemed that him and Diablo were more like twins than me and him. Soon as I walked in, smoking a blunt, he jumped straight into some business shit. Diablo had grabbed ten, and instead of giving Chico his cash back he grabbed ten too. So that left us with 35.

"I'ma probably hit niggas in the hood with two, another two goin' to Forty them, that'll leave us with 31…oh yeah, we gotta shoot them ten up the road. So it's 21 left. Shiid', that's at least another $300,000 and some change. Feel me?"

"It don't matter, as long as we stack bread and stick to the script. Everythang'll be everythang, yo." I continued. "Where yo' bitch Passion at?"

"She went out to run a few errands for me."

I stood up to leave. "I'ma go holla at Pop them next month, to introduce Denise to everybody."

"Let me know," Dutch said, standing to walk me out. "I might just ride with you."

As soon as I pulled out of my parking space the phone rung. It was Angie's crazy ass. She was already at my ole-girl's crib, so I shot 'round there. Angie was looking so good that if beauty was a crime she'd have been doing a life-long sentence.

Shortman was fresh. But then again, he always was. We all made sure of that, because he was my little man. As soon as they got in the car Shortman jumped in my lap. He loved to drive.

"What's up, lil' nigga?" I said as I drove off.

There was a fat ass half a blunt between my finger. Smoking around children wasn't cool in my book, so I was about to put it out when Shortman stopped me.

"Let me hit that," he said.

"Hit what?" I asked, surprised and staring at him hard.

"That joint."

"Lil' nigga, you can't smoke! Smokin' bad for you."

He looked upset. "EK let me hit his joints everytime he at our house."

I looked at Angie and she grabbed Shortman and put him in the back seat.

"What's up with that!" I asked, mean-mugging Angie.

"With what?" she played dumb.

"Bitch, you know them niggas smoke lace!"

"I ain't know that, Bo, damn…and you ain't have to call me out of my name."

The bitch was lucky that's all I did was 'call her out of her name'. I should've punched her ass in the mouth. I was heated! How she gon' have a nigga giving my little man drugs?

All kind of shit ran through my mind as I got on I-95, heading north. I had to hurry up and do something with this bitch, and soon before I blew my cool. For thirty whole minutes we rode in silence, finally pulling up to the hide-out.

As soon as we walked in Shortman looked and started screaming. I laughed to myself as he ran over to the pee-wee Ninja-50 that I'd bought him for his birthday. I was giving it to him early because I was going to be hella' busy in the coming days. He didn't care one way or another, he just wanted to ride it. He busted his little ass a few times, but he finally got it together. And he loved it. I was happy to see him happy. Something I missed as a child.

After he'd rode his self tired I got him ready for bed. Nothing had been said between me and Angie. She was sitting in the living room watching GET IT HOW YA' LIVE [the straight to DVD movie based on the novel by Big Gemo] when I came out of the room with Shortman.

"You got 90 days to get yo' shit together." I said point blank.

"Or what?" she shot back.

"Or I'ma fuckin' kill yo' ass and Shortman can come live with me."

I didn't yell or nothing. I just sat down and fired-up a blunt. She was looking at me trying to figure out whether my threat 'to kill her ass' was serious or a joke. Looking into my eyes and seeing no signs of a smile she got nervous and tightened up. I had the bitch's full attention. She'd heard the stories about me and Dutch, we were thuggin' for real. The shit that rappin' ass niggas like Trick and them were rappin' 'bout we were living.

"I'm sorry, Bo...I, I know you only mean good, but..." Angie started explaining in a sad whisper... "...but I ain't really tryna move and a bitch get stuck with all kinda' bills and shit. You said it yo'self, you could be dead or in jail at any given time....so, I'm not tryna live beyond my own means."

I looked at Angie and really felt sorry for her. She wasn't just afraid of me and the highly exaggerated stories of my squad's infamy, but she was scared of leaving a life that had given her *nothing*. Overtown was (and is) the poorest part of Miami – characterized by poverty, social collapse, and death. Which her and many more people (generations and generations) had grown to accept *as life*, but was nothing in comparison to what they could have if they'd only dare to have more. Some were just never given the opportunity, while Angie was being afforded every opportunity and was scared to take it.

I shook my head, no longer mad at her but sad. "That's all you had to do in the first place was talk. Girl, you won't be under no pressure. Yo' Section 8 goes everywhere! Whatever yo' bills are now it won't be much of a difference."

She sat there looking stupid for a minute. "Are you gonna live with us?"

"So you gon' make this about me? Angie, this ain't about me! It's about you and Shortman havin' more in life. Give him a fuckin' chance, even if you don't want one for yo'self." I blew on her.

"I'm not like you, Bo! I'm not strong! I can't hide my fuckin' feelings..." Angie said, crying.

She softened me up with that. I couldn't stand to see women cry – at least the ones that I cared about.

"Look ma, let's worry about one thing at a time. You already know I fuck with you, so what's yo' beef?"

"My beef is, Bo, I don't really want or ask for much...I mean, as long as me and my baby got a roof over our heads, food on the table and clothes on our backs, I'm straight with whatever...'Cause, I'm sayin', I coulda' got serious with a few dudes, but...man, you ain't blind. I want you."

"Angie, this ain't 'bout me. It's –"

"Nah nigga! It is 'bout you!" Angie said, still crying. "You can't see that I love you, nigga? Is you that caught up in yo' thuggin'? Or is this too much for Mr. 'In Control'? Yo' ass tough enough to tote guns and kill people, but you scared to love me! Or I ain't good enough for you?"

Angie was crying like crazy. I'd never seen no female trippin' like she was trippin'.

"Look Angie, slow down and stop cryin', ma." I hugged her. "I'ma meet you half way. Show a nigga that you ready to be with me and then we'll talk serious...but for real, ma, tell me this. Why would a nigga wife somebody who ain't what they want or need?" I let my words set in before I continued. "You ever ask yo'self that? You the one blind. I've been tryin' to move you into a better situation every since I put myself into one. Why? You ever asked yo'self why? Well I'ma tell yo' crazy ass. It's because I've been plannin' a future for 'us'! So think before you pop slick."

Angie didn't know what to say. We just stood looking at each other. I broke the silence by kissing her. She quickly hugged me extra tight. The only thing standing between me and her *good-good* was the little skirt she was wearing and opportunity.

"I, I...love you, Bo, baby." Angie whined as I slipped her panties to the side and inserted my finger.

Angie was what dudes in Miama referred to as *leakers*. At the mere hint of sex they got soaking wet.

While I fingered Angie's *good-and-wet*, she unzipped my pants and pulled out my little man. With no hesitation she went for her shot – deep throat. Her mouth was pure pleasure. I pleased her with three stiff fingers. The faster I slid in and out of her, the quicker her head bobbed up and down. I could tell that she was about to cum because she was applying more pressure with her jaw muscles, bringing me to climax with her. I looked and saw that my hand was drenched in cum. At that instance I ejaculated in her mouth. Angie didn't miss a beat! She continued to apply passionate pressure until she felt that she'd drained me completely.

Smiling, Angie searched my pants pocket for a condom. Once she found one, she tore the package open and placed the condom in her mouth. Then, with no hands, she slid it down my shaft with her mouth. She went so far down that I could feel the back of her throat.

Angie mounted me just as easily as she had put the condom on me. I was sitting on the couch, we were face-to-face as she slowly rode my dick. Up and down she went while I sucked hungrily on her breast. This went on for about ten minutes. She would suck and stick her tongue in my ear, then blow her warm breath over the cool saliva. Shorty really knew how to please a nigga.

With every bounce I pulled her back down harder. And before I knew it we were kissing. Usually Angie and I just freaked or fucked, but this time there was real passion in every moan or stroke. It was more like making love. I'd never seen Angie so turned on.

"I love you," she whispered between sucking my lips and tongue. "I'm cummin', Bo."

"Me too, baby." I heard myself say.

And we came together.

$$$

"So what, now?" Angie asked as we laid back smoking a blunt of 'dro.

"Shiid', nothing...either yo' ass comply with what I put down...or shiid', it's over. I ain't got time to waste on you. We done played long enough, ma. I could be using my energy somewhere else, on somebody that's gon' 'preciate a nigga."

With that said I got up and went to look in on Shortman. He was sleeping good. When I came back Angie was sitting up watching TRUE ROMANCE – sort of like the modern day Bonnie & Clyde. There was a bag of Flaming Hot Chips sitting in her lap that she was eating.

"So," I said, sitting down and grabbing the chips. "Whatchu' gon' do?"

She looked at me sadly. "I'm gon' get right...but look, I wanna ask one more thing of you."

"What?"

"Can we have a baby?"

"A baby?!?!" I asked.

"Yeah, a baby."

"Ma, that's a big ass responsibility. I'm sayin', da—"

93

"I could manage, Bo. You said—"

I cut her off by holding up my hand.

"Look, just say I say yeah. We gotta go get tested, and once we get tested all that fuckin' with other niggas is out." I looked at her seriously and continued. "That's something you gotta think about, 'cause there's a lot more that comes with what you askin'."

"Boy, first off, ain't nobody got no AIDS. But we can take the test if that's what you want...and long as I been 'round you, I know what you want and how you want it, just like I know what it's gonna be if I cross or betray you...damn, how many times we gotta talk 'bout that?"

I thought for a minute. Angie was talking real crazy...but for some nut-ass reason, I liked what she was saying. I knew that I was *wrong-as-fuck* for what I was doing, because I was about to be a married man. Still, I could not help myself.

"Aiight, set it up for next week. We gon' get tested and go from there." I told her. "But it defeats the purpose to go through all this shit and go fuck around with other niggas."

"Whatever, Bo. I know what I want."

"Yeah, me too...I know that I want yo' ass on somebody's job or in somebody's school, asap. Learn how to do hair or something. Find some shit that you're good at or like doing, and we'll put it together." I looked at her and began to rub her pretty face. "I'ma need you to really play yo' position, ma."

"I got you." Angie said simply.

"Aiight, well look, I gotta go handle a few. You and Shortman can just chill here until I get back."

Angie nodded her head yeah. She already knew not to open or answer the door. If somebody came over and they were important, then they'd have a key. Angie walked me to the door and I left.

$$$

94

On the way to Carol City I hit Denise at the crib to see what was up with her. I don't know if it was guilt eating at me or what, but I needed to hear her voice.

"Hello?" she answered.

"Whatchu' doing?"

"Just layin' here...thinkin' 'bout you."

"Aiight, well I'm tied up, so don't expect me until late."

"Aiight," she said and hung up.

When I pulled up in the Match Box the first person I saw was Kiki. She was kind of like my Reebok broad. I had been knocking the pretty little red-bone down for about a month – here and there. She was super-sexy! To the point that I over looked her not being thick.

"Oh, you act like you can't speak." Kiki said, hands on her little hips, neck and eyes rolling.

I laughed at her young ass. "What they do, lil' momma?"

"Why you ain't been callin' me back, Bo?"

"I told you that I'll call you when you grow up."

"Boy, I am grown up!" Kiki snapped.

"I can't tell."

"Well, aiight, I'ma just show yo' ass, okay?"

"We'll see." I laughed again.

Kiki sucked her teeth and walked off. Her little sexy ass was crazy. But I liked her though. We were beefing because she ain't want to suck me up. It had only been about a week and a half since I'd cut her ass off, so I was truly surprised that she'd broke so quick.

As I leaned on my car watching Kiki do her hoe-walk across the parking lot, Dutch and Diablo whipped up. I could tell off-the-rip that Diablo had problems.

"What's up, cuz?"

"Ain't shit," I answered.

Dutch just gave me some dap and posted up.

"The North Carolina spot is dead, my nigga."

"What happened?" I asked. That spot was really jumping off the hinges.

"Had to holla at some New York cats...shit got crazy, so we gonna let shit die down some. Feel me?"

95

I just shook my head. A nigga was really going to miss that bread.

Chapter 12

BO

After offering up that little bit of bad news Diablo cleared it. Me and my brother just posted up and watched the happenings in the projects – hoes hoing, niggas begging, and gangstas getting it. And though most of the shit we saw was really sad, we laughed our asses off from a great deal of it. Because niggas are some funny muthafuckas!

It seemed like the longer we sat out there the funnier shit got. Reason being, more of our men [team] kept pulling up and posting up with us. I was blowing big-boy 'dro and Dutch was sending Shod to the liquor store every twenty minutes for Henny and Green Bottles. We were all either tipsy or fucked up! Even my little brother Shod was tore down.

"Man, my nigga, dog, yall let's hit Miami Nights!" E yelled.

I really ain't want to go. Angie and Shortman were at the hide-out waiting on me, and my future wife Denise was at home waiting on me. Just as I was about to opt-out of going Dutch spoke up.

"Fuck it, let's go…come on, married ass nigga, hang out witcha' brutha."

Dutch was drunk as fuck! So I said "fuck it!" and went. We were surrounded by some good dudes, but couldn't nobody watch the twins' back like the twins. Plus, I was enjoying being with my brother. Since the money had gotten greater and we'd turned up the thuggin', it's like we rarely hung anymore. When it should've been the direct opposite.

When we left the Match Box it's like the whole projects was with us – ten cars deep. Including bitches and all, it had to be about 30 or 40 of us. After parking we shot straight to the club's entrance. The line of people waiting to go inside was off to the side of us. There was a little chain that they had to snap and un-snap to let you through. I looked at the bouncers and the doorman who was collecting money and stamping hands.

"Yo, all 'em with me." I said.

The doorman looked at the long line of project males and females that were behind us and whipped his forehead. "Damn, all 'em?"

Instead of repeating myself I handed him a stack and we all mobbed on through – and we were all strapped. The metal detector was beeping like it was 'bout to blow up. Everybody was staring as we mobbed over to our reserved spot. It was empty. It stayed empty even when we didn't come, 'cause everybody knew what it was with us – pressure.

As soon as I leaned on the wall and sparked up a blunt I seen that two waitresses and a bouncer were sitting a case of Budweiser, a case of Heineken, and two cases of Crystal on the floor in front of our tables. The two waitresses left and came back with four fifths of Remy Martin V.S.O.P. and some Alize.

I don't really drink, but I grabbed a Budweiser and pushed of through the club. Damn near half of the niggas that came with us moved with me. Then, when Dutch pushed off the other half moved.   There was major *larceny* in the air, niggas with *slight* because the twins made it. When for real, they should've been happy for a nigga and thanking God that we'd made it, because had we been still broke, every nigga and bitch outside of our circle would've been under pressure.

Anyway, a few real dudes was holla'in. Dudes that had came up through the trenches and knew what it was like to finally have something after never having nothing. Diamonds, gold and platinum, and big-boy 'drobes spelt success in my hood. Straight up! And me and my team was rocking all of the above.

So as I was making my way towards the food section I saw this bad little chick with a short tennis skirt on. She was tall with some pretty brown legs. Her back was turned to me, so I easily approached her from behind and whispered in her ear. Shorty quickly turned around with this mean as East-Unit tore across her face, like "I know this nigga didn't." But when she saw all twenty of them goons standing behind me she stuttered and found something more appropriate to say.

"Uumm', what did you just say?"

I was like, "What's up. Let's do breakfast." I smiled. "But you heard me the first time."

Let's do breakfast was a polite way of saying *let me fuck the air out of you.*

After about two long minutes of silence she started smiling and was like, "Bo, that's fucked up."

"What?" I replied, looking crazy. Because she'd just called me by my name.

"I guess you don't know a bitch when she got her clothes on, huh?"

I was puzzled as fuck, but my facial expression never changed.

She kept rapping, "You don't remember me? Tasha! Jessie's niece."

Then it hit me. Jessie was my sister's friend.

"Damn you look different."

She smiled, "I bet I do."

Women have a little thing that they do, sort of bounce on one leg with their hand on their hip and fan themselve's with the opposite hand. I guess it's equivalent to men brushing their shoulders off. Because for real, every bitch that did that shit, at least the ones that I had ran through, either had the best pussy and head in the world...or sho'nuff thought they did. And for real, I was trying to find out.

"So what's up?" I cracked.

"Whatchu' mean?" she shot back, still fanning and bouncing.

"I'm tryna go."

"You got my number and I still live alone."

The bitch kind of rolled her eyes along with her neck as she turned and walked off. *Fuck, it*, I thought, *I guess we ain't doin' breakfast.*

I screamed at a few more people before heading back over to our little reserved spot. When I got there I saw that the homies had somebody surrounded, so I rushed over. It was Dutch drunk ass!

"Dog check!" he yelled.

"Woof!!!" all of the homies called back.

"Dog check!"

"Woof!!!"

"Check, check, check!"

"Woof, woof, woof!!!"

"Check, check!"

"Woof, woof!!!"

Dutch little drunk ass looked around laughing at all of the niggas outside of our circle, then yelled, "Front, back, side to side!"

And all of the homies yelled, "Never let a *hoe-ass-nigga ride*!!!"

Dutch was tripping, "I said, front, back, side to side!"

"Never let a *hoe-ass-nigga ride*!!!"

It was crazy, but everybody knew that we did that shit everywhere we went. Once Dutch and them fools got drunk it was *whatever-whatever*. So *fuck it*, it was *whatever*. Niggas was mobbing up and looking for something to get into when I peeped Diablo in the cut drinking a Pepsi – 'cause he don't drink alcohol period. I guess the doorman or one of the scared-ass- niggas in the club had called him and told him that we was crew thick. For real, Diablo was the only person that could slow us down. It didn't matter who niggas were or what they had, when we *set-it-off* somebody was *fucked-ass-up!* Lucky though, ain't nobody jump their ass out there. We had a real good time and nobody got fucked up.

$$\$\$\$$$

When I got home Denise was upstairs in bed. She immediately sat up in the bed when I entered the room. I sat down next to her and rubbed the side of her pretty face. Denise was my baby, and I was

100

a very lucky man to have such a wonderful woman waiting for me at home.

"What's up, ma?" I spoke softly.

"Nothing," she said yawning.

"What did you do all day?"

"I went and picked up a few more of my things…that's about it."

"You ain't miss me?" I asked as I stood and stripped down to my boxer.

"I always miss you, bay."

Slipping beneath the sheets I took Denise into my arms. She felt so good. I instantly got an erection as the smell of her Peaches & Cream lotion filled my nostrils. We started kissing. I slid a finger in her wetness, then climbed on top of her.

"Oooh, baayy." Denise moaned.

The alcohol had me numb and spinning, but not so intoxicated that I couldn't feel Denise's sugar-walls gripping my dick super tight before she spasmed and came…

$$$

The next morning I jumped up bright and early. I had to run over to the spot to see Angie and Shortman. I'd left them there unattended all night, which I really had not planned to do. When I walked in the house they were sitting in the living room eating.

"Damn nigga, I thought you forgot about us." Angie said with a little attitude.

"How could I forget about my lady and my son?" I shot back, kissing Angie on the forehead.

"What's up, Bo?" Shortman asked.

"Nothing." I snatched him up in a big rough manly hug. "Wanna play me in the racing game?"

"Hel--," Shortman caught himself and looked at his mother. "I mean, yeah, I wanna play the racing game."

I sat around and kicked it with them until about 12 o'clock. Then they got all of their stuff together so that I could drop them off.

Soon as I got back in traffic my cell went off. It was a funny number so I did not answer the shit. It stopped ringing and started right back ringing. Not everybody had my number so I did not take kindly to strange muthafuckas calling me. Yet it was hard to just ignore the call, 'specially with the phone ringing *back-to-back-to-back*.

"What?" I finally answered.

"Cuz!"

"Who the fuck is this?"

"Me, nigga!" Diablo said. "Me and lil' cuz stuck, come get us."

"Where yall niggas at?"

He gave me the street and avenue where they were. I didn't ask any questions, I just shot over there. It only took me about eight minutes to hit the area, police were everywhere, and another two or three minutes to find them. They both jumped in sweating bad and breathing heavy. Dutch still had on the same outfit that he'd wore to the club last night – minus the jewelry.

"Drive, my nigga." Diablo said and laid down on the back seat.

As I drove Dutch filled me in. Diablo hadn't come to the club last night to babysit us, he was there laying on a dude from Opa Locka, Forty was with him. Seeing Diablo in the club spooked the dude, which Diablo already knew would happen, so Forty was posted in a rental waiting to follow the dude home. Once he got the address he called Diablo, Diablo called Dutch and they were waiting for dude when he came out of his house that morning. I knew better than to ask *did they kill him*. I did wanna know about my dog, though.

"Where Forty?"

"Mmaann'," Dutch said, looking back at Diablo.

"Crackas got 'im." Diablo answered. "Drop me off at the duplex and I'm 'bout to get the lawyer and the bondsman on it."

"So whatchu' want me to do?" Dutch asked.

"Tie up yo' loose ends, we leavin'…Bo, you takin' us, so be ready."

"When?"

"Tonight," Diablo said, taking my cell phone. "Get a hoe that can drive a van."

I thought about Denise, she was a G, but I didn't wanna put her freedom in danger. After all, she was wifey. Next my mind went to Angie, but I wasn't sure if I wanted her in family business like that. Especially with her still politicking with Brenda – the nigga Conrad's broad. I seriously didn't think that she would outright cross me, but unconsciously bitches just ran their mouth too much. Just as Diablo got out my phone went off again.

"Yeah, who this?"

"You rude," the sweet female voice said.

"And you playin' games…who this, befo' I hang up on yo' ass."

"Boy, this Kiki!" she snapped. "And you a trip. I was callin' to offer yo' butt something special, but you wanna act all stank and fuck up the mood."

I was about to cuss the bitch out for real, 'cause wasn't nothing special about her funky dick chasing ass. But then my brain reiterated my current plight – I needed a hoe-driver.

"My bad, ma. I didn't catch the voice." I mellowed out. "Can you drive a van?"

"What?"

"I wanna take you outta town and show you a real good time. But I ain't got no license and what-not. So can you drive a van?"

"Yeah, I can drive one." She piped back down and sweetened back up. "Where we goin'?"

"I'll tell you when we get on the road. Meanwhile, just be yo' ass ready tonight."

"Okay."

"And whatchu' got to offer me, all-of-a-sudden, that's so special?" I cracked.

Kiki giggled like a little girl. "It's two things…" she giggled some more. "And it's something I ain't never gave nobody."

"Well, we'll see." I said and hung up.

For real though, I knew what it was. That's why I had cut Kiki's ass off the first time – she was faking with the lips and tongue service. Now she was ready and her timing couldn't have been more perfect. I would be doing my part for the team – by getting us up the road – and getting my due service out of KiKi. Because one thing I knew for sure, *hoes got all the way off the chain when you got them out of their environment.* And I put that on stacks.

After running it by Dutch – he was cool with it – I dropped him off and shot back to the crib to tell Denise. I knew that she was going to be tripping, but hey, it was what it was.

$$$

"So why the fuck you gotta go?" Denise screamed on me. "I 'posed to just sit up in this big ass house, *by myself?* And how I know it's *business?* Why I can't go? I know you most likely got one of yo' foot draggin' ass bitches goin' witchu'."

She was crying and all. I just looked at her. She was emotionally unbalanced, that's the only reason I didn't blow on her crazy ass. That and the fact that *I did have one of my foot-draggin' ass bitches goin' with me.* So I let her have that little bit. Besides, Ma, my ole-girl, had already told me to excuse Denise because her hormones were changing, with the baby and all, so she'd get real emotional and crazy sometimes. With that in mind I hugged Denise.

"Look ma, it's business...strictly business, that's why you can't go. I don't wanna involve you in my bullshit."

"But I thought we was a team. How can I not be involved?" she whined, still crying like a baby as I held her.

"We are a team. It's just that 'everything' on the team's agenda ain't for 'everybody' on the team. That's why there's so many different positions." I lifted her chin and kissed her lips softly. "Play yours, aiight?"

She nodded her head up and down, indicating yes. "I'm tryin', Bo...I really am. I done damn near cut my family and all of my friends loose for you. Tryin' to live how 'you' want me to. And, and this ain't easy...but I'm tryin' real hard...me and this baby, we're a pair. So if you abuse one, you gon' lose us both."

I understood that she was emotional, however that was a fucking threat. So I checked the shit. "It seems as though you know that you have a lil' leverage or power over me as far as the baby goes...whatchu' don't know is how to use it, or when to pull rank...I don't just go around slappin' niggas and goin' in their pockets, even though I know I can. So in the same breath, I ain't gon' have 'nobody' pushin' my buttons because they have something I love or want."

"So whatchu' sayin'?"

"Don't let your little power destroy us."

She thought for a minute. "Sometimes, Bo, it's like I don't even know you anymore. And it's like the deeper we get, the more you change; the more I wanna love you, the more you wanna thug the streets; and while I'm lovin' you, you're in love with someone else."

Her tears were really running now.

"Look Denise, I know you ain't askin' me to choose between you and my brutha, 'cause he's my heart and I ain't leavin' him in the streets alone."

"I'm not stupid, Bo. I'd never ask you to choose between yo' brutha and me, because I know that I'd lose...so it's not that, it's the street, your lifestyle...that's what's gonna destroy us, not my power."

"Only if you let it." I kissed her again. "I told you from the beginning to *just be patient* with me. It ain't even been a year yet. You gotta give me some time to build 'our' future, aiight?"

She nodded her head up and down again. I kissed her once more and started packing my shit for the trip.

Chapter 13

BO

Diablo had rented a nice ass Dodge custom van. It had four captain seats, TV's and VCR, refrigerator, and a big ass couch bed in the back. The seven and a half hour ride to Tallahassee was smooth sailing in that big nice muthafucka with KiKi driving. Once we arrived we got rooms at the Sheraton right off I-10.

I dropped me and KiKi's luggage off in our room and we all got back in the van. Diablo had work down in Quincy – a little city about 45 minutes outside of T-town – so we shot that way. We had family there also – on my ole-boy's side. I had a 9mm Glock over to my cousin Die's house so we stopped there first. Properly strapped, we shot back to T-town.

"Swing in this Apply Bee's," Dutch said.

Which wasn't a bad idea. We hadn't had any real food since we left the Bottom. Dutch loved Apple Bee's because his little ass could get drunk while he ate. I wasn't tripping though, I had a few drinks with him, because I wanted to be *right* for KiKi when we got back to the 'tel. I guess she wanted to be *right* also, because every time I got a drink she got one too. Diablo spent his time on the phone, calling niggas to let them know that he was in town and needed to collect. He set everything up for the following day.

When me and KiKi got back up to our room she went to the shower while I checked out the news. The area that the reporter was in looked real familiar. I eased over to the TV so I could get a closer look. Sure enough, it was the same 'hood that I had picked Diablo and my brother up from earlier that day. I turned the volume up.

Earlier today this South Florida man [a picture of the dude flashed on the screen] was brutally shot to death in front of his Miami home [the camera man zoomed in on the house before showing the dude's dead body beneath a coroner's tarp] as he exited the house. 28 year old Zackery Paul worked as an electrical specialist at Rip-N-Ride Studio. He was recently released from Coleman U.S.P. where he served an eight year sentence for drug related offenses...witnesses reported two men assailing Mr. Paul with AK-47's, before fleeing the scene in a late model Honda Accord...police arrested a suspect, Everett Casado [a picture of Forty flashed on the screen]. As of now no...

I heard KiKi opening the bathroom door so I cut the TV off and sparked a blunt. She came out in a little red pajama type set. The top was tight like a bra and the bottoms were like loose fitting shorts. The lotion that she was wearing had the whole suite smelling like wild-cherries. She sat down on the bed, smiling, and asked to hit the joint. I passed it to her, realizing for the very first time just how bad KiKi was. Being that I was smashing so may hoes on the regular I rarely had time to seriously evaluate a hood bitch like KiKi. I mean, my nigga, I was probably about 16 or 17 and had done bussed about 800 bitches.

I know that I shouldn't have, but I kissed the hoe KiKi. Her lips were soft as wet cotton. I reached between her legs and started fingering her. She was wet as hell. I continued to finger her, now using two fingers, as she reached in my boxers and started jacking my dick. This went on for about 15 minutes before KiKi got up and stripped butt naked. Her young tight body was flawless. I slipped out of my clothes with the quickness. Kiki smiled and pushed me down.

"This what you want?" she asked.

I said nothing as she kissed and sucked my neck, then my chest. Her wet tongue continued down to my navel, the whole while I was smiling, knowing I'd struck gold. When her tongue stopped again it was what I call the jack pot. KiKi was a certified head doctor. I had done had my brains blowed by over 800 bitches, but KiKi made my dick melt in her mouth. I'm talking 'bout pure passion in her lips and tongue.

"Damn, ma." I moaned involuntarily.

107

Looking me in my eyes KiKi held my balls up and sucked them softly.

"You surprised?" KiKi wanted to know as she ran her tongue up and down the bottom of my shaft.

My only answer came in spasms. Tasting the pre-cum, KiKi sucked harder while jacking me at the same time. Nut started shooting everywhere! And KiKi was eager to consume as much as I could produce.

$$$

When I finally caught my breath and stopped shaking, I cracked wisely. "If that was yo' first time, I'd hate to run into you in a year or two...you gon' have some niggas fucked up and broke."

She just smiled, knowing damn well she'd been sucking dick since she was twelve...lying-ass-bitch. Hoes think they can lie to a nigga with that *I ain't never ate a dick shit,* and get a nigga to wife them. When in all reality, all they gotta do is be themselves, keep it 100 with a nigga, and if the head right a nigga gon' be there every night. That's on stacks!

So anyway, I laid her down, grabbed one of her legs and started to enter her. She stopped me.

"You ain't got no condoms?"

"It's too late for that." I said and rammed my third leg in.

"Ooooww, be gentle, bay...I, I ain't done nothing since you cut me off." KiKi whispered with her eyes closed.

I really didn't believe her, but for real, she was tight as hell. I could see that I was hurting her. Still, KiKi worked her hips like a big girl. After about five or six minutes of slow stroking KiKi was cummin' and digging her nails in my back. *Damn,* I thought, *Denise gon' kill my ass coming home with my back scarred up.* Pulling out of KiKi I told her to turn around. I stood on the side of the bed, her pretty red ass at the edge, and thought about Denise as I ram-rodded KiKi from behind. With every stroke I pulled her to me, violently slamming my dick into her. I could see that she was cummin' again. It also sounded like she was crying. Leaning forward I kissed the nape of her neck and filled her womb with the warmth of my sperm.

I was nowhere near tired and neither was KiKi. She poured us up some Absolut and Tom Collins, while I rolled up two blunts. The mood was real mellow as conversation flowed and knowledge of our pasts and future wishes were shared. Just looking at KiKi and the way that she carried herself you'd never know that she really had something to think with. I was really surprised. She listened to me as I spoke about Denise, our baby, and our future plans. I'm sure that both saddened and shocked her. However, it didn't stop her. When she finished her blunt and third glass of Absolut and Tom Collins, KiKi took my dick into her mouth and performed like eternal life and love hinged in the aftermath of her fellatio.

"Come on, bay." KiKi whined, turning around. "Put it in my ass."

I was kind of tipsy so I had to ask her, "do what, ma?"

"Put it in my ass, bay." She sang.

I got the lotion off of the dresser and lotioned up my dick and her ass. Placing my dick at the entrance to her lower intestine, I pushed and slipped in. It felt just like the pussy, only tighter and better. After getting over the initial shock of her request, I found my motion.

"Oh, oh, bay." KiKi whispered. "You hittin' my spot, you hittin', my, my, spot."

That really got me going. I started stroking faster and harder. From that point on I became the teacher, *because I taught up in that room for the rest of the night!*

After we both came KiKi got up and came back with a soapy rag. She cleaned me up, sucked me up, and road my dick like there was no tomorrow. Based on experience, I knew that every woman had their own cowgirl technique. Hers was grinding. She would go up and down, round and round, while rocking back and forth. Her grind was like no other I had experienced.

"I'm 'bout to, 'bout to cum." I said.

KiKi jumped up and took me back into her mouth. If I wouldn't have had Denise waiting at home, and Angie waiting to come off the bench, KiKi would've had me locked in.

As we laid there, sweaty, in each others' arms, KiKi looked at me and asked, "Well did you like your surprise?"

"Hell fuck yeah." I answered.

She smiled. "You got me sore."

"And you got me hooked."

We both laughed. Pretty soon we were both dead asleep.

The next morning I was awakened by someone beating on the door. After reaching for my gun and not finding it, I realized that I wasn't home. My dick was *sore as hell* and my head was killing me. *Last night must've been a muthafucka*, I thought, opening the door. It was Dutch and Diablo.

"Where red-girl?" Diablo asked.

"Who?"

"KiKi, nigga!" Dutch clarified.

"Oh," I looked around the room. "Man, I'on know where that bitch at."

That sweet ass Tom Collins shit and that Absolut had me fucked up.

As I sparked up a blunt everybody pulled out phones and started making calls. For what-ever reason Denise was not answering. I called about six or seven times before I said fuck it and called Angie, whom was talking and complaining like her period was on. I didn't want to hear that shit, so I rapped with Shortman and hung up. Just as I did KiKi came through the door with big bags. She was smiling brightly.

"Hey, yall! What's up?"

Everybody returned her greeting and kept doing what they were doing. Everybody except for me. "What's in them bags?" I asked.

"Breakfast," she replied, setting food out on the table. "I got up, thankin' I'm 'bout to eat something special, that continental breakfast shit, and all they give you is some toast and fruit!" KiKi said, took the blunt and hit. "And after the way you taught in here last night, I knew you was gonna want more than that."

Me and her bussed up laughing. Diablo and Dutch didn't get it, but they got down with the food. I ate a little something, but Denise had my appetite in the choke hold.

$$$

When we finished eating Diablo and Dutch left to handle the business of collecting money. I wasn't going no where! Me and KiKi had our own business to handle. For two days we didn't leave that room for anything. I must've nutted 30 times.

KiKi was a good little broad in a bad world. She'd came up bad, most likely in a single parent home, and had had a lot of bad relationships. She got on some Usher shit one night after I finished teaching and confessed to a nigga like, "Pat-Pat was my first. I loved that boy, and he dogged me...I called myself gettin' back at him by messin' with Pretty Pulla but he ain't do shit but fuck me and talk about me...then, it's like after that, I ain't really care. Every time I fucked a new nigga it got easier for me to fuck the next nigga with no pressure."

I could see that shorty wanted change, to be loved. But I also knew that she was fucked in the game. No dude was going to wife KiKi because she'd been labeled an animal. Which to me was unfair, because like I said, she really was a good girl.

Anyway, when it was time to clear it back to BadLand, I was given $93,000 and told that me and KiKi would be making the trip home without them. Dutch and Diablo had decided to stay missing a little longer – to let that murder shit die down some more. I wasn't tripping though I had KiKi doing 100 getting me home, because I still hadn't found Denise.

It was around 2 o'clock in the a.m. when we pulled up in the Match Box. KiKi was sort of sad and hesitant about exiting the van. I felt her though because I sort of hated to send her back to the gloom she called life. But I had a wife and a life of my own.

111

So to ease my conscience and show KiKi that I did care, I slipped her five stacks.

"You want me to hold this for you?" she asked.

"Nah, ma. That's you."

"No, Bo. You ain't gotta pay me. I had fun –"

"Nah, nah, ma. I want you to have that." I told her. "You're a real down ass chick. For real, you deserve more."

I kissed KiKi goodbye and shot straight to the crib.

When I got to the crib and opened the garage Denise's car wasn't in there. I parked and jogged up to the room. Looking around the room I could see that she hadn't been there in a few days. *Bitch!* I said as I dialed her number. No answer! I called and called until I got tired of calling and went to sleep.

At 6 o'clock the next morning I was up and at it. There were three messages on my phone. One was from my momma, one was from Dutch, and one was from KiKi; none were from Denise. After rolling and blazing a blunt, I returned my calls and tried Denise again, no answer. By then I wasn't mad anymore. I was worried. Maybe something had happened to her. I was just about to call her mother's crib when my phone started ringing.

"Yeah?"

"You called me last night, baby?"

"Girl, don't ask me no stupid ass shit like that! Where the fuck you at?"

"I'm, I'm down here to my momma house." Denise continued whining. "I got scared in that house by myself."

I tried that *take a deep breath and count down from ten shit*, but nothing could control my anger. "Listen bitch, this is yo' first and last time sleeping outside of this house...now get yo' ass home!"

I hung up the phone. If Denise would've been standing in front of me I would have kicked her ass. Maybe I was jumping the gun with the bitch, but I wanted to be there for my baby – if the muthafucka was mine. I could've been carrying Denise bad based on the cheating shit that I was doing. But whatever the reason, her ass was under the microscope from then on. All kind of shit ran through my mind before I remembered this shit from a mob movie that I'd seen. A father was talking to his son and stated, "when a wife betrays her husband with a lover, she allows a possible Trojan horse into their home...she can unconsciously leak secrets. She gives her lover power over her husband, because she has become a spy in a war...and love is no excuse for such treachery." *Treason,* I thought as I laid down for sleep, *is punishable by death!*

I don't know how long I was out, but I cracked my eyes and found Denise standing over me. The sneaky bitch was just standing there staring at me. I got up without saying one word to her and headed to the shower. It was so much that I wanted to say to her. I mean, I did what I did in the streets with other women, but I loved me some Denise and it really fucked with me to think that she might've been fucking another nigga.

When I finally got out of the shower, lotioned up and jumped fresh, Denise was still standing near the bed. I couldn't rightfully say whether that was guilt or fear replacing what was normally an energetic smile. If I had to guess I would've surmised that it was both. Yet seeing as I didn't get paid for guessing dumb shit, I just got my shit and cleared it. At that point my ego and pride were both fractured, so my attitude was *fuck Denise!* And I let it be known, because on my way out I yelled, "I want a blood test when you have that baby too!"

$$\$\$\$$$

For the next two days Denise was blowing my shit up! But I ain't answer, I had my ole-girl to call her back...*mannn, she hate it when I did that shit.* But I was with Angie and really didn't give a fuck what she didn't like. Yet my ole-girl got on some, "yall engaged, she having yo' baby, and you don't need to be doin' that girl like that. You actin' just like yo' daddy." Yeah, my momma was taking Denise's side again and she knew that bringing my ole-boy's mistreatment of her would make me go home....*mannn, I hated when she did that shit.* Still-in-all, I took my ass home.

When I walked in the house Denise was sitting there looking stupid. I was still a little fucked up with her, but I did love the chick.

"What's up?" I shot at her.

"I been callin' you for two days. I don' rode through the Match Box 100 times. Where you been?" Denise whined.

"That ain't important. What's important is you tried me knowing clear as day how I feel about bein' betrayed."

"But I ain't done nothing," she whined again, looking even stupider now. "I, I just had to clear my head."

"Is it clear?" I asked her dumb ass.

I'd always told myself that I'd never let my fate be decided by what a female puts in her mouth or vagina. Yet faith and loyalty were two of my highest principles. And both were predicated on trust.

"Yeah, it's clear."

"Good, 'cause ain't no turnin' back. You said this was what you wanted and now you got it, for a lifetime. You say you ain't did shit, but time gon' tell."

"Bo, baby, I haven't done anything." Denise stated firmly with tears in her eyes.

"I'ma take yo' word, ma. But you ain't got no more passes."

"I don't need no pass for sleeping at my momma house."

"You right," I said, staring at the lying bitch. "Go fix me something to eat."

As soon as she walked off I fired up a blunt and called Angie. I needed to get away from Denise before I ended up fucking her over. Because being a hoe was one thing, but taking me for a hoe was all together different. People got paid for the former and killed for the latter. Feel me?

Chapter 14

BO

Shit was progressing as far as getting money and thuggin' went, but my love life was a real mess. I mean, I had beaucoup bitches running for a young don, yet the relationship with the one I craved most was rapidly deteriorating, and that shit was killing me.

The baby was due any day. We barely did anything but argue, fuck, and exchange cold stares. It was her hormones I reasoned. While it was a nasty gut feeling that kept me distant and suspicious.

Shit had blown over with the police and the dead nigga from Opa Locka. Forty was out and my brother and Diablo were back in Miami. Aside from a few whispers of payback shit was chill.

Angie had landed a good job at a doctor's office. I was real proud of ma, because not only was she working, but she was attending school at night to get her real estate license and she was tearing the road down for me. Once a month she'd take five kilos of cocaine to Tallahassee for the team. With all of that going on and me fuckin' the breaks off of her, she'd stopped hanging Overtown altogether.

I went home almost every night, but I spent all of my time in the Match Box with KiKi or out with Angie. Both of them were following my instructions and stacking their paper up.

Everything was good until I got a phone call telling me that Forty got shot up while riding with his son and some other nigga.

"Is he dead? I mean, dog gon' live?" I asked, heart pounding.

"I don't know, Bo."

I hung up and shot 'round Dutch's spot. Him and Passion was over there having a threesome with some *badass* little thang name Tangaray Red. Lil' Momma might've been the baddest bitch on the planet.

"What's up, boy?" Dutch asked, looking crazy. "You tryna get down? Shorty a cold animal."

"Not right now, dog. Niggas done hit Forty up."

"What?"

"Yeah, fucked him over too."

"Who?"

"Them bitch-ass niggas from 'Town. Rome bitch-ass done got with them niggas on some military campaign type time."

Dutch laughed. "Fuck 'em! It's revenge on the niggas who played us and all the cowards that was down with it."

"I feel you."

Dutch laughed some more. He always laughed before he fucked somebody up. At present, that somebody was about to be Rome. We knew that he'd been giving them niggas from 'Town k-cutters and feedin' them work. I had already told Dutch when I first heard the whispers that we needed to deal with fool before him and his new little team became a real problem. But Dutch and Diablo brushed it off, and now Forty was fucked up.

$$$

We found Diablo in the safest spot on earth, the Match Box. When we pulled up he jumped right in the car. His nose was sweatin'. Which meant he wasn't happy about something.

"What's up?" Diablo asked.

"War, nigga!" Dutch stated.

Diablo smiled his devilish smile. He my cousin, but dude was the black devil for real. With him, we had a six-tight clique so vicious that they could've sent us at Noriega; all we would've needed was the proper intel' and the right equipment and he was a done deal...*my word!* So dealing with these little cunts wasn't going to be no pressure at all.

116

"Look," I said. "Angie lil' partner, Brenda fuck with one of the main niggas. So I'ma send her to see what the lick read."

"Can you trust her like that?" Diablo asked, nose still sweating.

"She the one been drivin' work up the road. Hell yeah I can trust her."

"Fuck that drivin' work shit! Can you trust her wit' yo' life?"

"Cuz, lil' mommas with us all the way." I said, praying I was right.

"Say no more then." Diablo opened the car door. "Call me when it's Choppa season."

He closed the door and walked back over to where he'd been when we pulled up.

We got back in traffic. I couldn't believe those fuck niggas had tried us like that. Dutch drove around checking our splacks and k-cutters. Everything seemed to be everything, so he dropped me back off. I jumped in my car and shot straight to the crib. Denise was laying there dead sleep. She was big as hell! At seven months she looked like a whale. Her feet were swoll up and some more shit. Normally she'd be up, ready to argue and fuck. But since she wasn't I slipped in bed and went to sleep.

$$\$\$\$$$

The next morning I was up before the sun and gone before Denise ever knew that I was there. When I pulled up at Angie's spot she was up waiting.

"Why so early?" she asked.

"'Cause I want this shit over wit'. Them suckas gotta lil' spot, so they gotta move during the day." I said, grabbing my mask and gloves.

As soon as we were in Angie's car behind tints, I popped my regular clip and put in my extended clip. That Tupac "Me and My Girlfriend" played as we hit I-95 South. She got off by the Miami Herald building so that we could come through the back way.

"So whatchu' plan on doin'?" Angie asked.

"Talk to 'em." I laughed. "What, you scared?"

"No, ain't nobody scared. I just wanna know."

"Well you'll know when I decide."

By the time we got in Overtown the sun was up. We rode through 22nd Street twice. I laid ducked off on the passenger side while Angie hit every block in 'Town looking for them niggas or trying to spot one of their cars. We hit every parking lot and duck off but hadn't seen nothing, so we hit the Swamp. Pay dirt! I wasn't expecting to see Conrad out there. The nigga was sitting outside of the store eating a breakfast tray. He never even looked up.

"Look Bo, that's him right there." Angie said excitedly.

"Yeah, I see 'im. Keep goin'."

We hit 8th Street, in front of the Bar BQ Pit, and made a left. I already knew the alley where he was sitting led to a one-way street going towards 3rd Avenue and 10th Street, right across Range Park was another one-way that went towards 11th Street and 7th Avenue. There was an abandoned building that sat right on 10th Street, so when the shit popped off I wouldn't have to worry about being seen.

"Look Angie, go all the way back 'round by the one-way and drop me off in front of the building." I told her, rolling my mask up on top of my head like it was a skull cap.

"Want me to wait right here?" there was less fear and more excitement in her voice.

"Nah, go to the light and I'll meet you on the 11th Street side."

I jumped out and hit the abandoned building. Fuck all that planning shit, soon as I hit that cut I was going to hit everything moving! No bullshit, I was a little nervous, but I knew that I had to dead-these-niggas or die.

I dropped my mask and pulled on my gloves. I went to letting off, *Boom! Boom! Boom! Boom! Boom! Boom! Boom! Boom! Boom!* Running towards him at full speed, firing as fast as I could. *Boom! Boom! Boom! Boom!*

My first few shots missed him, causing him to jump up and drop his breakfast plate. Which made my job easier, because with

118

him standing I had a bigger target. Conrad reached, but never cleared his waistband.

Boom! Boom! Boom! I let off, nailing his brave ass to the side of the store. By the time he slid to the pissy concrete, leaving a thick nasty trail of blood and flesh on the store's wall, I was standing over his stupid ass. He looked up, tears in his sad eyes, trying to talk and apply pressure to his many burning wounds, but both attempts were fruitless. Blood was running from his shaking lips, causing a gurgling sound. And he had so many holes in him it would've took eight octopuses to pressure all of his wounds. Conrad was a done deal.

"Make sure you tell Trav and the rest of yo' bitch ass homies that Bo said fuck 'em!" I laughed and emptied my 30 round clip in his ass.

I ran back through the cut. Angie was right there. I jumped in and she pulled off slowly. She hit the expressway by ICDC. Once we were safely on I-95 Angie turned the radio all the way down and slightly turned towards me.

"Did you get him?"

"Girl, watch the road."

I knew I didn't have no business doing that shit with her. The lick was just too sweet to pass up. I only hoped that I hadn't made a 'life sentence' mistake.

"Where we goin'?" she asked, attitude in full play.

"Look Angie, this shit serious. And you can't ever, I mean 'ever', talk about this shit with nobody!"

"Boy, I ain't pussy and I ain't stupid." Angie shot back, poking out her sexy lips. "I been told yo' ass I'm the real deal, nigga."

"True that, you real." I smiled at her wanna be thug ass.

She smiled back. "Now, did you get him?"

"Nah, 'we' got him." I said and lit a blunt. "His ass outta here."

As we rode along towards her crib, I flipped open my phone to hit a few of my double agents. I needed to know what people were saying they 'thought they saw', because you'll always have a million different versions of the same story, and in this instance it wasn't any different.

"Bo, baby, three lil' boys jumped outta van with assault rifles and shot that boy down like a dog...My nigga, Bo, them boys had k-cutters! From how they came, they had to be parked on the expressway...Twin, I don't know what Conrad was into, but that shit was a profession hit. I was out there and we never seen nobody. They hit fool with a sniper rifle..."

I laughed my ass off! Because those were just three of the wild ass lies I heard from my spies. But once we got to Angie's crib I checked the news. The reporter said that they were looking for a black or dark-blue Toyota Camry. I kissed Angie and left to holla at Dutch.

$ $ $

When I got to the hideout Dutch was sitting on the couch watching TV. He was there alone, which was strange. Dutch never slept alone. I sat down on the leather love seat and gave him the scoop on Conrad's timely demise.

"Nigga! Is you crazy?" Dutch hopped up, yelling. "Maannn, you tripped out! Why you did that with that hoe!?!"

"Chill, my nigga. I got Angie. Plus, dog, it was just too sweet to pass up." I explained.

"Them niggas shootin' to kill, my nigga!"

I shrugged. "That's the chance I took."

Dutch blew a bunch of hot air and sat down. The room was real quiet for a few minutes. That's the first time that I'd seen my brother that upset with me. He was mad enough to fight. But I wasn't tripping. I'd only did what I felt was necessary. Because in the game that we was playing, slippers counted, and the more of them niggas I got rid of, the less I'd have to worry about getting caught slipping by. So fuck 'em!

"Look, man." Dutch finally said. "You gotta stop lil' momma from hittin' that road."

"Why, what's up?"

120

"'Cause she doin' too much. If she get jammed on that road ain't no tellin' what she might say, my nigga. Shit was different before you took the hoe on a mission."

"But I got Angie, dog."

"Yeah, I hear ya', but she comin' off that road. You made yo' call and now I'm makin' mine." Dutch got up and fixed himself a drink. "Besides, my nigga, Passion gotta start earnin' her keep, anyway. I'ma put her money spendin' ass on the road," he paused, hit his liquor and stared at me. "Bo, was the hoe nervous or shaky, my nigga?"

"Nah, dog. She was calmer than some of the niggas we done rode with."

Dutch kind of smiled a little, then sat down. We talked money, chopped up hoes, and then made a few family plans. The game was getting real old to me. I hated being in the streets just as much as I hated going home. Yet when you're loving and thuggin', where else was a fool supposed to go?

"So whatchu' gon' do?" Dutch asked.

"I'ma go fuck Angie." I said, getting up. "I'ma fuck with you later, yo."

$$$

Angie was laid up looking sexy when I hit the spot. But I had shit to do, so that freak shit was out for the time being.

"Put some clothes on ma, we gotta ride for a minute." I told her.

I broke the .40 that I splashed Conrad's bitch ass with into a million pieces. Then Angie drove me to Silver Blue on 103rd, the 'partments on 119th, and then to the 135th Street 'partments. At each stop I threw pieces of the gun behind the 'partments in the lake and canal. Once the gun was gone we shot back to Angie's crib and I fucked her brains out! The pussy had always been bomb as fuck, but after taking lil' momma on that caper and seeing her perform under pressure, the sex seemed better. Probably because I had more respect for shorty's mind. Angie was really shaping up into a real gangsta.

"Look, ma," I spoke as she laid on my chest after sex. "The road is out. No more outta town for you. No more unnecessary chances, because I ain't tryna be yo' way outta jail."

Angie sat up quickly, shooting daggers at me with her angry eyes. "Nigga! I can't believe you just laid up there and said no fuck-ass-shit like that!" she paused, breathing hard. "Boy, I'd die or do a hunid' years for you...that's my word."

"Look, I know you a gangsta. But we gotta be smart and that means doin' what's best for everybody, 'cause it's more than me and you involved. Things gotta be done, we do them and never talk about them. You don't try to justify them, 'cause they can't be justified. You just do them and forget about them. You feel me?"

"Yeah," she answered dryly.

"Yeah what?" I checked her sternly.

"Yeah, I feel!" She snapped, then checked herself just as quickly. "I mean, I understand, Bo."

"Good." I stated, then stood and started getting dressed. "I gotta go."

BOOK 2WO

* * * * *

THUGGIN'

By PLEX &
Bo Brown

WHEN LOVE FAILS [Poem by John T. Bussey]

Where Are We
Stuck Between Heaven And Hell
With Really No Place To Be
Now I'm Deferring Love
For Fear Of Love
When Love's Always Been My Most Consistent Yearning
Why Has Love Left Me Down And Out
Constantly Telling Myself
This Can't Be What She [Love] IS Truly About
MAD AT MYSELF
Screaming DAMN! WHAT AM I DOING WRONG
Seems Yesterday Was Short Lived While Forever's Too Long
Not Understanding Why Emotional Walls Are Built
Only To Be Ripped Apart
Leaving That Zig-Zagged Coursing The Center Of The Heart
Why!
I'm Tired Of Love Building Me Up
Only To Tear Me Down
Too Ashamed To Cry
Too Afraid to Stop Trying
Dejected In This Ole' Life
Back On The Battlefields Of Sin
Unprotected
THUGGIN' AGAIN
Knowing This Life Has Given Me Nothing But Heartache And
Bad Weather
I Only Pray That LIFE AND LOVE
Somehow Bring Us Back Together

Chapter 15

"Look, this him on the other line, so I gotta go." Denise whispered into the phone. "I'll get back with you later, okay?...I love you, too." She said and clicked over. "Hey baby."

"What's up, ma?"

"You." Denise answered, smiling from ear to ear. It had been almost three days since she'd last spoken to Bo, and she missed him like crazy.

"What was you doin'?"

"Nothing. Just sittin' here thinkin' 'bout you."

"Yeah, I bet you was." Bo responded, then asked. "Where Susan?"

Denise sighed, somewhat jealous of her own daughter. "Sometimes I think she's all you care about," she stated before answering his question. "Yo' momma came and got her two days ago."

"You talked to my brutha?"

"Nah," she said slowly. "You know Dutch don't really vibe with me since you been gone."

"I wonder why?"

"Well I don't care, 'cause I ain't done nothing to him."

"Whatever, Denise." Bo cut her off before she got started. "Come see me, asap."

"Okay, want me to bring something?"

"Nah, I'm good."

"I bet you is," she sassed.

"Man, bye." Bo said, laughing at her little attitude.

"Bye," Denise half said and hung up.

I shouldn't even go see his ass, she thought to herself, knowing that she was splitting time with Angie. *Let that hoodrat ass bitch deliver ya' lil' messages,* she continued, knowing that his request for a visit was strictly about business. *His business!* Because every since she'd had the baby it seemed that there was no more 'them', only 'him and the baby', and rarely if ever 'her'. It was a situation that she genuinely hated, but had absolutely no power to change.

Love had failed her. *And that's exactly why I do the shit that I do,* she thought, pulling off her T-shirt and panties. She needed to shower and get dressed, because she had *business* of her own to handle before going to that filthy ass county jail to visit a nigga that no longer loved her. It was torture to sit opposite him, knowing what they'd once shared, yet living in the darkness of what they now were.

Standing beneath the warm spray of the shower, a few drops of liquid sorrow ran from her eyes and mingled with the water as it flowed over her large breast and down her thick curvaceous body. With her eyes closed tightly, Denise moaned a rueful sigh and thought. She reflected on all of the games and lies…*too ashamed to apologize…too afraid to stop trying.*

$$\$ \$ \$$$

Ten Months Ago
Bo walked in the house and found Denise bent over aiming for a straight shot up the rail. After rocketing the ball up the table and into the corner pocket, Denise turned around and faced him, her thug. She loved him so much, because he'd done so much for her. Yet he never really seemed to understand her, her need to be first.

Denise stared at him, knowing he'd just left one of his bitches, because he reeked of a fragrance that wasn't her own. Composed, she lifted her chin and pretended like everything was everything.

"You must be bored." Bo asked, kissing her.

"Not really. I just ain't played in a while, so I was just shootin' around."

126

Bo rubbed her big stomach gently. "You know you can't be bendin' over like that."

"I know," Denise answered, slightly irritated with her shape, her predicament, her life. Everything changed. Everything that was right was now wrong. She was due any day and couldn't wait.

"Come on," Bo said, taking the pool stick from her and racking it. "Let's go upstairs."

He could sense that something was bothering her. And he also knew what it was. It was the trips out of town, the tight relationship that he and Dutch shared, and most of all the other women. But why was she mad? He wondered. She knew from the beginning what she was signing up for. Yet he felt a need to soothe her.

"Look ma, I got a little tied up today. So maybe tomorrow we can go shoppin' or something." Before she could respond his cell phone rung. "Yeah?" he answered. "Oh, what's up Diablo?...Nothing, just chillin'...I'm at the crib...Right now?...Aiight, gimme a few minutes, I'll be through there."

"So you gotta go?" Denise asked, attitude in place.

"Yeah."

"You comin' back?"

"Yeah. I just gotta go holla at my cousin right quick."

"Well bring me back some Boston Market."

"Aiight," Bo said, laughing. He knew that that was her way of making sure that he came back home.

Denise laid there thinking. She knew for sure that his cousin Diablo had been the caller on the other end, but what had he wanted? After all, all men were dogs once you'd given yourself to them. So Diablo could've easily been calling Bo for some bitch that he had waiting in the wing. The whole idea of him being off with some chick, enjoying himself while she sat home miserable with his baby insider of her brought tears to her eyes.

I'm leavin', she told herself and tried to stand, but a sudden wave of light headedness overwhelmed her, and a sharp sneering pain erupted in her pelvic area. *Ooooh, God!* Denise groaned as the clear liquid ran down her leg. She immediately seated herself on the bed and picked up the pone. Her first call was to her doctor. Her second call was to Bo.

"My water just broke," she whined as soon as he picked up.

"I'm on my way!" he shouted, excitedly.

"No, just meet me at the hospital. I already called my doctor."

$$\$\$\$$$

By the time Bo made it to Miramar General they'd already prepped Denise and had her in the delivery room. He was nervous and it showed. A nurse approached him, smiling.

"Are you the father?"

"Yes," he answered.

"Is this your first time?"

"Yeah, this both our first time."

The nurse laughed. "Do you want to be in the delivery room with your wife?"

He hesitated for a moment. Not sure if he really wanted to witness such a sight, or if he could handle it. The cute nurse grabbed his sweaty hand.

"It's not that bad," she said.

"Okay, well, I'll do it."

"Good," she squeezed his hand reassuringly. "Follow me."

They entered a room where they both washed their hands, faces, and forearms with the greenish-blue solution, and changed into doctor's scrubs. Bo was then instructed to follow the nurse through another door which brought them into the delivery room.

Denise was crying and her face was sweaty. He could see that she was scared and in pain. Over and over the nurse instructed her to breathe deep and release slow. Bo walked over and held her hand. It trembled in his own. She was so frightened, but was being so brave. And in his eyes, she was doing it all for him.

Her trembling hand began to squeeze his tightly as the doctor instructed her to push. Then *breathe...push again…breathe…one more big push.* They commanded Denise before he heard the doctor yell, "here it comes!"

The nurse signaled for Bo to walk around to where she stood. Blood was everywhere! Bo looked and nearly passed out. He'd shot many people in his young life, but never before had he seen so much blood. A head popped out, Denise cried out loud and then came the entire baby. *Goddaammnnn!* Bo said to himself, amazed at how wide Denise's pussy had stretched open. He could not believe it.

A baby's cry broke this train of thought. The nurse handed him the baby and asked, "what's her name going to be?"

"Her?" Bo asked, thrown by the whole ordeal.

"Yes, sir, it's a beautiful little girl."

"Susan. We gon' name her Susan Paige Brown." Bo replied, beaming with pride.

The baby weighed seven pounds and eights ounces. Yet she seemed so tiny in his hands. He held her carefully, afraid that he might somehow hurt her. He smiled. There was a new respect for life building inside of him. And a new love for two women, Susan Paige Brown and the soon to be Mrs. Denise Brown. Something about holding little Susan made him love her again.

$$$

"Excuse me, Ms. Nurse." Bo called out to the thick brown-skin nurse who'd been such a big help to him. Denise was in her private room recovering and the baby was in the nursery.

"Yes, how may I help you?"

"How yall go about blood tests?"

Very quickly the cute, well proportioned nurse explained everything concerning the blood test. It all seemed pretty simple to him as she explained, so he agreed to take one.

"Thank you nurse," he said, smiling at her.

"You're welcome, sir." She smiled back.

"Don't call me, 'sir'. You make me feel old."

She laughed, blushed, then laughed some more. She was a real cutie.

"Do you have a name besides 'nurse'?" Bo popped at her.

"Yes I do. It's Shanika."

"That's a cute name to go with yo' cute face and beautiful figure," he said, removing a pen and paper from the counter to write down his number. "Here, take my number and call me sometime."

"Sir, aren't you here with your wife? And you're up here flirting with me?"

"For one, I'm too young to be married. And for two, didn't you just swab me for a DNA test? If shit was all good at the crib, would I need a DNA Test?"

She shook her head, stuck the number in her pocket and walked off.

"Aiight now, don't make me have to come back out to the hospital 'cause a certain Nurse Taylor ain't call me." Bo yelled to her.

After Nurse Shanika Taylor had walked off, Bo rounded the corner to Denise's room. He'd had no idea that the room was so close to where he'd been hollering at Shanika. He also had no idea that Denise had heard almost everything that he'd said.

When he walked in she was laying in the dark crying.

"You aiight?" Bo asked, taking a seat in the chair next to her bed.

Bitch! I almost died havin' yo' fuckin' baby and you 'round her disrespectin' me with that nurse bitch. How the fuck you figure I'm aiight? Denise thought but said, "I'm good," wiping her sad eyes.

Bo looked at her, truly surprised by her strength. She'd given him life, a baby girl. It was enough to make him overlook the small shit, the petty differences that they'd had. He really did want a family. With this in mind he called Dutch and Diablo to inform them that they were uncles. He then called his mother, Bee and Naomi; and lastly he called Denise's mother and sister. Everyone was pleased with the news of a healthy baby girl, and all promised to be there first thing in the morning.

While Bo was making his phone calls the nurse came in and brought him a pillow and blanket.

"Thank you," he said, smiling at the nurse.

"You're welcome," she replied. "Sleep tight."

Denise rolled her eyes at the exchange. "You ain't got to stay."

"Why wouldn't I stay?"

"Because you probably got thangs to do, people to see." Denise said sadly.

"If I was the one layin' up in pain, I'd expect you to be by my side."

Denise stared for a minute and nodded her head yes, as if to say, "I would."

Bo leaned in and kissed her forehead, her nose, and then her lips. "Sleep tight, ma. I got you," he whispered to her and made himself comfortable in his hospital chair.

Chapter 16

Denise climbed out of the shower feeling better, yet worse. *Damn I sho' wish shit was like it used to be,* she thought lotioning her naked body. The body that Bo once loved and couldn't seem to ever get enough of. The body that had birthed him a beautiful and healthy daughter. For a brief moment she wondered what had gone wrong. Yet just as quickly she remembered. It was the lonely nights, the streets, and the thuggin'. It was the money, the lack of love, and the temptation.

She dressed in a yellow Gucci skirt set and matching Jimmy Choo stilettos. With her wavy black hair pulled into a neat shoulder length ponytail and a coat of Mac lip gloss on her soft edible lips, Denise grabbed her oversized Nadia Terrell purse and headed for the door. However, before she could exit the house the phone began ringing. *Who the hell is this?* She sighed angrily, seeing that the caller ID read *private.* Thinking that it was Bo her anger rose further. *I told this crazy nigga I was comin'!* Denise thought, snatching up the phone. *This is a collect call from an inmate in the county jail...* Denise quickly hit 1-1 before the computer animated voice recording could play all the way through.

"Boy what?" Denise blew. "I woulda' been in the car by now if you ain't blow the line up."

"Excuse me?" the female voice questioned. "But, umm', is this Denise?"

"And who is this?" Denise shot back, surprised at the female voice.

"I don't mean to be rude and I apologize for callin' yo' house. But this is an emergency and I really –"

Denise cut her off. "Who – is – this!"

"This is Angie. And, well I'm locked up and I –"

Denise's laughter cut her off again. "Them crackas done finally caught yo' broke ass stealin' they shit, huh?"

"Excuse me?" Angie said, not believing what she was hearing. "I really think you have me confused, sweetheart, with yo' light-handed ass. Because last time I checked, me and my baby's closet was fulla' shit that you stole! So please 'miss me' with that shit and let Bo know that I'm jammed up on some bullshit 'bout my car bein' seen –"

Denise hung up the phone and strolled out of the house.

$$\$\$\$$$

Diablo, Dutch, and Shod were fresh to death as they exited Mall of America. They all were carrying big boy bags filled with expensive gear, even though it all belonged to Shod. It was his birthday, so Dutch and Diablo took him out and dropped a stack and a half a piece on him. Shod was happy as hell too! He only wished that Bo would've been out so he could've gotten another $1500 dropped on him.

The three men loaded all of the bags into the rented Volvo's trunk and climbed in. They'd been at the mall for most of the day. Dutch was eager to drop Shod off so that he and Diablo could go scoop up Forty and go *mobbin'*. Since Forty had gotten shot up and Bo had killed Conrad, things had really gotten *off-the-chain* in the streets. Niggas shot Bush up on 60th and left him in a wheelchair; James got killed in Opa Locka, Red Boy got shot up at the Rollex, and their other man Darrell got shot up and paralyzed on 95th and 17th.

Behind dark tinted windows, Dutch backed out of the parking space, MAC-11 resting on his lap, and crept through the crowded parking lot. As they drove along he peeped a pearl-white Q45 whipping into a parking space. The plates read *TWIN ONE*.

"Ain't that Bo shit?" Shod asked, pointing at the car.

"Yeah, that's it." Diablo answered, then asked. "What she doin' down here?"

"You know her sista' and ole-girl live down here," Dutch informed them. "Lemme see if this hoe heard anythang on Bo."

Dutch turned the Volvo in that direction and cruised slowly towards the Q45. But before he could reach it, Denise hopped out in a tight little yellow skirt and heels. Exposing her matching yellow thong when she reached back in the car to retrieve her purse. Denise quickly locked the vehicle and sashayed over to a money-green Expedition. She hopped in and the SUV sped off.

"You see that shit?" Diablo asked.

"Yeah," Dutch replied. "Did you see who was in it?"

"Nah."

"You wanna follow that bitch?"

Diablo thought for a minute. "Nah, cuz, fuck it. It probably ain't nothing. You know them hoes be goin' stealin' and shit."

Dutch wasn't sure. Why would she meet up at the mall, change cars, then go to another mall to steal? It didn't make sense, while at the same time he had other business to attend to. He'd fix Denise's *little red wagon* later.

$$$

The Expedition had barely cleared the parking lot's exit when the Volvo sped by it. Paying the car no mind, Denise sat smiling with her back to the window, facing the driver. He was dark and handsome. Sort of gentle. She loved that about him. Bert was her Baby Face in a world of Tupac[s] and Trick Daddy[s].

"You get that for me?" he asked, never looking in her direction.

Denise sucked her teeth. "Boy, Bert, do not sit up there and act like you pressin' me and shit. 'Cause, for one, I done told yo' ass –"

"And how was your day, Denise?" Bert asked, cutting her tirade short before she could really get started. "Did your husband stress you out at visit today?"

134

Denise sucked her teeth again. "Boy, don't play with me...and how you know I went to see Bo, you stalkin' me?"

"Nah, ma." Bert smiled, flashing a wall of pearly whites. "You always come to me with stress and attitude after you leave him," he replied charmingly. "That's all, ma. But ain't no pressure though...we good."

Denise wanted to slap his face, because he was right and she was wrong. *Always wrong!* Everything about her situation was wrong. She had no business creeping in the shadows with Bert. A dude, though sweet as nectar from the lips of an angel, that couldn't provide her with shelter for one night, let alone shelter her from the certain death that grew nearer everytime she'd succumb to her vain desires for his shallow offerings of pleasure. Nervous and frustrated, Denise dug in her Nadia Terrell handbag and removed $2,200. She tossed the crispy new bank notes, lightly, hitting Bert in the face.

"You happy now?" Denise inquired, anger in her tone.

Bert didn't answer. He simply pulled the SUV over on the shoulder of the express way.

"What are you doin', boy?"

Maintaining his silence, Bert turned, and in one swift motion he snatched Denise's legs up, causing her to yelp as her voluptuous bottom slid from beneath her and she suddenly found herself on her back, staring up at the SUV's roof. Bert didn't waste anytime ripping away her thong and diving face first into her gapping center of pleasure.

"Ut'un, Bert...no, not right...right here, booyyy. I ain't no, no mutt, booyyy." Denise protested trying to push Bert's head out of her hot leaking pussy.

Undeterred, Bert roughly jacked her legs up further and sucked harder on her moist mound of hot flesh. The car rocked steady as speeding cars zoomed by on the busy expressway. The thrill of being exposed on the highway seemed to heighten the waves of pleasure that swam through the both of them.

"Oh Bert...Bert, baby....Please, Bert...Yes! Yes! Yes! Bert!" Denise whined and moaned as her sugar walls fell and covered Bert's thick lips and tongue.

Shivering from the orgasm, Denise laid, legs spread out on the vehicle's dash and head rest, primed for every inch of the naked dick that Bert was about to deliver. With his knees on the truck's bench seat, he leaned in and sank the full length of his stiff manhood into her.

"Oooh, Bert!" Denise moaned out, scooting back. "Go slow, Bert...go slow!"

But Bert pounded. Emptying and refilling her sloshing middle. Each stroke quicker and harder than the last. The pleasure of the pain travelled from Denise's burning insides to her sweaty face, where it expressed itself in a sinful grimace, which was illuminated by the lights of passing vehicles as they shone through the dark tinted windows.

Unable to scoot back any further, Denise bit her bottom lip and began working her hips. She threw the pussy back at him with everything she had. They cores collided for less than five minutes before Bert began to shiver and drool. But not before he removed himself and shot his hot load all over Denise's $2,000 Gucci skirt and blouse. It was then that the reality of Bert having fucked her without a rubber sat in. *OhmyfuckingGod*, she thought. However, it was too late, and she was too exhausted to bitch about it.

$$$

"Who that right there?" Forty asked from the back seat.

"Where?" Diablo asked in return.

"Over there by the pay phone" Forty pointed from behind the tinted windows of the gray four door Acura Legend. "The nigga with the blue and red short set on."

Diablo looked, navigating the stolen car slowly through the streets of Overtown.

"That's Lil Tron. He ain't on nothing."

"Shiid', he be with 'em!" Dutch responded from the passenger seat.

"Nah, I fuck with Tron." Diablo shot back, dismissing the idea of fucking his little partner over.

The three had been out riding for over two hours. There wasn't a trace of Rome, Crab, Stanka, Dorry, Zack, or Dell. Diablo took one more dip and cruised until he got to the Orange Bowl. Snaking along the back streets they came through the 40's and rode some more. The air conditioner was piping. Yet with the worrying and heavy gear – bullet proof vests, thick army issue cargo suits and ski masks – the three heavily armed men perspired severely.

Coming west on 54th Street, Dutch looked to his right and what he saw almost made his eyes pop out of their sockets. He couldn't believe that disloyalty and good fortune could run together.

"My nigga, look!" he said, nudging Diablo.

"What?"

"Right there, yo."

Forty also looked in the direction in which Dutch was pointing. "Ain't that Naomi?"

"Yeah," Diablo replied, then looked further into Dutch's reasoning for pointing her out. "Ay', ain't that that nigga Kay?"

"Yep," Dutch said, nodding his head and gripping his AK-47.

"Hold up," Forty asked. "Ain't Kay the nigga that got lil' cuz on hold?"

Just as they'd made the realization on Kay and the situation at hand, the light changed and Kay and Naomi pulled off. And without being told, Diablo took off behind them.

Kay had picked the wrong day to rear his hard head.

$$$

"Ssshhhiiiitttt!" Shawanna moaned as she rode Rome's face backwards and watched her partner -- in both sex and crime, go the distance with his stiff dick. She'd come twice already and couldn't figure out if it was Rome's head or the sight of Von giving him head that turned her on the most.

The three of them had been going at it for over an hour. Rome was a boss-freak and Shawanna, Von, and their other partner White Girl, whom was in the other room getting freaked and flipped two ways by Crab and Stanka, loved him for it. Because in their line of work, and especially with their reputation, it was uncommon to find a big-money-nigga that tricked off stacks and ate the pussy. Rome and his boys were a heaven-sent to Shawanna and her girls, whom all had children and bills to take care of.

Boom! Boom! Boom! Sounded at the room door. Rome pushed Shawanna's juicy black ass out of his face and snatched his .9mm off of the dresser. "Bitch, move!" he instructed Von, who was still polishing his dick with her big lips and long tongue. "Who that?" Rome yelled, nearing the door.

"Crab!" the voice on the other side of the room door replied.

Crab was Stanka's man. His cousin had gotten killed earlier in the beef with the twins, before Rome himself was involved. Crab was a soldier, but not too bright and surely not too loyal. Rome only dealt with him, or any of his newfound Overtown associates, because he needed them. They had a mutual foe in the twins, and with his money and Stanka's muscle, he felt confident that they could murder Bo, Dutch, Diablo and everybody around them. Rome was a fool, he didn't underestimate the twins, but felt that they were fools for underestimating him. *Did they really think that I was pussy enough to let them fuck me out of 30 kilos and let it ride?* He wondered this for many days as he'd struggled to repay the connect and get back on his feet. Because of the twins and their treachery he'd had to sell his girl's Benz, all of his jewelry, and their home. However, because of them he was now stronger – he had a bigger, nicer split-level pad out west, his girl had a new Benz, and he now had a killer clique from Overtown to back him. Rome now had more money than he'd ever seen! Because not only was he supplying Stanka and his other clientele with boss cocaine, but Stanka had introduced him to the heroin game, and the two of them locked Overtown down as well as parts of Opa Locka.

"What, Crab?" Rome asked, cracking the door.

"Joe out here."

"So?"

"He say he need to holla."

"So why you comin' to me?" Rome asked, feeling his power. "Yall holla at Stanka!"

"Man, Stanka locked in with White Girl. He said holla at you." Crab shot back, twisting his short dread locks as he spoke.

Rome sighed, blowing the smell of Shawannas pussy in Crab's face. The man frowned, but before he could speak, Rome spoke. "Go get Stanka outta that room, yo. I'll be out there in five minutes."

After cleaning up and dressing himself, Rome stepped into the living room of his play pad, a nice little three bedroom duck-off in Miami Shores. He found Crab, Joe, Stanka and White Girl sitting on the couch and love seat blowing coc', drinking, and passing a blunt. Rome sat on the edge of the coffee table and lit a Newport.

"Bitch, get the fuck outta here. We 'bout to be on something," he growled at White Girl and watched as she stood, hot shorts wedged deep up in her big fat vagina, and shook what little booty she had as she went in the room with Shawanna and Von. Rome made a mental note to freak off with White Girl when their little meeting was over. He had a real fetish for her big titties and super-slut nature. "So what's the problem, yo?" Rome questioned, turning his attention back to his men.

Crab snorted some more coc'. Joe looked at Stanka. Stanka smoothed his wavy black hair and stood up. "We gotta do something 'bout them niggas," he stated, looking at Rome.

"Okay, and?" Rome shot back, blowing a cloud of Newport smoke. "I bought yall niggas thirty sticks and enough ammo to fuel a war in Pakistan. So whatchu' want now, a tank?"

"Nah, nigga!" Stanka sat back down. "We gotta spread some more money 'round. Niggas scared to open shop because them niggas ridin' hard. Everytime they peep shop open they tear up the block. Them niggas shot Zack up two days ago and Joe just said the niggas was out ridin' today."

Rome thought for a minute. "Call Dorry and Dell and tell 'em to get two splacks. We gon' do some ridin' too. 'Cause I

139

want shop open today. Right now!" he looked at Joe. "Whatchu' waitin' on, yo? Go open up the spot!"

Joe looked at Stank. Stank nodded his head and Joe slowly lifted himself from the couch and left. Rome walked back towards his bedroom, where White Girl was.

"Rome, what's up?" Stank called out, knowing they had some riding to do.

"I gotta handle something right quick…get them cars and gun and meet me back here in a hour." Rome commanded and closed his room door. He needed a little more loving before he went out thuggin'.

Chapter 17

Bo returned from his visit with Denise and fell back on his bunk. He was drained, both physically and mentally. The visit had only lasted a matter of minutes, 49 to be exact, and he could not understand how such a short amount of time could deplete him of so much vivacity. Lately there had been a great deal of shit that he couldn't quite bring himself to understand, whereas his relationship with Denise was concerned. Everything was bittersweet, hot and cold, muddled. He had to admit though, she looked good enough to smother in molasses and swallow whole, with her short tight yellow skirt on and cleavage revealing blouse. The baby hadn't hurt her body at all. Denise was even finer now, Bo thought, remembering how her yellow thong was cutting into her pussy lips at visit. It had been a while since he'd allowed her to visit him. Seeing her, conversing with her, was like *old times*. Times when they were happy. Yet something inside of him didn't want him to be happy...not with Denise. But how could he not be happy with the mother of his beautiful daughter? Denise was supposed to be his wife.

Unable to sleep, though hella' tired, and unable to clear his mind of thoughts of Denise, he pulled his stash of contraband from its stash spot and walked over to his smoke spot. He rolled one, fat and tight. Firing it up, he pulled hard and held long. The 'dro tickled his lungs and throat, threatening to gag him. Bo released the potent smoke, and without looking, passed the blunt to his left where Dewey the iron lung sat smiling with his hand out. Dewey took the blunt to the face and choked hard before passing it back. At this feet sat two peanut butter jars of *buck*. Bo wasn't much of a drinker, but under the circumstances, and being as though session crashing ass Dewey had paid for it, Bo took one and guzzled hard. The shit was nasty as hell, but it was pure gas! Bo looked at a smiling Dewey through glassy eyes, passing him the blunt back. The two continued smoking in silence until the roach was swollowed. Bo knew what Dewey wanted to ask, but he didn't make the situation easy for him. Dewey wanted to know had he ran the spiel down to his woman to convey to his brother. He had, and the situation was all good, but he wanted Dewey to sweat a little longer.

Wasted, Bo got up and staggered back to his bunk. Denise was now even heavier on his mind. He missed her. He wanted her. He fell back on his bunk and thought about his last days with her and the situation that had separated him from her…

$$\$ \$ \$$$

Ten Months Earlier

Baby Susan had been born for all of two days. Bo had been spending almost every minute of the day at her side, comforting her and playing with his baby girl. Denise's family and his family, Dutch and Diablo included, had also been coming in and out of her private hospital room, leaving flowers and gifts for the baby everywhere.

On his way to and from Denise's room, Bo had also been seeing a lot of Nurse Shanika. And she was exactly what he loved to see – pretty baby doll face, full woman sized breast, small waist, accented by booming hips and a huge round ass. Often times he'd sit in the little hospital café and watch her work the floor in her tight nurse's uniform. Always wondering did she wear G-string panties or none at all, because he never once peeped a panty line through her thin tight pants. She would always be smiling and in good spirits, unlike Denise. And though he constantly shot clever remarks laced with endearment, Nurse Shanika would simply smile, speak, and continue her rounds. At which times, he'd return her smile and head back to Denise's room.

"You gonna spend the night again?" Denise asked, flipping through the cable stations.

"Yeah, unless you expectin' company." Bo joked, then pulled $4,000 out of his pocket. "My cousin, Diablo, gave me this for you and the baby."

"Denise's eyes lit up. She was surprised. It was at times like this that she truly appreciated being Bo's lady. His family was strong and they expressed their love through their strength.

"Thank you...baby. And tell yo' cousin thank you too." Denise whispered.

"Ain't no pressure, ma." Bo paused, looking into her eyes. She was physically weak from delivering the baby, yet so brave and strong in his eyes. Those were qualities that his mother displayed, so he had to appreciate them in Denise. His mother liked Denise, and so did Bee and Naomi. Dutch was another story. But Dutch didn't have to live with her, he did. And in living with her, things hadn't been perfect, yet neither had he. He was thuggin'. And in doing so it was hard, if not impossible to trust. For in thuggin' you learned to trust only what you could see and explain. While the most beautiful things in life, the most beautiful thing being love, was rarely seen and could never truly be explained. So most thugs, Bo being the thugginest, feared love and felt an extreme sense of malaise in its presence. Still, for whatever reason, he fought it. "Summer 'bout to roll 'round, ma. When you gon' be ready to hop a few islands?"

"Whatchu' talkin' 'bout, Bo?"

"The Bahamas, Jamaica, whatever. We can just get missin' for a minute."

Denise smiled. This was the Bo she'd fallen in love with. Her mind asked her, *how long will this Bo be here, the loving Bo, before the thuggin' Bo replaces him again?* In a sense it didn't matter, because she needed them both. "Whenever you ready is fine with me."

"Next week then."

Denise nodded her head yes. "Thank you, Bo."

"For what?"

"Thank you for being by my side like you have."

Bo leaned forward and kissed her lips softly. "That's what I'm here for."

Denise and the baby were released from the hospital the very next day. And for the next two days Bo never left their side. Except maybe to go get Denise's order of Boston Market or sour cream and onion potato chips with ice cream. On such trips he communicated with Angie and KiKi, which only added to his callosity of muddle emotions. Angie was his soldier. KiKi was his solace. While Denise was the one source that had provided him life – Baby Susan. So his responsibility was to her.

On Denise's third day out of the hospital Bo received a beep from an unfamiliar number. It was after 10:00 at night, which further puzzled him. With Denise and the baby laying next to him sleeping, he decided to go downstairs to call the number back. A female answered on the third ring.

"Talk," he said.

"Talk?" the female voice repeated. "Is this Bo?"

"Yeah. Who this?"

Without answering his question she replied. "I figured since yo' peoples been released from the hospital it's safe for me to call you now."

Bo immediately recognized the voice. "Damn, ma. About time you called."

"Boy, stop," she laughed. "I woulda' felt funny callin' you knowin' I had to look at yo' baby momma. 'Cause this is not a good look."

"Well, she gone and you done called, so that's nothing to discuss."

"Ex-cuse- me, then." Nurse Shanika said, laughing again.

Her laugh was cute, Bo thought. "Do you have kids?"

"Yes."

"Where you from?"

"Lil' River."

"When are you free?"

"Anytime before 5:00 p.m. and after 1:00 a.m."

Bo thought for a minute. "Well, I'ma be tied up for the next few days, but we can hook up this weekend some time."

"Boy," Shanika laughed. "Who said we was gonna hook up?"

"Come on, ma. You ain't call just so we can talk."

"Please stop illustratin', Mr. Bo…You seem a little too sure of yo'self."

"I hear that a lot."

"I wonder why?"

Bo heard something, someone moving. Figuring it was Denise he cut the conversation short.

"Look, ma, I gotta go. But this is my cell number, use it."

"Aiight."

"One."

When Bo got back upstairs Denise was putting Baby Susan in her crib.

"You good?" he asked.

"Yeah," she said simply and climbed back into bed.

Bo climbed in behind her. His chest to her back, he held her. No words, just cuddling. The warmth of her body, combined with the sweet smell of her fragrance and the softness of her ass pressed up against him caused an erection. Still, Bo continued holding her, playing the loving supportive gentleman.

"Bo, you know I can't do nothing for six weeks."

"Ain't no pressure, ma."

"I can't tell." Denise said, thinking of the bits and pieces of his conversation that she'd just heard. She didn't want to lose Bo. "Want me to suck it?" she asked, turning to face him.

"I said ain't no pressure, Denise. I'm good."

"No you ain't. You on hard," she said, massaging his stiff penis. "So that means either I take care of it now, or you'll get somebody else to take care of it later."

Before Bo could put up any further protest, Denise went to work. She sucked his penis as if her life depended on it. Because in her mind, it did. She did not want to lose him to some *jane-come-lately* ass bitch with dollar signs in her eyes. Denise had known Bo before he'd really established himself as a major figure, and therefore she deserved to share in all that he had. Not some other bitch. And she meant to prove it. With all lips, tongue, and throat muscles, Denise applied extreme pressure. Causing Bo to moan and quiver as his loins exploded, shooting an abundant load of warm semen into her hot mouth. Denise swallowed and continued milking him until his hose was dry.

The following days passed in relatively the same fashion. Bo would cook breakfast for Denise. Play with the baby. Get head from Denise. And run back and forth to twenty different stores to kill whatever strange food cravings Denise was having. But Bo didn't really mind, because he spent those times away on the phone. Angie, KiKi, and now Shanika, whom he'd really been talking to a lot more. In fact, he talked to her the most. She seemed to be different and he really wanted to get to know her better.

$$$

It had been two weeks since Bo had hit the streets. Denise was moving around a lot better and he needed out. Dutch had been handling his end of the drug trade for him, but he needed to thug again. To move around, visit with goons, and most of all, to see his hoes. Bo hadn't had any pussy in two weeks!

He got up early, as he always had, fixed breakfast and jumped fresh. Denise had sensed that he was getting restless. But what could she do?

"You goin' out today?" she asked, slowly.

"Yeah."

"I mean, like, goin' out, out?"

"Yeah, I'm goin' out, out." He laughed and kissed her. "The bills gotta get paid, ma. Plus we gon' need some spendin' money for our island vacation."

Denise smiled faintly. "I know...will you bring me some stewed and fried conch from the Bahamian Pot when you come in, please?"

"Yeah, you got that, ma." Bo said, kissed her and the baby and cleared it.

As soon as Bo pulled out of the driveway in Denise's car, his cell phone went off. It was Shanika. It seemed like she enjoyed talking to him just as much as he enjoyed talking to her. The two still had not seen each other since Denise's last day in the hospital. Bo had tried but couldn't bring himself to leave Denise at home while she was feeling weak. So he'd put their rendezvous on hold, even though he suspected a lot of Denise's pains and light headedness were conditions concocted to keep him at home. But *fuck it*, he owed her that much.

He talked with Shanika the entire ride from his home to the Match Box. Two weeks seemed like two years. However, nothing in the old ragged apartment complex had changed. Young *loose-ass-hoes* were still dragging their feet and talking loud about nothing, while niggas that couldn't spell cat or count pass fifty were trying to scheme up on a session. Bo whipped in and spotted KiKi's pretty, sexy ass posted up in front of her partner Kelly's crib. The minute Bo hopped out, .40 in hand, she ran over and hugged him.

"What's up, ma?"

"You! 'Bout time you broke away to see a female," KiKi said, smiling and excited.

"You know what it was." Bo capped, gripping her soft ass. "You hungry, ma?"

"Yep."

"Get in the car, then."

As KiKi got into the car Bo peeped a white Box Chevy with dark-boys on it. The car was cruising slowly through the parking lot. Bo stepped away from the car, closer to the steps, gripping his gun and waiting to *pop off*. The Chevy stopped, Bo aimed, and Pressure World hopped out, laughing.

"Damn, boy! What's up? You don't fuck with yo' dog no more?"

Bo lowered the .40 and waved his long time friend off. "Play with it, now. You kee-keeing, but I'll air that shit out."

"Slow down, outlaw!" Red Boy shouted, hopping out of the passenger side.

Bo shook his head sadly. See, Pressure World was one thing, but him and Red Boy together spelled *some muthafuckin' bullshit*. Because first off, both of them were from Overtown and rarely came across 36th Street unless they were robbing, killing or

147

begging. Pressure loved 'Town so much that he'd refused to leave when the beef popped off, that's how he'd gotten *shot-ass-up* and damn near killed. And Red Boy was a damn fool! Bo fancied himself as a flamethrower, sort of a muscle man for the cause, while Red Boy just bussed his guns and robbed niggas because he could. He was the wildest nigga that Bo had ever met.

"Man, what yall niggas want?" Bo asked, already knowing the answer.

"A nigga fucked up, boy." Pressure said, dapping Bo up and passing him a big ass blunt.

"This airplane?" Bo asked before hitting it.

"Yeah, fool, I know you don't smoke lace." Pressure snapped.

Bo hit the weed and held it. It was *fire-green*. Which was not surprising, because Pressure World always kept fire weed. Bo hit it again and passed it to Red Boy, who simply passed it to Pressure without smoking.

"Yo, I'm good on that, my nigga." Red Boy said, looking around with a mean scowl on his face. "But a nigga fucked up, Bo. A nigga need a lick, boy."

Bo, Diablo, Dutch, Forty, and everybody else in their circle had tried to put the two of them down. Yet they'd hustle for a while, fuck up the bread, and it was back to the bullshit. Bo figured that they must've already struck out with Dutch, Diablo and Forty, so he was their last recourse before they robbed a corner store and killed an Arab.

"Here, man." Bo said, removing a knot from his pocket. "I got my own child at home and my own problems, yo…$500 a piece, yo." Bo stated, pissed off with his two partners. "I'ma try to put something together, yo. But that's it!"

Red Boy took the money and passed Pressure his before popping slick. "Nigga! My nigga stop cryin', nigga. You know a nigga got yo' cryin' ass, yo!" he got back in the car. But before closing the door yelled, "And make sure that lick is a ten piece or better, my nigga! We ain't on that petty shit." Red Boy slammed the door, still talking shit.

"Bet that up, Bo!" Pressure said and jumped back in the car.

148

Bo got in the car and whipped out. KiKi was sitting on the passenger side looking and smelling good. Her little sexy legs were turning him on in those little booty shorts she was wearing. She looked finer to him.

"KiKi, girl, whatchu' doin'? You on them periactive shits or something?" Bo looked at her legs and titties again. "You done got kinda' thick, girl."

KiKi just laughed. "You crazy, Bo." She looked away before continuing. "I ain't on no periactives...I'm, I'm pregnant."

"Pregnant? Damn girl. Why you just tellin' me?"

"'Cause I'm just seeing you," she said. "And I'm keepin' it."

"Why wouldn't you keep it?"

"So you not mad?" KiKi asked, surprised.

Bo whipped the car up into Esther's parking lot. But just as he did, an Expedition whipped in beside him. He automatically upped his .40. The nigga Bert got out of the big SUV and approached the driver side window, smiling. Bo lowered the tinted window, gun on his lap.

"You straight, fool?" Bo asked.

Bert stutter-stepped and lost his smile. He looked like he wanted to run.

"Oh, umm', wh-what's up, Bo, boy?" Bert managed to say.

"Shiid', that's what I'm tryna see." Bo shot back, eyeing Bert hard. "Who you was lookin' for in this car?"

"Umm, nah, my dog gotta car like this. I thought you was him, dog." Bert said.

"Yeah, aiight Bert." Bo said, knowing the nigga was lying. Then again, there were a lot of similar models floating through the streets of Dade county. *Fuck it,* Bo thought, getting out with KiKi in tow.

The two walked in, ordered, and came right back out. Bo had sort of lost his appetite. The fact that Denise used to fuck with Bert hadn't escaped his mind. Still, he prayed that it was just a coincidence...For their sake, because if he found out otherwise, both of their lives were on the line.

"So, umm', you ain't gon' say nothing?" KiKi asked once they were en route to Carol City. They had been riding along in complete silence.

"Have you been fuckin' anybody else?"

"Boy, are you crazy? I ain't like that, Bo." KiKi snapped, obviously upset.

"Don't get in yo' feelings, yo."

"Nah, Bo, you wrong for even askin' me that shit."

"Oh, so if I wouldn't have asked, would you have volunteered the info'?"

"Whatever, Bo."

"Hold up." Bo said, pulling up in the Match Box. "You trippin' 'cause I asked you a *punk-ass* question?"

"Put yo'self in my shoes, Bo...I'm 'round here waitin' on you, being good, while you home with wifey. Niggas and bitches laughin' and callin' me stupid, yet you wanna try me."

"Look, KiKi, that wasn't nothing for you to get in yo' body 'bout." Bo copped out, looking into her watery eyes. "If I offended you, ma, I'm sorry. It wasn't meant like you took it."

KiKi looked and tried to smile. Bo wiped the lone tear that escaped her eye, then kissed her lips. That brought a real smile to her pretty face.

"I love you, Bo." KiKi whispered.

"Love? That's a powerful word, ma."

"I know." KiKi said and kissed him again. This time with tongue and passion. "I mean it, too." And without another word being passed between the two of them, KiKi got her food and got out.

Bo's head was spinning as he pulled out of the Match Box. He had wanted some pussy when he left home, now all he wanted was to lay down. After hollering at Dutch and checking a few traps, he shot over to Angie's new place. Shortman was happy as hell to see him. Angie was happy to get the plate of Bahamian Pot that he hadn't eaten. She hated cooking. Bo sat around there for about three hours and decided to go home. He needed to get away. Far away! So he called his travel agent and made plans to leave on a seven day cruise with Denise. He didn't tell Dutch, Diablo,

Angie, KiKi or nobody else. The only person that knew was Ma, and that's because she had to babysit Susan.

$$$

The boat was bigger than either one of them could've imagined. There were restaurants, a shopping mall, two different night clubs, pools [indoor and outdoor], a movie theater, and all sorts of gambling activities. Anything you could think of, they had on the cruise ship.

They visited the Paradise Island where Bo had reservations at the resort. While there, browsing through the gift shops and jewelry stores, Bo fell in love with a nice four carat diamond set in white gold. He knew that Denise would love it. And after all the passionate loving she'd blessed him with – orally and anally – he knew that she deserved it. So without a second thought, he dropped the $6,900 that was written on the price tag. Pocketing the ring, he planned to surprise her not only with the ring, but with a proposal of marriage. Why not? Nobody was perfect and time wasn't going to stand still while he searched for someone who was.

Ma had explained to Bo, so had Bee, that a woman can be tore up emotionally after having a baby. Some because of the weight gain, others because of the hormone imbalance, insecurities concerning other women, and some woman suffered from *all of the above*. So Bo did his best to make her feel special and deeply appreciated. He wanted her to have the best time of her life.

They only had four days in Nassau and three days in Bimini. They toured both islands and hit every club that was open. Bacardi Rum, Mango, Orange, and Coconut. They sipped it all. Cush, Sour Diesel, Purple Haze, Cotton Candy and Red Cinnamon Sinsemilla. They smoked it all. And the food was *off-the-chain*. They both might've put on ten pounds from eating so much fresh conch and exotic island delicacies. Everyday while there they did something different. Fishing, scuba diving, jet skiing and hang gliding. Hiking, bike riding, and plenty shopping. Before it was all said and done, Bo had spent over $14,000. But it was worth it, because Denise laughed and smiled the entire seven days. Yet he still hadn't brought himself to give her the engagement ring and propose.

$$\$\ \$\ \$$$

When they returned and exited the ship, Denise was puzzled to find that her car wasn't parked where they had left it. Angry, she scanned the parking lot, cursing beneath her breath while Bo looked on laughing.

"What's funny?" she finally asked him.

"You," he laughed, handing her the keys to the brand new Infinity Q45 that was parked where her old car once was. "You been upgraded, ma."

Denise looked, mouth hanging wide open. "Oh, Bo! Oh, I love you!" she yelled hugging him tightly.

"Okay, ma." Bo laughed, pulling her arms from around his neck. "Don't choke me to death. It's only a car."

They loaded it with all their stuff and Denise whipped out of the lot in style. Bo cut the power on and his cell phone started ringing immediately. *Damn!* He thought, seeing Bee's number.

"Hello?" he answered.

"Bo! Bo! Where you at?" Bee yelled.

But before Bo could answer, Bee started yelling into the phone.

"Wait! Bee, slow down, I can't understand you."

"Bo, Naomi's boyfriend came over here to fight her." Bee cried. "Bo, and when I tried to stop him…he, he pushed me down and kicked me, baby."

"That nigga did what?" Bo yelled, scaring Denise.

"He pushed me down and kicked me." Bee cried.

"Is this the same nigga she been fuckin' with, Kay?"

"Yeah, that's him." Bee answered and Bo hung up.

"Go to 54th and 6th Avenue." Bo ordered Denise.

"Baby, what's wrong?"

"Just get me there and go yo' ass home! I don't wanna talk about it!"

Bo jumped out at the hideout, ran in and got a .357 that he kept there and the keys to the G-wagon that they had parked out front. He shot straight around 71st and 13th, where the nigga Kay hung out. When he rounded the corner, he spotted three young niggas sitting in a yard. Kay was one of them. Bo whipped up and jumped out. One of Kay's little homeboys tried to up. Bo started bussing.

Boom! Boom! Boom! Boom! The .357 cut loose, causing homeboy to drop his .38 and haul ass! They both ran, leaving Kay to suffer for self.

"Hold up, Bo, bruh. I –"

Bo stood over him and slapped the fuck out of him with the .357. The young dude hollered like a real bitch. Bo continued to slap him repeatedly with the big revolver. Then he stood back and bussed the screaming dude in the leg, *Boom!* Kay stopped screaming and passed out.

Jumping back in the G-wagon, Bo fled. But someone had called Metro and they were all over him. Bo flushed it and tossed the gun. Coming up 12th Avenue, past North Western Senior High School, he wrecked the truck and jumped out. Police were everywhere by then and he had nowhere to run.

"Get down! Hands up! Hands up, now!" the police yelled.

Bo laid it down and was hauled off to the county jail. Where he's been ever since. The attempted murder was serious, but it carried a bond. It was the armed robbery charge that had him stuck, and only Kay and his two homeboys could straighten it...

Chapter 18

"Boy, Bo, what's up famalam?" Dewey said, smiling like a supreme devil. "I'm outta here, boy."

Bo just looked up at him through sleepy eyes. He hated when Dewey came waking him up. It had become a habit of his. Always disturbing his groove for something to fill his ever craving lungs. "Fuck is you on, Dewey? What I told you 'bout wakin' a nigga up?"

Dewey continued smiling. "What I'm on? Boy, I'm on cloud nine! You did it, boy! Yo' people came through. They got to Trent and him and his girl recanted their statements...They just called my name, the Hound outta here."

Bo shook his head slowly, registering the information. It had been a month since he'd given the message to Denise in regards to Dewey's situation. He was pleased to see that she had delivered the message to Dutch and he'd moved out promptly. Now there was the matter of Dewey keeping his word.

"That's good news, Dewey, my nigga. I held up my end, now you gotta hold up yo' end. Get with my brutha', get Trent his shit, and my nigga, get me mine." Bo stated with the authority of a true don.

"Don't trip lil' homie. The Hound gon' take care of everythang. That's on Black Flag, boy. I'ma take care of everythang." Dewey said, smiling wickedly.

"I don't know shit 'bout that Black Flag shit, and I ain't tryin' to. Just keep it gangsta, yo, 'cause my face on that." Bo reiterated as he stood.

Him and Dewey hugged and exchanged dap. Bo wrote down Dutch's phone number and Dewey walked off towards a new tomorrow.

After tightening up his hygiene and getting his lungs out of pawn, Bo strolled over to the phone. Every since their visit a month ago, Bo had been making it a habit to call Denise every morning. Something about that visit had rekindled a sea of desirous feelings for her. Visits had been more frequent and enjoyable, now that he himself allowed it. And in doing so Denise had become a new person. A better person in his eyes.

Bo still had not given Denise the expensive four carat rock that he'd purchased, and had yet to request her hand in marriage. Though he planned to as soon as he got home.

Denise picked up on the first ring. "Hey baby!" she greeted him excitedly.

"What's good, ma?"

"You," she replied. "I've been sittin' here waitin' on yo' call."

The two conversed the entire 30 minutes that he was allotted per phone call, exchanging *I love you's* and reflecting on the better days of their strained relationship. They were happy again, though uncertain. For they both had unwarrantable skeletons in their closets. Bo had a baby and Denise had a deadly affair with a lover from her past. Neither secret likely to go undisclosed.

As soon as he hung up with Denise he tried Angie's home phone for the millionth time. It had been a month since he'd heard anything from her, which was strange. She normally visited him twice a week, wrote often, and he called her every two days. Yet after he'd told her "not to come because he needed to holla at Denise about some important business," he hadn't seen or heard anything else from her. *I know this bitch don't call herself in her feelings 'cause I asked her not to come that day*, Bo thought as he rolled a blunt of 'dro. *But if she is, fuck her!* He reasoned. It only made it easier to gravitate towards Denise.

Bo studied his handiwork. The blunt was a perfect baseball bat. However, before he could put the flames to it the C.O. called his name. "Brown! Lawyer visit! Lawyer visit for Brown!" *Damn!* Bo cursed to himself. *Crooked ass lawyer don't want shit but some more money*, he mused as he passed Red, the houseman

155

whom he'd known from Overtown, his stash of weed and cigarettes and left the cell block.

$$\$\$\$$$

Angie sat in the women's annex, cold and confused. She did not know what to do or think about her situation. It had been 32 long trying days since the police pulled her over en route to the Bay Club on 11th Street. They wouldn't even so much as allow her to pick up Shortman and secure shelter for him. As she sat, horrified at her plight, she did not know where her son was and it was driving her crazy. It also did not help matters any that no one from Bo's family had reached out to her. *Maybe he's trippin' because I called his house*, Angie thought, fighting back tears. But what else was she supposed to do? Her mother, nor his mother, had collect on their phones and she did not have his brother or cousin's number. So calling his house was her only recourse. She knew that it was wrong, but she had absolutely no other choice.

Why? Why? Why? Angie questioned her dire situation. Hopelessness fermented and excited an element of rage within her as she looked at her surroundings; at the trifling ass females that seemed to have found joy in her denigration. It was not bad enough that they were all being held in dirty, overcrowded cell houses that forced them so close that they could smell one another's menstrual when it flowed; the toilet sat out in the middle of the floor, where women, because of over capacitance, laid their moldy piss stained mattresses and slept. Angie hated the place, while all the miserable bitches there seemed to hate her. She'd heard the foul whispers and slick comments as she exited the shower and sat around by herself...*Miss Bo Brown, hmp', might as well be Miss Nobody Brown, because Bo and nobody else ain't thankin' 'bout that bitch...Miss High-sediddy over there puttin' tissue in her panties 'cause she can't even buy no pads...Bo ain't stuttin' that bitch. You know my lil' cousin KiKi got his ass wide open. Yeah girl, she just had that bitch baby, girl...These bitches stupid, girl. Sittin' in jail for these messy ass shonin' niggas while*

156

*the niggas wifyin' other bitches…*Angie had heard it all, and it took everything in her to keep from snapping and dragging one of those roxy ass hoes. They were envious and sad. They were worst than the police detectives who'd said much of the same shit, trying to get her to flip on Bo…*We know who did this. You think he cares about you? You better think about yourself and your son…Help yourself Angie, because he's finished. He can't help you. He can't even help himself. We're going to bury his ass on this murder. So if you don't want to spend the rest of your life fighting off dykes and crying over your son, who'll end up a ward of the state, you better start talking now…*And Angie had talked. She said four simple words, "I want my lawyer." Those words ended the interrogation, but not the nightmare that she'd found herself living in.

Angie wiped away the beginning of a tear that tried to form in her pretty eyes. She had to be strong. If not for herself, she had to be strong for Shortman and Bo. Her men! Bo was her man and he loved her, she told herself over and over. The police, nor the low-life, hating ass bitches surrounding her could change that. Angie found a little comfort in her thoughts. *Things will get better, girl.* She told herself and laid down. Hoping that tomorrow would be better than today.

$$\$\$\$$$

"Damn Zack, do something for a nigga, fool." Man-Man damn near begged. "I gotta ball, my nigga."

"I'll give yo' ass four quarters, nigga. Get it and go, I got no time for brain wrestlin' and rappin' witcha', fool." Zach shot back, constantly scanning the block.

"Damn Zack, my nigga! A nigga been runnin' all day for yall boys. Come on, maannn!"

"Fuck out my face, yo."

Zack had been out all day pitching $25 bags of BLACK LABEL heroin. He had half a bundle left of the 100 bundles that Stanka had dropped him, and he was ready to haul ass. Still peeking around for the Boe-Nine and killers, he spotted Dorry in the cut holding the block down with a M-16. Crab cut his conversation short with some *shones* and walked over to where Man-Man stood, still begging Zack for a deal.

"Whatchu' got left, Zack?" Crab asked.

"25 bags."

"Whatchu' tryna do, Man-Man?"

"Maann, I'm tryna go."

"Whatchu' got?" Crab asked, irritated slightly.

"I gotta hundred dollars, yo."

"Give it here," Crab took the dirty crumbled up bills. "Give 'im the 25 bags, yo."

"Who?" Zack asked, looking crazy at Crab.

"You, nigga! Give the man the shit!" Carb snapped. "You done done 100 fuckin' bundles, 50 bags a bundle, and this man done ran for you all day. That's $125,000 you done turned, and $2,500 of that money's yours. Stop trippin' nigga, I'm ready to go!"

Crab snatched the brown paper bag from Zack and threw it to Man-Man, who caught it and briskly shot up the block. Crab turned and waved to Dorry, who disappeared in the shadows. It was time to count up the bread and get the fuck.

Four hours after entering the stash apartment, the three men came out carrying duffle bags and big guns. They quickly jumped into a four door Dodge Intrepid with limo tints on it, and pulled out. It seemed to be another successful day in the trap.

Dorry brought the car up 20th Street, Bust-Down's *WAS IT WORTH IT* played as they cruised. Dorry and Zack bobbed their heads, both caught up in the music. But Crab was in the back seat, on coc' and peeping everything. He noticed the same lights had been on their ass since they'd passed Lensy Hopkins Adult Education Center. Without saying a word to Dorry or Zack he lifted his cell phone and called Stanka.

$$$

158

The light-brown Grand Marque had been laying on the BLACK LABEL heroin hole every since 7:00 p.m. Patiently waiting for the men to close shop and make their way to the bigger stash house. There was blood on every dime of the money that the crew had made, and now it was time to pay for it.

As soon as the Dodge Intrepid sailed past the school, the Grand Marque jumped in behind it. Trailing it, the driver noticed that they seemed to be riding aimlessly. Which was rather strange for three dudes with guns and a large sum of money on them. Figuring that he'd been made by someone in the Intrepid, and assuming he knew where they were headed anyway, based on their beginning route, the Grand Marque gambled and turned off. Because even if he was wrong about their destination he could always pick up their trail the following day in a different slider. The odds and time were both on his side. He could make several mistakes, as it stood, they could afford to slip but once.

$$$

*...livin' in a land where hearts are cold / ya-e-ya-eeee' yall / livin' in a land where thugs don't live that long...soooooo / thuggin' day for day with the G's and we pray / help us Lord / 'cause I'm / livin' in a land where thugs don't live that long...*Trick Daddy's song played at a whisper as the Grand Marque sat four houses down from where the driver assumed the Dodge Intrepid was going. And true to his guesstimation, the Intrepid rounded the corner. *Bingo!* The driver smiled, easing his .40's from his lap and melting away in the shadows. Quickly, the distance between him and his lick was closed, placing him just beside the Intrepid as Zack hopped out, duffle bag in hand.

Boom! Boom! Boom! Boom! Boom! The assailant fired into Zack's back, sending his lifeless body back into the car, while the duffle bag that he'd been holding was promptly snatched up.

Tat! Tat! Tat! Tat! Tat! Crab let loose from the rear seat, sending shots through the back window and into the duffle bag.

Boom! Boom! Boom! Boom! Boom! Boom! Boom! Boom! Boom! Boom! The assailant fired with both .40's, having dropped the duffle bag with intentions on killing everyone in the vehicle.

Fuck! Crab yelled in his mind. In his panic he dropped his weapon and rolled out of the rear passenger side door, where he found Dorry outside the car trying to chamber the M-16 with unstable hands. Crab snatched the M-16 from Dorry just as death was rounding the rear of the car. But before the .40's could sing again a dark-blue mini-van slammed on brakes, causing the man holding the two .40's to spin around; and when he did there were three M-16's trained on him.

Dell, Joe, and Stanka quickly jumped out of the van, followed by Rome, whom was the driver. With weapons still aimed, and pain in their eyes, they slowly approached Dewey.

"My nigga, what is you doin', Hound." Dell asked.

"What it look like, fool?" Dewey replied, a crooked grin fixed on his face. "Yall boys know what it is. I rode for yall and yall left me stuck."

It was only then that Crab realized who he'd been exchanging shots with. The shit had happened so fast and he was so scared that he hadn't been able to take in Dewey's face. He was now up and standing beside his old friend. "It wasn't like that, Dewey, my nigga." Crab managed to say.

"I can't tell, fam." Dewey picked up the duffle bag. "Yall boys eatin', while the Hound was on ice. Now I need mine."

"We coulda' rapped 'bout this Dewey!" Stanka said.

"And we still can," Dewey said, turning to leave, duffle bag in hand. "Call me later, 'cause them crackas comin' now."

Joe was about to up and gun Dewey down as he ran off, but Stanka pushed the rifle down before he could.

"Let 'im go." Stanka said calmly. "Push Zack outta the car and get rid of it Joe...Crab, get them other two bags outta the car and in the van. We gotta clear it."

It hurt Crab to have to leave Zack's body out in the streets like that, but he had no other choice. He promised himself that he'd look out for Zack's people, and jumped into the van as Rome gunned it up the block, leaving Zack behind, with no clues of the killer.

160

Chapter 19

Denise sat outside by the pool, thinking and watching the sun as it hung seemingly just above the roof of their two-story house. She was lonely. However, she knew that this was one of the *not-so-glamorous* essentials that came with loving a nigga that was *thuggin'*. Because she truly did love Bo, *indubitably*. She'd been assured over the past 21 days. Her every thought was of him. Her only regret was having came to this powerful realization after cheating on him with Bert, whom she'd been ducking like a bad cold as of lately. She'd maybe spoken to him three times and had only seen him once since he'd fucked her raw on the expressway. Denise cared about Bert, and probably always would, but her love rested solely in the heart of Bo Brown.

Looking up into the darkening sky, Denise observed the soft-orange sun, with its almost yellowish core, just hanging there in the Heavens as if it was refusing to go down. Denise viewed it with enmity. For as long as the sun stayed its course it would be all the more longer before she got her morning call from Bo. Time just appeared to stand still between their recent visits and phone conversations. What they'd found as of lately was really looking up, and Denise wanted more and more and more of it.

Her reflections were suddenly invaded by the ringing of her phone. Hoping to see *Private* on her phone's display, Denise was both disappointed and disgusted to see Bert's number. Denise simply sighed and let the phone continue to ring. *Niggas just don't get it*, she said to herself. It was over between them. It should've never been between them. The worst mishap in her life had been *them*.

The phone continued to ring off and on as she sat. Every call was from Bert. Tired of the constant ringing, Denise turned the ringer off and walked into the house. A nice hot bubble bath was what she needed. After getting the water just the way she wanted it, Denise poured herself a glass of *Ecco Domani* and stipped naked. The hot waster was soothing to her body and mind. She slowly sipped the smooth alcoholic beverage with thoughts of Bo racing through her weary mind. She closed her eyes and pictured Bo standing naked before her. His hard black dick standing at attention. Pouring the last of her drink briskly down her throat, Denise envisioned herself zealously engaging the thick black penis orally. With one hand below the water tickling her throbbing clit' and filling her hot insides, she unconsciously worked her head back and forth. A warm chill enveloped her and invoked jubilation so intense that she could taste the viscid whitish fluid coat her tongue and slide down her throat. Removing one hand from her vaginal inlet, she sucked it into her mouth and quickly filled her wanting center with three fingers from her other hand. The already simmering water seemed to bubble as her sexual intensity boiled within her, hankering release.

"Oh Bo!" Denise screamed as her pressure flowed from her in fervent sprays and powerful spasms. For a moment the rapture was so consuming that her next breath seemed unlikely to come. It was volcanic...fantastic...It was unreal...an infernal illusion. A misconception that left her taxed and empty. Even the tear that had formed in her eye did not have the temerity wherethrough to fall.

$$$

Dewey had gotten rid of the light-brown Grand Marque and was now bending corners in a smoke-gray Mark VI with limo tints and a high performance engine. His partner Bobby from down south flipped the vehicle for a mean two stacks. Now, with fresh wheels he could move around a little better. With the exception of Crab, Stanka, Rome and their little crew, only Bo and Bobby knew that he was out. Dewey hadn't even been by the house or his hideout to fuck Traci or Juliette. He had business to settle and the sooner it was settled the better life would be.

Dewey looked at the digital clock on his Sony radio. It read 12:06 p.m. Not much traffic was out as he cruised the streets, seeing exactly what he could see. On the seat beside him sat a .32 revolver with a silencer on it, a fresh roll of duct tape, and eight dumby brick of coc' that he'd personally took the time out to mix, weigh, and tape up to perfection.

Coming off of the 826 expressway, Dewey slid back street to back street until he found himself parked in front of a neat four bedroom crib with a 500 Benz and a Benz wagon parked out front. Dewey smiled like the true devil he was, tucking the small caliber pistol and bagging the bricks and duct tape before stepping out. Seeing that no one was out on the street, Dewey strolled up the walkway. He planned to take care of his business with Trent and be gone, in and out. He hit the doorbell and within seconds the curtain to the picture window moved, allowing a peek. Next he heard locks sounding and the door cracked. Trent stood there, a trace of fear outlined his handsome face. Dewey looked down and noticed the .9mm in Trent's hand.

"Damn fam, what's good?" Dewey greeted his cousin, smiling.

"Ain't nothing." Trent said, looking behind and around Dewey. "Come in."

Trent's crib was really nice. Dewey had to give it to Trent, he was a real hustler and first-class family man. Him and his girl, Zondra, took pride in their home and the rearing of their child.

"Where Zondra?" Dewey asked, tossing the eight kilos on the couch.

"In the room sleep." Trent said slowly. He did not trust Dewey one bit. His eyes shifted nervously from Dewey to the bag on the couch and back.

Dewey smiled and raised his hands in mock surrender. "That's you fam. I just want you to check one so I can go…I gave them boys my word that I would give you back eight and leave you alone, and I'm keepin' my word. That's you."

At the mention of *them boys* Trent relaxed a little. Because everybody knew that Diablo and his little cousins were truly about their business. In fact, he was surprised that they'd even came to him concerning a low life like Dewey. But they had came to him and he was expected to respect their call if he wanted to continue living. So he had, and it amounted to Dewey returning eight of the twelve kilos he'd robbed him for.

With a little reluctance, Trent sat the .9mm down next to the bag and lifted one of the heavily taped squares. *Prrph! Prrph! Prrph!* The little .32 sounded with minimum recoil. Trent's body did not tumble or spasm. It simply dropped to the couch. Dewey lifted the duct tape from the bag and journeyed into Trent's daughter's room. He quickly snatched her up and duct taped her to a chair. He then carried the chair into Trent's room where Zondra laid peacefully. Placing the chair with their daughter in it at the foot of the bed, Dewey laid down beside the half naked woman. Her body was beautiful.

"Baby...who was that?" Zondra asked, never raising her head or opening her eyes.

"The nigga you shoulda married." Dewey answered.

Zondra jumped up, shocked at hearing the strange voice. At the sight of Dewey, Zondra opened her mouth to scream but Dewey pointed to the foot of the bed.

"You don't wanna scare the baby, do you, baby?" he stated, smiling wickedly.

Upon seeing her daughter duct taped to a chair Zondra tried to run to her, but Dewey snatched her roughly by her long curly weave and placed the .32 to her head.

"Ut'un, sit yo' ass down, bitch." Dewey growled. "You already done got my sucka-ass cousin killed wit' the bullshit...now, don't make me kill you and lil' momma too." Dewey paused, letting his words marinate. Once he was sure that Trent's murder had soaked into her mind, he continued. "Now yall called the crackas on me and tried to get me 60 something years. But since I slumped Trent I feel like we even. I'm willing to let bygones be bygones. We can start fresh. But baby, I'ma need something from you." Dewey finished, hungrily eyeing her exposed body.

Zondra whimpered and pulled the cover over herself. "Please, Dewey...D-don't hurt me."

Dewey laughed. "Bitch, don't flatter yo'self. I want the money and drugs, now!" he snatched her up by her hair. "Empty

164

the safe! Empty the cabinets, the freezer, yo' jewelry box, and anythang else with them valuables in it." He shoved her into the wall. "Move, bitch! Don't play! Because I hate repeatin' myself. If I thank for ann' minute that you bullshittin', I'm sendin' lil' momma to be with her dead ass daddy."

Zondra ran from the room crying. She passed Trent's dead body as she went into the kitchen. There was $75,000 wrapped up in the large freezer. In the cabinet she found the $20,000 that Trent kept in Honey Graham boxes. From there she went into the garage and returned with a tool box that contained $50,000. She gathered the entire $145,000 and carried it in the room to Dewey.

"Ain't no safe," she cried and pulled out a lower drawer and removed a jewelry box. "All of our jewelry's right here..." she handed him the large box. "The stuff's in the tool shed, out back."

Dewey smiled. "You did good, Zondra baby," he whispered, rubbing the side of her crying face. Zondra was a straight up dime, and he couldn't help but to let his free hand roam everywhere that his eyes had. She trembled as his fingers entered her dry slit, causing him to laugh again. Removing his finger he smelt it. "Smell like water, girl... and since you kept in one hunid' and you keep yo' pussy clean, girl, I'm gon' look out...yeah, I'ma kill you first, so you don't have to witness yo' daughter die."

"No! Dewey, ple—"

Prrph! Prrph! Two shots put her to rest.

Dewey turned and placed the gun right between the little girl's eyes. "Lord, please bless her innocent soul." Dewey prayed before squeezing the trigger, *prrph!* Knocking the chair over and sending the little girl on to the next life.

$$$

Denise woke up to a sliver of sunlight nipping at her bare breast. Another morning alone. Only in the physical though, because the ringing of the phone, which brought a smile to her cute face and

165

joy to her lonely soul, assured her that Mr. Bo Brown was thinking of her. Denise eased out of bed, naked, and picked up the phone.

"Hey, baabeee'." Denise sang into the phone as she entered the bathroom of their master bedroom.

"What's good, ma?" Bo replied.

Denise sat down on the padded toilet and let her bladder go. The rush of silver waste pouring from her brought relief and a loud distinct sound.

"Girl, you pissin' with a nigga on the phone?"

"Yeah, what's wrong with that?"

"You ain't got no manners, girl."

"Bo, you crazy." Denise said, wiping herself and flushing the toilet. "You my man. I don't need no manners 'round you."

"Whatever, girl. You finish?"

"Yeah, why, you wanna hear my stuff make some different kinda' noises?" Denise questioned with a trace of lust in her tone.

"Don't play with me, Denise." Bo shot at her, playing hard.

"Boy, I ain't playin'…you want me to play in my pussy?"

"I thought it was my pussy?"

"Oh, baby, it is…and it's drippin' wet, Bo…Oooh, listen to it."

Denise put the phone between her legs and stuck two fingers into her wetness. In and out she worked herself until she was wet enough to insert three, then four. Her legs trembled and her pussy sloshed with each plunge. Denise began to sing in the background.

"Oooh, Bo…baby…I miss you…I need you home…I need you, baby!"

Bo listened intently. His nature was hard as homework. Damn he missed his girl, his soon to be wife. But it wouldn't be long. Bo hadn't told anyone, but he was due home in one week. The visit from his lawyer had been a good one, and well worth the additional $43,000 that he owed him once he touched down. Someone, Bo figured that it had been Dutch or Diablo, had finally caught up with Kay and made him get his mind right. So on his next court appearance, which was next week, Bo would be walking out of the courtroom free. And he couldn't wait! Because he needed to be home just as much as Denise needed him to be there.

When the sloshing and moaning ceased, and Denise came back to the phone, she was breathing heavily. The two sat saying nothing. With the exception of Denise's breathing there was complete silence until Bo finally spoke.

"Ma, you aiight?"

"Yes, I'm aiight...but baby, I need you home."

"And I wanna be home." Bo said. "You just hold me down until I get there."

"I will baby."

"Good, 'cause we gon' be aiight."

"I know," she whined in a child's tone. "I love you, Bo."

"I love you too, ma." Bo was able to reply just before the phone hung up.

Denise laid there in the huge king sized bed for a moment longer, thinking. Things were better between her and Bo now than they'd ever been. *And we will make it through this*, she said to herself.

Knowing that she'd turned the ringer off last night and had no doubt missed a few calls, Denise began checking her messages. The first missed call was from an irate Bert. Denise quickly erased the message before even hearing it through. The second message was from her sister. The third message almost sent her into cardiac arrest... "Ut'un, Bert...no, not right...right here, booyyy. I ain't no, no mutt, booyyy." She could faintly hear the sound of cars zooming by in the tape's background. "Oh Bert...Bert baby...Please Bert...Yes! Yes! Yes! Bert!" Denise heard herself whine before the message ended. She was mortified as she sat listening to the next message. "Pussy ass hoe! You thank it's a muthafuckin' game, huh? Then play with it. If I don't hear from yo' stank ass in 24 hours I'ma be sure to play our tape to Dutch, bitch!" Bert's message played before she simply hung up and cried like a child receiving a severe ass whipping.

Chapter 20

Dewey hung up his cell phone and hopped out of an all black Buick Century with classic limo tints and Momos. It was another flip that he'd purchased from Bobby. As soon as his black Forces hit the concrete he smoothed his black Dickie set and scanned the parking lot. He was rocking about $40,000 in jewelry and didn't mean to be anybody's vic' tonight. *Fuck this nigga at?* He asked. Dutch was supposed to have met him at club WET WETZ at 10:00 p.m., sharp. Just as he was about ot whip out his phone and call Dutch up, he spotted some flashing lights up towards the entrance. Dewey walked up towards the car. He was surprised to see Diablo get out of the car with Dutch.

Smiling, he greeted Dutch. "What's up, fam?" he dapped Dutch up. "Who you got with you, bruh?" Dewey asked, knowing full well who Diablo was.

"Ain't shit, boy." Dutch shot at his old partner. "This is my cousin, my nigga. He straight. You got that? 'Cause I got shit to do, my nigga."

"Damn, fam!" Dewey whined, throwing his hands up. "It's like that? You ain't seen ya' boy in 'bout three years, yo. 'Come on, man, lemme at least buy yall boys a bottle of bubbly."

"Nah, Hound." Dutch shook his head. "I gotta be somewhere in the morning. We just stopped to get this shit and go."

"Ut'un, fam. I ain't takin' no for a answer." Dewey shook his head in return. "It ain't but 10:15, man...yall boys saved the Hound, and I aim to show my appreciation," he turned and began walking towards the club's entrance. "Come on, yall boys!" Dewey yelled over his shoulder.

Dutch looked at Diablo, whom seemed sour about the whole ordeal. Neither man had any desire at all to go inside and have a drink with Dewey. They'd came on business and wanted it to remain strictly business. While at the same time, Dutch had no desires to burn bridges or offend.

"Just one drink, cuz." Dutch said to Diablo.

"This fucked up, cuz. We 'posed to be out, my nigga."

"I know, cuz. We gon' run in, one dance, one drink, get the two bricks and we gone, cuz. We'll be outta here by 11:00." Dutch finished, checking his Rolex.

Diablo sighed loudly and followed his little cousin into the club.

$$\$\,\$\,\$$$

"Hello, Big Bert speakin', who this?" Bert answered his phone arrogantly, already knowing exactly whom the caller was.

"B-Bert, this Denise," she paused, searching for words. "What's goin' on, Bert? Why did you put that message on the phone?"

Bert laughed at her. Bitches could be so damn dumb, Bert thought. Having once been truly in love with Denise, it was difficult for him to do as he was doing. Yet she'd played with his heart, leaving him for a young nigga like Bo simply because Bo had more money than him, so now she was going to be forced to respect his mind, even if it meant doing some sucka shit.

"Stupid ass bitch! Don't play no muthafuckin' games with me. You know exactly what's goin' on, and yo' loose stuntin' ass know exactly why I put that message on yo' phone." Bert paused to let his words shake the bitch a bit. Sucka' shit aside, Bert was thuggin', and Denise was going to respect that. "You 'round her duckin' me hoe?! Playin' with a nigga love! Bitch you think it's all about you?! You think I ain't got no feelings?!"

"Nooo, Bert! It's not like that. I swear. I've just been talkin' to Bo and I'm tryna do right –"

"Bo?!" Bert said, cutting Denise off. "Bitch, fuck Bo! You done played me one time for him and now you think I'ma just let you play me again? Hoe, you think I'm pie?"

169

"No, Bert, nooo. It's just that –"

"It's just what? You such a gold diggin' ass stunt that you gon' let the nigga run over you just 'cause he got money? All them nights yo' ass was left alone in that house, sad. Who the fuck stayed up talkin' to you on the phone? When yo' ass was pregnant and ain't know who the daddy was, who crept 'round with you, treatin' you special and fuckin' yo' fat ass when Bo ain't want you? Bitch, who was there for you?"

"Yyyooouuuu was, Beeerrrttt! You was." Denise cried into the phone.

Bert knew that he had her then. But truth was, he wanted to cry too. Denise had the firest' head in Dade County. Plus her pussy was bomb. He'd known Denise most of his life, and had always cared about her. The bitch was his heart. But why did she choose to play him? Was money that important? Well since she loved money so much and chose Bo and his money over him, he was about to play them both out of a lot of it.

"Well, if I was there Denise, why you chose him?" Bert whispered, tears filling his eyes.

"I, I, don't know Bert. I, I, I love him, Bert...B-bu-but, I love you too. Why you can't jus—"

"Just be a sucka for you...again. Nah, ma. Them days are over!" Bert declared. There was a severe ache in his heart; however, he was certain that time would heal it. Love had failed him, again. But for the last time. He was about to thug it until the wheel fell off. "Where you at?" he asked her.

"Umm', I, I'm at home." Denise whined, big funeral tears falling from her eyes.

"What's the address?"

"What?"

"Bitch, you heard me! What's the muthafuckin' address?"

"Ppplleeeaaassseee, Bert...Don't do this...I – I'll meet you anywhere you want, okay...But please...I can't let you –"

"And bitch you can't stop me, either...Now gimme the muthafuckin' address before I go holla at Dutch. I bet he'd love to hear our tape."

I know he would, but I can't let that happen, Denise thought. It was no military secret that Dutch disliked Denise. That tape would've been all that he needed to get the *green-light* from Bo or their crazy ass cousin Diablo, to kick her out on the streets and cut her off financially...or worst, have her killed. No, Denise could not allow Bert to give Dutch that tape. So she called out the address to Bert, hating herself for once again betraying Bo. *This is all gonna end bad*, she told herself, *I just know it.*

"Well, wash yo' ass, 'cause I'll be there in 'bout 30 minutes to get me some. You want me to bring you something to eat, drink, or smoke?"

Denise did not answer. She just sat there crying and sniffing over the phone.

"Bitch, you hear me talkin' to you?" Bert barked.

"Yeah, Bert, I, I hear you."

"Then answer me, then."

"No, I don't want nothing," she whispered.

Well I'ma get yo' dogg ass something anyway. Tonight gon' be a night to remember, Bert said to himself, smiling. "Aiight, then, see you in a minute." Bert said, hanging up the phone as he pulled up to Locket's crib. Locket was the pill man. He always had *Pink Naked Ladies* and *Green Clovers*. Bert ran in and copped six pills. Three of which he chewed before exiting Locket's pad. The other three he pocketed and sped off to Denise's house for a night of pressure and pain.

$$$

Denise hung up the phone feeling defeated and lost. All she could think to do was cry. Cry and question her dire situation. If Bo or Dutch found out about Bert coming to the house she was dead. Yet she'd allowed it. She had to. Bert had that damn tape and she needed to get it away from him. And if that meant him coming to the house, getting his dick sucked, and maybe fucking her, then so-be-it. It's not like she'd never fucked or sucked a dick before, she tried to reason with herself. But it didn't help the matter any. Because it wasn't just the tape, it was her love for Bo. Things were finally going right for them. *Now this!?!* Why couldn't Bert just understand? It was true that he'd been there for her when Bo was running the streets and giving her his ass to kiss, and especially when she found out that she was pregnant and didn't know who the daddy was. The situation had nearly drove her crazy. Yet Bert had been there. Listening to her and comforting her with his kind words and great sex. Sometimes, when she was really really low in her self worth, she'd wished that her baby was Bert's. However, she was too relieved to find out that it was Bo's. *Now this! Now this! Now – fuckin' – this!* Denise cried, punching a pillow. She fell to the bed and just sobbed. The ringing of the phone startled her. Denise looked and saw OUT OF AREA. She knew that it was BO. *Oowww, I need to hear his voice*, she thought. But guilt would not allow her to pick up the phone. How could she confess her love to him knowing that she was about to betray him? She could not. Denise just stared at the phone as it rung, wishing that it would stop. For every ring was like an alarming reminder of what she was about to do. The ringing finally stopped. Only to begin anew. It was Bo again. Denise simply got up and walked to the bathroom. She turned the hot water up and allowed the bathroom to steam up before she removed her T-shirt and tight panties. Beneath the hot spray of water Denise cried. Yet she convinced herself that it was for the last time. She would do *whatever* Bert wanted her to do for the *very last time*. Once the tape was in her hand, she'd destroy it and concentrate on her future with Bo.

$$$

12:43 p.m.
"Boy, Hound, you a muthafuckin' fool, boy!" Dutch said, laughing as they exited Club WET WETZ. They'd had a real ball. At least, they did. Diablo was pissed! He had somewhere to be. He and Dutch were supposed to pick up two bricks and be gone. But instead, they'd been inside bullshitting for the past two and a half hours.

"You know how the Hound do, my nigga! All black everythang, my nigga! Ball 'til we fall!" Dewey yelled in the empty parking lot.

Diablo just shook his head in disgust. He'd known Dewey for only two and a half hours and already hated his guts. Dewey was pure animation. Something Diablo couldn't stand. He held deep seated contempt for *extra* ass niggas.

"My nigga, that hoe Slushy the real one!" Dutch exclaimed.

"Nah, fam-a-lam, Slurpy." Dewey corrected. "The hoe with the ten pack, right?"

"Yeah, that hoe! Lord-have-mercy! My nigga, we gotta –"

"Dutch," Diablo cut his little cousin off. "We gotta go, homie. No disrespect to your man, but yall can rap about that shit later." Diablo walked over to Dewey. "Come on, homie, let's get that…Dutch, get the car and meet us in the back."

Dewey looked at Dutch like, *what's good?* Dutch nodded like, *yeah, go 'head*, and turned to get the car. Diablo walked off behind Dewey. Dutch told his self that once they got the work and rolled out, he was going to holla at Diablo about all of that *extra* shit. True enough he was little cousin and Diablo was *big homie*, but Diablo was not his muthafuckin' daddy. *I'm a grown ass man, my nigga. If I wanna stay to this bitch 'til they close it, that's my muthafuckin' business*, Dutch thought as he fumbled around his pockets for the keys. Once in hand, he unlocked the door and slid in. The six bottles of Gold Aces that him and Dewey had downed with Slurpy and her partner had him on lean. *Damn*, he thought, *Slurpy. She for the streets*, he smiled and tried to find the ignition.

$$\$ \$ \$$$

Dewey staggered over to his car with Diablo lagging behind him. A big dumb ass smile was plastered across his freckled red face. He loved Slurpy and Gold Aces, the two went together like weed and lace.

Easing the keys from his pocket Dewey hit his alarm and slid in on the driver's side. Diablo walked over in front of him.

"You got that, homie?"

Dewey laughed a little. "Man, you know I got it...it's in the back seat, on the passenger side. Take the whole bag...just make sho' I get my muthafuckin' bag back...yall niggas don't never return no nigga bag..."

Dewey's voice trailed off as Diablo rounded the car. The car had dark tinted windows so Diablo had to open the door to locate the bag. However, the space between Dewey's car and the van next to it was very narrow. *Dumb ass nigga*, Diablo cursed as he squeezed between the vehicles and pulled the door handle. The bag sat right there as Dewey had said, but when Diabo reached in to get it, flames leapt from the rear seat and pain exploded in his stomach.

Tat! Tat! Tat!...Tat! Tat! Tat! The M-16 rattled off in three round burst. The impact sent Diablo's body crashing back into the van. *Tat! Tat! Tat!* Crab fired again from his spot on the back seat.

Dewey mashed the gas, causing the Buick to smoke its tires as it fish-tailed out of the parking space. *Doom! Doom! Doom! Doom! Doom!* A big gun sounded, bringing down the rear window as Dewey fled. Glass flew everywhere. *Doom! Doom! Doom!* Three shots entered the car, striking the dashboard and front windshield.

"Crab! Crab! Answer that shit, boy! Shoot back, nigga!" Dewey yelled, ducking and side-swiping parked vehicles.

Tat! Tat! Tat!...Tat! Tat! Tat! ... Tat! Tat! Tat!... Crab laced the entire front end of Dutch's car, killing the engine. *Doom! Doom! Doom! Doom!* Dutch fired back in desperation as the Buick hook-slid and hit the block bailing.

Dewey floored the car, sending it flying down 121st Street. He bent a right on Gulf Drive, laughing. He was scott-free. Traffic was light so he sailed across 119th Street and took Guld Drive all the way up to McDonald's – across from Miami Dade Community College.

"We did it, boy! We got that nigga!" Dewey said, parking the car. "Yall 'round here fakin' with them niggas...I told yall that nigga was touchable...Fuckin' with the Hound, anybody can get it. Ya' heard me?"

Crab didn't answer.

"Crab!" Dewey yelled, looking over the backseat. A smile crossed his evil face.

Poor Crab was slumped down on the floor board with a baseball sized hole in his head.

"You can't be layin' down on the job, Crab." Dewey laughed. "You lose like that every time, but you don't hear me, though." Dewey laughed some more at his own twisted humor.

He then popped the trunk and removed the gas canister. Opening the canister he began dousing the car with the canister's content before stopping all of a sudden. Dewey smelt the canister.

"Well kiss my red ass!" he said, cursing Crab. "Dutch couldn't have killed a better nigga. I told this stupid, bitch-ass-nigga, to brang me gasoline! This nigga done brought me kerosene."

Fuck it, it's flameable, Dewey thought as he contined to douse the car, taking special care in soaking Crab's body. "Just don't know...nigga saved me from havin' to kill yo' sorry ass," said Dewey as he stepped back and flicked his Bic.

The car slowly flamed up. Dewey stood there long enough to make sure that it would indeed burn before he ran off across 27th Avenue where he had a change up car parked at the rear of the college on 32nd Avenue.

Chapter 21

The hot Miami sun beamed through the second story picture windows, giving light to Denise's misdeeds. The large eloquently decorred room was funky, causing Denise to crinkle her nose. She looked to her left and saw that Bert was no longer there...Maybe he'd never been there. Perhaps she'd dreamt the terrible nightmare. Her perfidious sense of conviction quickly disintergrated when she noticed the dried remnants of Bert's semen on her cheek, breast, and inner thigh. Beneath her was further testimony of her wrongful acts. The satin sheets that Bo had bought for their king sized canopy bed, sheets that he'd made love to her on on so many occasions, were stained with her love juices. Juices that Bert had drawn from her body like only he could. Because Bert knew her body so well. Denise hated what she'd done...what she'd become. A liar. A cheat. A traitor. Not only to Bo, but to herself.

Denise slowly climbed from the bed. Her thights and anus ached. Bert had really worked her to no end. Nonetheless, she survived it. Now she had the tape and Bert could no longer hold it over her head. Today would begin a new chapter in her life. One filled with promise and dedication to her man, Bo. Denise swore to God and herself that she'd *never ever* do anything to jeopardize the love that her and Bo had.

After soaking in the tub for an hour, Denise lotioned up and dressed in a navy-blue Familiar Line sweatsuit, with matching navy-blue Nike cross-trainers and a gray Nike T-shirt. She then began the process of eradicating the evidence of her infidelity. The lingerie she'd worn, along with the sheets and the tape, were all bagged and taken to the backyard to be burned. Denise sipped a warm glass of Chardonnay and stared into the flames. Tears streaked her face as she recounted the things that Bert had done to her. The awful things that he'd said to her. Yet he claimed to have once loved her. *How could he?* She wanted to know as she cried, sipped, and remembered.

$$$

Denise quickly showered and slipped into something real sexy. She then downed three big glasses of Chardonnay. Her nerves were burning and her confused mind was spinning, because she knew without a doubt or contradiction that she was treading on dangerous ground. If somehow this got out, that not only was she whoring around, but that she was fucking another nigga in Bo's house, *she was dead.* The thought made her drink another glass of wine. Just as she'd sat the glass down the door bell rang. Very nervous and quite tipsy, Denise willed herself to the front door. Knowing already who and what waited on the other side, she simply opened the door and allowed Bert to come inside of Bo's world.

"Where's the tape, Bert?" she'd asked.

Bert smiled an evil smile. "Right here," he replied and seated himself in the lovely living room.

"Give it here," she demanded.

"Nah, come sit down first."

"The living room is not for sitting. We can go –"

Bert quickly cut her off. "Denise, you better get yo' ass over here…besides, we ain't 'bout to do much sittin', we 'bout to do some fuckin'."

Denise sighed heavily and made her way to Bert's side. He didn't waste any time sticking his hand between her thick soft thighs. His middle finger was the first to disappear inside of her. She was dry and tense. Yet neither of which mattered to Bert, because he soon had his index and ring finger deep inside her as well.

Denise had tried with all that she had not to enjoy it. However, she found herself wet and moaning softly. It wasn't long before her ass and hips started grinding to the strokes of

Bert's hand. At which point she closed her eyes and accepted the moment for what it was...*a means to an end*, Denise reasoned. Although she knew that her reasoning was simply justification for her weakness.

Bert removed his cum soiled fingers from Denise's boiling well of pleasure and slipped them into her mouth. Her sexy lips covered his slippery members and quickly sucked them clean of her own juices. With his free hand Bert slipped out of his pants and boxers. He then began easing Denise's head into his crouch.

"Ut'un, Bert." Denise whined, resisting his play for fellatio. "You know I don't be –"

"Bitch!" Bert snapped, roughly grabbing Denise by the back of the neck and squeezing. He forced her face down towards his erect penis. "You better suck this dick!"

Scared and in pain, Denise wrapped her full lips around his dick and began sucking. With nothing but tongue and the roof of her hot wet mouth, Denise applied pressure. Pressure that caused Bert great pleasure. The pills that he'd chewed before arriving at Denise's house made her head game 100 times better. Thereby causing him to coat the back of her throat with thick warm semen. Denise gagged and tried to pull away. But Bert forced her head down, making sure that she caught every drop of his creamy lust.

"Bitch, and don't you spit," he groaned, trembling as his load shot out into her mouth. When the last drip had been swallowed, Bert raised himself from the sofa and spun Denise around. His dick was still swollen and hard. With her face down in the sofa's cushions and her big wide ass up in the air, Bert ripped away her g-string and slammed his ten inches of frustration into her. Denise groaned and bucked, but there was nowhere to run. So she bit down on her bottom lip and took it like a big girl. She could almost feel Bert's dick in her stomach, however, she'd decided that she wouldn't whimper or cry, giving him the pleasure of knowing that he had her in pain.

Grabbing both of her big soft ass cheeks, Bert spreaded them apart. Her fat moist pussy and pink asshole were both so beautiful. He continued to punish her with long hard strokes, while slowly easing a finger into her ass. Sweat poured from both of their bodies. The scent of their sex filled the air. Occasional murmurs and sighs gave cadence to their spurts of pleasure. Bert, retrieving two of his remaining x-pills, chewed one and pushed the other deep up into Denise's rectum. And within minutes sweat really began to pour from her. Her soft sight turned into loud passionate screams. The evidence of her pleasure covered Bert's shaft and leaked onto the couch.

"Oh, Bbbeeerrrttt!" Denise wailed. "Fuck me, Bert! Fuck this pussy, Bert!"

Feeling himself about to cum, Bert pulled out and began ejaculating on her ass and back. Denise felt the hot liquid spilling onto her body and briskly spun around, taking Bert's spurting shaft into her mouth, sucking it dry of its offerings.

Bert smiled. The pill had her gone. *I shoulda been slipped this bith a pill,* he thought to himself.

Denise released Bert's still hard dick from her mouth and got up. Taking his hand she pulled him upstairs where she freaked him like he'd never been freaked before. For hours Bert fucked Denise in every hole in her body. Always ending by shooting off in her mouth or face. And she loved it! Denise begged Bert to fuck her over and over again. And before he'd finally fucked her to sleep, Bert had made her open Bo's wall safe and give him the $12,600 that was inside. In return, Denise received the tape and the fucking of her life, literally and figuratively.

$$$

Denise found herself moisting between her smooth shapely thighs and cringed. Anger overwhelmed her because she wasn't supposed to be feeling this way. Denise drained the glass of Chardonnay and pitched the glass into the flames with the rest of her burning guilt.

Turning from the small fire, Denise made her way back into the house. The place felt used, unclean. Very much the same way that she felt about herself. Denise sighed, wiped away a final tear, and began the process of cleaning up her life; which would begin with an extensive cleaning of the house.

Upon entering her bedroom she saw that she'd missed twelve calls. According to the caller ID, four were from Bo, one was from Cola, five were from Dutch. *I wonder what the fuck his evil ass want*, Denise wondered. There was also a call from her sister, and Denise almost died when she saw that Bert's number was displayed. *Oh, no he didn't! That bitch can just lose my number because we are so over*, she thought to herself and jumped head first into her cleaning.

$ $ $

"Fuck is this dumb bitch at?" Bo asked out loud. "I can't believe this shit."

He was .38 hot. Of all the times to go AWOL, why did Denise have to choose today? Bo had been released from the county for over an hour and could not reach anyone. Ma had a collect block on her phone and Angie hadn't picked up the phone in so long that he'd decided not to call anymore. Maybe she'd heard about KiKi and the baby. Whatever the reason was, Bo was pissed and meant to clean house now that he was back on the turf. But first he had to get the fuck from in front of the courthouse. And being as the courthouse was only a stone's throw from Overtown, he was lightweight out-of-bounds with no gun and no ride.

Fuck I'ma do? He asked himself for the hundredth time. The property line was long as fuck! *Nah, I ain't fuckin' with that*, he told himself. Bo had a rule. The rule was, *leave everything in jail in jail*. He never picked up property after being arrested. Jewelry, cash money, car and house keys, he left it all and simply replaced it. To him, the shit was bad luck once the police had touched it.

Again he tried Denise, *no answer*. Maybe she'd heard about KiKi and the baby also, Bo thought. Then it hit him. He only hoped that shorty had call collect on her phone. It had been a while since they'd talked, but he knew that she didn't leave for work until around 2:30. Bo picked up the phone and dialed her

180

number. *Yes!* He silently celebrated as the phone began ringing. A sleepy female voice came across the line before the automated operator cut in...*this is a collect call from – Bo!...Will you accept the charges?*

"Damn stranger."

"What's good, ma?"

"Sure enough not being woke up out of my *beauty rest for a durn' collect call*," the female said, laughingly.

"Don't trip, ma. I gotchu'. But first I need a big favor."

$$$

The phone rung and rung as Denise tidied up the large house. She spilled bleach, sprayed disinfectant, and scrubbed. Seeing that Bo had called again gave rise to her guilt, which made her clean even harder. She thoroughly scoured, mopped, dusted, and vacuumed. From room to room she went. When she finally finished the scent of pine oil hung thick in the air. Floors, cabinets, and table surfaces gleamed. All bed settings had been changed and so had Denise's spirit. Sweat covered her forehead and soaked through the armpits and crouch area of her sweatsuit, yet a wide smile creased her pretty face. *The house is clean*, she said to herself. *Now I need to wash my funky self and go see my man.*

Denise sat soaking in the tub until the water got cold. She then dried herself, lotioned her thick body, and laid naked across the fresh silk sheets that she'd put on the bed. The cool sheets felt so good against her naked body. Had Bo been there with her Denise felt that she could just lay there forever. *Damn! I love and miss you, Bo.* She thought before drifting off.

$$$

Denise woke up with a stir. Not quite sure how long she'd been out, Denise turned towards the digital clock that sat on the nightstand, next to the pictures of her and Bo in the Bahamas. The

181

clock read 11:50 a.m. He body was so tired. And she felt a little dehydrated. It seemed that she'd been asleep for hours, while in actuality she'd only been out for forty-five minutes. *Oh well,* she said, easing from the comfortable bed. Just as she stood her flat stomach rumbled. Denise couldn't remember the last time she'd eaten. *Oh well,* she repeated, *I guess I gotta eat.*

Still naked, Denise headed off towards the kitchen. The closer she got, the hungrier she realized she actually was. Her mind recalled the list of food items that were shelved in the kitchen. Still, Denise did not know exactly what she wanted. She was midway the living room, about to veer left into the kitchen, when the front door flew open. Denise turned towards the door and froze. Staring at her naked body was Dutch. There was anger in his glance. Denise used her right arm and hand to cover her full breast, the left hand she used to shield her exposed vagina. Without a word being spoken between either of the two, Denise turned and ran upstairs. Dutch watched her big ass bounce as she ran. He then turned and locked the front door.

When Denise returned ten minutes later, wearing only her pink silk bathrobe and matching slippers, she found Dutch seated in the kitchen, drinking from a fifth of Remy V.S.O.P. that Bo kept in the cabinet. His angry eyes were still in place.

"What's up, Dutch?"

"Is you deaf?" Dutch screamed on Denise.

"No…I mean, whatchu' talkin' 'bout? You ain't said –"

"Bit—" he caught himself. Because even though he thoroughly hated Denise's sneaky ass, his brother loved the bitch so he had to respect her. "I been callin' you all muthafuckin' night! And I done called here at least six times today."

"Oh, I'm sorry Dutch. I've just been out of it. You see how you caught me." Denise referred to their earlier encounter. "I was just wakin' up."

Dutch eyed her. He did not believe Denise for one minute. For all he knew, there was probably a young nigga with a slick rap and a hard dick upstairs in his brother's house as they spoke. "You talked to my brutha'?"

"Umm', not today."

"Well you need to go see 'im, today." Dutch stated before taking a big gulp from the bottle. "Tell 'im to call back 'round here at 9:00. I'll be here, because I really need to holla at 'im. Shit done gone crazy."

"Okay," Denise said, trying to figure out where Dutch was going with what he'd said.

Dutch hit the bottle again and stood. "Denise, don't get caught."

"Caught doin' what?" she asked, her heart about to jump out of her chest.

"I'ma let you figure that out."

Dutch screwed the cap back on the bottle of fine cognac and headed out of the door.

Chapter 22

"Thanks for pickin' me up, ma." Bo said, eyeing the fat print of Nurse Shanika's pussy as she pushed the light-gray Nissan Altima through early noon traffic.

"You better be thankful, because I almost pulled off and left you." Shanika stated with a sly grin plastered across her pretty brown face. "Standing out there looking like Wolfman Jack, with those wrinkled clothes on and all that nasty hair all over your face…boy, you look a mess."

"So my appearance make you think less of me?" Bo quizzed her.

"No, I was just saying…At the hospital you looked –" Shanika shook her head as she stopped at the red light. "Never mind, man. Forget I said that…what was you doing down there at the courthouse, anyway?"

Bo thought before laughing at her. "What it look like I was doin'?"

"Panhandling," she said and they both busted out laughing.

"Nah, smart ass. I just got outta jail."

"Oh, so that's why you haven't been calling me…I thought that maybe I wasn't your type."

"Nah, never that." Bo stated, eyes looked on that fat mound of flesh between her legs. "I definitely believe you my type. I just need to test drive the car before I buy it. Fell me?" he finished with a nasty grin of his own.

"*Not!*" she said, laughing. "You already got a baby-momma, and I'm not trying to add to that. I'm *wifey*, honey…Besides, I'm a virgin and my first got to be special."

"Yeah, right!" Bo busted out laughing. "If yo' ass a virgin, Eddie Long ain't fuck them lil' boys!"

184

"He didn't," she replied before erupting in laughter also. "No, for real, I have a little girl. It's just us. I don't be dealing with dudes like that because yall have a lot of shit with yall, and I can't have that around my daughter."

"I can respect that."

The two rode in silence for a while before Shanika spoke up.

"So, since you done woke a female up all early and stuff, where are you taking me to eat?" she popped.

Bo smiled. "I ain't tryna buck you or nothin', because I 'preciate the ride...but, I ain't got no money, ma. That's why I called you," he laughed. "Plus, you don't wanna be seen eatin' with no panhandler, do you?"

Shanika shook her head knowingly. There was something about this *Mr. Bo* that really sparked her interest. And she like it. "You got all the sense, don't you?!"

"What?"

"What, my behind," she popped back. "We're going to eat. And I'm going to pay. But your butt owe me...and I always get what's owed to me. Believe that."

"Well, teach, then." Bo said, laughing. Shorty was cool. And if it was up to him, she surely would get everything that she had coming.

$$$

"What do you mean, *he isn't here?*" Denise asked, raising her voice. She'd stood in line for forty-five minutes and now the little ugly woman on the other side of the counter was giving her attitude.

The woman, about 5'5", 113 pounds, stood up from behind her computer. Her uniform was extra tight, showcasing her camel-toe, beer gut and flat ass. The bitch's body was busted and her attitude matched. "Like I told you the first two times, *he-ain't-here!*"

Denise sighed. She wanted to strangle the little weasel looking chick. "Okay, listen…I understand that he's not here. But where he at? Transfer, court, medical? Can you –"

"Ut'un, honey." The woman cut Denise off, giving her *the hand*. "That's classified information," she lied, knowing damn well she could've simply told Denise that Bo had been released that morning. However, she was miserable. So she wanted the beautiful woman that stood before her in the tight yellow Juicy Couture jeans and the studded white and yellow baby-t that read *George Washington Owned Slaves*, to feel just as despondent as she did.

"Okay," Denise said and spun on her white studded Ferragamo heels. "Thank you…for nothing, bitch!"

"Ut'un, no that bitch didn't just call me no bitch," she said to herself, steady popping her bubble gum. She briskly looked around to see if any of her co-workers had heard the exchange. Seeing that none of them had, she simply sat back down to her computer and wished that she was Denise.

$$\$\$\$$$

Where the hell is he? Denise asked herself as she entered her Q45. It dawned on her as she sped off that that's why he'd been constantly calling the house. Something was, or had changed in his situation, and he'd been calling to inform her. But she'd been so down and confused that she'd just ignored him. Now she'd lost him, she thought as big sorrowful tears welled up in her sad eyes. And before she knew it, she was crying uncontrollably. Somehow in her selfish desire to hold on to Bo, she'd unwittingly let him down again. Lord knows she did not mean to. And she hated herself for it. Had she been more hands on with his situation, maybe she would've had a better relationship with his lawyer and a better understanding of what he was going through. Because as things stood, not only did she not know where he was, but Denise never even bothered to find out what Bo was charged with or how much time he was facing. Only now did she realize how fucked up that was. Bo had been extra good to her. And she hadn't done anything but cheat and mislead him.

Wiping away her tears, Denise vowed to make things right. But first she had to replace the money that she'd took out of the safe. She had two choices, *sell some ass or go stealing*. Selling pussy was *out of the question*, so she called up Cola. Denise knew that her old stealing partner was always down for whatever.

"Hello?" Cola answered.

"What's good, sis'?"

"Bitch, whatchu' want?"

"Damn, that's how you feel?" Denise questioned.

"Yep, now what yo' scank ass want, 'cause I'm busy."

"Busy doin' what?"

"I'm 'bout to hit the mall. What else?!"

"So where you want me to meet you?"

Cola looked at the phone and then placed it back to her ear. "Excuse me?! Not miss *I don't steal no more, my man don't want me stealing*...bitch please. Is you aiight?"

"Okay, you got that, hoe." Denise laughed. "But I really need to hit a few licks. I fucked up some money and I need to hurry up and put it back."

"Whatever, hoe. Just meet me at Westland. I'll be there in twenty minutes."

Denise hung up and pushed her Infinity towards Hialeah.

$$\$\$\$$$

After dining at Artoria's and sharing a few laughs, Shanika pulled her car into the driveway of Bo's 54th Street hideout. As soon as she put the car in park Bo leaned over and tongued her down. At first she tried to pull away from his soft lips and aggressive tongue, but that only caused him to tongue her harder. For three minutes he sucked her lips and licked her face; and for three minutes she moaned and pulled his tongue. She'd never been kissed so passionately. Her libido was raging and her thong was soaking wet. And had he not pulled away from her, ending the kiss, he could have surely fucked her right there in the car.

"Thanks again for the ride and the lunch," he smiled at her. "I owe you one."

"Yeah," she said, trying to calm herself. "You sure do."

"I gotchu'."

Bo climbed from the car, only to be stopped by Shanika's voice.

"Bo! Hold up," she whined. "When I'ma hear from you?"

"I gotta lotta runnin' 'round to do today...I'll hit you late night. Maybe we can do breakfast...my treat," he smiled.

"Okay, that sounds nice." Shanika kissed him once more and drove off towards home.

$$\$\$\$$$

The first thing that Bo did was take an hour long shower. The privacy and steaming hot water felt damn good. A million and one thoughts ran through his mind as he showered. There were so many things that needed to be done. After drying off and donning a red Dickie outfit and red and white retro Jordans, Bo opened the small floor safe and removed five $1,000 stacks and a black plastic .40 Glock. The keys to the white Volvo S60 Turbo that was parked out back were on the breakfast nook. Taking the keys, he tucked the .40 and cleared it.

Driving was strange after not driving for such an extended period. But as the old adage went, *it's like riding a bike, you never forget how to do it.* So he easily found his groove and pushed the S60 Turbo towards Little River. He needed a haircut and nobody could trim and gossip like Mr. Frank at Central Barbershop. When Bo entered the large barbershop there were beaucoup hoodrats, dressed in the sleaziest clothes they could find, with children galore and plenty of attitude. Bo knew and had fucked most of them because he came through the barbershop at least three times a week.

"Well look what the dog done drug in," a thick straggly looking red-bone called out, causing everybody to turn towards the door.

"What's good, everybody..." Bo spoke, smiling to everyone. "And you too, Rhonda." He shouted at the *pass her prime* red-bone that had made the slick comment towards him.

"Nigga, you anything," she snapped back.

You would know, Bo thought to himself. "You sent Diddy that money and the letter that I gave you?"

"Boy, yeah." She lied. "You got some more for him?"

"Yeah, I'ma give it to you when federal parole come back," *lying ass bitch*, he thought and took his seat in Mr. Frank's chair.

"Ut'un! My son was next!" yelled a slim dark-skin chick with body like Beyonce and a face like a chihuahua. And the worst part about it was the fact that her poor son looked just like her.

"Tiasha, calm yo' lil' self down. Bo here is a special customer, with a lot goin' on. So I gotta get him in and outta here." Mr. Frank explained.

"Yeah, plus Mr. Bo gon' pay for everybody's haircuts...right Mr. Bo?" Rhonda capped.

Bo smiled at her fast hustling ass. "Yeah, yall got that. It's all on me, Mr. Frank."

When Bo exited Central Barbershop he was feeling and looking like a brand new man. With the Volvo back out in traffic, he shot straight to Angie's spot. The bitch had a lot of explaining to do. Of all the chicks that he had in his life, he expected the most from Angie. That's why he was always so hard on her. That's why he'd always gone the extra mile in schooling her. And that's also why she had an ass whuppin' coming as soon as he stepped foot in her house. As he flew up the street BG pimped through the Volvo's sound system.

...I bats the fuck outta bitch quick / 'cause these hoes ain't shit / the only thing they good for / is puttin' they mouth 'round my dick...I gotta put my foot down / keep 'em in check / 'cause if I let 'em disrespect me / they gon' always disrespect me...Pimpin' ain't easy / gotta keep these hoes from talkin' back [Oh I'll give Daddy

*respect or get batted]...Ain't nothing but a G-thang baby / these
stank ass hoes goin' crazy...*

Bo jumped out of the car and quickly made it into the
house. The place was completely ramshacked and smelt as if a
dead body was inside. Pulling the .40 from his waistband, Bo
slowly made his way though the house, checking each and every
room before finding himself back in the living room. It was
evident that no one had been inside the house in quite a while. *But
what the fuck is that smell?* He asked himself. Bo then decided to
check the backyard. Walking through the kitchen he suddenly
found the cause of the vile smell. The power was off and
everything inside of the fridge and deep freezer had spoiled. *Man,
where and the fuck is this bitch at?* He thought, fuming with anger.
On stacks, I'ma bat this bitch right in her muthafuckin' mouth! He
checked the phone. It was still in service. Dialing the number to
his house he hoped that Denise was finally in. *Answering
machine!* He hung up and called her cell phone. *Answering
machine!* Bo slammed the phone down. *I'ma kill both of these
bitches!*

Back behind the Volvo's tinted windows Bo headed to the
Match Box. Nobody was out when he pulled up, which was fine
by him, because he wasn't in the mood to socialize. He shot
straight to KiKi's apartment. Her mother opened the door holding
his baby. Looking at his child and how small he was made Bo
realize that change was in order. He had to get KiKi and Lil Bo
out of the projects. True, KiKi was a certified animal, but she'd
proved her worth. She hit the road whenever he needed her to and
she'd produced him a healthy son that looked just like him.

Before he could give Lil' Bo back to KiKi's mother, KiKi's
fine ass came out into the small cluttered living room looking good
enough to eat. *Damn!* Bo said inwardly as she strolled over to him
and hugged him tightly. It was his first time seeing her since she'd
had the baby, and Lil' Bo had put weight on her in all the right
places. It felt good holding her in his arms. And he could tell that
she felt the same way, because she quickly pulled him off to her
bedroom and expressed just how much she'd missed and loved him
– using her mouth not only to tell him, but to show him.

$$$

Denise followed Cola from Westland Mall to the Dolphin mall. They'd only hit about four stores in Westland and ripped them for about $4,000 worth of clothes, handbags, and shoes. Some items going for as much as $700. But being as they had to let it go for half price on the street and then turn around and split the profit 50/50, $4,000 worth of shit was chump change. So they decided to hit the Dolpin Mall for at least another four grand.

The two fast hustling chicks browsed a few stores together before splitting up. Normally they worked together. But Denise felt that if they each worked solo they could get twice as much done. Cola didn't like it but had no choice but to agree.

Denise hit Nieman Marcus and tore them off for $1,100 – two pair of boots and a belt. After taking the items to the car she browsed The Bonanza. They had Dior and Kimono pieces ranging from $75 to $500. However security was tight ass hell. Denise purchased a pair of panty hose and quickly got the fuck on. Walking the large mall, filled predominantly with white folk, Denise stopped at Ronald's – an exclusive high-end handbag store. A Spanish chick in a badass cream and peach Dior skirt set approached her. She was a sales representative. Denise briskly shooed her away. A nice crowd of rich upper-class, tea drinking, nigga hating Ofays filled the store. Denise saw off rip what she wanted. The feeling that she got from stealing was almost as blissful as an orgasm. And it had been so long. She was a little rusty, but smooth nonetheless. A smile. Three quick hand gestures. Denise shifted her position and walked to the other end of the crowded shop. More smiles, two more waves of her fast manicured hands and Denise dipped for the parlay. Her manipulation of the circumstances surrounding her was a grand scheme to behold. Denise moved like an epicence counselor in a remote institute stocked with fine young girls, it was simply hers for the taking. Smiling, she purchased a small $290 Emily Embellished suede Antik Batik purse and cleared it. But not without the Ted Baker *Tube Chain* leather shopping bag, valued at $570; the three-color gray *Super Dooney*, that Dooney & Bourke

191

wanted $840 for; and the Jimmy Choo *Sylvia large* grained leather bag, which was hitting for a cool $1,995. She walked out of that store feeling like she'd lost her virginity all over again. She only hoped that Cola had been as successful. Because if so, they'd struck jewelry! A few more good days like this and she'd have Bo's money replaced.

Bo? She thought, walking towards the exit. How she loved and missed her Bo. Denise reached the main exit and her short reverie imploded with a firm grip on her right arm. Denise spun around to find a tall Asian looking man holding her arm. Beside him stood a husky, badly build black man and an ugly white woman. Before Denise could utter one word the woman removed a badge. Without protest Denise allowed them to escort her to an office located in the rear of the mall. Cameras and screens covered the walls...Tears streaked her face...And Cola sat before her crying as well.

$$$

Bo left KiKi's pad feeling totally revived. KiKi had fucked him, sucked him, fed him, and went out to get him some *sticky-green* weed and a box of El-Po's. He almost hated to leave. Yet he had to. There was a lot that still needed to be done.

The sun had just fell and he still had not seen anybody. Pushing the Volvo towards home he hoped that Denise's ass had finally made it there. *She gon' fuck 'round and lose her position...her and Angie ass,* he thought, remembering some of the shit that KiKi had just done to him. After kicking Denise's ass, he planned to catch up with Dutch and Diablo. He knew that they'd seen the nigga Dewey by now. With his share of the *free-money* that they'd gotten off of the two kilos that Dewey promised, he was going to get KiKi a nice two bedroom pad somewhere. Shorty deserved it.

Pumping that Tupac, *ME AGAINST THE WORLD*, Bo flushed it down 826, loving every minute of his *thug-living*.

Chapter 23

...You probably crooked as the last trick / wanna laugh how I got my ass caught up with this bad bitch / Thinkin' I had her but she had me in the long run / just my luck I'm stuck with fuckin' wit' the wrong one...[Unh'] Wise decisions / based on lives we livin' / scandalous time / Game's like mines religion...You could be rollin' with a thug...

Tupac piped as Bo pulled up to his beautiful two-story home. It was dark outside. The neighborhood quiet. Flood lights lit up the walkway as Bo strolled up to the door, tripping the flood light's sensor in the process. It had been a long time since he'd stepped foot in his house. Yet it was just as he'd left it; quiet, clean, and dark. Dropping the keys to the Volvo and the spare house key that he'd taken from beneath the flowerpot onto the glass coffee table, Bo started up the stairs. He could already see that Denise wasn't home, which was strange. Everything about his day, including his release from the county, had been crazy. Angie was missing. Denise was missing. And a very strange feeling had been riding him all day. A premonition that something terrible was in the works. The feeling shook him to his very core as he took the last step on the staircase and turned towards his room. Then, suddenly he found himself being shoved up against the wall, a gun barrel at his dome.

"Bitch-ass-nigga! You move and I'ma put it in yo' life!" The hight pitched voice squealed in the darkness.

Bo sighed heavily. "Dutch, if you don't let me go. I'ma kick yo' lil' drunk ass!" he yelled, pushing off of the wall. He could smell the alcohol oozing out of his twin brother's body.

"Bo!" Dutch squealed, flicking on the hallway light. "Boy, when you jumped?"

Bo did not answer. He simply embraced his flesh and blood. He could see that Dutch was going through it. His clothes were wrinkled. He needed a hair cut and a shave. Not to mention, Dutch, rarely if ever, came to the house because he hated Denise. So Bo knew that something had to be seriously wrong. Which brought him back to the strange feeling that he'd been having, prompting him to question his brother.

"What's wrong, bruh-bruh?"

"Bo, my nigga, cuz dead." Dutch whispered.

"What cuz?" Bo asked, but really he already knew. A big ass knot formed in his stomach as he stared at Dutch, waiting to hear the obvious.

"Diablo, bruh...bitch-ass-niggas killed him."

Tears rolled down Bo's face. "Who?"

"You man...the nigga Dewey. He with Rome and 'em."

"What?!" Bo screeched. "You talkin' 'bout Hound? Dewey who I sent you to holla at Trent 'bout?"

"Yeah. Trent, his girl, and his lil' daughter dead too. Shit crazy." Dutch whispered.

"Nah, dog! How the fuck —"

Dutch cut Bo off and explained everything. The two sat talking and crying for what seemed like forever. Bo could not believe his ears. Dewey had played him like Alicia Keys played a piano. And as a result he'd never get to see his big cousin again. Diablo had always been there for him. Acting as mentor, big brother, and somewhat of a father. Now he was gone. Gone forever. And no matter how he flipped the scenario or twisted the précis his mind, when it all boiled down, it was his fault.

"I'ma kill Dewey and everything that he love." Bo stated, staring blankly at the wall.

"It's whatever, bruh-bruh...I'm just glad you home. 'Cause for real, I ain't feel safe ridin' with nobody else."

"You seen Pressure and Red Boy?"

"Nah, but they ain't hard to find."

"Then find 'em, 'cause I got some work for 'em."

Chapter 24

Denise sat on the floor next to the pay phone crying. She was a mess. After being booked she'd been stripped of her hair pins, makeup, and her expensive wardrobe. Everything that she was had been taken from her. Now, sitting there on the hard dirty floor, she was just an average chick, longing to be released like all of the others surrounding her.

Denise had a bond, but after calling every bitch that she knew, still she sat. Nobody, not even her mother, had $1,000 that they were willing to part with. How she wished Bo was out. He'd be mad ass hell! He might have even kicked her ass. However, Denise had no doubt that he'd bond her out. Bo was her everything! And times like this proved it. She had no one else to lean on. Nobody else to turn to. Except? *Ut'un*, Denise told herself. She was not about to go there. How could she? Then again, how could she not? After all, she would not have been in this position if it wasn't for his ass. Anger replaced her sadness. Rage dried her tears. Denise lifted herself up from the floor and dialed Bert's mother's house. After six rings a female voice picked up. It was Bert's mother. She quickly accepted the call and got Bert to the phone. From the sound of his cranky voice Denise knew that he'd been asleep.

"Yeah? Whatchu' want?"

"I need you to come get me, Bert."

"Oh," he smiled inside. "You miss me?"

"No, I'm in jail." Denise snapped, almost on the verge of breaking down again.

"In jail? For what?"

"Does it matter, Bert?"

Bert thought for a minute. He wanted to carry her high-sididdy ass bad. But the truth was, Bert loved Denise to death. "Where you at?"

"Downtown."

"I'm comin' now."

Tears welled up in Denise's eyes. "Thank you, Bert."

"Yeah, aiight." He replied and hung up.

$$\$\$\$$$

It was 1:00 a.m. and Denise still was not home. Dutch was passed out in the TV room, while Bo sat up thinking. Worrying. Both of his women were still missing in action. His thoughts constantly drifted from Denise, to his dead cousin, to Angie, to killing Dewey and his entire family, and back to his cousin's death. In the process he'd smoked two packs of Newports and a half ounce of sticky-green. Picking up the phone he dialed Denise's cell number for the one hundredth time. Voice mail. He then decided to call Denise's mother's house.

"Hello?" a sleepy voice whispered.

"Is Denise there?"

Denise's mother recognized Bo's voice. "Umm', no baby. She left here maybe ten or fifteen minutes ago...I ain't been feelin' to good so she stayed here with me for a while," she lied, knowing damn well that the last time she'd spoken to her daughter that Denise was in jail.

"Did she say she was comin' home?"

"Nawl, baby, I didn't ask."

"Okay, thank you." Bo said and hung up.

Chapter 25

"So how much is that?" Rome asked, sliding eleven $2,500 bundles into a green duffle bag. Shop had been closed for over two hours and him, Stanka, Joe, Dorry and Dell were still counting money.

"With that $27,500 you just took, that make $96,000 off the hard and soft." Dell said, turning to Joe. "Whatchu' do off the boy?"

"Shiid'," Joe looked up, fatigue showing on his face. "Them black bags did $54,000, and we ain't even finished countin'."

"Damn!" Stanka shouted. "Shit done went to whammin'!"

Rome smiled. "Yeah, that's how shit go when you handle yo' business."

Stanka frowned at Rome. Because he knew that the comment was made in reference to his inability to murk Diablo. Yet Dewey had done it almost effortlessly. Still, Stanka had to admit, with Diablo no longer around things had really gone into overdrive.

"Man, fuck Dewey!" Stanka said, steady counting money. "I don't see him or them fuck niggas."

Rome laughed. "Well, you might have to see 'im tonight." Rome stated, checking the time on his iced-out Rolex. Just then, a knock sounded at the door. "'Cause that's him right there."

Stanka sucked his teeth. He and Rome had argued about whether or not they should fuck with Dewey. Rome acted like the nigga was Maddog Cole reincarnated. While Stanka wanted absolutely nothing to do with him. Dewey was a rotten snake with no love or loyalty for anyone besided himself, and Stanka did not want to be around when the poisonous muthafucka struck again. Nor did he want to be around the nigga when Bo got out. Stanka felt it was better to just pay the nigga for what he'd done and be done with him altogether. Obviously, Rome felt different.

Dell got up and opened the door. Dewey walked in, smiling, fresh to death in a dark-gray Dame Dash two-piece suit. The suit coat was open, showcasing the expensive black silk shirt, and the .40 Glock that rested in a black holster beneath his left armpit. His gray and black alligators click-clacked against the bare cement floor as he strolled over towards the group of men counting money. A gleam radiated in his evil eyes as he peeped the heavy amount of paper being counted.

"Look like the Hound's right on time," he smiled big. "What's good, family?"

Everybody returned his greeting except for Stanka, who never looked in Dewey's direction. Instead he busied himself with the task at hand, counting money.

Dewey made a mental note of the slight and sat with his back to the wall, keeping everyone in front of him in case shit went bad. His left hand rested on the butt of the .38 snub that he had holster beneath his jacket on his right hip.

"What's up, Stanka?" Dewey spoke, a sneer across his face.

"Oh, what's up." Stanka replied dryly, as if he'd just noticed Dewey for the first time.

Dewey smiled maliciously. "You got me, Rome?"

"Yeah," Rome answered, sliding several bundled stacks over in front of Dewey.

Dewey eyed the pile before lifting a stack to inspect it. He then dropped the money and growled at Rome. "You tryin' me, my nigga?"

"How you figure? That's $17,500, Hound."

"And that's a helluva lot more money than yall boys was seein' before I offed fool," Dewey countered, pointing at the bags of money. "Yall thank I'm stupid? Yall forgot I touched yall for that bag when I jumped? I saw what yall boys was pullin', and it wasn't near this much!"

"So whatchu' want?" Stanka asked.

"In! Nigga, I want in!" Dewey stated. "You don't think I know what's next? I might be dead tomorrow for what I did for yall niggas. And you thank I'ma accept 17,500 punk ass dollars? Nigga, my life on the line!"

Rome slid another $17,500 over. "How 'bout that and another $10,000 a week to be my number one hammer?"

"How 'bout you kiss my ass!"

"Here, man!" Stanka tossed a duffle bag to Dewey. "That's $75,000. Now take it and get the fuck on!"

"Oh yeah?" *Boom! Boom! Boom!* The .38 banged, catching Stanka square in the chest.

"What the fuck?" Joe yelled, jumping up from his seat.

"If you don't sit yo' bitch-ass down, Joe, I'll put this whole clip in yo' life." Dewey said, flashing the .40 Glock in Joe's direction; the .38 still trained on Stanka's dead body.

Without a moment's hesitation Joe found his seat. The room was deadly quiet until Rome spoke up.

"Damn, Dewey...Man, why you killed Stanka?" Fear lined his face. A deep-seated gloom filled his words. Stanka was not a childhood friend, yet he'd been a friend indeed.

"Fuck Stanka and any nigga that gotta problem with 'im bein' dead!" Dewey barked, eyeing each man individually. "Any of yall gotta problem?" Nobody voiced a contrary opinion. "Good! 'Cause I ain't opposed to wholesale murder...now, with Stanka, Sam, Crab, Ty and Cash dead, every nigga that crossed me is dead. Them bitch-ass-niggas left me in the county for dead! Now they dead, and everybody even...so you can let me walk outta here with $50,000 and whatever percentage of the business that Stanka used to have, or I can kill everybody in here, walk out with everythang in here, and that'll be that. It's yo' choice."

"I ain't trippin'," Dell said, raising his hands in mock surrender.

"Shiid', me neither." Dorry replied.

"Aiight," Rome said. "Joe, clean this shit up...come on Dewey, we gotta talk."

With that the two new business partners exited the spot.

$$$

Bert woke up tired and dehydrated. He looked around the cheap motel room in search of a cup. After finding one he filled it with tap water and quickly drained the cup, only to repeat the process thrice more. He loved the roll that x-pills gave him; however, when compiled with three hours of freaky sweaty sex, it took a lot out of the body. Knowing that Denise was probably just as thirsty – after all, he'd pushed a pill and a half up her anus during sex – he filled the cup again for her. She was naked beneath the dingy covers when Bert began to shake her. She stirred, barely opening her sleepy eyes.

"What...Bert...I'm sleepy," she whined.

"Here, we gotta go." Bert said, passing her the cup.

Denise quickly drank the water. "Thank you. Damn I was thirsty."

"I bet you was...now come on."

The two showered and dressed. Denise was tired and sore as hell. Bert had really fucked the shit out of her. Every inch of her body ached. But that was the price she paid for being bonded out. After Bert had came and got her from the womens' annex she'd simply thanked him and asked to be dropped off at home. However he'd had other plans and she'd had no choice but to oblige him.

"Bert," Denise started as they neared his SUV.

"What?"

"Umm', could you get my car for me?"

He laughed. "And whatchu' gon' do for me?"

"Bert, come on, now." Denise huffed. "I wouldn't even be in this mess if I wouldn't have gave you Bo's fuckin' money."

"Bitch, you wouldn't have had to give me Bo's money if you wouldn't have gave Bo my pussy."

"Bert, I ain't no bitch, first off. And I'm Bo's lady, so this is Bo's pussy."

"Then tell 'Bo' to getcha' muthafuckin' car for you...gold diggin' ass bitch."

Denise slammed the SUV's door as she got in. "Come on, Bert. Don't act like that. You know I ain't got no money and I need my car," she began crying. "Please, Bert. I'll pay you your money back for the car and my bond."

"Whatever, Denise. Where the car at?" Bert asked, mad as hell at her. How could she sit there, look him in his face, and say she's Bo's lady? Especially after the shit they'd just finished doing. Couldn't she see the love in his eyes as they grind and exchanged body fluids? Wasn't the passion evident in his every stroke? Couldn't she sense the tenderness of his touch? Bert loved her and she should've known it. Why else would he have gotten out of bed in the middle of the night to bond her out of jail? The same reason he'd played second fiddle to Bo after she'd left him. Love! He did it all because he loved her…

$$$

"What if these niggas ain't out here?" Dutch questioned his brother as he navigated the splacked bark-brown Lincoln through the bowels of Overtown.

"Then it's just me and you." Bo responded. "We ridin'."

Dutch thought for a minute as he drove. "My nigga, we might need to go up to the bar and holla at Chico, Bush, Vinny, or Forty, my nigga…you remember what big cuz said."

"Dutch, no disrespect to Diablo's word, but cuz is gone. He ain't here no more, yo. It's just us, you and me!" Bo stated, a little flustered at his brother's lack of fire. "I fuck with Forty and 'em and all, but bruh-bruh, we gotta make our own name. And we can't do that by runnin' to them boys when the bullshit pop off…my nigga, after we crash these fuck-niggas niggas gon' be runnin' to us for help. Feel me?!"

"Yeah, I feel you, bruh. I'm just sayin' though."

"It ain't nothin' to say, yo. We 'bout to let these K-cutters do all the sayin'. Straight up!" Bo emphasized by chambering his Ak-47. "I got this, yo. It's me and you. You handle the finances and I'ma sponsor all the funerals…and that's on stacks."

The two rode the next two blocks in silence.

"Yo, that's them right there."

"Damn sho' is. Pull up."

Dutch pulled the Lincoln up to the old dilapidated building that they'd once called home.

Bo jumped out. The red dude with the low-caesar flinched. He was of medium build and wore a mean sneer with his dark-blue Dickie set.

"It's too late for all that," Bo said, approaching Red Boy.

"Yeah, fuckin' with Pressure will get a nigga killed."

"Fuck you, nigga." The chubby short man with long dreadlocks and a mouthful of gold teeth said, lifting himself from the crate he'd been sitting on.

Bo hugged Red Boy and Pressure World.

"When you jumped, boy?" Pressure asked his childhood friend.

"Yesterday."

"Oh yeah?"

"Yeah, and I'm out to get it."

"Whatchu' out to get?"

"Blood!" Bo stated.

"Well, we with whatever." Red Boy told him. Diablo had been his man as well, so he knew how Bo was feeling.

Before they could resume their conversation a badass bitch rounded the corner. She was straight dime status. Making eye contact with Bo she pouted her sexy lips and rolled her eyes, never breaking her stride.

"Damn Brenda, what's good witchu'?" he said, grabbing her arm.

"Ut'un, don't be grabbin' me."

"Damn, it's like that? You actin' like I killed yo' brutha' or somethin'."

"You know what, fuck you Bo! You thank I don't know you killed Conrad?"

"Killed Conrad? Bitch you crazy! I ain't killed nobody." Bo lied.

"Whatever, nigga." She popped her lips. "If you ain't do it you had something to do with it, or else the police wouldn't have never locked Angie up."

"Locked Angie up?" Bo repeated her, not quite clear if he's heard her correctly.

"Nigga, don't play dumb. She locked up and yo' ass gon' be too." Brenda said and spun off.

Red Boy and Pressure World stared at Brenda's big round ass as it jiggled away. However, Bo was lost in thought. He could not get over the words that Brenda had just hurled at him, "if you ain't do it you had something to do with it, or else the police wouldn't have never locked Angie up." Now he understood why all of his calls had gone unanswered, and why her house was in shambles. A pang of guilt crept over him. Thoughts of Angie being jammed up for his mess made him sick.

The sound of the Lincoln's horn brought him back from his trip of self-condemnation.

Dutch leaned out of the Lincoln's window. "Man, what yall gon' do?"

Bo waved him off. "Yall boys ready?"

"You got fi' for us?"

"Already, yo...let's ride."

The three men hopped into the stolen Lincoln with Dutch and rolled out.

$$\$\$\$$$

Joe came out of the trap apartment carrying a soiled brown paper bag filled with quarter sacks of Black Label heroin. It was his third re-up of the day and it wasn't even 10:00 a.m. Of course, the heroin always pumped heavy in the earlier part of the day and close to closing time – around 11:00 p.m. But in between those hours crack and powder cocaine reigned supreme. At times Joe couldn't believe how much money they pulled in. Especially since Diablo was out of the way. It sort of bothered him that Stanka was gone, but what could he do?! It was business. At least that's how Rome had explained it. Rome had also upped his, Dell's and Dorry's pay to $7,500 a week. Which was love.

As Joe made it down the stairs and rounded the cut Dorry was completing a transaction with Man-Man, their runner, and two white boys.

"Here," Dorry said, handing Joe $325 and taking the brown bag from him. "That money clear me for the last boy-bomb, and I got $1,000 in dimes and raw quarters, plus $2,500 in dime rocks and quarter slabs...how much we got upstairs?"

"Shiid', 'bout $100,000 in everythang."

"We boomin'...we boomin'...we boomin'," Dorry sang.

"Nigga, you crazy." Joe laughed at his partner before checking his stainless steel Citizen watch. "Man, Dell ain't back from takin' fool that brick?"

"Nah."

Just as the words left his mouth a line of dopefiends began to form. Man-Man was at the head of the line, smiling. He was the best runner in all of Overtown, because he was honest and had a monster habit. So once fiends saw him copping or running to a particular spot they automatically followed suit. One after another, Dorry exchanged their crumbled up bills for black packages of heroin. And the more he served, it seemed even more walked up, all clutching amounts of $25 and up.

Joe sat on the building's steps and busted a black-cherry Swisser, which he promptly filled with brown weed and cocaine. It was his first blunt of the day. He put the flames to it and pulled hard, releasing a heavy cloud of potent smoke. The mixture brought a calmness to his restive nerves. Joe was about to pull his blunt again when he heard the familiar call of an AK-47. *YAK! YAK! YAK!* But before he could get up he felt a barrol being pressed up against his head.

"I'll burn yo' bitch-ass up...now play with it."

"You got it, my nigga...just don't killa' nigga, dog." Joe pleaded and prayed that the dude wouldn't kill him.

"Get yo' fuck-ass up! Come on, move!"

Joe got up and saw that three more dudes with AK's were already walking Dorry up the stairs to the apartment. There was no talking. Once inside the AK-47 was slammed into Joe's neck. The blow sent him to the floor. Then, *YAK! YAK! YAK!* Joe jumped, covering his head. Three hard kicks to his ass, ribs, and chest caused him to uncover his head and scurry towards the wall. He found himself mere inches from Dorry's lifeless body. His whole torso had been ripped away.

"Where it at?"

"Over...over...over..." Joe kept repeating as he pointed towards the bedroom.

One of the four men jogged off towards the room.

"Where Rome at, yo?"

"Over...over...over..."

YAK! YAK! YAK! Bo let his AK go. "The nigga in shock...Red Boy, let's go!"

Red Boy came running out of the room with a duffle bag. "I got it!"

They all turned and ran back to the Lincoln.

$$\$\$\$$$

"What the fuck?" Dell asked as he rolled up the street leading to the spot. Police and emergency vehicles were everywhere. They had the whole front of the building yellow taped off. "Fuck!" he yelled, already knowing that at least one of his partners was either dead or seriously fucked up.

Dell skated past the building, parking his car two blocks over. There was a burner and $27,500 in the car, and he did not want to get popped off with either. After parking he jogged back over and mingled with the crowd of nosey people. He was just in time to see them bring Joe and Dorry out of the building – dead. Dell felt himself about to cry, then he felt a hand on his shoulder. It was Man-Man.

"What happened, my nigga?"

"Maann," Man-Man said, shaking his head. "Four niggas ran up with sticks, my nigga. Niggas ain't stood a chance. They caught them boys down bad as fuck."

Dell looked at Man-Man, scratching his ashy black neck and batting his eyes. He knew that Man-Man was high. But what did that matter? His two homeboys were dead.

"Did you see who it was?"

"Umm, I saw 'em...but umm, I don't know who it was." Man-Man ducked a few times and sucked his finger. "They was in a do-do-brown Lincoln."

Dell was mad as hell. Then he realized, had he not left to serve that kilo of cocaine to Skip up in Deerfield, he probably would've been dead too. The thought caused more anger to well up in him.

"You ain't notice nothing else 'bout the niggas?"

"Hhhhmmmm, hhhmmmm." Man-Man moaned. "Thuggin'."

"Man-Man!"

The young dope fiend jumped. "Umm, yeah...the guns. They had big ass guns."

Dell sucked his teeth and walked off. He needed to talk to Rome.

Chapter 26

After splitting the loot from the Overtown hit – $100,000 in drugs and another $34,000 in cash – Bo and Dutch jumped in the Volvo and went over to the lawyer's office. Bo neither Dutch wanted anything to do with the individually packaged bundles of heroin and cocaine, so they gave it all to Red Boy and Pressure World and kept the $34,000 in cash; $8,000 of which Bo handed over to Ms. Ward, their lawyer.

Their next stop was TGK, where Bo put $500 on Angie's account. Ms. Ward, after receiving the eight grand, jumped right on top of Angie's situation, and promised to contact Bo with some news before day's end.

Next Bo found himself at his mother's house. She was so happy to see her son. So was his daughter, Susan. She'd gotten so big since he was away. His mother, Ms. Sue, did not waste any time feeding her two sons. She fixed fried chicken, seasoned yellow rice, green peas and corn muffins. As they ate and Bo spent some quality time with his daughter, Ms. Ward called.

"This is what we have…Angie's being held for murder. Her car was spotted leaving the area after one witness 'alleges' she saw a black man with a gun get into Angie's car…Angie won't tell the police who got into her car. In fact, she says that she wasn't even in the area."

"So where she stand?" Bo asked nervously.

"Nowhere, really. We know for a fact that Angie didn't kill anyone…it's all a pressure move on the state's behalf, but it will not work. Angie doesn't have a record and best of all, she has me for a lawyer."

"Bond?"

"We have to have a hearing, fourteen to twenty-one days. But I'm more than sure she'll be given a bond."

"Did she give any statements?"

"Yes, she did."

"W-wh-what she said?" Bo asked nervously.

"I have it right here...let me see." Ms. Ward shuffled through her paper. "Yes, okay, here we go...Yall people tripping. I have not done shit, and I want to make my phone call. I ain't signing shit and I don't know nothin'."

"That's it?"

"Yes, that's it."

Bo beamed with pride. Angie had just raised herself ten more notches in his life. She'd aced her most important test, *never fold under pressure.* "Okay, look. Tell Angie to put me on her visiting list and I'll be there to see her in a few days. I put $500 on her books and my ole-girl already workin' on gettin' Shortman."

"Will do," Ms. Ward replied cheerfully.

"Thanks again, Ms. Ward."

"It's my pleasure."

As soon as Bo hung up the phone Dutch began questioning him.

"So what the hoe said?"

"Which one?"

"The one you just hung up with."

"She say it's all good."

"So Angie ain't say nothin'?"

"Man, I told you before, she's all in with us."

"So what now?"

"I'm goin' to see her so we can really talk. Once that's done, it's all out warfare on them bitch-ass-niggas."

"We gotta find Rome, though!" Dutch shouted, pounding his fist against the wall.

"Yeah, he the head. We kill him and the body dead."

"You right," Dutch replied, stopping to think for a minute. "Bo, my nigga, in this war shit you can't be havin' feels, gettin' emotional and shit."

"Whatchu' sayin'?"

"Like when I told you we need to holla at Forty and 'em. You went on 'bout some other shit. Bruh, fuck who kill the niggas as long as they get killed."

208

"They dead ain't they?"

"Yeah, but I think we made a mistake."

"How?" Bo asked.

"By fuckin' with Pressure 'em." Dutch answered, shaking his head. "It was 'posed to been a straight hit. But just 'cause them two thirsty ass niggas doin' bad we ended up robbin' the spot. And you gave them the drugs. Whatchu' thank they gon' do with that shit?"

"They gon' sell it."

"And it's gon' lead right back to us." Dutch stated.

"Good!" Bo said, standing. "'Cause I'll be here when they come. Fuck 'em!"

"Aiight, it's yo' call, my nigga. But I don't like it."

"Dutch, you do the finances, bruh-bruh. I'll handle the funerals." Bo said and left for home.

BOOK 3HREE

* * * * *

LOVE

&

THUGGIN'

By
PLEX

A YOUNG BOY'S FASCINATION
[Poem by Billy 'Dollar Bill' Richardson]

As a young boy I was fascinated by a female's clear complexion; As a grown man I've realized that even a clear complexion cannot cure a female's emotional complexity...

As a young boy I have always had a fascination with sparkling brown eyes and a pretty smile; As a grown man I realized that those qualities didn't outshine the little white lies...

As a young boy I was fascinated by naturally beautiful females that needed no further enhancement; As a grown man I realized that not even enhancements could hide a female's sneaky or deceitful ways...

As a young boy I was fascinated by a female's physique – wide hips, juicy lips, pretty toes, thick legs with tapered calves and bodacious asses; As a grown man I realized that although these are beautiful exterior attributes, nothing could compare to the hidden treasures that lay within...

As a young boy...Now a grown man...

Chapter 27

DENISE

The steaming hot sprays of the shower *good as hell* felt pummeling against my sore body. I was so glad to be out of that fucking nasty ass jail around those dykes and sorry crack head bitches. How could I have allowed myself to fall so low? After all that Bo had given me, all that I'd suffered through, only to find myself in a worster position than I'd started. *What a tangled web we weave when we practice to deceive...* That's what my momma has always said.

Opening my mouth I drank thirstedly from the shower head. My throat was so dry and my tired body seemed overly dehydrated. I'd never felt this way before. Well, except the last time that Bert and I had had sex. *Bert?!* He was doing something to me. Something that no one had ever done to me. Sexually, he made my whole body vibrate! The slightest touch or even the feel of his breath against my skin caused me to shiver. Just thinking about it had my pussy wet and throbbing. And I did not want that. I did not want Bert. I simply wanted Bo home. I wanted things to be back the way that they were when we vacationed on the islands. Bo loved me and has always had my best interest at heart, regardless of what he did in those damned streets. And the truth was that I not only needed him, but I also loved him.

$$\$\$\$$$

I got out of the shower to the ring of the phone. I hoped that it was Bo. I was naked and eager to hear his voice. It had been nearly 48 hours since I had talked to him. *He is gonna cuss yo' ass out, Denise.* I told myself, rushing to catch the phone before the answering machine picked up, and one look at the caller ID killed my spirits. *Bernise Williams*, it read. I turned off the ringer and lotioned my body. Bert was a *da dun dun.* Fuck how good the dick and head was. Fuck how he made my body convulse and brought real tears to my eyes during moments of climax. Nah, fuck all that. The nigga had done fucked me, fucked over me, and made me steal from my man. He did that, *da dun dun!* Now it was time to shut him down, *basement!* And if that muthafucka tried to fuck over me again in anyway, it would surely be his last. Bert was gon' respect my mind or I was gon' kill his ass. Simple as that. *Shiid'*, my momma ain't raised no punk-bitch.

$$\$ \$ \$$$

Still thirsty as hell I walked naked to the kitchen. My plans were to simply drink me a tall glass of spring water. But after getting a glass and taking the half-gallon jug of water from the fridge, I sat my bare ass in one of the cool leather kitchen chairs and the cold sensation that the leather gave my ass and pussy felt tooo' good! Hmmph, I got my tired ass up, put that damned water back, and got the bottle of Chardonnay. I poured myself a glass and downed it in three quick qulps. It was just what I needed. The last two days of my life had been a real bitch and it was starting to fuck with my nerves. *Seriously!* Raped. Robbed. Cheated. Stupid little me. But no more. Ut'— to the muthafuckin' — un. Downing another glass of wine really had me loose and a little horny. I poured myself another glass and switched seats because the one that I'd been sitting in had lost its coolness. Mmmm', I purred, taking my new seat. It was cold against my pussy. I drank from my gass, my eyes closed tight, I pictured Bo and began grinding my nakedness against the chair's seat. *Shiit,* it felt good. It felt so good that I began to finger my clit and pinch my nipples. I was zoning. At one point, nearing orgasm, I thought that I heard a noice. But I wanted to cum. So I blocked that shit out and got me, me. *Ooooh, yes!*

Chapter 28

BO

I hate a muthafuckin' hard headed bitch. I swear I do! When I pulled up to the crib Denise's car was parked in front of the garage, something that I'd told her about before. What if a nigga was just out *ridin' and lookin'* and just so happened to peep her Q45 out front? Just that easy a nigga would have our location and probably be in the muthafuckin' bushes waiting to kill me and rape her funky ass. Why the fuck did she think I paid the extra $12,000 for the four car carage? But then again, what did it really matter? I'd get the bullet [if or when the niggas killed me] and she'd get a nut [if or when the niggas gang raped her].

Mad as a muthafucka, I parked behind her car and hopped out. Using the spare key again I opened the door and quickly locked it before turning towards the stairs. The house was dark and quiet. I was about to take the first step when I heard a noise in the kitchen. Turning, I found Denise naked, exiting the kitchen with a glass in her hand. Upon seeing me her eyes blinked quickly and bucked as wild as dinner plates. The glass fell from her hand and crashed loudly against the marbled floor.

"Bo! Bo!" Denise shouted and ran to me. "Oooh, bay! It's you!"

She grabbed me in a bear hug. I could tell that she'd been drinking like a fucking fish, because her words were slurred and she smelt like strawberry cream and prison hooch.

"Denise," I said, pushing her hard. "Get yo' drunk ass off of me!"

She stumbled and damn near fell.

"B-b-bay…what's wrong? Why you pushin' me?"

215

I shook my head sadly at the stupid bitch. "What's wrong, huh? I was hopin' that maybe yo' slick ass could tell me."

"Slick? Baby whatchu' mean?" Denise whined and approached me again. "I ain't did nothin' slick."

"Then where the fuck you been? I been callin' yo' ass for two days and you ain't answered yo' cell phone or the fuckin' house phone."

"I seen yo' calls, bay. And I knew you was gon' be pissed. But bay, I ain't did nothin'. I been runnin' 'round for my momma and tryna —"

I cut her ass off quick. "Fuck all that shit! What the fuck I told yo' dog-ass 'bout sleepin' out?" She stood there looking stupid as fuck. "Where the fuck you was last night? And before you lie and make me kill yo' ass in here, I know you wasn't at yo' momma house."

The bitch just stood there playing with her fingers and batting her sad eyes at me. A single tear ran down her cheek as she looked at me. More tears joined in before she'd formulated her thoughts. Denise stepped closer to me and grabbed my hand. Hers trembled as she held me.

"I...I was...I was in jail," she finally whispered.

"For what?"

"They caught me and Cola stealin'."

I sighed. Denise was a stupid bitch and I wanted to kick her ass. Here we were in a house that valued in the six figures, big-boy whips in the garage, and me being valued at a mill', on the low. My life was on the line everytime I left the house – the possibility of getting murked or arrested and sentenced to life was ever present. I didn't do the shit that I did for kicks or to impress no bitches. I did it for my ole-girl [Susan], my daughter [Susan Paige], Denise's selfish ass, and KiKi and my son. Of course Dutch, Angie and Shortman were also priorities.

"Why, Denise?" I simply asked. I'd never been so mad at Denise as I was at that very minute.

"Cola asked me to. And plus –"

"Shut the fuck up!" I barked on her. "Because you sound stupid! Fuck what Cola wanted or need. What the fuck did I tell you? Huh? Is Cola fuckin' you and takin' care of yo' ass?"

"No."

"Then why the fuck is you listenin' to Cola?"

"Bo, I'm sorry. I don't know why I let –"

"I know why." I said, cutting her short again. "But when you finally figure it out, call me and let me know…if it ain't too late by then."

I turned and started for the door, hating the fact that I'd ever walked my ass through the door in the first place.

"Whatchu' mean *too late?!* And where you goin'?" Denise screamed, chasing me out the door naked. "You just got out, Bo! Why you leavin'?...Bo! I love you! Please don't go."

I ignored all of her futile pleas. The bitch was crazy. I jumped into the Volvo and sped off. *Damn, damn, damn! Angie*, I thought, she should've been home. Turning the car towards the east I headed to the Match Box, to KiKi's crib.

Chapter 29

DEWEY

"So hold up, my nigga." I sat listening to Rome giving Dell the 21 questions. "Did the crackas get the bread and the dope too, my nigga?"

Dell blew hot air and rubbed his face. Rome had already asked the man that shit like forty times already. "Rome, man, I don't know what the crackas found. I was gone. When I got back from servin' fool them the crackas had the spot roped off. All I know is that them boys is dead and the lil' shit that Man-Man told me, that's it."

"But I'm sayin'...tell me this then." Rome continued with his frivolous interrogation. And even though I knew that shit was serious, the whole shit was funny to me. Dell was sad as hell over the loss of his dogs and Rome's scared ass was getting scareder by the fucking minute and tripping off of the money loss. I truly didn't give a fuck. Fuck Joe, fuck Dell, fuck Dorry, fuck Stanka, fuck Rome, and fuck the niggas on the other side. I was getting paid regardless. And when Rome couldn't pay me no more or the situation got to hot for my liking, the Hound *outta there!* Fuck what a nigga thank.

My phone rung, taking me away from Dell and Rome's convo'. It was one of my partners from 'Town. "Yeah," I answered. "Oh yeah?...Get the fuck outta here...You sure?!...Boy, bet that up!...Yeah, I gotchu'. Don't even trip."

When I hung up Rome and Dell were staring in my mouth.

"What's up? Who that was?" Rome's scary ass asked.

"A friend of a friend."

"Come on, Dewey, my nigga. Ain't no time for games. What's up?"

"Bo out." I said simply.

"F-fo-for real. How you know?"

Rome looked like he was about to shit on his self.

"Friend of a friend told me."

"So what we gon' do?" Dell asked.

"Ask yo' boss-man," I said, pointing to Rome. "'Cause that ain't the worst of it."

"Whatchu' mean?"

"My man said it's niggas in the blue building sellin' black bag."

"So?!"

"So that's our shit!" I told Rome's scared ass. "Bo and his brutha' used to trap in the blue building. They got people in the blue building…My nigga, that's who hit us."

Rome sighed. "So whatchu' gon' do?"

"Shiid', whatchu' wanna do?"

"Nah, killa. It ain't *what I wanna do*. Killin' people was Stanka's job. You killed Stanka so it's *whatchu' gon' do!*" Rome lightweight checked me. "I'm 'bout to duck off. Call me when them pussy-ass twins dead."

Chapter 30

BO

I pulled up to TGK feeling damn good. KiKi truly was the real one. After Denise had done pissed me the fuck off, KiKi made everything better. Bomb-ass head! Sweet submissive attitude. And some fi' ass pussy! It was hard to believe that Lil Bo had just came out of her. It's like the pussy was tighter and better than before. She even had breakfast in bed for a real boss when I got up. Then to top it all off, shorty had me an after breakfast blunt of that purp' rolled and ready for me. Yeah, KiKi was on her wifey shit and I was feeling it. Because that's exactly what a nigga needed after running the streets all day. A nigga [a real nigga that provides for his family and respects the crib] should never have to fall off in the crib to drama from his ole-lady. When a nigga come, pockets   swoll   up   with G-stacks, trigger finger sore from handling that iron, and nerves on edge 'cause them people looking for him; it should be peace and love waiting at home.

Anyway, floating off the purp', I made it into the building. I couldn't wait to see Angie. She'd really held a nigga down. When all this shit was finally over, I had something real special planned for her, because she deserved the best.

The CO took me upstairs. I could see Angie's unit in the back as I walked up. She was sitting down smiling on the other side of the glass. She looked so good in her little jeans and matching jean jacked. Under her jacket she wore a tight colorful T-shirt with the matching tennis.

"Hey," she said, still smiling.

I smiled back at her. She had her hair jelled down and pulled into a ponytail.

"Hey yo'self." I shot back. "So you a real hardcore convict now, huh?"

"Boy, forget you!" Angie laughed. "It seem like every hoe in here either know you, know of you, done fucked you, or know a hoe who done fucked you."

"Damn, ma." I laughed at her trying to be all serious like she was checking me. "Is that good or bad?"

"Nigga, I'm just sayin'. That shit ain't funny. These hoes been tryin' me, callin' me all type of *stupid bitches* and talkin' 'bout *you locked up for that nigga and he got KiKi pregnant and his ass 'bout to marry Denise*...I couldn't find you. I ain't had no money for food or hygiene. I don't even know where my fuckin' son is, Bo."

Angie was openly crying at this point. I felt bad as fuck.

"I apologize, ma...but it's all good 'cause a nigga here now. My ole-girl goin' to pick Shortman up today, you got money on yo' books, a fi' ass lawyer on yo' case, and the realest nigga in the world on yo' team."

Angie tried to smile a little smile. "Bo, bay you just don't know. I've been really fuckin' stressin'. I thought you had done left me or was mad at me."

"Left you? Why the fuck would I leave you? Ma, you trippin'. Why would you think some stupid shit like that?"

"Because nobody ain't get at me." Angie said sadly. "I know I shouldn't have called yo' house, but I ain't have nobody ---"

I cut her off. "Hold up! You called my house?"

"Yeah. I'm sorry, but –"

"Nah, fuck all that. When did you call, and who you talked to?"

"I called when I first got arrested. Denise accepted the ---"

I cut her off again. "You talked to Denise?"

"Yeah."

"And you told her that you was locked up?"

"Yeah. I told her my situation, apologized to her for callin' her house, and asked her to please let you know what was goin' on."

"This stank selfish bitch!" I said out loud.

221

"She didn't tell you?" Angie asked.

"Nah, the bitch ain't tell me. I would've never left you hangin' like that. I just got out myself. I ran into Brenda triflin' ass and she told me."

"Fuck Brenda."

"Yeah, now you see why I always told yo' ass to keep that bitch outta our business. Brenda some shit! Just like the rest of them cakin' ass jealous hoes from 'Town."

"You right," she whispered. "I love you, Bo."

Tears were falling from her eyes again.

"I love you too, ma."

"For real?" Angie asked, truly surprised. I had never said those words to her.

"Yeah, for real." I laughed. "I been felt it. I guess I'm just realizing how much. You my heart, ma."

"Oh, Bo...that's so sweet," she whined. "I would've been came to jail for yo' ass if I woulda' knew this was gon' be the outcome."

"Girl, you crazy."

We both laughed. Angie was that baby. And Denise was the damn devil. I could not wait to see her selfish ass.

"Bo, tell me again."

"What?"

"That you love me."

"I love you, Angie."

She smiled so brightly. The smile was so bright that it dried up all of her tears.

"Thank you, Bo."

"For what?"

"Thank you for makin' me get my shit together. I hated it when you used to get on me about school, a job, and leavin' Overtown. But now I see and understand why you did and said the things you did."

"Well, I'm glad you understand."

"I do. And I love you more than anything in this world, baby."

I returned her sentiments of love as our visit came to an end. Now it was back to the streets and on with the thuggin'.

$$\$\$\$$$

As I drove up 32nd Avenue smoking a blunt, I reflected on Angie's last question to me at visit, *Do you love her?* Yeah, I'd answered. She was looking crazy, but hey, she asked so I answered. Rarely did I lie to bitches. Lying wasn't my thing, so I also told her the truth about KiKi and Lil Bo. And being a big girl, Angie respected it and I respected her for respecting it.

My thoughts then drifted to Denise. I'd done so much shit for her deceitful ass. How could she play games like that with me? What if Angie would've flipped the script and told the crackas everything because she felt that I'd left her to rot in jail? Simply because Denise's stupid ass failed to do the right thing, I would've been facing the electric chair.

I didn't regret any of the nice things that I'd done for Denise. She was my baby's momma and had given me a beautiful little girl – my very first child. So I had to do right by her. I truly did want to be there for my baby and her mother. I wanted what I'd never had growing up, a fucking family.

The ring of my cell phone troubled my groove. I hoped it was Denise's ass, but I did not bother to check the caller ID, I answered with my true feelings in my greeting.

"What?"

"Ut'un?! You rude," the female voice came across the line. "Did I catch you at a bad time? 'Cause I could call you later."

Recognizing the sweet voice I lightened up and almost smiled. "My bad, man. What's good with you?"

"Boy, you are a mess. Why did you stand me up?" Nurse Shanika asked with a slight attitude.

"Damn, ma. Again, my bad. These streets 'bout to drive me crazy."

"Hmmph, so why you won't get out of 'em?"

"That's a whole nother conversation that I'm not prepared to have just yet."

"Just like I said, *you are a mess.*"

"You think you can help me get it together?"

"Probably could," she said with boss confidence. "But I ain't sure it'd be worth it."

"And why you say that?"

"I've done dudes like you before, lil' movers and shakers...got the lil' money over bitches attitude and whatnot. You might come 'round when you wanna escape the streets and just relax, but baby, I need more than an occasional fling with love and that might be more than you're willin' to give."

Shorty had her little spiel together. She was just running that shit on the wrong nigga. So I had to teach her. "First off, ma, you ain't never *done dudes like me before,* because ain't nann' nigga like me. And as far as my finances, hell yeah I put 'em before bitches. But that's something you'll never have to worry about because I don't consider you to be a bitch. You feel me?" I popped at her. "Now let me come through. We can both escape for a few hours. We'll deal with what comes of it when it's time."

The line was quiet for a moment. Shanika sighed, then finally spoke. "Where you want me to meet you at?"

Chapter 31

DENISE

I hung up the phone highly pissed. For the thousandth time I called Bo's phone and I was sent to voicemail. And for what? Just because I got caught stealing and went to jail? Nah, his ass was tripping off some other shit and it wasn't fair. But you know what? *I am not goin' to keep kissing his ass! Here I am, call myself keepin' it real with him; done had his fuckin' baby, done rode with him on his lil' bid, sittin' my stupid ass by the phone waitin' on his fuckin' call, and I done put up with all his cheatin' and havin' a fuckin' baby with that loose-deep bitch KiKi. And what did it get me? His ass to kiss. But fuck him! And fuck this shit.* I thought as I got super-hoe fresh and left the house. If he could twirk something and live his life then so could I.

It was a Tuesday night so I knew that the *off-the-chain* spot was gon' be *CLUB WET WETZ.* So where was I headed? Muthafuckin' *CLUB WET WETZ!* I had on my pussy-pink sheer Dior mini-dress, pink and yellow Barbie doll wig, yellow lipstick, and a yellow thong and bra set to match my pink and yellow Ferragamo heels. Can yall *stunts* say *super-bad-bitch*? If yall can't then just imagine it. I jumped out of my Q45 and handed the valet my keys. The line to get in was long as hell, and I *do not* do lines, so I worked my jelly – chunking ass and swaying hips – past all of those hoes and *wanna-be-ballas'* going second-class and handed the doorman $150 for the velvet rope. My walk was extra nasty and my attitude smelt like spoiled salmon. Everything about me screamed, *suck my pussy and pay me!* Yeah, Bo really had me fucked up.

As I sashayed through the club, my titties and ass bouncing, my pretty lips pouted and my yellow thong showing through my dress, all I heard over Raw-Nitty's *MY BITCH'S PROPER* was niggas yelling *pink and yellow, pink and yellow*. I contracted my neatly arched brows in a show of displeasure and continued slinging my wide ass as hard as I could to the VIP area.

I didn't bother to look around. There was no need to, becaue I was more than sure that everybody in the room, male and/or female was already locked in on me. With a booth to myself I sat down. The little waitress broad didn't waste anytime bringing me a complimentary bottle of bubbles. You know the cute little champagne bottle that look like a skinny 22 oz bottle water? *Exactly*. She brought me one of those and a plastic wine glass. I tossed the glass and drunk it straight from the bottle.

The vibe was nice. My body vibrated with the loud sound system as Tupac's HOW DO YOU WANT IT pumped throughout the club...*so tell me is it cool to fuck / Whatcha think I came to talk / Am I a fool or what...Positions on the floor / It's like erotic / Hypnotic and I'm somewhat psychotic / Hittin' switches on bitches like I've been fixed with hydrolics...My up and down like a roller coaster...*

I closed my eyes and worked my arms and upper body as I swayed to the music in my booth. I loved me some Tupac. Bo was always playing his music when we rode out. *Damn*, I loved me some Bo! And I missed my baby sooo' much. But what could I do besides me? He wanted to leave me and *run the streets with his thugs*. Well, I was gon' run them too.

When I opened my eyes I noticed a handsome brown-skin *trade* surrounded by three tender young sexies. He was definitely balling outta control. His necklace, watch, earrings, bracelet, and rings had more ice in them than the six big silver buckets that held the dozen or so bottles of champagne at his table. The pretty chicks that encircled him at his booth seemed to be catering to his every whim, however playboy couldn't keep his eyes off the prize – me.

Being the boss bitch I was, I coursed my sensuous lips with my tongue, making sure that he saw me, and finished my small bottle of bubbly. Still vibing to the music, of course there was more emphasis on the motion of my big titties, I purposely avoided eye contact with him. *Let his ass sweat*, I told myself. And just like clockwork, the waitress from earlier approached my booth.

"Excuse me, Miss, the dude over there with the ice on," she turned and pointed. "He told me to come over here and take your order for whatever. So, what would you like?"

I looked over at him, he smiled and lifted his glass. Turning back to the waitress I placed my order. "Honey, bring me a six-pack of these." I said, holding up my empty bottle.

"Umm'," she began. "It would be cheaper to just –"

"Honey," I cut her off. "Do I look cheap? No! Okay, exactly." I corrected her ass, moving my freshly manicured hands, which showcased big rocks in my Rolex, rings, and diamond bracelets. "Now go get me what he's payin' for and maybe you'll learn enough tonight to quit yo' tired ass job. Okay?!"

She was young and very cute. In fact, she probably was a bad lil' bitch in her own weight class. Baby wanted to pop fly sooo' bad, but the bitch knew better. She turned and went to get my shit just like I told her to. *Hmph!* I would've drug her little ass in that club.

$$$

Little Ms. Thang came back shortly and placed my buckets on the table. Without even somuch as looking in dude's direction I downed two bottles. Bo really had me fucked up. I mean, I really-really loved his ass! He had no reason to be trying me the way he was. Yeah, I fucked Bert, but so *fuckin' what?!?!* He was probably out fucking some bitch right now, and the nigga had a fucking baby on me; and even more, nobody knew about me fucking Bert. So that was not justification to dog me. Just thinking 'bout the whole fucking ordeal had me vexed as fuck! I downed another bottle just as my jam came on.

...yo / I be buyin' things / So all the girls be eyein' Cease / Waitin' back stage / Dyin' to get please...They watch me / They clock me / Versace and linen / While I'm skinnin' and grinnin' with lots of sexy woman...Why you speed-ball wit' cards...

227

I snatched up a bottle of bubbles and hit the little dance area near my booth. I slightly dropped it and worked my wide hips to the beat. My big titties bouncing in sequence. All eyes were on me as I sipped at my bottle and shook my ass. I never noticed the handsome baller slide up behind me. However, I felt his body press up against my voluptuous ass. I turned and frowned on his ass just as my girl Kim's verse came on.

...yo shorty / Let's go get a bag of the lethal / I'll be waitin' in a bra that all see through / Because all I want to do if freak you...You can keep your stone set / I got my own baguettes / And I'll be doin' thangs that you won't forget...

I rapped along to the lyrics, eyeing this nigga like he was new money. Because to me, he was. Bo was on one of his trips and I wasn't about to keep kissing his ass. No baby...

Shall I proceed / Yes indeed...I'ma through shade if I can't get paid / Blow you up to your girl like an army grenade...You can slide on my ice like an escapade / It's the ichy ichy yaya' with the marmalade...

I rubbed my sex-spot on that note and smiled for the very first time. He was open. So I turned and left his ass right there on the dance floor. *Yes I did,* castigating him and every bitch that was viewing my ass as I walked like a hoe.

After seating myself I popped a bottle and swigged deeply as I caught my breath. It had been a long time since I'd hit the dance floor. When I brought the bottle down from my lips Mr. Handsome was seated beside me, smiling.

"You think you the shit, huh?"

I fanned away a few imaginary flies and drunk my drink.

He laughed and shook his head. Light reflected from his golfball earrings and lit up our area. "You are a real fly chick. What's yo' name?"

"Why do you think you need to know my name?"

"That's usually how people get to know each other."

I rucked my brow. "And why do you think we need to get to know one another?"

He really was handsome. Beneath all of that ice he wore pink tailored slacks, a soft-blue silk button-down, a thick Polo sweater with the pink, yellow, and soft-blue argyle pattern. He topped the get-up with some nasty-ass soft-blue gators. I couldn't front, *he was hurtin' them*.

"This is so new to me," he said, laughing at his self. "Ma, do you know who I am?"

"Let me guess..." I pretended to be thinking, index finger in my mouth and all. "Umm, Keeky B? 'Cause you sho' ain't Young Jeezy."

Before he could respond we were rudely interrupted.

"What's good, Denise?"

I looked up and saw Bert staring down at me.

"Oh, what's good, Bert?"

"You," he replied, looking towards my company. "What's happenin'?"

I turned up my bottle. My company rose and passed me a C-note. His number was on it.

"I'll see you later, Miss Lady." He nodded to Bert and walked back over to his three young freaks.

Bert sat down. I could see that he was light-weight hot with me. He'd been calling me all day, but I'd simply been ignoring his ass. Yeah, he was fine, the dick was *the bomb*, his head was on fire, and he was super-nice at times. But I wanted my Bo back! And if I couldn't have Bo, well, I needed a nigga that was at least on his level; and Bert surely was not on his level. So, Bert was not getting within sniffing distance of this pussy ever again.

Chapter 32

BO

Last night was *off-the-chain!* After picking up Shanika yesterday we really hung out. Shorty has a real sweet personality and some *come-back* pussy. We spent all of yesterday in the streets; Bay Side, the movies, and Artoria's. Then we spent all of last night in between her sheets. She wanted to hit Club WET WETZ, but after sampling that wet-wet she had between those thick thighs of hers, ain't no way I was leaving her crib to hit no club. Like that nigga Biggie said, *no Crytal tonight..we fuckin' tonight.*

I ran through two packs of rubbers on ma. After properly fucking her to sleep I jumped up and cleared it. For whatever reason I just couldn't sleep. Every time I closed my eyes I thought about Denise. *Why the fuck I love that bitch so much?* I keep asking myself. And though Shanika was real cool to be around, I kinda' felt like I was wrong for being with her. Like maybe I was *cheating on Denise.* I just drove around smoking 'dro and listening to Tupac. Eventually I ended up going to my baby-momma KiKi's house. She was happy as fuck to see a nigga, even though it was 4:00 in the morning. We just sat up and talked. Shorty had a few things on her mind. And I gave her my word that I'd help her accomplish her goals.

As I traveled down 27th Avenue leaving KiKi's apartment in the Match Box, my phone started to ring. I checked the caller ID to make sure that it wasn't Denise, because I was not in the mood to hear her bullshit. The screen read *PRIVATE CALLER.* Now, normally I don't answer no shit like that, because hoes be hitting all type of *68 and shit like that.

"What?!"

"Damn, do we always have to go through this?"

A smile crossed my face. "Oh, nah. You know we good, ma. I just ain't know who it was callin' me with all this *private* shit. You feel me?"

"Pssst, boy, you a trip." Shanika said. "If you ain't give so many *stunts* the number you wouldn't have to screen yo' calls."

I laughed. "After the fun we had yesterday and last night, you called me to argue?"

"Nah, I ain't call to fuss yo' slick self out. I was just makin' sure that we was straight..." she paused to arrange her next line. "A female like me woke up to an empty bed and all, the only thing I could think was *damn, the pussy wasn't good to him.*"

"Ma, you a trip." I laughed. "It ain't nothin' like that, ma. You know you got that *come-back.*"

"Oh, well let me know something...you 'round here pullin' disappearin' acts. Normally I have to put a nigga out of my house."

"Girl, you crazy."

"Nah, you ain't seen crazy yet." Shanika said seriously. "You done got my stuff, boy. Now you ain't gon' just be playin' with me."

"I hear you, Miss Boss Lady." I joked and kept laughing.

"Bo, I-am-not playin' with you...Am I gon' see you later?"

"Yeah. Call me before you to go to work."

"Okay."

"Bye."

As soon as I hung up the phone rung back.

"Hello?" I answered, feeling better since talking to Shanika.

"Myniggatheydonekilled him!!!" somebody yelled all in one breath.

"Who the fuck is this?"

The person was crying. They held the phone sniffling for a while before speaking again. "My nigga...they, they done...k-killed him."

"Pressure, this you?"

"Yeah, my nigga..." he continued crying in the phone. "They gunned him down right in front of me, my nigga."

231

A chill ran through my body and my heart started pounding. I just knew that my brother was dead. *Damn I hope he ain't talkin' 'bout Dutch,* I silently prayed.

"P-P-Pressure. Who, my nigga? Who they gunned down?" I asked nervously.

"Red Boy. They killed Red Boy last night, my nigga. They killed him in the blue buildings. I tried to call Dutch, but he ain't answerin'…my nigga, Bo, what we gon' do?" Pressure World said and broke down crying again.

"Where you at?"

"I'm 'round Lottie house."

"Fuck you doin' 'round my sista' crib?"

"My nigga, I had to get from 'round there."

"Well just stay right there. I'ma hit Dutch and we'll be through there."

I hung up sad for Red Boy, because not only was he a soldier he was my muthafuckin' dog. *Damn I'ma miss Red Boy,* I thought as I drove. My jaws were tight, but I didn't cry. I was too mad to cry.

Picking up my phone again, I was about to speed dial Dutch when the phone rung. "Yeah?" I answered without checking the I.D.

"Good morning, Mr. Brown."

"Who is this?"

"Ms. Ward, your lawyer." She said cheerfully.

"Oh, hey Ms. Ward. What's goin' on?"

"I have some great news."

"What's up?"

"Are you busy?"

I really was but I needed to know what she knew, because I knew that it was concerning Angie. "Nah, I ain't on nothin'."

"Great! Meet me at TGK in an hour. And bring $10,000."

"Aiight." I said and hung up.

There was a few dollars in the safe at my house, so I turned the car in that direction. Besides, I really did need to see Denise. Shorty really had my heart. I'd simply run in, grab the money out of the safe, let Denise know that we were going to iron everything out tonight when I got home, and head back out to meet Ms. Ward.

Chapter 33

DENISE

I staggered out of my car with my expensive heels in hand, my see through dress hiked up around my shapely hips, and my hair looking a damn mess. I was so dehydrated that my tongue felt swollen, and my pussy and ass were both burning like somebody had a blow torch flaming over them. *That damn Bert*, I growled inwardly. On a stack of Bibles I'd swore to me, Jesus and God that I was unequivocally through with his cutthroat, extortion for sex ass. Yet I sat my stupid, depressed, weak for some dick ass right there and let him talk me into leaving with him *for breakfast*. I hate myself for that shit. *Oooowww*, and I hate his good-dick-ass even more.

I popped open the front door, dropped my shoes by the door, and damn near ran into the kitchen for something to drink. Popping the top on a half-gallon of orange juice, I took it straight to the head – no glass, straight from the jug. After draining damn near half of it I stopped to catch my breath. My breathing was strange, clear. I felt light headed and tingly. *Damn*, I whispered as a roll of sweat and hot energy ran through my body. Even my aching pussy suddenly cooled and throbbed for attention.

What the fuck is wrong with me? I questioned myself. My intake of air was so cool that it burned my nose. I felt horny...drugged...dopey...turned on...I felt...I felt like I did whenever I was with Bert...Bert!?! *I know this bitch-ass-nigga ain't been slippin' me no fuckin' drugs.* I spun around to go get my phone and dropped the container. Orange juice spilled everywhere.

"Bitch, where the fuck is my money?"

"B-B-Bo, b-bay, where you been?" I squealed in absolute shock. "I been callin' you for two days and you ain't answered yo' phone. I been worry –"

"Denise, save all that shit!" Bo yelled. His eyes were fire-red and anger covered his dark face. "Where the fuck is my money?"

"What money, baby?"

"Bitch, the money I left in the muthafuckin' safe!"

"Oh, the safe money...umm', I umm', had to take care of some things for my momma and my sista'. Plus remember when I went to jail, I had to pay the bondsman...and before that I had went shop—"

"Denise, do I look stupid?" Bo asked, inching closer to me. "You gon' stand here in my muthafuckin' house and lie in my face?"

"Nooo, bay, I ain't lyin'. I just –"

"Shut the fuck up!" he snapped. "Where the fuck you just comin' from? Sellin' pussy."

"Ut'un, Bo." I said, tears running down my face. "You ain't gotta disrespect me like that."

"Disrespect you? Bitch you come in my house 8:00 in the morning, dressed like a fuckin' prostitute, but cryin' 'cause I asked you 'bout sellin' pussy!? You lucky I ain't beatin' yo' funky ass."

I just stood there crying. Bo had never talked to me like this before. I felt nasty and ashamed. My eyes, filled with tears, fell to the floor, unable to stare into Bo's angry face.

"Bo, I'm sorry." I cried. "But I ain't been doin' nothin'."

He reached and lifted my face, now staring into my eyes. "You on dust or somethin'?"

"Nooo. You know I don't use no drugs."

Bo shook his head. "And you stank! Who you been fuckin'?"

I knew he was just trying to pick me, because even though I looked raggedy as hell, I knew I wasn't stank because I'd washed up at the hotel.

"Bo, I swear on my daughter's life, I ain't fuck nobody last night...I ain't fucked nobody but you since I moved here with you...I swear."

He looked like he wanted to punch me, but instead he just shook his head and sort of laughed at me. "Bitch, I can't believe you."

"You ain't gotta keep calling me all them bitches, Bo."

"Whatever, Denise." He turned and headed to the door. "You better have spent that money out the safe wisely. 'Cause you'll see the coming of Jesus before you get some more from me. I promise you that."

"Where you goin'? Why you leavin', Bo? Why you always gotta go?" I yelled, following him to the door.

He turned to face me. "Denise, we through...you can stay here until you get yo'self together, but you gotta go...until then, don't call me for shit. Don't ask me for shit. And don't ask me shit 'bout me, but when can you see Susan."

"Ut'un, Bo, please!" I cried. "Don't go, Bo, please! I'll do anything, Bo! I'll do anyting! Just—don't—don't—leave—me—please!"

He turned and walked off as I fell to the floor crying.

Chapter 34

BO

I was fi' hot when I left the crib. For the very first time in life, well, the first time in our relationship, I seriously started to kick Denise's muthafuckin' ass. Never, I mean never, had I ever felt so disrespected by a bitch. Not only had she gone against *every principle of both love and thuggin'*, the bitch was high. I know the bitch was high because I've known Denise for years and I've never seen her look or act like that. Wondering whether Denise had spent my money on drugs, I pulled up to my mommas house. Her and my daughter were sitting at the kitchen table eating when I came in. After kissing them both and exchanging a few words with the ole-girl, I cracked the safe in my old room and got the money for Ms. Ward. Shortman was in me and Dutch's old bunkbed fast asleep. My momma had gotten him back from child protective services and I was about to get his mother back from the county lock up.

$$$

"Bo!" Angie yelled as she came through the door with Ms. Ward and the bondsman. There was a broad smile on her face and big tears running from her pretty eyes. "Oh, Bo, I missed you sooo much," she whispered, hugging me tightly and kissing all over my face.

"I missed you too, ma." I replied, giving her a deep tongue kiss. "Now let's get outta here. I hate bein' 'round jails."

Angie got in the car with me and we hit the highway. I needed to see Dutch concerning Rome's bitch ass. *I can't believe these fuck niggas killed Red Boy*, I thought as I drove.

"Baby, where we goin'?" Angie asked sweetly from the passenger seat.

"Oh, ummm', to the mall out in Sawgrass. I know you wanna go shoppin'."

"Shoppin'? Boy, if you don't pull this car into a hotel I'ma catch another case." Angie exclaimed, looking at me all sex starved. "I need some of that *thug lovin'* and I need it *right now!* So fuck that mall shit."

"Well, yes ma'am, Miss Boss Lady." I laughed and turned into a Holiday Inn.

I got us a nice little suite on the top floor. It wasn't the Executive or the 'W', but it served our purpose. We made love like lovers do, then we fucked like tomorrow wasn't coming. With each sexual act we expressed appreciation and devotion. I assured her that the future was ours, together...and she allowed me to forget that my dog was dead and my home was a wreck.

Chapter 35

DEWEY

"Listen baby, I'll be home as soon as me and Dewey get through clearin' these niggas out. You know this beef shit is serious and I don't wanna take no chances on no niggas followin' me back to the crib. You hear me?" Rome explained to his main piece as I sat laughing to myself.

Rome was a real funny nigga to me. Always lying to his hoe about *me and Dewey clearin' niggas out*, when me, him, and his hoe knew damn well that he wasn't *clearin' shit out*. Shit was crazy, niggas was getting flipped and I was doing all the flipping. Dell was running the traps.

It had been about a month since they hit our spot and I turned around and killed their man Red Boy. Niggas must've thought I was pussy because I was running with Rome. *How you gon' hit my trap, kill my workers, and push my pack in the same city without even changin' the bags?* That stupid ass nigga either had the heart of a District Attorney or just wanted to die, because he tried *anything*.

"Okay, baby...I love you too," the simple nigga Rome said into the phone and hung up.

"Ay', Rome, my nigga, when you and yo' people havin' pillow talk over that wireless phone, which the crackas don't need a warrant to tap the line, don't be sayin' my muthafuckin' name. I done told you that befo', fam-O." I bassed on the nigga.

"You right, Dewey, my nigga. That's my bad. Wifey just been buggin' the shit outta nigga, you feel me?! She know a nigga out here thuggin' it. You feel me?" Rome finished all animated like his was *based on a true story*.

"Yeah, I feel you, fam-O. But don't you think you'd be trippin' too if yo' people hadn't been home in a damn month?" I popped at him, gauging his emotions. "I'm saying, 'cause seem like you and the new lil' bitch you been shonin' tryna take this shit somewhere else...what's really good, hood?"

Rome sighed and poured his self a double of Henny. After downing the drink he looked over at me, "shorty the real one, Dewey Hound, my nigga...I mean, she get a nigga right and keep a nigga feelin' good. You feel me?!"

Pussy whipped as sucka, I'ma playa, how the fuck I'ma feel yo' love struck ass? I said to myself, but popped to Rome, "It is what it is, fam-O...Just don't lose sight of the yellow brick road, 'cause we on it."

Before the *sucka-for-love* ass nigga could respond his electric dog collar rung.

"Hello?" Rome answered. "Oh, what's up ma? I was just thinkin' 'bout you...Nah, I ain't got shit on my agenda for the nigga...Don't play, lil' momma. You know you ain't gotta ask to swing through...Okay, what time?...Aiight, bring a movie and some carry out from Bistro's...I love you too, bye."

I damn near threw up listening to this *soft-body* ass nigga. *I love you too.* Nigga, you don't even know this bitch, so how the fuck do you *love her too?!* I wanted to ask his ass. I also wanted to know, *how the fuck you end up with money? 'Cause you ain't just pussy, you stupid.* But I held my tongue and played my position.

"You know them lil' twins hit our new spot in the 40's and shot Junk?" Rome moreso stated than asked.

"Yeah, I know."

"So?"

"So what?"

"So whatchu' gon' do?"

"I'ma kill them lil' bitches when I catch 'em. But 'til then, we gon' keep it movin'."

"Well you need to fix yo' *catcher*, 'cause my patience is gettin' thin and I'm losin' money fuckin' with them two lil' muthafuckas. So you had better finish 'em befo' I start lookin' into shit myself."

"Yes, sir, Mr. Rome." I said laughing to myself, 'cause this nigga was too funny to me.

Rome grabbed his Glock .40 and left.

Chapter 36

DENISE

I left from with my new lil friend two-thirds satisfied. His head was *stupid-dumb*, which I absolutely loved the way he sucked my pussy and ate my ass; his money was long as a little black girl's dream, which could run on forever, and I had $13,000 in my Coach overnight bag to prove it. Yeah, I shook this hot pussy on him and teased him with the fi' head. Then I got quiet and cried on him. Naturally he wanted to know what was wrong, and naturally I lied to his ass. I told him that *my man* was getting suspicious about me staying out all night.

"So what the nigga said?"

I wiped at my tears. "He, said…that, that he knew I was out cheatin'…and, and that I had to either stop what I was doin' or get out."

"How he knew you was cheatin'?"

"He, he said…he knew because I don't let him touch me no more…but, baby, I can't help it…after, well after bein' with you I just don't feel him like that no more." I lied and really put on. Tears, shaking, snot and everything.

He pulled me tight to him. "So whatchu' wanna do, ma?"

I looked up into his eyes, still crying, and whispered, "I wanna be with you."

Playboy got beside himself and almost cried with me. But instead, he walked over to a drawer and came back with some money. "Fuck that nigga, ma. This is $13,000. Go find a lil' condo or something. Once you get in it, I'll furnish it and pay it off. But look…"

"What baby?"

"You can't be fuckin' no other nigga! 'Cause I'm sayin', I—"

"Baby," I cut him off with a deep tongue-kiss. Then I put him to bed with some of this *bomb-ass-head*.

$$\$ \$ \$$$

Just like that, I smiled as I drove home. Well, to what was once home. Bo's mean ass had told me that I had to 'get out', so I was making moves 'to get'. Fuck him! His ass was gonna pay for playing me. I promised myself that.

After checking the messages and stripping naked, I pulled out my big black electric dildo. I always had to *re-fuck* myself after fucking Mr. *Two-Thirds Satisfaction*. The one-third that he was missing was *pipe-game*. No, his dick wasn't small. He had a nice eight and a half on him. *He just didn't know how to work the muthafucka!* Or maybe it was me. Or maybe it was that sneaky, no good muthafucka, Bert. Whatever his ass had done to me, sex without him was so depressing. *Bert's ruined me!* I thought as I worked the big dildo in and out of me. It felt sooo' good. My juices were flowing. The big rubber dick was good and greasy with my vaginal secretions. Greasy enough to slip right up in my big loose, juicy ass. *Oooooowwww,* I sceamed as I pushed most of it up inside of my rectum. Working it in and out, I used my other hand to play with my throbbing clit. *Oh, oh, oooh, shiiiiit'!* I screamed as my orgasm exploded. I lay there motionless. Trying to compose myself. Bo crossed my mind. Then Bert...I needed to see my daughter. But to do so I had to speak with Bo. With no reluctance what-so-ever, I sucked my pussy-juices from my fingers, tossed the dildo to the side, and picked up my phone to call Bo.

Chapter 37

BO

Me, my son Lil Bo, my daughter Susan, my ole-girl and Dutch all sat around playing and enjoying the new environment. The crib was right across Countyline and was perfect for its intended purposes. With my mother's signature and a nice down payment I'd purchased the house and had it furnished. It was nice – three bedrooms, two car garage, sunken den, three bathrooms, and a very nice backyard with screened patio. My son and daughter had been running around the patio since they'd arrived.

"Where ole' girl at, Bo?" Dutch asked for the one-thousandth time.

"On her way, yo. She was just gettin' in Broward when you asked me the nine-hundred ninety-ninth time." I shot back.

His crazy ass just looked at me. I don't know why he was stressing. It wasn't the first time we'd sent KiKi up the road and it wouldn't be the last. She'd only taken eight bricks to T-town, so I really didn't see what was bothering him.

"Man, she need to hurry up. I got shit to do," he said, pacing the new carpet.

"Yo, you need to chill befo' you fuck up my new carpet."

Before he could respond my cell phone rang.

"Yeah?...where you at?...Okay, hold up...Yeah, the white house wit' the black trim...hold up, let me open the garage." I told KiKi and went outside. Pointing the remote I hit the garage door for her to pull in.

Me and Dutch met her inside. I gave her a big hug and a kiss. Dutch shot straight to the car and removed the two duffle bags.

"Oh, Dutch." KiKi said. "That money's $49,000 over. Yo' boy wanted two, so I told him to just send the money."

Dutch smiled. "See, Bo, that's what I'm talkin' 'bout. I like lil' momma." Dutch said. "KiKi, you wanna be my sister-in-law?"

"And you know I do." KiKi said, hugging me and placing another kiss on my lips.

"I'ma work on that for you." Dutch said. "But first Bo gotta lil' surprise for you."

"Damn, yo...roxy-ass-nigga."

Dutch laughed and left the garage.

"Whatchu' got for me, baby?" KiKi asked.

"You standin' in it."

KiKi's eyes stretched and her mouth flew open. "Oooh, Bo! For reeal?"

"Girl, you know I don't play games...I promised to get you and Lil Bo outta the projects and I did it. Ain't no big deal, just me keepin' my word."

"Oh, Bo." KiKi said again and damn near stuck her tongue all the way down my throat.

She was happy and rightfully deserved to be. Riding with me and keeping it one-hundred had its rewards when you fucked with real dudes and/or females. The ringing of my phone broke our moment. I didn't recognize the number. And for real, I shouldn't have answered it. But I did.

"Who the fuck is this?" I asked.

"Must you be so rude?"

"Denise?"

"Yes, Denise, yo' baby momma, who ain't heard from you in a month!"

"Hold on." I told her ass and turned to KiKi. "Go and let my momma show you the house. I gotta take this call."

"Okay," KiKi said and kissed me again before walking off.

Once she was out of ear shot I returned to Denise. "How the fuck you got my number?"

"I got it from yo' momma."

"My momma?" I asked knowing damn well I'd told my ole-girl not to give *nobody my new number, especially Denise.*

"Yeah, she gave it to me because she was tired of me blowin' up her phone askin' her to see my muthafuckin' daughter."

"Oh, so now you wanna see Susan?"

"Bo, please. Do-not-play with me. I love my daughter. You the one 'took her from me'…so, when can I see her?"

"I don't know, Denise. I been real busy and –"

"Ut'un, nigga! Whatchu' mean, *you don't know*'? Bo, regardless of whatchu' think about me, that is my daughter, and I have not done anything to deserve this. You left me, *for nothin'*, and that I can't change. But, Bo, baby I love our daughter and I want to see her…okay, please?" Denise whined.

I broke. That shit melted me inside. I loved Denise. But I also knew that we couldn't be together. Too much had happened. Shit that I couldn't understand.

"Look Denise, I'll call you tomorrow. We'll meet and you can get Susan for a few days. But I don't want no bullshit when it's time to –"

"Oh, Bo, thank you. I won't give you no problems. I swear."

"Aiight."

"Thank you!"

"Aiight."

"I love you, Bo." Denise whined.

"Aiight," I repeated and hung up.

$$\$ \$ \$$

While my children played together in the den, me, Dutch, KiKi, and my ole-girl counted the money. Satisfied with what we came to, me and Dutch broke the ole-girl off proper and she left with both of my kids. Dutch then made a few phone calls before putting the rest of the money up in the third bedroom, which was his bedroom. No matter which one of us bought a house, and no matter who we'd bought the house for, the other always had a key and a room.

245

"I'm gone, my nigga. I'ma see you tomorrow." Dutch said, lifting his Scorpion *fully automatic* .223 from the table.

"Where you headed?"

"To Annie crib. She gotta new lil' hoe for me." Dutch stated, laughing.

"Have fun, yo."

"I'll let you know."

When Dutch left I had my own fun. I taught up in that muthafucka! In the living room, in the den, in the kitchen, in all three bedrooms and in two of the bathrooms. I fucked KiKi like she had the last pussy on earth. We ended up on the patio talking as I smoked a blunt.

"Look ma, responsibility comes wit' this crib." I told her point blank.

"I know. I finally got a real home and real chance at life. So tomorrow I'ma get out and find me a real job. I don't care what it is. Then, once I'm workin', I'ma take some night classes at Miami Dade. I know yo' momma or my momma will watch Lil Bo for me."

"All that sounds good. But until things change, I'ma pay all of your bills. So you can just stack yo' checks…and KiKi, you can't bring nobody to this house. Not yo' sista', yo' homegirl, not even yo' momma. You hear me?"

"Yes, I hear you, Bo. And I promise, I will not let you down. You the only person in life that ever really gave me a chance. Even though I had a lil' bad rep' or whatever, you didn't let that stop you from gettin' to know the real me. I love you, Bo. And I'll never let go of you. I don't care how much thuggin' you do. I'ma always love you and be right here when you need me."

KiKi had tears running down her face. I'd only done what was right. What I'd want a nigga to do for Lil Susan if I wasn't around.

"It's all good, ma. You just keep it one-hundred and the sky's the limit."

Chapter 38

DENISE

It had been three long days since I'd talked with my baby-daddy about getting my daughter and his ass just *finally* called me back to meet him and Lil Susan at The Doll House. It was her very favorite place to hang out. Sort of like Chuck-E-Cheese only one-hundred times better.

I was filled with excitement as I drove. Seeing my man and my daughter was exactly what I needed. Especially seeing his ass! I had a sho'nuff trick for him. Since he wanted to be tough and play games, I had a few *tough games* I was about to play for him.

I jumped out of the cream Grand Cherokee Sport, yess, the fully loaded demo that my *new lil' friend* had rented me. I was looking a *hot mess*! Rocking the pants to my Familiar Line sweatsuit, they were lime-green, two sizes too small and all up in my pussy and ass, because I ain't had on no drawers. Yes, ass just jiggling and pussy breathing as I walked. I also had on my red and white Cavi skull studded baby-T. My big titties bouncing and turning all eyes. No make up, just some Mac lip gloss and my hair pulled back in a simple ponytail. I wanted to look sexy, but also used and in need. So I had on my low top Ice cream Keds. Besides, I supported real niggas. And in my book Dame Dash was a real nigga. So even though them Keds was *ugly as fuck!* I made it my business to cop like two pair every month or so to grocery shop or clean up in. *Nothin' heavy.*

"Mmmmaaaaaa, Ma!" Susan yelled and took off running to me.

I snatched her up in my arms and spun her around. My little girl! She was getting big and heavy. So I sat down with her

247

and talked girl talk. I could see Bo eyeing the hell outta me, because I know I was fine as hell and that he missed my body. Plus, I didn't so much as look in his direction. *Mr. Wanna Be Tough*, I acted like his ass wasn't even there. I'd told that nigga that *I loved him* during our last two conversations and he didn't have the damn decency to say it back. Well, I had a trick for his ass...*use Denise, you'll lose Denise*. I swore by that.

All the while me and my daughter laughed and ran back and forth to the different games and food counters, Bo just sat there looking at us. I knew Bo like nobody else. He was stressing. And I believe that it had *something to do with us,* but there was also other things eating at him. Deep in side, I kinda' felt sorry for him. He was too much to too many people. Too kind hearted. Never able to settle and enjoy himself. *Damn, I love you, Bo!* I wanted to yell and hug him. To comfort him and make love to him until all of his stress disappeared. But I couldn't...because Bo didn't want me anymore.

Finally after being there for almost three hours, Susan had played me out. I was too tired and wanted to sit down, but she wanted to play in the ballroom.

"That's it, baby. Momma tired." I said.

She just made her little mean face, looking just like Bo and said, "Well, I'm goin' by myself." And that's just what she did.

I just laughed at her little mean butt and drunk some of my cherry soda. She was a real mess. And some little boy, in about twelve years, was gonna have his hands full.

Playing with Susan had me tired. I stretched my body and turned to find Bo staring at me.

"What's up?" I finally spoke to him.

"Man, what is you doin', yo?" he asked me, shaking his head.

"Whatchu' mean?" I responded, playing the nut role.

He laughed at me. "Yo' clothes. Yo' hair. Who truck is you drivin', and where you get them ugly ass shoes from?"

Got his ass! I thought before lowering my head to avoid his eyes. "Shit been rough, Bo. I don't wanna go out stealin' and shit...that's what got us all in the mix right now. So, I'm just tryna get by."

"You still ain't said who truck that is."

"Oh, umm', that's...that's my friend's truck."

"Yo' friend?!" Bo damn near shouted.

Got his muthafuckin' ass! I thought and looked up in time to witness his shocked expression. "Yeah, my friend. It ain't nothin' real serious. He just help me out a lil' bit and I didn't wanna disrespect you by havin' him in the car you bought me." I lied my ass off and watched him *eat it up.*

"So who is the nigga?" he asked, trying to mask the anger in his words.

I could see that he was fucked up. I could also see that he wanted to know more than my friend's name. *You fuckin' the nigga? You sucked his dick? He got bread? You love the nigga?* Bo wanted to ask all of that and more. Yet his pride wouldn't let him. I played on that.

"He ain't nobody. Just a lil' dude outta Carol City." I understated. "I told him that you wanted me outta yo' crib and all...and well, he wanna help me but he ain't got it like that. So, umm', if you could let me hold somethin' until I get a job, I swear, we'll pay you back."

Bo had fire in his eyes. "Denise, how could you be so stupid?"

"Whatchu' mean?" I whined, faking like I was on the verge of tears. Or was I really faking? Who was I fooling? I loved Bo and that nigga knew it! So yeah, I had real tears in my eyes.

He just shook his head sadly. "Look Denise," he said and reached in his pocked. "I'm doin' this for Susan. You my baby-momma and no matter who you with, you reflect me. People ain't gon' be sayin' *look at dude girl or Denise look a mess.* Nah, they gon' be sayin' *look at Bo baby-momma, he need to be ashame of his self.* That's what they gon' say."

He passed me a nice lil' wad. It was probably 'bout three-four stacks.

"Thank you, Bo. And I promise –"

"Denise, save that shit. 'Cause I don't wanna hear it. Take that bread and do whatchu' gotta do...I'll give you some more when I pick up Susan...and Denise, if I find out you givin' a nigga my money!"

"Bo, please! Do it look like I can afford to give a nigga anything? Please, I am not *that stupid*, okay."

"Well, I'm just tellin' yo' ass. Be—" his phone rung, interrupting his little tirade.

"Yeah?" he answered and my nosey ass listened. "I'm at The Doll House…What?!…You sure it's Rome?…Yeah, follow his bitch ass and keep me posted!…Yeah, I'm 'bout to hit Dutch now…You positive it's Rome, though?…Aiight, we on our way…" Bo said and started to rise.

"Bo, umm', what's wrong?"

Bo had death in his eyes. "Business. Nothin' for you to worry 'bout," he tossed two one hundred dollar bills on the table for our tab. "I gotta go. Tell Susan I'll see her in three days. She has my number, she can call me."

"Okay, but Bo…wait for a minute. Umm', I heard you say 'Rome'. What Rome are you talkin' 'bout?"

Bo looked at me crazy. "Brown skin, tall nigga outta Carol City. Why, you fuckin' the nigga?"

"Psstt'!" I sucked my teeth. "You really got me fucked up. You'll just say anything out of yo' mouth."

"Whatever Denise. I'm gone," he said and jogged off to his car.

I really got his muthafuckin' ass now! I thought. Him and Rome, my Rome, my *new lil' friend*, had major issues, huh? Well, I knew what to do. I knew exactly what to do! *Mr. Wanna Be Tough* gon' play me and call me stupid. Well, we'll see who's stupid when I'm finished with his ass, I thought and went to go get Susan outta the ball room. Momma had a cake to bake.

Chapter 39

DEWEY

"Bitch! You want me to knock yo' fuckin' front teeth out?" I asked the stupid yellow bitch that had her face buried in my crotch as I pushed my cocaine-white big body Cadillac bubble. I had fresh 20" Mirrors and low boys on that bitch, limo tints and all white leather interior.

"Ut'un, Daddy, nooo'. Don't knock my teeth out," she whined, holding my dick as she spoke.

"Well you better keep yo' fuckin' teeth off my shit." I dictated. "Matter fact, get up and get in the back. Let Black eat some of this dick."

Yellow-bone climbed her big wide ass across the seat. She was thick as fuck! Had big ass titties, a second chin, a lil' gut, and some cellulite. But she was pretty as hell and that ass was on donk! Bitch was perfect to me, except for the fact that she was stupid as hell and popped pills.

Now Black, on the other hand, was ugly as that nigga Flavor Flav. Nappy-bald headed lil' bitch. But boy, her body was boss perfect – 5'3", 117 pounds, with measurements 30, 24, 38. I coulda ate the hoe alive. Only she was a pill animal just like Yellow-bone. I caught the two hoes outside of Tic-4-Tac on 95th Street and 17th Avenue. Just out making my rounds and ran into them hoes. I ain't even had to say shit. My Caddy Bubble did all the speaking. They jumped in and got ass naked. We'd been riding every since.

Black's head was smooth as the Cadillac's ride. Which was a $8,000 gift from Rome for killing Red Boy. He gave me $30,000 to snatch one off the lot, but I went to my man Bobby from down south and got the bitch flipped for eight stacks, rims and all. Bobby was a beast with that plating shit.

"Dewey, can I have another pill, pleeaasseee?" Yellow-bone begged from the back seat.

My phone rung before I could answer.

"State yo' business, gangsta." I called into the phone. "What?! Where you at?...I'm 'bout five minutes from you...yeah, I'm in the 'Lac...You in the blue Suburban?...Aiight, brang 'em down 183rd into the Flea Market parking lot...yeah! But you sho' they followin' you?...aiight, and it ain't the police?...aiight, brang 'em through, I got 'em!" I hung up with Rome's ultra-scary ass and stopped the car. "Yall hoes get out."

"What? Whatchu' mean, Hound? What happened, Daddy?" Black's ugly ass asked, still holding my big dick.

I snatched my dick outta her hand and zipped up my pants. "I said, *get the fuck out!* Is yall hoes deaf and dumb?"

The two hoes mean-mugged me and started getting dressed.

"Nah, hoes! Do that out there!" I snapped, reaching over Black and popping the passenger door open. "Get yall nasty asses out!"

Black sucked her pretty even teeth and got out half naked. Big sexy Yellow-bone followed suit, only she was completely naked. I went in my pocket and peeled off $300. I also pulled out the pill sac. I chewed three blue dolphins and tossed the sac to Black, along with the $300. They both smiled, but I sped off before they could express their jive ass appreciation.

As soon as I entered the Flea Market's parking lot, I snatched up the rear seat cushion and pulled out my AK-47. Then I circled the lot. Over near McDonalds I saw Rome's Suburban come in. And sho'nuff, a brown Lincoln was hot on his ass. The windows were tinted. Still I was able to peep two heads inside, one driving and the other in the back seat. Rome had called exact money. Those wasn't no police, them was some niggas tryna kill his ass.

At an easy pace I crossed the lot. Yet before I could make the scene, a big gun went off. Yyyyyyyyaaaaaaaaaakkkkkkkkkkk!!! that big muthafucka sounded. The nigga had to have let off 'bout 70 rounds. All of them went into the Suburban, causing Rome to

252

crash into a row of parked cars. I punched it as I noticed the shooter jump out flipping his clip.

I sped up and jumped, *Yak! Yak! Yak! Yak! Yak!* Dude dove for cover between the Suburban and a wrecked car. As I advanced on him another gun exploded. *Boom! Boom! Boom! Boom! Boom!* I spun around to the driver, who was shooting at me. *Yak! Yak! Yak! Yak! Yak! Yak! Yak! Yak! Yak! Yak!* I let off, bringing down the windows and peppering the hood of the car. *Yyyyyyyyaaaaaaaaaakkkkkkkkkk!!!* The shooter turned and ran around towards the fleeing Lincoln. I ran over to the Suburban. Snatching the door open I saw Rome cowering on the floor board, his .40 Glock in hand. Dell was on the passenger side, *dead as a muthafucka.* It was also a dead bitch on the back seat.

"Come on," I yelled and pulled Rome out. "Go to the Lac and lay down."

I took off my Polo jacket and wiped the door handle, the door panel, the steering wheel, the console and the ignition. The keys I snatched out.

When I got back to my Caddy Rome was sitting there shaking like a stripper, gun still in hand. I put it in gear and smashed off...

Chapter 40

BO

"Fuck!" I yelled as I dove onto the Lincoln's back seat. "Drive! Get the fuck, yo!"

The car zoomed from the parking lot. I looked back to see Dewey's bitch-ass helping Rome outta the car.

"Fuck!" I yelled again. "I almost had his bitch-ass!"

I'd never been so mad in my life. I was so fucking close to ending this shit. I turned on my phone to try Dutch again. We needed a change up.

"Damn, bruh-bruh, I see you been callin' the shit outta me." Dutch spoke into the phone, all happy-go-lucky and shit. "What's good?"

"Nothin', man, where the fuck you at?" I snapped, 'cause if he woulda answered his phone earlier Rome woulda been dead.

"I'm over at Annie crib. What's the muthafuckin' problem, my nigga?"

"Look, I'm on one. Shit went crazy and I need a change up."

"What? Man, is you crazy?" Dutch asked.

"Man, you comin' or what, yo?"

"Where you at?"

"Comin' up 32nd, 'bout to hit Countyline."

"Meet me at the Sports Authority, my nigga."

Broward be on that bullshit! So I wiped down the *stick* and threw it out the window. The gloves and mask I put in my pocket to be burned later. A nigga can't just be tossing shit that held DNA.

"Go to the Sports Authority." I told my driver.

"Okay."

"And gimme that gun."

Angie looked at me through the rear view mirror and passed me the Glock .40. I wiped it down and threw it out of the window also. My nose flared and my eyes were blood shot red. I was mad at myself for missing, but I was super-hot with Dutch for not being there.

"You aiight, baby?" Angie asked as she drove.

"Yeah, thanks to you...you saved my life back there, ma."

"That's what I'm here for, Bo. I'm not just a pretty bitch out to get yo' money. I'ma rider, Bo. I'll do whatever for you," she proclaimed. "Besides, you been saved my life."

"And how I did that?"

"By schoolin' me. By takin' me outta the projects. By just bein' there for me and drivin' me to want more outta life."

"You deserve even more, ma." I said sincerely.

"Then why won't you give it to me?" Angie asked, eyeing me in the mirror. "You know I'll do anything for you. I've proved myself time and again, Bo."

"So whatchu' want, Angie?"

"I wanna have yo' baby and wake up with you every morning for the rest of my life. I want you, me, Lil Susan, Shortman, Lil Bo, and our new baby to be a real family. A family like you've always talked about."

"Aiight, it's done." I simply stated.

"You mean it, Bo?" Excitement filled Angie's question.

"Yeah, 'cause you right. You played yo' position and now it's time that I reward you for yo' work."

"So what about Denise?"

"Ain't no Denise. We over. Now it's yo' turn to live in my devotion."

"Thank you, Bo! I'll never let you down."

I didn't comment on that because what was known didn't really need to be spoke on. Angie spotted Dutch just as I did. He was standing beside a silver Lexus. She parked next to it and we all jumped in the Lexus and cleared it.

"So what happened, my nigga?" Dutch asked as he drove.

255

I explained everything form meeting Denise with Lil Susan, to getting the call from Angie, to not being able to contact him, and finally the whole shoot out at the Flea Market.

"Damn, Bo, my nigga, I'm sorry." Dutch said.

"It's all good."

"And Angie, my nigga, thank you for holdin' my brutha' down. You just got yo' G-pass from me, and I don't give hoes G-passes. You the real one, and I'm on yo' team from here on. If you need anything, just holla at me…you hear me?"

"Yeah, it's all good." Angie answered, tryna sound like me.

"Bo, my nigga, that's two number one draft picks in a row. I take my hat off to you, my nigga."

"Two?" Angie asked, staring at me.

"Dutch, you roxy-as-fuck, yo!"

We all bust out laughing at his crazy ass.

Chapter 41

DENISE

I was Dooney and Bourke'n it, off the Vachetta Mazatlan and Juicy Couture. Walking like I had never in life took a shit and my pussy didn't bleed once a month. Yes, I was feeling me and I wanted the entire globe to know it.

Lil Susan was with me and she was sooo' cute in her Baby Phat outfit with the little baby heels. For whatever reason, Red Lobster was her favorite place to eat. So I decided to meet Bert's nasty ass there for lunch. He'd been blowing my phone up non-stop! Leaving me all kinda' fucked up messages and threats like he was fucking losing his rabbit ass mind. But I'd had enough. I knew Bert like the days of the week. So I was about to fix his ass once and for all, and end all the bullshit.

"Damn, what's up, pretty ladies?" Bert greeted us as we neared the table that he occupied.

"Hey!" Susan greeted.

"What's up, Bert?" I said dryly.

The waiter came over and took our orders. We had the Alaskan snow crab legs, lobster, shrimp and steak. Bert and I both had extra large daiquiris with quadruple shots of 1800. Susan had a virgin. We ate and drank in silence. I watched his ass good too. He wasn't about to slip shit in my food or drink. Not this time. I had his muthafuckin' number. *Damn rapist!* I thought as I eyed him. I could easily see that something was on his mind. Yet he couldn't get it off with Susan sitting there. She quickly fixed that.

"Momma, can I go look at the funny fish in the tank over there?"

"Yes, go ahead. But don't touch the tank."

"Okay," she replied sweetly and ran off.

I sipped the last of my daiquiri. Bert broke the silence.

"Who truck?"

"Mine."

"Where you got it from?"

"Why?"

"Look Denise, don't play with me!" Bert tried to bass. "I been callin' yo' ass and you been duckin' me."

"Bert, honey," I said with a noticeable smirk on my face. "I do not have to duck you. I don't owe you shit, and you ain't my man...sssooo'."

"Okay, smart ass bitch. I'ma give Bo and Dutch the tape, stupid bitch!" Bert laughed. "I know you ain't think I gave you the only copy?"

I gave Bert a fake applause and laughed at his dumb ass. "I don't think Bo or Dutch cares to hear yo' lil' blackmail tape. Especially since I'm no longer *doin'* Bo. Maybe you should try passin' it to Rome, my new man. But, I don't think he'd give a fuck. Especially since it was *wwaaayyyy* befo' his time...sssssoooo, Mr. Blackmale artist, anymore bright fuckin' ideas? Huh? Would you like for me to order another drink so you can try to drug me with some more pills. Huh?" I pushed his fucking buttons.

"Bitch! Bitch, I ain't gotta drug no *loose-deep* bitch like you! Fuck-ass-bitch!" Bert yelled, his eyes red and his face trembling.

"No, yous a bitch, bitch! Fuck you! Fuck you, bitch-ass low-life nigga! Yous a lil' su—"

Whop! The straight right damn near blinded me. All I saw was black and blue flashes and my eye stung like hell! I had expected to get hit, but not in my muthafuckin' eye.

"Mmmmmaaaaa!" I heard Lil Susan yell.

I got yo' ass, Bert! I thought and laughed inside. Yet in reality I grabbed my eye and cussed Bert the fuck out.

"You got that, soft-ass-nigga! But you'll never fuck me again, hit me again, or see me again, broke-ass-nigga!"

I grabbed Susan's hand, still holding my eye, and stormed outta the restaurant. My head was killing me as I drove off. Susan was crying her little eyes out.

"Don't cry baby."

She continued to cry.

I drove her to her grandmother's house, Bo's mother.

"Susan, look at me…don't tell yo' daddy, okay?"

She nodded her head up and down. Of course, I knew better. Bo had her trained. They kept no secrets.

"I love you," I sang.

"I love you too," she said and got out of the SUV.

$$$

After dropping my daughter off I drove around for a minute. My eye was killing me. I looked at it in the mirror and cried. My fucking eye was black and purple, and it was completely swollen shut. *Thank you so much, bitch. 'Cause I got yo' no good ass now,* I said to myself, placing my $300 Nadia Terrell *stuna-shades* on. I called Rome.

"Hello?" he answered.

"I need to see you, baby…I, I need –" terrible sobs rocked me, cutting off my words.

"Denise. Denise! What's wrong?" Rome asked with much concern in his voice.

"I, I need to, to see you, baby." I cried.

"Where you at? What's wrong?"

"I'm on the expressway."

"Well, come to the Miami Lakes apartment. Come right now."

"Okay, baby. I'm, I'm on my way."

I hung up and laughed. I shoulda' been an actress. *Denise,* the black Erica Cane. My fat, good pussy got wet at the thought. I was about to pay *everybody back.* After today, I'd have no more drama, like my girl Mary J.

$$$

Rome buzzed me into the main building and I ran up to the apartment. Conveniently my big sad tears were back in place. Rome swung the door open as I ran up the hall and into his arms. He held me. Slowly rocking me and caressing my back.

"Easy, lil' momma, easy." Rome said, pulling me inside of the apartment. "What's wrong, Denise? Tell me, what happened."

I cried uncontrollably. I rocked and I snotted. Rome continued to console me.

"Come on, ma. You drivin' me crazy. What's wrong?"

I didn't bother to say shit. I just took off my shades.

Rome's eyes fluttered quickly before bucking wide ass open. "What the fuck happened to yo' eye?"

"M-m-my, my ba-baby daddy hit me." I stuttered and fell out crying again.

"For what?" Rome held me. "Why the fuck he blacked yo' eye?"

I cried hard for at least ten minutes before I spoke again. *Fakin' good!* I don't know where all of those tears came from, yet I'm glad I had them. Maybe it was all of the frustration and disappointment in life finally coming to one big head.

"Listen, Denise. You gotta talk to me." Rome raised my head to look into his sincere eyes. "Why did he hit you?"

"B-b-be-ca-cau-because of you." I stuttered, lying my ass off.

"What?" Rome asked in shock.

"I told him t-tha-that I was le-leavin' him for you...t-th-that-that I didn't wanna be with him no more. A-an-and he just snapped." I sobbed hard at this point. "He puched me and st-sta-started yellin' *fuck Rome* and callin' me all kinda' nasty names."

"Damn, ma...we gon' fix this. Who's the nigga?"

Before I could fix my tongue to lie again my cell phone rung. It was Bo and he was *right on time*. I turned the volume up before answering it.

"Hello?" I answered, tears and pain in my voice.

"Denise, where the fuck you at?" Bo yelled into the phone.

"With my friend. Why, what's wrong with you?"

"You know what the fuck is wrong with me!"

"Look, not right now, please."

"Denise, you got twenty fuckin' minutes to get yo' ass over here!"

"Please, Bo, no –"

"Twenty fuckin' minutes!" he yelled.

"Okay, where are you?"

He told me and hung up.

Rome was fi' hot! "Who the fuck was that?"

"My-my b-ba-baby daddy."

"The nigga that hit you and said *fuck me*?"

I nodded my head yeah.

"What he want?"

"He wanna talk to me."

"Good, 'cause I wanna holla at him."

"No!" I hugged Rome. "No, please. Let me handle this, please…because he's crazy."

"Crazy? Denise, do you know who I am?"

I didn't answer that question. Instead I said, "Please Rome, let me handle this. I'm just gonna go talk to him. Then I'ma file a restrainin' order. So we ain't gonna have to worry 'bout this no more." I rubbed his chest as I spoke.

"Aiight, but who is the nigga?"

"Bo."

Rome's eyes fluttered and bucked wide ass open again. He looked like he's seen a ghost. "W-wh-what Bo? T-h-the-t-twin, Bo?"

I nodded my head up and down slowly. "What, you know him?" I asked as if I didn't already know.

"N-na-nah, I don't know, fool. I j-ju-just heard the name before." Rome lied.

And I knew right then and there that *I had his muthafuckin' ass! I had them all!*

"Well look, baby." I whispered innocently. "I'ma go meet him."

"Where?" Rome asked anxiously.

"At Foxy Ladies on 79th Street and 18th Avenue. Why?"

"Because, I need to know where you at. Just in case."

"You so sweet, baby." I sang, smiling for the first time. "But you gotta promise not to come up there, Rome."

261

"I'm not."

"I mean it, Rome." I said with authority.

"I said, aiight!" Rome bassed back with more authority.

"Okay, well, give me yo' gun." I said, holding my hand out.

"My gun?"

"Yeah, yo' gun." I repeated.

"For what?"

"So I'll know that you're not comin' up there. Because you don't go anywhere without yo' gun."

Rome stared at me real hard before handing over the all black Glock .40. He was surprised when I checked it to make sure that one was in the chamber. I smiled. Bo had a million of these guns.

Kissing Rome deeply, I rubbed his face and left.

Chapter 42

BO

I sat up in Big Mac's, Foxy Ladies to the suckas and lames, fi' ass hot! I'd never been a drinker, yet I drunk four straight doubles of E&J as I replayed my daughter's phone call in my head.

"Da-da-daddy. A man beat my momma up." Lil Susan had cried to me.

"Where yo' momma?"

"She gone."

I hung up and called her funky ass, and the bitch had the nerve to play dumb. The liquor and loud music was fucking with me, so I tucked my 9mm and walked outside to smoke a joint. Denise was one dumb bitch! And that nigga was dead, whoever he was. Not because he had hit *Denise,* but because he'd hit *Bo's baby-momma in front of Bo's baby girl.* Yeah, his ass was baked chicken, *whoever he was.*

I sparked up a blunt of 'dro and just thought. I looked up into the heavens and wondered was it really a God. And if so, did He really fuck with *thug niggas?* Because life was really hell for a nigga. Here I was, a nigga that ain't never really had shit, doing his best to see that my people was straight. Yet every turn I made it was an obstacle there to throw a nigga off...*bad dope...a crooked cop...a jealous ass nigga...a hatin' ass hoe...a cutthroat ass nigga tryna take mine...the wrong hoe in my life...a fake ass friend...the loss of one of my dogs...*I almost cried. Instead I prayed. It was something I'd read in a novel by Anthony Field, *God help me through the night...and protect me from my friends, I can handle my enemies...*

Just as the prayer left my mind, and hopefully reached God's ears, Denise's trifling ass rolled up. She jumped out of the

263

Cherokee and sashayed over to me. *Damn!* She looked so good. I really missed her.

"Look Bo, I don't know –"

"Shut up, Denise! Because I'm really gettin' tired of yo' bullshit." I spassed on her.

"Bo, I ain't did nothin'!" she snapped back.

"You gotta nigga beatin' yo' ass in front of Susan?" I stated more so than asked. "Yeah, Susan told me."

"Look, Bo, it really wasn't nothin'."

"Bitch is you crazy? Take them ugly ass glasses off!" I demanded.

Denise dropped her head and tried to walk off, but I grabbed her arm, spinning her. Her back was now to the club, facing the parking lot. I stood directly in front of her, my back to the parking lot...

"Denise, I ain't gon' tell yo' ass no more, take 'em off!"

Denise broke down crying as she removed the glasses.

"Damn!" I winced at the sight of her swollen eye. I mean, her shit was closed! My blood boiled. "Who did it?"

"Bo, I'ma get a restrainin' order, okay. Please, just let it –"

"Bitch, shut up! I don't wanna hear shit but who did it!"

She stood there looking crazy before finally coming clean. "Bert."

"Who?"

"Bert."

"You fuckin' Bert again?" I asked, not believing what I was hearing.

"No!"

"Then why he hit you?"

"I was at the spot with my new dude," she started out. "And Bert just walked up trippin'. Feelin' all on me and shit. I told him to *leave me the fuck alone*, and told him I was with dude. Then, when he seen my dude he really started gookin'. Callin' me all type of bitches and sayin' how I keep *messin' with soft ass Carol City niggas instead of him.* He said, *first you let that bitch ass nigga Bo get you pregnant, now you fuckin' this lame ass nigga*...he was just snappin'. So I said, *nigga fuck you! You just*

264

jealous of Bo, bitch! And he punched me in my eye." Denise was crying me a river.

I was madder than I'd ever been. "Where he be?" I asked her.

"Umm, over at that lil store by the alley on 32nd Avenue and like 81st or 85th. You know, over by Madison."

I pulled out my phone. "What he had on?"

"A red, white and blue Tommy set."

"Hello?...yeah, Pressure, I need you. Where you at?...Good, pick up Cliff, Terry and two AK's...yeah, and go to that lil' store by Madison...yeah, the one by the alley...aiight, when you get there, look for Bert...yeah, that Bert. I want him dead! I want that nigga dead tonight! You hear me?...aiight, call me when it's done. I got twenty stacks for you. Dog 'im! Close casket, yo...aiight, one." I hung up and could've swore I saw that bitch smiling. But that wasn't the case. She was crying.

Chapter 43

DENISE

Yes! Hell yeah! I thought as Bo gave the orders to have Bert's bitch ass killed. Lil Susan's *roxy-ass* had done just what I wanted her to do, *tell her daddy that a nigga had hit me.* I knew that she would. Just like I knew how he'd react. That's why I'd taken her little big mouth ass in the first place. Now everythin' was in motion. *One nigga down and one to go,* I thought as the black Impala crept by for the second time. Then it stopped. The door opened. A hooded figure emerged.

Bo, with his back turned to the car, re-lit his blunt and hit it hard. "Look, Denise, you got me in a real fucked up spot...whatcha' nigga did when Bert popped yo' ass?"

"Ran!"

"Ran? What type of fuck-ass-niggas you fuckin' with? The nig---"

"Bo!" I yelled, "Look out!"

Bo spun around and the hooded figure froze. I squeezed off. *Boom! Boom! Boom! Boom! Boom! Boom!* My shots levitated his ass, up and into the asphault.

Then *Boom! Boom! Boom! Boom!* A deep burning pierced my side. The force drove me into Bo, sending us both to the ground. Bo fired, *Tat! Tat! Tat! Tat! Tat! Tat! Tat!* I turned my head in time to see a skinny red dude spin and grab his stomach. *Tat! Tat! Tat! Tat! Tat! Tat! Tat!* Bo continued firing. The dude dove and returned fire, *Boom! Boom! Boom! Boom! Boom!* I felt another hot sensation numb my body. Bo rolled from under me and yelled for someone to call an ambulance. My plan had been perfect. Rome was dead. Now Bo didn't have to worry about him anymore. But what about me? Was I gonna die? I didn't want to.

266

I only wanted to be his shero'…I only wanted my Bo back. Who was the red dude with the big red beard? Where did he come from? Why did he spoil my plan?

I saw Bo. He was teary eyed. He was sad. He was holding my hand and kissing my face. I wanted to kiss him back. *Hold me, Bo, I'm cold,* I wanted to say.

"Hold on, Denise! Hold on, ma! I need you to hold on for me and Susan. We need you, ma…just hold on, please!"

I wanna hold on! I wanna be with you, baby! I love you, Bo! I – love – you! I thought but couldn't say. Something was strangling my voice…my breath…then my vision. *Oh God, please! Don't let me die tonight!* I pleaded and pleaded with God.

I heard Bo's phone ring. "Hello?" I heard him answer and then say, "you sho' he dead?...aiight, good. Pick up yo' money tomorrow, I'm busy."

He hung up with Bert's killers and I blacked out thinking, *what a tangled web we weave…*

Chapter 44

BO

Denise went into surgery that night. She stayed under for six hours. Three bullets had hit her. Two entered her side and one hit her in the back. Fortunately, they were able to remove all three projectiles. Unfortunately, the one that they'd removed from her back left her paralyzed from the waist down. I was crushed! Because it was my fault. *All my muthafuckin' fault!* I sat outside the hospital in my car that night and smoked blunt after blunt. I wanted to smoke myself to death. But I couldn't. I had to be there for Denise. If it wasn't for her Rome would've killed me. But no, Denise took three bullets that were meant for me…

$$\$\$\$$$

When I walked into her hospital room the next morning I like to have broke down crying. Denise was strapped down on this big circular bed that constantly rotated. Tubes and different wires were running from every part of her body. She looked terrible.

Her eyes slowly opened as I approached her bedside. Stains of dried tears covered her face. And before I could sit down and whisper my apologies Denised looked at me and hissed, "get out!"

"But wait, ma. Let me –"

"Go!...it's…you…fault…I…hate…you!" Denise managed through labored breaths.

My tears fell. "I'm sorry, ma. I swear. I'ma kill everybody that I thank had somethin' to do with this."

"That…won't…help…me…walk…again."

New tears appeared and ran down her face.

I fell down on one knee and tried my damnest to kiss them all away.

"Look Denise, I'll do anythin'. I'll do whatever you need me to do to get 'us' through this. Whatever! You just say the word and it's done."

"Marry...me...never...leave...me...Bo...please...I'm...so ...sc-scar...scared..."

Still down on one knee I kissed her forehead...her eye lids, both, one at a time...her nose...then her lips.

"It's done, ma. You set the date." I said and fell back in the chair. Our lives were officially ruined. Mine, hers, KiKi's, and Angie's. And it was all my fault...Thuggin' and running the streets. You can't do that shit and have a family. 'Cause it ain't no love when you're thuggin'...

$$\$\$\$$$

The days that followed were brutal! I rode day and night, six times a day! And I rode with no remorse. My conscious was blood thirsty and my Choppa was heartless. I crippled, paralyzed and killed. Yet I felt no better. Still I could not stop. I did dirt, never coming home or visiting KiKi and Angie. I couldn't face any of them after I'd let them all down...my promise, my word had been broken. Something which had never happened before.

Still unable to catch Dewey I went home the day before my wedding. Denise was so excited to see me. I hugged her and kissed her. She was like a little child. My ole-girl, a live-in housekeeper, and Lil Susan had moved in with us. It was home, but I wasn't happy.

$$\$\$\$$$

I came up the aisle to teary sad faces and hard stares. Angie and Shortman held hands and cried openly. KiKi held Lil Bo in her

269

arms, a faint smile on her sad face. She was trying to be strong like I'd taught her, but I could see that she was mad and hurt.

The music played and the people watched. Denise smiled brightly from her wheelchair. It was her big day. The preacher read the vows. Tears fell from everyone's eyes as Denise screamed *"I do!"* Then it was my turn. I looked out at the crowd, expecting somebody to speak up…to say something…*to save me.* It was then that I noticed my brother Dutch wasn't there. He hated Denise! His absence made me mad to a degree. *"I do,"* I finally said.

"Does anyone here have any reason why this coulple shouldn't wed?" the preacher asked.

Then it happened. "Federal Agents! Everybody step aside! Mr. Brown! Mr. Brown! Hands where we can see 'em! People, step aside!" the twenty or so agents seemed to all be screaming at once, guns drawn. Denise screamed as they forced me to the floor and cuffed me.

"Man, what yall doin'? I ain't did shit!" I protested.

KiKi put Lil Bo down and rushed to help me, but agents quickly subdued her. Angie didn't move. She just watched, tears streaming her face.

"Man, cracka, let her go! Get off her!" I yelled, tryna free myself in order to help KiKi.

"Pipe down, Mr. Brown…you have enough problems. You're under arrest for felony murder. You have the right to remain silent. Anything you say may be held against you in the court of law…"

"Save the speech, cracka! I know what it is…I've been thuggin' for years."

A Grown Man's Realization

[Poem by Billy 'Dollar Bill' Richardson]

As I grew from a youngn' into a grown man my fascination matured, I began respecting a female's intuition and understood her suspicious mind. I realized that there's nothing better than a female that has evolved into a woman of strong characteristics...

As a grown man I'm more fascinated with a woman's spirituality. I realize that any woman of substance has built her foundation on concrete principles. Respect is her platform. Trust is a must! Loyalty is her shield. Integrity is her sword...honesty's her sole conviction...

There are so many things to be fascinated about whereas a woman's concerned...her intelligence...her aggressiveness...her independence...her sexuality and freakish nature...her sense of humor...her compassion...her wisdom and understanding...and her ability to maintain a down-to-earth attitude under the worst of circumstances...

I realize that a docile woman or a fake female has no longevity in my fascination or realization...

BOOK GANG MEDIA [Special Bulletin] had a chance to sit down with the author and co-author of this year's most anticipated novel LOVE & THUGGIN'. The interview was indeed interesting and read as follows. We hope that you enjoy.

Interview by Hayward Coleman

HC: **What it do, ya'll boys?**
BB: Chillin', man.
PLEX: Maintainin'.

HC: **Okay, how did the book LOVE & THUGGIN' come about?**
PX: When Bo ran into me he already had the book and was trying to shop it. BOO BABY was already popping and I told him I'd help him get it off if he waited. He waited and I'm glad he did. LOVE & THUGGIN' is my favorite book on our catalog.
BB: To me it wasn't nothing heavy. I just put a bunch of my thoughts on paper.

HC: **How long did it take to complete the book?**
BB: I wrote off and on for about two months.
PX: Even though the book was finished when I got it, I spent about four months [off and on] on it. I only changed the end and freaked the middle. Bo did his thing.

HC: **Who or what inspired you to write a book?**
BB: My co-defendants, PLEX and Mike Harper.

272

PX: The Honorable Elijah Muhammad and my two road dogs Bradshaw Palmer and Nathan 'Big Nation' Welch.

HC: **What are your thoughts on the current state of the book game?**

PX: It's divided. The people who are already 'in' don't want to share the cake and the people forcing their way 'in' don't realize that if we don't work together, we won't get the cake. The economy's f#@ked up and buyers are getting pickier. So resources need to be pooled to make things easier and less expensive for everybody [especially the readers]. Which is what BOOK GANG MEDIA is all about.

BB: I don't know about all that sh#@. All I know is "Ain't Nobody Fu#@ing with BadLand. We got next, point-blank, period.

HC: **So, who would you like to work with right now?**

BB: Big Gemo and K-1 [Lil One]. They're two up and comers.

PX: I want to do a full-length novel with LaMont 'Big Fridge' Needum [we already have the anthology entitled MONEY, POWER & BETRAYAL] and one with Nathan 'Big Nation' Welch. That is where my heart's at.

HC: **What's something about you that most of your readers would not know about you?**

BB: That I'm married...nah, for real. That I have a very good heart but it can and will get ugly.

PX: That I do this sh#@ for ya'll, because I'm not making no money. Every penny that I get goes right back into the grind. I eat noodles so that we could hit ya'll with ten books in twelve months. Of course, the money will come.

HC: **Which character in LOVE & THUGGIN' is your favorite and why?**

PX: I'm really feeling KiKi but Denise is my favorite. Why? Because I really got to know her and I respect her ambitions [run with me or run from me].

BB: Of course mines is Bo. He reminds me of me in some ways.

HC: **What's next for the two of you?**

BB: POINT SEEN, MONEY LOST...That's my next book dropping on BadLand. It's BadLand forever, baby.

PX: BOOK GANG MEDIA. It's big. My man Willie Dutch, The Soulman Seth Ferranti, LaMont Needum, Troy Cannon, Pam Quigley, Cedric Killings, myself, and my son Big Gemo's the boss. We're about to combine resources with Kim and Tracey and flip the book game. Look for the bodies to start falling soon.

HC: **Give us a favorite [book, movie, author, actor or actress, rapper, song, etc...], any favorite.**

PX: One of my favorite people in the world is Summer Rose. She's so unselfish. She never stops giving. My favorite teams are

the Miami Heat and the Miami Dolphins.
My favorite pass time is preparing for
tomorrow because it's coming and I know
it'll be better than yesterday.

BB: Tupac was and still is the best rapper of all
times [my favorite]. BOO BABY is the
best urban book I've ever read [my favorite].
I can't wait for part 2 [PIMP &KILL].

HC: **Quick, what is it that you bring to BOOK
GANG's table that makes you
invaluable to them, BadLand and PLEX
PRESENTS?**

PX: I bring that Dame Dash shit. I hustle, hustle,
hustle! I'll fall back when they kill   me.
Until then I want all of my ni#@as to have
their share.

BB: Just check my credentials. They speak
volumes.

HC: **How would you like for the world to
remember you?**

BB: As a loving father, son, brother, husband and
friend. Family is all that really matters to
me. What everybody else says or thinks
really don't matter to me.

PX: As that ni#@a that wouldn't quit. The ni#@
that despite his circumstances makes a way
for everybody that believed in him [a
difference maker].

HC: **Anything you'd like to share in closing?**

BB: Yeah. Being in the pen [prison] you get to
see everybody for who they really are.
So to all of my real people, I salute ya'll…If

I didn't salute you, then you wasn't   worthy
...ya'll already know who's worthy   and
who ain't.

PX: I want to tell my sons [specifically Arthur
        III, Isaiah and Artraveous] that LOVE
        made ya'll and THUGGIN' took me away
        from ya'll. The streets are a trap that you
        three don't have to be a part of...I did it. I
        f#@ked up! Learn from my mistakes...I
        love ya'll...

PLEX PRESENTS:
NO TURNING...

Nathan "Big Nation" Welch

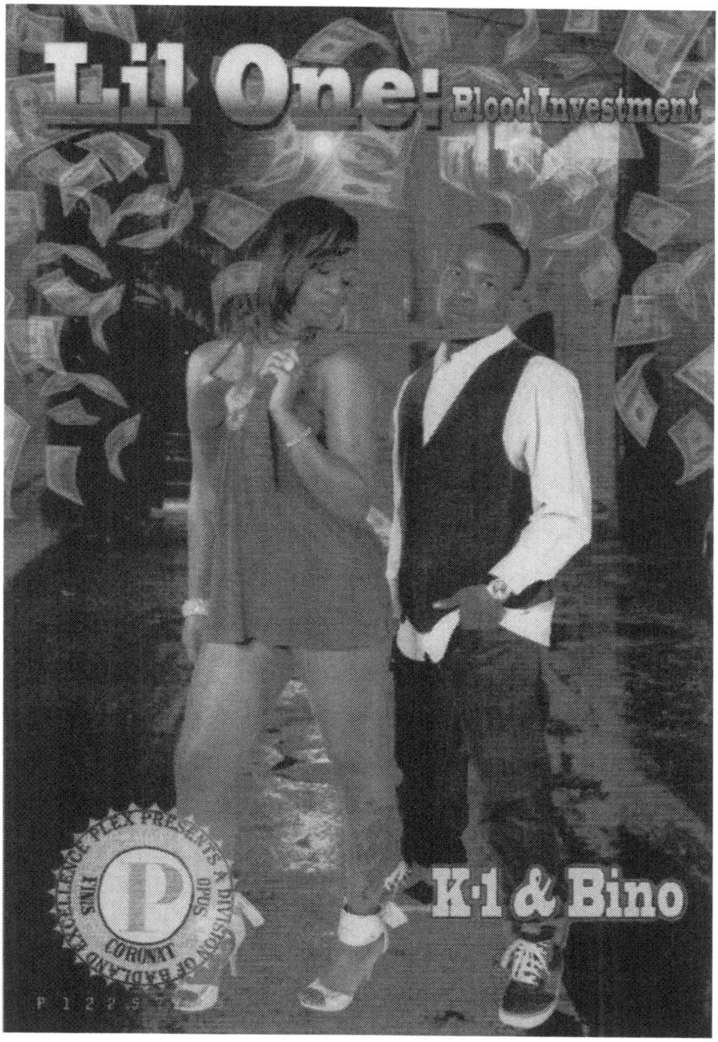
Lil One:
Blood Investment
K-1 & Bino

BOOK GANG MEDIA
PO Box 2114
Clinton, MD 20735
(301) 856-7797

Shipping address

Name:_____

Address:_____

City:_____State:_____Zip:_____

Title	Author	Price
STREET RAISED: The Beginning	Mike Harper	15.95
BOO BABY: The Secret Of...	PLEX	15.95
SERVED: With No Regard!	PLEX	15.95
STREET RAISED: The Raw Deal	PLEX	15.95
NO TURNING...	Big Nation	13.95
FOREIGN EXCHANGE	A. Glaster	14.95
CRUMBS TO BRICKS	Capo Cat	15.95
SUGAR	Mike Harper	15.00
PRISON STORIES	Seth Ferranti	15.00
STREET LEGENDS Vol. 1	Seth Ferranti	15.00
STREET LEGENDS Vol. 2	Seth Ferranti	15.00
STRAIGHT SAVAGE	LaMont NeeDum	15.00
ONE LOVE	PLEX	13.95
BUCKIN 'DA 'DICE	Book Gang	15.95
LIL ONE: Blood Investment	K-1 & Bino	15.00
EROTIC DESIRES	Seven Supreme	12.95

3.75(S&H) for 1-3 Books _____
For Quantities over 3 add $ .75 per book _____

Made in the USA
Lexington, KY
12 September 2012